D0685090
The
SCHOOL
for
GOOD
AND
EVIL
A WORLD WITHOUT PRINCES

GIRLS
The
SCHOOL
for
GOOD AND EVIL

BOYS

Soman Chainani

The School for Good and Evil

A World Without Princes

Illustrations by

Iacopo Bruno

Scholastic Inc.

ISBN 978-0-545-91379-9

12 11 10 9 8 7 6 5 4 3 2 1 15 16 17 18 19 20/0

Printed in the U.S.A. 40

First Scholastic printing, September 2015

Typography by Amy Ryan

For Maria Gonzalez

IN THE FOREST PRIMEVAL

A SCHOOL FOR GOOD AND EVIL

TWO TOWERS LIKE TWIN HEADS

ONE FOR THE PURE

ONE FOR THE WICKED

TRY TO ESCAPE YOU'LL ALWAYS FAIL

THE ONLY WAY OUT IS

THROUGH A FAIRY TALE

The
SCHOOL
for
GOOD
AND
EVIL
A WORLD WITHOUT PRINCES

PART I

1

Sophie Makes a Wish

There is an uneasiness that remains after your best friend tries to kill you.

But as Agatha gazed out at her and Sophie's golden statues, towering over the sun-speckled square, she swallowed it away.

"I don't know why it has to be a musical," she said, sneezing from the carnations on her pink dress.

"No sweating in your costumes!" Sophie barked at a boy struggling in a ferocious plaster dog head, while the girl roped to him stumbled around in her own cuddly dog head. Sophie caught two boys labeled Chaddick and Ravan trying to swap outfits. "No switching schools either!"

"But I want to be an Ever!" RAVAN groused, and pulled at his dumpy black tunic.

"My wig itches," mewled BEATRIX, clawing her blond hairpiece.

"Mummy won't know it's me," whined a boy in the SCHOOL MASTER's shiny silver mask.

"AND NO SULKING ABOUT PARTS!" Sophie boomed, branding DOT on the blacksmith's daughter before stuffing two chocolate ice pops in her hands. "You need to gain twenty pounds by next week."

"You said it'd be small," Agatha said, eyeing a boy teetering on a ladder as he painted two familiar green eyes on the massive theater marquee. "Something tasteful for the anniversary."

"Is *every* boy in this town a tenor?" Sophie squawked, inspecting the males with these very same eyes. "Surely *someone*'s voice has changed? Surely *someone* can play Tedros, the most handsome, charming prince in the—"

She turned to find red-haired, bucktoothed Radley in tight breeches, puffing his chest. Sophie gagged and stamped him HORT.

"This doesn't seem small," Agatha said, louder, watching two girls pull the canvas off a ticket booth with twenty neon Sophie faces silk-screened across it. "And it doesn't seem tastef—"

"Lights!" Sophie called to two boys suspended from ropes—

Agatha spun from the blinding detonation. Through fingers, she peeked up at the velvet curtain behind them, embedded with a thousand white-hot bulbs spelling out:

CURSES! The Musical
Starring, Written, Directed, and Produced by Sophie

"Is this too dull for the finale?" Sophie said, whirling to Agatha in a midnight-blue ballgown with delicate gold leaves, a ruby pendant around her neck, and a tiara of blue orchids. "That reminds me. Can you sing harmony?"

Agatha swelled like a tick. "Have you lost your mind! You said it'd be a tribute to the kidnapped children, not some fairground burlesque! I can't act, I can't sing, and here we are having a dress rehearsal for a vanity show that doesn't even have a scrip— What is THAT?"

She pointed at the sash of red crystals across Sophie's dress.

Ball Queen

Sophie stared at her. "You don't expect me to tell our story as it happened, do you?"

Agatha scowled.

"Oh, Agatha, if we don't celebrate ourselves, who else will?" Sophie moaned, looking out at the giant amphitheater. "We're the Gavaldon Curse Breakers! The School Master Slayers! Larger than life! Greater than legend! So where's our palace? Where's our slaves? On the anniversary of our kidnapping from this odious town, they should adore us! They should worship us! They should bow down instead of trolling around with fat, badly dressed *widows*!"

Her voice thundered across empty wooden seats. She turned to find her friend studying her.

"The Elders gave him permission, didn't they," said Agatha.

Sophie's face darkened. She spun quickly and started handing sheet music to the cast.

"When is it?" Agatha asked.

Sophie didn't answer.

"Sophie, when is it?"

"The day after the show," Sophie said, sprucing the garlands on a giant altar set piece. "But that might change once they see the encore."

"Why? What's in the encore?"

"I'm fine about it, Aggie. I've made my peace."

"Sophie. What's in the encore."

"He's a grown man. Free to make his own decisions."

"And this show has nothing to do with trying to stop your father's wedding."

Sophie twirled. "Why would you ever think that?"

Agatha glared at the fat, homeless hag, slouched in a veil under the altar, stamped HONORA.

Sophie shoved Agatha music. "If I were you, I'd be learning how to sing."

When they returned from the Woods nine months before, the hubbub had been frightening. For two hundred years, the School Master had kidnapped children from Gavaldon to his School for Good and Evil. But after so many children lost forever, so many families torn apart, two girls had found their way back. People wanted to kiss them, touch them, build statues for them, as if they were gods fallen to earth. To satisfy demand, the Council of Elders suggested they hold supervised autograph signings in the church after Sunday services. The questions never changed: "Did they torture you?" "Are you sure the curse is broken?" "Did you see my son?"

Sophie offered to endure these on her own, but to her surprise, Agatha always showed. Indeed, in those first months, Agatha did daily interviews for the town scroll, let Sophie dress her up and slather her with makeup, and politely endured the young children her friend loathed.

"Totems of disease," Sophie grumbled, dabbing her nostrils with eucalyptus before signing another storybook. She noticed Agatha smile at a boy as she autographed his copy of *King Arthur.*

"Since when do you like *children*?" Sophie growled.

"Since they beg to see Mother when they're sick now," said Agatha, flashing lipstick stains on her teeth. "Never had so many patients in her life."

But by summer, the crowd had thinned. It was Sophie's idea to do posters.

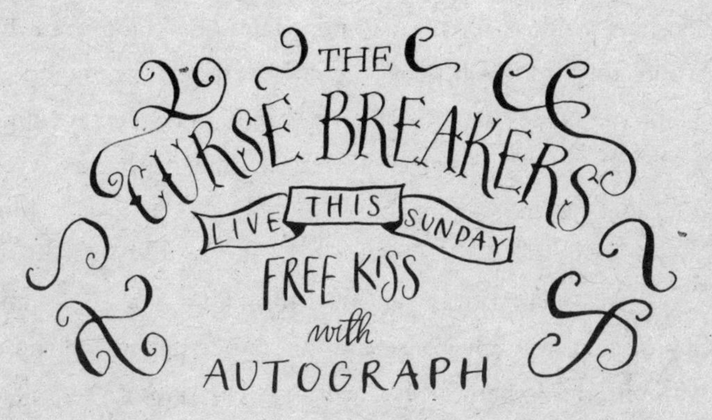

Agatha gaped at the sign on the church door. "Free *kiss?*"

"On their storybooks," Sophie said, puckering garishly red lips into a pocket mirror.

"That's not what it sounds like," said Agatha, pulling at the clingy green dress Sophie had loaned her. Pink had noticeably disappeared from her friend's closet after they returned, presumably because it reminded her of her time as a bald, toothless witch.

"Look, we're old news," Agatha said, yanking at the dress's straps again. "Time to go back to normal like everyone else."

"Maybe it should just be me this week." Sophie's eyes flicked up from the mirror. "Perhaps they sense your lack of enthusiasm."

But no one except smelly Radley showed that Sunday or the next week, when Sophie's posters hawked an "intimate gift" with every autograph, or the next, when she promised a "private dinner" too. By the fall, the Missing signs in the square had come down, the children had shoved their storybooks in closets, and Mr. Deauville put a LAST DAYS sign in his shop window, for no new fairy tales had come from the Woods for him to sell. Now the girls were just two more fossils of the curse. Even Sophie's father had stopped treading gently. On Halloween, he told his daughter he had received the Elders' permission to marry Honora. He never asked for Sophie's.

As she hurried from rehearsal through a hard, ugly rain, Sophie glowered at her once-shining statue, spotted and runny with bird droppings. She had worked so hard for it. A week of snail-egg facials and cucumber-juice fasts so the sculptor would get her just right. And now here it was, a toilet for pigeons.

She glanced back at her painted face beaming from the distant theater marquee and gritted her teeth. The show would remind her father who came first. The show would remind them all.

As she splashed out of the square toward soddy cottage lanes, trails of smoke wafted from chimneys, and Sophie knew what each family was having for dinner: breaded pork with mushroom gravy in Wilhelm's house, beef and potato cream soup in Belle's, bacon lentils and pickled yams in Sabrina's. . . . The food her father loved and never could have.

Good. Let him starve, for all she cared. As she walked up the lane to her own house, Sophie inhaled for the smell of a cold, empty kitchen, a smell that reminded her father of what he'd lost.

Only now the kitchen didn't smell empty at all. Sophie inhaled again, a smell of meat and milk, and felt herself running to the door. She threw it open—

Honora hacked into raw pork ribs. "Sophie," she panted, wiping plump hands. "I had to close at Bartleby's—I could use some help—"

Sophie stared through her. "Where's my father?"

Honora tried to fix her bushy, flour-crusted hair. "Um, putting up the tent with the boys. He thought it might be nice if we all have dinner toget—"

"Tent?" Sophie charged for the back door. "Now?"

She barreled into the garden. In gusty rain, the widow's

two boys each manned a roped-down stake while Stefan tried to loop the billowing white tent around a third. But just as Stefan succeeded, the tent ripped away, burying him and the two boys beneath it. Sophie could hear them giggling before her father poked his head from under the canvas. "Just what we need. A fourth!"

"Why are you putting up the tent?" Sophie said, ice-cold. "The wedding is next week."

Stefan stood tall and cleared his throat. "It's tomorrow."

"Tomorrow?" Sophie went white. "*This* tomorrow? The one after today?"

"Honora said we should do it before your show," Stefan said, running a hand through a newly grown beard. "We don't want to distract from it."

Sophie felt sick. "But . . . how can—"

"Don't worry about us. We announced the date change at church, and Jacob and Adam here will have the tent up in no time. How was rehearsal?" He hugged the six-year-old to his brawny flank. "Jacob said he could see the lights from our porch."

"Me too!" said eight-year-old Adam, hugging his other side.

Stefan kissed their heads. "Who'd have thought I'd have two little princes?" he whispered.

Sophie watched her father, heart in her throat.

"So come on, tell us what's in your show," Stefan said, smiling up at her.

But Sophie suddenly didn't care about her show at all.

Dinner was a handsome roast, with perfectly cooked broccoli, cucumber salad, and a flourless blueberry tart, but she didn't touch any of it. She sat rigid, glaring at Honora across the cramped table as forks speared and clinked.

"Eat," Stefan prodded her.

Next to him, Honora rubbed her neck wattle, avoiding Sophie's stare. "If she doesn't like it—"

"You made what she likes," Stefan said, eyes on Sophie. "Eat."

Sophie didn't. Clinks petered to silence.

"Can I have her pork?" Adam said.

"You and my mother were friends, weren't you?" Sophie said to Honora.

The widow choked on her meat. Stefan scowled at Sophie and opened his mouth to retort, but Honora grabbed his wrist. She dabbed at dry lips with a dirty napkin.

"Best friends," she rasped with a smile, and swallowed again. "For a very long time."

Sophie froze over. "I wonder what came between you."

Honora's smile vanished and she peered down at her plate. Sophie's eyes stayed locked on her.

Stefan's fork clanked against the table. "Why don't you help Honora in the shop after school?"

Sophie waited for Adam to answer him—then saw her father still looking at her.

"Me?" Sophie blanched. "Help . . . *her*?"

"Bartleby said my wife could use an extra hand," Stefan pushed.

Wife. That's all Sophie heard. Not thief. Not tramp. *Wife.*

"After the wedding and the show is over," he added. "Get you settled into normal life."

Sophie spun to Honora, expecting her to be as shocked, but she was just anxiously slurping cucumbers through dry lips.

"Father, you want me to—to—" Sophie couldn't get words out. "Churn *b-b-butter*?"

"Build some strength in those stick arms," her father said between bites, as Jacob and Adam compared biceps.

"But I'm famous!" Sophie shrieked. "I have fans—I have a *statue*! I can't work! Not with *her*!"

"Then perhaps you should find somewhere else to live." Stefan picked a bone clean. "As long as you're in this family, you'll contribute. Or the boys would be happy to have your room."

Sophie gasped.

"Now *eat*," he spat, so sharply she had to obey.

As he watched Agatha slip on her old, saggy black dress, Reaper growled suspiciously, sucking on a few trout bones across the leaky room.

"See? Same old Agatha." She slammed the trunk on Sophie's borrowed clothes, slid it near the door, and kneeled to pet her bald, wrinkled cat. "So now you can be nice again."

Reaper hissed.

"It's me," Agatha said, trying to pet him. "I haven't changed a bit."

Reaper scratched her and trundled away.

Agatha rubbed the fresh mark on her hand between others barely healed. She flopped onto her bed while Reaper curled up in a moldy green corner, as far away from her as he could.

She rolled over and hugged her pillow.

I'm happy.

She listened to rain slosh against the straw roof and spurt through a hole into her mother's black cauldron.

Home sweet home.

Clink, clink, clink went the rain.

Sophie and me.

She stared at the blank, cracked wall. *Clink, clink, clink* . . . Like a sword in a sheath, rubbing against a belt buckle. *Clink, clink, clink*. Her chest started pounding, her blood burning like lava, and she knew it was happening again. *Clink, clink, clink*. The black of the cauldron became the black of his boots. The straw of the ceiling, the gold of his hair. The sky through the window, the blue in his eyes. In her arms, the pillow became tanned muscles and flesh—

"Some help, dear!" a voice trilled.

Agatha jolted awake, gripping her sweat-stained pillow. She lurched off the bed and opened the door to see her mother lugging two baskets, one teeming with stinky roots and leaves, the other with dead tadpoles, cockroaches, and lizards.

"What in the world—"

"So you can finally teach me some potions from school!" Callis chimed, eyes bulging, and plunked a basket in Agatha's hands. "Not as many patients today. We have time to brew!"

"I told you I can't do magic anymore," Agatha snapped,

closing the door behind them. "Our fingers don't glow here."

"Why won't you tell me anything that happened?" her mother asked, picking her oily dome of black hair. "The least you could do is show me a wart potion."

"Look, I put it all behind me."

"Lizards are better fresh, dear. What can we make with those?"

"I forgot all that stuff—"

"They'll go bad—"

"Stop!"

Her mother stiffened.

"Please," Agatha begged. "I don't want to talk about school."

Gently Callis took the basket from her. "When you came home, I'd never been so happy." She looked into her daughter's eyes. "But part of me worries what you gave up."

Agatha stared down at her black clump shoes as her mother towed the baskets into the kitchen. "You know how I feel about waste," Callis sighed. "Let's hope our bowels can handle a lizard stew."

As Agatha chopped onions by torchlight, she listened to her mother hum off-key, like she did every night. Once upon a time, she had loved their graveyard haven, their lonely routines.

She put down the knife. "Mother, how do you know if you've found Ever After?"

"Hmmm?" said Callis, bony hands scraping a few roaches into the cauldron.

"The people in a fairy tale, I mean."

"It should say so, dear." Her mother nodded at an open storybook peeking from under Agatha's bed.

Agatha looked down at its last page, a blond prince and raven-haired princess kissing at their wedding, framed by an enchanted castle . . .

THE END.

"But what if two people can't see their storybook?" She gazed at the princess in her prince's arms. "How do they know if they're happy?"

"If they have to ask, they probably aren't," said her mother, jabbing a roach that wouldn't drown.

Agatha's eyes stayed on the prince a moment longer. She snapped the storybook shut and tossed it in the fire under the cauldron. "About time we got rid of these like everyone else."

She resumed chopping in the corner, faster than before.

"Are you all right, dear?" Callis said, hearing sniffles.

Agatha dabbed at her eyes. "Onions."

The rain had gone, but a harsh autumn wind raked across the cemetery, lit by two torches over the gates that clung to skipping flames. As she approached the grave, her calves locked and her heart banged in her ears, begging her to stay away. Sweat seeped down her back as she kneeled in the weeds and mud, her eyes closed. She had never looked. Never.

With a deep breath, Sophie opened her eyes. She could barely make out an eroded butterfly in the headstone above the words.

LOVING WIFE
&
MOTHER

Two smaller gravestones, both unmarked, flanked her mother's like wings. Fingers covered by white mittens, she picked moss out of the cracks in one, overgrown from the years of neglect. As she tore away the mold, her soiled mittens found deeper grooves in the rock, smooth and deliberate. There was something carved in the slab. She peered closer—

"Sophie?"

She turned to see Agatha approach in a tattered black coat, balancing a drippy candle on a saucer.

"My mother saw you from the window."

Agatha crouched next to her and laid the flame in front of the graves. Sophie didn't say anything for a long while.

"He thought it was her fault," she said at last, gazing at the two unmarked headstones. "Two boys, both born dead. How else could he explain it?" She watched a blue butterfly flutter out of the darkness and nestle into the carving on her mother's decayed gravestone.

"All the doctors said she couldn't have more children. Even your mother." Sophie paused and smiled faintly at the blue butterfly. "One day it happened. She was so sick no one thought it could last, but her belly still grew. The Miracle Child, the Elders called it. Father said he'd name him Filip."

Sophie turned to Agatha. "Only you can't call a girl Filip."

Sophie paused, cheekbones hardening. "She loved me, no

matter how weak I had left her. No matter how many times she watched him walk to her friend's house and disappear inside." Sophie fought the tears as long as she could. "Her friend, Agatha. Her best *friend*. How could he?" She cried bitterly into her dirty mittens.

Agatha looked down and didn't say a word.

"I watched her die, Aggie. Broken and betrayed." Sophie turned from the grave, red faced. "Now he'll have everything he wanted."

"You can't stop him," Agatha said, touching her.

Sophie recoiled. "And let him get *away* with it?"

"What choice do you have?"

"You think that wedding will happen?" Sophie spat. *"Watch."*

"Sophie . . ."

"*He* should be the one dead!" Sophie flushed with blood. "Him and his little princes! Then I'd be happy in this prison!"

Her face was so horrible that Agatha froze. For the first time since they returned, she glimpsed the deadly witch inside her friend, yearning to unleash.

Sophie saw the fear in Agatha's eyes. "I'm s-s-s-sorry—" she stammered, turning away. "I—I don't know what happened—" Her face melted to shame. The witch was gone.

"I miss her, Aggie," Sophie whispered, trembling. "I know we have our happy ending. But I still miss my mother."

Agatha hesitated, then touched her friend's shoulder. Sophie gave in to her, and Agatha held her as she sobbed. "I wish I could see her again," Sophie wept. "I'd do anything. Anything."

The crooked tower clock tolled ten times down the hill, but loud, doleful creaks thickened between each one. In each other's arms, the two girls watched the hunched silhouette of old Mr. Deauville as he wheeled a cart past the clock with the last of his closed-down shop. Every few paces he stopped, laboring under the weight of his forgotten storybooks, until his shadow disappeared around the corner and the creaks faded away.

"I just don't want to end like her, alone and . . . forgotten," Sophie breathed.

She turned to Agatha, trying to smile. "But my mother didn't have a friend like you, did she? You gave up a prince, just for us to be together. To think I could make someone happy like that . . ." Her eyes misted. "I don't deserve you, Agatha. I really don't. After all I've done."

Agatha was still quiet.

"Someone Good would let this marriage happen, wouldn't they?" Sophie pressed her softly. "Someone as Good as you."

"It's late," Agatha said, standing up. She held out her hand.

Sophie took it limply. "And I still have to find a dress for the wedding."

Agatha managed a smile. "See? Good after all."

"Least I can do is look better than the bride," Sophie said, swishing ahead.

Agatha snorted and grabbed the torch off the gate. "Wait. I'll walk you home."

"How lovely," Sophie said, not stopping. "I can smell more of that onion soup you had for dinner."

"Lizard and onion soup, actually."

"I really don't know how we're friends."

Through the groaning gate, the two slipped side by side, torches lighting up their long shadows across overgrown weeds. As they waded down the emerald hill and out of sight, a gust flew back through the cemetery, igniting a flame on a candle dripping onto its mud-stained saucer. The flame grew over a blue butterfly settled curiously on a grave, then stoked brighter, long enough to illuminate the carvings on the two unmarked graves beside it. A swan on each. One white.

The other black.

With a roar, the wind lashed between them and blew the candle out.

2

Agatha Makes a Wish Too

Blood. It smelled blood.

Eat.

Smashing through trees, the Beast hunted their scent, grunting and slobbering on all fours. Claws and feet pounded the dirt, faster, faster, shredding vines and branches, bounding over rocks, until at last it could hear their breaths and see the trail of red. One of them was hurt.

Eat.

Through a long, dark, hollow trunk it slunk, licking up the blood, smelling their terror. The Beast took its time, for they had nowhere to go, and soon it heard their whimpers. Bit

by bit they came into view, silhouetted in moonlight, trapped between the end of the log and a thick patch of briars. The older boy, wounded and pale, clutched the younger to his chest.

The Beast swept them both up and held the boys as they cried. Snuggled in briars, the Beast rocked them gently until the boys stopped weeping and knew the Beast was Good. Soon the boys breathed heavier against the Beast's black breast, nestling deeper into its arms, hugging them tighter . . . harder . . . bonier . . . until the boys gasped awake . . .

And saw Sophie's bloody smile.

Sophie flung up from bed and knocked into her bedside candle, splattering lavender wax all over the wall. She whirled to the mirror and saw herself bald, toothless, pockmarked with warts—

"Help—" she choked, closing her eyes—

She opened them and the witch was no longer there. Her beautiful face stared back at her.

Panicked, Sophie checked her shivering white skin for warts, wiping away the cold film of sweat.

I'm Good, she calmed herself when she found none.

But her hands wouldn't stop shaking, her mind racing, unable to shake that Beast, the Beast she'd killed in a world far away, the Beast that still haunted her dreams. She thought of her rage in the graveyard . . . Agatha's petrified face . . .

You'll never be Good, the School Master had warned.

Sophie's mouth went dry. She'd smile at the wedding. She'd work at Bartleby's. She'd eat the widow's meat and buy toys for her sons. She'd be happy here. Just like Agatha.

Anything to not be a witch again.

"I'm Good," she repeated into silence.

The School Master had to be wrong. She'd saved Agatha's life, and Agatha had saved hers.

They were home together. The riddle solved. The School Master dead.

The storybook closed.

Definitely Good, Sophie assured herself, snuggling back into her pillow.

But she could still taste blood.

The fog and winds of the night cleared to a blinding sun, so strong for November that the day seemed blessed for love. Every wedding in Gavaldon was a public occasion, but on this Friday, the shops were all closed and the square deserted, for Stefan was a popular man. Under a white garden tent behind his house, the entire town mingled over cherry punch and plum wine, as three fiddlers strummed in the corner, exhausted from playing a funeral the night before.

Agatha wasn't sure if her dumpy black smock was appropriate attire for a wedding, but it suited her mood. She'd woken up miserable and couldn't put a finger on why. *Sophie needs me to be happy,* she told herself as she tromped down the hill, but by the time she joined the crowd in the garden, her frown was a scowl. She needed to snap out of it or she'd make Sophie even more depressed. . . .

A flash of pink surged through the crowd and bear hugged her into a poofy, ruffled gown.

"Thank you for being here on our special day," Sophie cooed.

Agatha coughed.

"I'm so *happy* for them, aren't you?" Sophie mooned, dabbing nonexistent tears. "It'll be such a thrill. Having a new mother, two brothers, and going to the shop each morning to churn"—she gulped—"butter."

Agatha gaped at Sophie, back in her favorite dress. "You're pink . . . again."

"Like my loving, Good heart," her friend breathed, stroking pink-ribboned braids.

Agatha blinked. "Did they put toadstools in the punch?"

"Sophie!"

Both girls turned and saw Jacob, Adam, and Stefan trying to fix crooked blue tulip garlands over the altar at the front of the tent. Standing on pumpkins to reach, the boys beckoned her with waves.

"Sweet little munchkins, aren't they?" Sophie smiled. "I could just eat them both u—"

Agatha saw her friend's green eyes chill with fear. Then it was gone, and the only traces left were the bruised circles beneath them. Nightmare scars. She'd seen them on Sophie before.

"Sophie, it's me," Agatha said quietly. "You don't have to pretend."

Sophie shook her head. "You and me, Aggie. That's all I need to be Good," she said, voice shaky. She clasped Agatha's arm and looked deep into her friend's dark eyes. "As long as we keep the witch inside me dead. Everything else I can bear if I try." She gripped Agatha tighter and turned to the altar. "I'm coming, boys!" she shouted, and with a strained smile, swept off to help her new family.

Instead of feeling touched, Agatha felt even more miserable. *What's wrong with me?*

Her mother came up beside her and handed her a glass of punch, which she downed in one gulp.

"Added a few glowworms," Callis said. "Brighten that sour face."

Agatha spat a spray of red.

"Really, dear. I know weddings are putrid things, but try not to look hostile." Her mother nodded ahead. "The Elders already despise us. Don't give them more reason."

Agatha glanced at three wizened, bearded men in black top hats and knee-length gray cloaks, milling between seats and shaking hands. The length of their beards appeared to indicate their relative ages, with the Eldest's funneling down past his chest.

"Why do they have to approve every marriage?" Agatha asked.

"Because when the kidnappings kept happening, the Elders blamed women like me," her mother said, picking dandruff from her hair. "Back then, if you weren't married by the time you finished school, people thought you were a witch. So the Elders forced marriages for all those unwed." She managed a wry smile. "But even force couldn't make a man wed me."

Agatha remembered when no boy at school wanted her for

the Ball either. Until . . .

Suddenly she felt even grimmer.

"When the kidnappings continued, the Elders softened their stance and 'approved' marriages instead. But I still remember their terrible arrangements," said her mother, digging nails into her scalp. "Stefan suffered worst of all."

"Why? What happened to him?"

Callis' hand dropped, as if she'd forgotten her daughter was listening. "Nothing, dear. Nothing that matters anymore."

"But you said—" Agatha heard her name called and spun to see Sophie waving her into a front-row seat.

"Aggie, we're starting!"

Side by side in the first pew, a few feet from the altar, Agatha kept waiting for Sophie to crack. But her friend clung to her smile, even as her father joined the priest at the altar, the fiddlers began the procession, and Jacob and Adam strewed roses down the aisle in matching white suits. After months of fighting her father, fighting for attention, fighting real life . . . Sophie had changed.

You and me, Aggie.

All Agatha had ever wanted was to be enough for Sophie. For Sophie to need her as much as she needed Sophie. And now, at last, she'd won her happy ending.

But in her seat, Agatha didn't feel happy at all. Something was bothering her about this wedding. Something worming through her heart. Before she could pinpoint it, the fiddlers slowed their tune, everyone under the tent stood, and Honora waddled down the aisle. Agatha watched Sophie carefully, expecting her friend to finally betray herself, but Sophie didn't flinch, even as she took in her new stepmother's bulbous hairdo, pudgy behind, and dress smudged with what looked like cake frosting.

"Dearest friends and family," the priest began, "we are gathered here to witness the union of these two souls . . ."

Stefan took Honora's hand, and Agatha felt even more dismal. Her back hunched, her lips pouted—

Across the aisle, her mother was glaring at her. Agatha sat up and faked a smile.

"In love, happiness comes from honesty, from committing to the one that we *need*," the priest continued.

Agatha felt Sophie gently take her hand, as if they both had everything they needed right here.

"May you grow a love that fulfills you, a love that lasts Ever After . . ."

Agatha's palm started to sweat.

"Because you chose this love. You chose this ending to your story."

Her hand was dripping now, but Sophie didn't let go.

"And now this ending is yours eternally."

Agatha's heart jackhammered. Her skin burned up.

"And if no one has any objections, then this union is sealed forever—"

Agatha pitched forward, sick to her stomach—

"I now pronounce you—"

Then she saw it.

"Man and—"

Her finger was glowing brilliant gold.

She let out a cry of shock. Sophie turned in surprise—

Something flew between them, throwing them both to the ground. Agatha wheeled to feel another arrow graze her throat before she lunged away. She could hear children crying, chairs falling, feet stumbling as the mob stampeded for cover, dozens of golden arrows whizzing past, gouging holes in the tent. Agatha spun for Sophie, but the tent tore off its stakes, toppled over the shrieking crowd, and swallowed her, until she couldn't see anything but muffled shadows flailing behind the canvas. Breathless, Agatha crawled on all fours over a shattered altar, hands clawing through mud and trampled garlands as arrows landed ahead with shearing rips. Who was doing this? Who would destroy a weddin—

Agatha froze. Now her finger was shining even brighter than before.

It can't be.

She heard a girl's screams ahead. Screams she knew. Sweating, shivering, Agatha skimmed under overturned chairs, shoving the last fringe of tent off her, until she felt a blast of sunlight and scraped into the front garden, expecting carnage—

But people were just standing there, silent, still, watching the skyfall of arrows from every direction.

Arrows from the Woods.

Agatha shielded herself in horror, then realized the arrows weren't aimed at her. They weren't aimed at any of the villagers. No matter where they came from out of the Woods, their shafts curved at the last second, tearing toward one and only one target.

"Eeeeeyiiiiii!"

Sophie ran around her house, ducking and batting arrows away with her glass heels.

"Agatha! Agatha, *help*!"

But there was no time, for a shaft almost sliced off her head, and Sophie ran down a hill, fast as she could, arrows following her all the way.

"Who would want me *dead*?" Sophie wailed to stained glass martyrs and statues of saints.

Agatha sat beside her in the empty pews. It had been two weeks since Sophie started hiding in the church, the only place where the arrows didn't pursue her. Again and again she tried to break out, but the arrows returned with vengeance, slashing from the Woods, followed by spears, axes, daggers, and darts. By the third day, it was clear there would be no escape. Whoever wanted to kill her would wait as long as it took.

At first Sophie saw no reason to panic. The townspeople brought her food (taking heed of her "fatal allergies" to wheat, sugar, dairy, and red meat), Agatha brought her the herbs and roots she needed to make her creams, and Stefan brought assurances he wouldn't rewed until his daughter was brought home safe. With the townsmen uselessly combing the forest for the assassins, the town scroll branded Sophie "the Brave Little Princess" for taking the burden of yet another curse, while the Elders ordered her statue be given a fresh coat of paint. Soon children clamored once more for autographs, the village anthem was amended to "Blessed Is Our Sophie," and townsmen took turns keeping watch over the church. There was even talk of a permanent one-woman show in the theater once she was out of danger.

"*La Reine Sophie,* an epic three-hour celebration of my achievements," Sophie raptured, smelling the sympathy bouquets that filled the aisle. "A bit of cabaret to stir the blood, a circus intermezzo with wild lions and trapeze, and a rousing rendition of 'I Am but a Simple Woman' to close. Oh, Agatha, how I've longed to find my place in this stagnant, monotonous town! All I needed was a part big enough to hold me!" Suddenly she looked worried. "You don't think they'll stop trying to kill me, do you? This is the best thing that's ever happened!"

But then the attacks got worse.

The first night, firebombs launched from the Woods and annihilated Belle's house, leaving her whole family homeless. On the second night, boiling oil flooded from the trees, immolating an entire cottage lane. In smoldering ruins, the assassins left the same message, burnt into the ground.

By the next morning, when the Elders took to the square to calm rioting villagers, Stefan had already made it to the church.

"It's the only way the Elders and I can protect you," he told his daughter, bearing a hammer and padlocks.

Agatha wouldn't leave, so he locked her in too.

"I thought our story was over!" Sophie cried, listening to a mob of villagers outside chanting, "Send her back! Send her back!" She slumped in her seat. "Why don't they want *you*? Why am *I* always the villain? And why am I always *locked in*?"

Next to her, Agatha gazed at a marble saint in a frieze above the altar, lunging for an angel. He stretched his strong arm, torqued his chest, as if he'd follow the angel wherever it went . . .

"Aggie?"

Agatha broke from her trance and turned. "You do have a way of making enemies."

"I tried to be Good!" Sophie said. "I tried to be just like you!"

Agatha felt that sick feeling again. The one she'd been trying to keep down.

"Aggie, do something!" Sophie grabbed her arm. "You always fix things!"

"Maybe I'm not as Good as you think," Agatha murmured, and pulled away, pretending to polish her clump. In the silence, she could feel Sophie watching her.

"Aggie."

"Yeah."

"Why did your finger glow?"

Agatha's muscles clenched. "What?"

"I saw it," said Sophie softly. "At the wedding."

Agatha threw her a glance. "Probably a trick of light. Magic doesn't work here."

"Right."

Agatha held her breath. She could feel Sophie thinking.

"But the teachers never relocked our fingers, did they?" her friend said. "And magic follows emotion. That's what they told us."

Agatha shifted. "So?"

"You didn't look happy at the wedding," Sophie said. "Are you sure something didn't make you upset? Upset enough to do magic?"

Agatha met her eyes. Sophie searched her face, seeing right through her.

"I know you, Agatha."

Agatha gripped the pew.

"I know why you were sad."

"Sophie, I didn't mean it!" Agatha blurted—

"You were upset with my father," said Sophie. "For all he put me through."

Agatha goggled at her. She recovered and nodded. "Right. Uh-huh. You got me."

"At first I thought you'd done the spell to stop his wedding. But that doesn't make any sense now, does it?" Sophie said with a snort. "That would mean you sent the arrows for *me*."

Agatha croaked a laugh, trying not to look at her.

"Just a trick of light," Sophie sighed. "Like you said."

They sat in silence and listened to the chants.

"Don't worry about my father. He and I'll be fine," Sophie

said. "The witch won't come back, Aggie. Not as long as we're friends."

Her voice was more naked than Agatha had ever heard it. Agatha looked up, surprised.

"You make me happy, Agatha," said Sophie. "It just took me too long to see it."

Agatha tried to hold her gaze, but all she could see was the saint above the altar, hand lunging towards her, like a prince reaching for his princess.

"You'll see. We'll come up with a plan, like always," Sophie said, reapplying pink lipstick between yawns. "But maybe a little beauty nap first . . ."

As she curled up on the pew like a cat, pillow to her stomach, Agatha saw it was her friend's favorite, stitched with a blond princess and her prince, embraced beneath the words "Ever After." But Sophie had revised the prince with her sewing kit. Now he had boxy dark hair, goonish bug eyes . . . and a black dress.

Agatha watched her best friend fall into sleep a few breaths later, free from nightmares for the first time in weeks.

As the chants outside the church grew louder—"Send her back! Send her back!"—Agatha stared at Sophie's pillow, and her stomach wrenched with that sick feeling.

The same feeling she felt looking at the storybook prince in her kitchen. The same feeling she felt watching a man and wife exchange vows. The same feeling she felt as she held Sophie's hand, growing stronger, stronger, until her finger had glowed with a secret. A secret so terrible, so unforgivable, that she'd ruined a fairy tale.

For in that single moment, watching the wedding she'd never have, Agatha had wished for something she never thought possible.

She wished for a different ending to her story.

An ending with someone else.

That's when the arrows came for Sophie.

The arrows that wouldn't stop, no matter how much she tried to take her wish back.

3

Breadcrumbs

That night they flattened Radley's house first, with a boulder lobbed over the trees, then the crooked clock tower, which tolled broken moans as screaming villagers fled through the square. Soon whole lanes went up in splinters as parents clung to their children in wells and ditches, watching rocks fly across the moon like meteors. When the blitz ended at four in the morning, only half the town remained. The trembling villagers looked out at the theater, illuminated in the distance, the lights on its red curtain rearranged:

SOPHIE OR DIE.

While Sophie slept calmly through all this, Agatha sat trapped in the church, listening to the screams and thumps. Give them Sophie, and her best friend would die. Don't give them Sophie, and her whole town would die. Shame burnt her throat. Somehow she'd reopened the gates between the worlds. But to who? Who wanted Sophie dead?

There had to be a way to fix this. If she'd reopened the gates, surely she could close them!

First she tried to make her finger glow again, focusing on her anger until her cheeks puffed—anger at the assassins, anger at herself, anger at her stupid, unlit finger that looked even paler than before. Then she tried doing spells anyway to repel the raiders, which went about as well as expected. She tried praying to stained glass saints, wishing on a star, rubbing every lamp in the church for a genie, and when it all failed miserably, she pried Sophie's pink lipstick from her fist and scratched "TAKE ME INSTEAD" on the dawn-lit window. To her surprise, she got an answer.

"NO," flames spelled across the forest fringe.

For a moment, through trees, Agatha saw a glint of red. Then it was gone.

"WHO ARE YOU?" she wrote.

"GIVE US SOPHIE," the flames answered.

"SHOW YOURSELF," she demanded.

"GIVE US SOPHIE."

"YOU CAN'T HAVE HER," Agatha scrawled.

A cannonball smashed through Sophie's statue in reply.

Sophie stirred behind her, mumbling about the connection between poor sleep and pimples. Banging around in the dark, she lit a candle that streaked the hemlock rafters with bronze glow. Then she did a few bumbling yoga moves, nibbled on an almond, rubbed her face with grapefruit seeds, trout scales, and cacao cream, and twirled to Agatha with a sleepy smile. "Morning, darling, what's our plan?"

But hunched in the windowsill, Agatha just stared out the broken glass, and then Sophie did too, at the leveled town, the homeless masses picking through rubble, and her severed statue head gaping at her from the church steps. Sophie's smile slowly vanished.

"There's no plan, is there?"

CRACK!

The oak doors shivered as a hammer bashed away a padlock.

CRACK! CRACK!

"Assassins!" Sophie cried.

Agatha leapt up in horror. "The church is hallowed ground!"

Boards snapped; screws loosened and clinked to the floor.

The girls backed against the altar. "Hide!" Agatha gasped, and Sophie ran around the lectern like a headless chicken—

Something metal slipped into the door.

"A key!" Agatha squeaked. "They have a key!"

She heard the lock catch. Behind her, Sophie fluttered uselessly between curtains.

"Hide *now*!" cried Agatha—

The door crashed open, and she spun to the dark threshold. Through weak candlelight, a hunched black shadow slunk into the church.

Agatha's heart stopped.

No . . .

The crooked shadow glided down the aisle, flickering in flamelight. Agatha dropped to her knees against the altar. Her heart was rattling so hard she couldn't breathe.

He's dead! Ripped to pieces by a white swan and thrown to the wind! His black swan feathers rained over a school far, far away! But now the School Master was creeping towards her, very much alive, and Agatha cowered against the lectern with a shriek—

"The situation has become untenable," said a voice.

Not the School Master's.

Agatha peeked through fingers at the Elder with the longest beard, standing over her.

"Sophie must be moved to safety," said the younger Elder behind him, doffing his black top hat.

"And she must be moved tonight," said the youngest at the rear, stroking his meager beard.

"Where?" a voice breathed.

The Elders looked up to see Sophie in the marble frieze over the altar, pressed against a naked saint.

"*THAT'S* where you hid?" barked Agatha.

"Where will you take me?" Sophie asked the Eldest, trying in vain to extricate herself from the nude statue.

"It's been arranged," he said, replacing his hat as he walked towards the door. "We'll return this evening."

"But the attacks!" Agatha cried. "How will you stop them?"

"Arranged," said the middle, following the Eldest out.

"Eight o'clock," said the youngest, trailing behind him. "Only Sophie."

"How do you know she'll be safe!" Agatha panicked—

"All arranged," the Eldest called, and locked the door behind him.

The two girls stood in dumb silence before Sophie let out a squeal.

"See? I told you!" She slid down the frieze and smushed Agatha in a hug. "Nothing can ruin our happy ending." Humming with relief, she packed her creams and cucumbers in her pretty pink suitcase, for who knew how long it'd be before they'd let her friend visit with more. She glanced back at Agatha's big dark eyes fixed out the window.

"Don't fret, Aggie. It's all arranged."

But as Agatha watched the villagers sift through ruins, glowering bloodshot at the church, she remembered the last time her mother said the Elders "arranged" things . . . and hoped this time they'd have better results.

Before sunset, the Elders allowed Stefan to come, who Sophie hadn't seen since he locked her in. He didn't look the same. His beard was overgrown, his clothes filthy, his body sallow and malnourished. Two of his teeth were missing, and his left eye socket was bruised blue. With his daughter protected by the Elders, the villagers had clearly expelled their frustrations on him.

Sophie forced a sympathetic look, but her heart twinged

with glee. No matter how Good she tried to be, the witch inside still wanted her father to suffer. She looked over at Agatha, chewing on her nails in a corner, pretending not to listen.

"Elders said it won't be long," Stefan said. "Once those cowards in the forest realize you've been hidden, sooner or later they'll come looking. And I'll be ready." He scratched at his blackened pores and noticed his daughter wincing. "I know I'm a sight."

"What you need is a good honeycream scrub," Sophie said, digging through her bag of beauty products until she found its snakeskin pouch. But her father was just staring out at the demolished town, eyes wet.

"Father?"

"The village wants to give you up. But the Elders will do anything to protect you, even with Christmas coming. They're better men than any of us," he said softly. "No one in town will sell to me now. How we're going to survive . . ." He wiped his eyes.

Sophie had never seen her father cry. "Well it's not my fault," she blurted.

Stefan exhaled. "Sophie, all that matters is you get home safe."

Sophie fiddled with her pouch of honeycream. "Where are you staying?"

"Another reason I'm unpopular," her father said, rubbing his black eye. "Whoever's after you blasted the other houses in our lane, but left ours alone. Our food store's all gone, but Honora still finds a way to feed us every night."

Sophie gripped the pouch tighter. "Us?"

"Boys moved to your room until all's safe and we can finish the wedding."

Sophie spurted him with white gobs. Stefan smelled the honeycream and instantly started scrounging through her bag—"Anything here the boys can eat?"

Agatha could see Sophie about to faint and stepped in. "Stefan, do you know where the Elders will hide her?"

He shook his head. "But they assure me the villagers won't find her either," he said, watching Sophie whisk her bag as far across the church from him as she could. Stefan waited until she was out of earshot. "It's not just the assassins we have to keep her safe from," he whispered.

"But she can't last long alone," Agatha pressed him.

Stefan looked through the window at the woods shutting Gavaldon in, dark and endless in the fading light. "What happened when you were out there, Agatha? Who wants my daughter dead?"

Agatha still had no answer. "Suppose the plan doesn't work?" she asked.

"We have to trust the Elders," Stefan said, averting his eyes. "They know what's best."

Agatha saw pain cloud his face. *"Stefan suffered worst of all."* That's what her mother had said.

"I'll fix this somehow," Agatha said, guilt squeezing her voice. "I'll keep her safe. I promise."

Stefan leaned in and took her face into his hands. "And it's a promise I need you to keep."

Agatha looked into his scared eyes.

"Oh good grief."

They turned to see Sophie at the altar, bag clenched to her chest.

"I'll be home by the weekend," she frowned. "And my bed better have clean sheets."

As eight o'clock approached, Sophie sat on the altar table, surrounded by dripping candles, listening to her stomach rumble. She'd let her father take the last of her butterless bran oat crackers for the boys, because Agatha had practically forced her. The boys would gag on them, surely. That made her feel better.

Sophie sighed. *The School Master was right. I am Evil.*

Yet for all his powers and sorcery, he hadn't known there was a cure. A friend who made her Good. As long as she had Agatha, she'd never be that ugly, horrible witch again.

When the church darkened, Agatha had resisted leaving her alone, but Stefan forced her. The Elders had been clear—"Only Sophie"—and now was not the time to disobey their orders. Not when they were about to save her life.

Without Agatha there now, Sophie suddenly felt anxious. Was this how Agatha used to feel about her? Sophie had treated her so callously back then, lost in her princess fantasies. Now she couldn't imagine a future without her. No matter how hard it was, she'd endure the days ahead in hiding—but only because she knew she'd have her friend at the end of it. Her friend who had become her real family.

But then why had Agatha been acting so strange lately?

The past month, Sophie had noticed a growing distance. Agatha didn't laugh as much on their walks, was often cold to the touch, and seemed preoccupied with her thoughts. For the first time since they met, Sophie had started to feel she had more invested in this friendship.

Then came the wedding. She had pretended not to notice Agatha's hand, dripping, trembling in hers as if wanting to slip out. As if gripping a terrible secret.

"Maybe I'm not as Good as you think."

Sophie's pulse hammered in her ears. Agatha's finger couldn't have glowed that day.

Could it?

She thought of her mother, who too had beauty, wit, and charm . . . who too had a friend she had long trusted . . . only to be betrayed by her and die broken and alone.

Sophie shook off the thought. Agatha had given up a prince for her. Almost given her life for her. Agatha had found them a happy ending against all odds.

In the cold, dark church, Sophie's heart skittered out of beat.

So why would she ruin our fairy tale?

Behind her, the church doors creaked open. Sophie turned with relief and saw the shadows waiting in their gray cloaks, black hats in hand.

Only the Eldest was holding something else.

Something sharper.

The problem with living in a graveyard is the dead have no need for light. Besides the flittering torches over the gates, the cemetery was pitch-black at midnight, and anything beyond just an inky shadow. Peering through her window's broken shutters, Agatha caught the sheen of white tents down the hill, pitched to house those left homeless by the attacks. Somewhere out there, the Elders were about to move Sophie to safety. All she could do was wait.

"I should have hidden near the church," she said, and licked a fresh scratch from Reaper, who still acted like she was a stranger.

"You can't disobey the Elders," said her mother, sitting stiffly on her bed, eyes on a mantel clock with hands made of bones. "They've been civil since you stopped the kidnappings. Let's keep it that way."

"Oh please," Agatha scoffed. "What could three old men possibly do to me?"

"What all men do in times of fear." Callis' eyes stayed on the clock. "Blame the witch."

"Mmhmm. Burn us at the stake too," Agatha snorted, flopping onto her bed.

Tension thickened the silence. She sat up and saw her mother's strained face, still staring ahead.

"You're not serious, Mother."

Sweat beaded on Callis' lip. "They needed a scapegoat when the kidnappings wouldn't stop."

"They *burnt* women?" Agatha uttered in shock.

"Unless we married. That's what the storybooks taught them to do."

"But you never married—" Agatha countered. "How did you survive—"

"Because I had someone stand up for me," her mother said, watching the bones strike eight. "And he paid the price."

"My father? You said he was a rotten two-timer who died in a mill accident."

Callis didn't answer, gazing ahead.

A chill prickled up Agatha's spine. She looked at her mother. "What did you mean when you said Stefan suffered worst of all? When the Elders arranged his marriage?"

Callis' eyes stayed on the clock. "The problem with Stefan is he trusts those he shouldn't. He always believes people are Good." The long bone ticked past eight. Her shoulders slumped with relief. "But no one is as Good as they seem, dear," Callis said softly, turning to her daughter. "Surely you know that."

For the first time, Agatha saw her mother's eyes. There were tears in them.

"No—" Agatha gasped, a red rash searing her neck.

"They'll say it was her choice," Callis rasped.

"You *knew*," Agatha choked, lurching for the door. "You knew they weren't moving her—"

Her mother intercepted her. "They knew you'd bring her back! They promised to spare you if I kept you here until—"

Agatha shoved her into the wall—her mother lunged for

her and missed. *"They'll kill you!"* Callis screamed out the window, but darkness had swallowed her daughter up.

Without a torch, Agatha stumbled and tripped down the hill, rolling through cold, wet grass until she barreled into a tent at the bottom. Mumbling frantic apology to a family who thought her a cannonball, she dashed for the church between homeless dozens stewing beetles and lizards over fires, wrapping their children in mangy blankets, bracing for the next attack that would never come. Tomorrow the Elders would mourn Sophie's valiant "sacrifice," her statue would be rebuilt, and the villagers would go on to a new Christmas, relieved of another curse. . . .

With a cry, Agatha threw the oak doors open.

The church was empty. Long, deep scratches ripped down the aisle.

Sophie had dragged her glass slippers all the way.

Agatha sank to her knees in mud.

Stefan.

She had promised him. She had promised to keep his daughter safe.

Agatha hunched over, face in her hands. This was her fault. This would always be her fault. She had everything she wanted. She had a friend, she had love, she had *Sophie.* And she had traded her for a wish. She was Evil. Worse than Evil. She was the one who deserved to die.

"Please . . . I'll bring her home . . . ," she heaved. "Please . . . I promise . . . I'll do anything . . ."

But there was nothing to do. Sophie was gone. Delivered to

invisible killers as a ransom for peace.

"I'm sorry . . . I didn't mean it. . . ." Agatha wept, spit dripping. How could she tell a father his daughter was dead? How could either of them live with her broken promise? Her sobs slowly receded, curdling to terror. She didn't move for a long time.

At last Agatha slumped up in a nauseous daze and staggered east towards Stefan's house. Every step away from the church made her feel sicker. Limping down the dirt lane, she vaguely felt something sticky and wet on her legs. Without thinking, she wiped a gob off a knee with her finger and smelled it.

Honeycream.

Agatha froze, heart pounding. There was more cream on the ground ahead, spurted in a desperate trail towards the lake. Adrenaline blasted through her blood.

Nibbling his toenails in his tent, Radley heard crackles behind him and turned just in time to see a shadow swipe his dagger and torch.

"Assassin!" he squeaked—

Agatha swung her head back to see men explode out of tents and chase her as she tracked the honeycream like breadcrumbs towards the lake. She ran faster, following the trail, but soon the globs turned smaller and smaller and then sprayed to specks in every direction. As Agatha hesitated, searching for another sign to guide her, the men reached the lake, racing east around the shore towards her. But there were three figures across the lake, hunting her from the west. In their torchlight, she saw the shadows of three long cloaks and beards—

Elders.

They'd kill her.

Agatha spun, waving her torch in front of her, as both sides converged. *Sophie, where are you*—

"Kill him!" she heard a man's voice cry from the mob.

Agatha swiveled in shock. She knew his voice.

"Kill the assassin!" the man screamed again as his mob ran towards her.

Panicked, Agatha stuttered forward, swinging the torch at the trees. Something heavy whizzed past her ear, another past her ribs—

Then a sparkle flared ahead and she froze her flame on it.

The empty honeycream pouch lay at the forest edge, snake-skin scales glinting.

A hard, cold blow smashed into her back. Agatha buckled to her knees and saw a jagged rock on the ground beside her. She turned to see more men aiming stones at her head, less than fifty feet away from the east. Rushing in from the west, the Elders held up their torches, about to glimpse her face—

Agatha hurled her torch in the lake, plunging her into pitch darkness.

With confused cries, the men whisked torches wildly to find the assassin. They saw a shadow sprint past them for the trees. Like lions to a kill, they charged in a grunting, vengeful mob, chasing faster, faster, one breaking from the pack, and just as the man who screamed for blood caught the assassin by the neck, the shadow whirled to face him—

Stefan gasped in shock, long enough for Agatha to press her lips to his ear.

"I promise."

Then she was gone into the labyrinth, like a white rose into a grave.

4

Red Hoods Ride

Agatha heard the men's shouts recede with the light of their torches. Kneeling against a wet, crumbly tree trunk in darkness, she folded her shivering arms into her black dress.

A few distant hoots and skitters muffled to silence. Agatha didn't move, her spine throbbing where the rock hit her. All this time she had focused on rescuing her best friend and going back. Back to what? Murderous Elders? More assassin attacks? A village that wanted Sophie gone?

She thought of innocent women burnt publicly in a square, not so long ago, and her stomach turned over. *How can we ever go home?* Their future in Gavaldon was just as dark as the Woods around her now. To go home, she couldn't just rescue Sophie. She had to defeat these assassins—whoever they were—and stop their attacks once and for all.

But she had no idea how to even begin looking for her friend. For hundreds of years, the villagers had stormed into the forest, seeking its lost children—only to come out the other side, right where they started. Like all the missing children, she and Sophie had seen what lay beyond the forest: a dangerous world of Good and Evil that had no end. They had been the lucky ones to return, sealing the gates between reality and fantasy forever . . . or so she'd thought. One wish, and the gates had reopened.

Wherever Sophie was, she was in terrible danger.

Rising from a crouch, Agatha stepped into the Endless Woods, clumps crunching on dead leaves. Inching forward, she probed blindly with her hands, feeling splintered bark, cobwebbed branches. . . . Her head smacked into a tree and a shadow flung out, spewed something wet at her face, and vanished with a hiss. In response came a chorus of grunts and groans, all through the woods, like a sleeping enemy called to arms. Dazed, Agatha scraped the goo off her face and pulled Radley's dagger from her pocket. Scuffling sounds came from beneath her feet.

Through dead leaves, she saw pupils open and shut in the undergrowth, yellow and green, glinting in one place, reappearing in another. Agatha shrank against the tree, trying not to blink. Little by little, her eyes adjusted, just in time to see eight slinky shadows unfurl from the ground in a circle around her, like coiling trails of smoke.

Snakes.

Only they were thicker than snakes, black as ash, with flattened heads and needle-sharp barbs through every scale. They rose higher, higher around Agatha, angling towards her with long, overlapping hisses, opening their full-fanged jaws wide—

All at once, they spat.

Gobs of mucus pinned Agatha to the tree, and she dropped the dagger. She tried to wrench free, but sour film smacked into her mouth and eyes so all she could see was a ring of blurry, spiny silhouettes. They all aimed at different parts of her body, then curled their trunks around her, barbs piercing into her skin. Flailing silently, Agatha saw a last one, bigger than the rest, lower from a branch and loop its cold, black tail around her neck. As its barbs pricked her throat, she gasped for more breath, but the monster's head was slithering up her face now. It pressed its fat nose against the film over her cheeks, glaring at her through thin, acid-green pupils . . . and started to squeeze. Agatha choked and closed her eyes.

She felt no hurt, only her soul searching for a memory. . . . She was sitting on a lakeshore, head on someone's shoulder. Arm in arm, they held each other, sun drenching their skin, breaths quietly matched. Agatha listened to the silence of happiness, Ever After in a single moment. . . . Then sharp, stabbing pain flooded her body and she knew the end had come. Gripping the arm beside her, Agatha gazed into their lake's reflection, needing to see her happy ending's face, one last time—

It wasn't Sophie's.

Light speared the darkness. The snakes recoiled with screams and scudded back under dead leaves.

Agatha opened her eyes. Dazed, she looked around for the source of light. Through the veil of goo, she saw it was her fingertip, burning gold for the first time since the wedding. She was at once relieved and sickened. Both times it had happened thinking of *him*.

Magic follows emotion, Yuba had warned. She'd lost control of both.

This time, however, her finger didn't dim. Agatha held it up, confused. She focused on her need to get off this tree, and suddenly the glow pulsed brighter, as if waiting for instructions. Agatha's heart pumped faster. She'd crossed into the fairy-tale world. Her magic was back.

Bursting with pain and stuck to a tree, Agatha was hardly in shape to remember spells from school. But when her breaths settled, she managed a basic melt jinx, and the mucus rinsed away with the blood, leaving her black dress sticky and soaked. Still, she was alive somehow, and with a wretched groan, Agatha picked up Radley's dagger and pried off the soggy bark.

Finger aglow, she swept it like a torch through knotted trees, searching for a path, like Yuba had taught them. Like all the group leaders at the School for Good and Evil, the old gnome had used the Blue Forest, a lush, tranquil training ground meant to mimic the Endless Woods and prepare students for what they'd face. Agatha squeezed between two rotted tree trunks, trying to ignore the burning cuts all over her body. Now the Blue Forest seemed like the School Master's cruel joke.

Agatha wrenched between more webbed trees towards a gap in the thicket, hoping it'd be the path. She didn't dare call Sophie's name and signal the assassins she was on their trail.

With each step, Agatha felt a growing sense of doom. She'd been in the Endless Woods twice before, but this time it was different. There was no school to save her. There was no Tedros.

Her fingerglow pulsed brighter.

Tedros of Camelot.

Finally she said his name to herself, here, alone in the Woods. The last time she'd seen her prince was in the twilight of her and Sophie's kiss, a kiss he thought would be his. As he watched her disappear into thin air, he reached for her, choking a scream—*"Wait!"*

She'd had the choice to take his hand. She'd had the choice to stay as his princess. She felt it as her body glowed to light, trapped between worlds.

But she chose Sophie, and then Agatha was gone.

She was so sure she'd made the right choice. It was the only ending she ever wanted. But the more she tried to forget him, the more her prince came. In dreams, day and night . . . his pained blue eyes . . . his body lunging . . . his big, strong hand, reaching for hers . . .

Until one day she reached back.

Just find Sophie, she gritted, remembering her promise to

Stefan. All she wanted was Sophie home alive—charming, maniacal, ludicrous Sophie. She'd never doubt her happy ending again.

As she waded through a mess of fallen branches towards the gap in the trees, Agatha held up her lit finger and saw it wasn't a path at all. It was a vast cesspool of mud, rusted red, stretching east and west as far as she could see. She picked up a rock and lobbed it into the pool. The splash wasn't shallow.

Suddenly Agatha noticed two shadows down the bank, probing at the red mud with dark hooves: a horned stag with his female deer. After a few more testing prods, the stag seemed satisfied, and both slid into the mud side by side, swimming towards the distant bank. Relieved, Agatha rolled up her dress to follow them—

Something snatched the female deer and Agatha stumbled back in shock. Three long, spiny white crocodile snouts rose from the mud, thin and rectangular, with enormous round nostrils and black shark teeth, tearing into the thrashing female. They pulled her under, ignoring the bigger male completely as he flailed whimpering to the far shore.

Agatha didn't try to cross.

Tears in her eyes, she staggered back the way she came, sweeping her fingerglow across the maze of trees. Where was her friend? What had they done with her? Trying to stifle her sobs, she limped towards the forest edge, seeing nothing but the shadows of skeletal branches . . . slivers of dark clouds . . . a hot glow of pink. . . .

She stopped her finger on it, pulsing like a beacon to bad behavior. Anyone else would have mistaken it for an animal's eye. But Agatha knew.

Only one animal on earth made a pink like that.

She tore through trees, fighting her pain, following the pink glow fading weaker in the distance. As she neared, she began to see smears of blood on trees, like the trail of a wounded beast. She plowed through broken branches and ripped away vines, hair snaring on nettles, until she caught wisps of lavender perfume. Agatha jumped over a log, heart bursting from her chest, and charged into the small glade—

"Sophie!"

Sophie didn't respond. Facing away, she was slumped on her knees behind a far tree, arms over her head. The second finger on her right hand pulsed her signature pink glow a few last times and dulled to pale.

"Sophie?" Agatha said. Her own gold fingerglow went cold.

Sophie still didn't move.

Agatha approached the tree, dread rising. She could hear her friend's shallow breaths. Slowly Agatha reached out and touched bare shoulder through Sophie's torn dress.

There was blood on it.

Agatha spun her around. Sophie's hands were lashed to a branch with braided horse reins. There were shallow knife pricks in each of her palms, from which the Elders had taken blood and smeared a scarlet message on Sophie's chest.

TAKE ME

Frantic, Agatha cut Sophie down with her knife, trying in vain to think of a spell to wash away the blood. She scrubbed at her friend's skin with shaking palms. "I'm sorry—" she choked, severing the last rein. "I'll get us home—I promise—"

The instant she was free, Sophie covered Agatha's mouth with ice-cold hands. Agatha followed her wide, bloodshot eyes. . . .

There was something on all the trees ahead, flapping milky white in the darkness. Agatha held up her glowing finger.

Parchment scrolls crackled in the wind like dead leaves, tacked to the trunks. Each one was the same.

The face on the posters was Sophie's.

"That's impossible!" Agatha cried. "He's dea—"

She froze.

Between trees she caught glints of red. Something was coming.

Agatha grabbed Sophie's wrist and dragged her behind a trunk. Muffling Sophie's moans with her hand, Agatha slowly peeked out.

Through tangled branches, she saw men in red leather hoods, eyeholes cut away. They carried fire-tipped arrows, which lit up their sleeveless black leather uniforms and bare, muscular arms. She tried to count how many there were—10, 15, 20, 25 . . . until she counted one whose violet eyes glared right at her. Grinning, he raised his bow.

"Down!" Agatha yelped—

The first arrow singed Sophie's neck as both girls dove into dirt. Neither spoke as they floundered through snarls of black briars, dozens of flaming arrows barely missing them and igniting trees left and right. Hand in hand, the girls fled deeper into the Woods, looking for somewhere to hide, red hoods gaining, until they came to a break in the trees and finally glimpsed the forest path, serene in moonlight. Wheezing with relief, they ran for it and stopped short.

The path forked into two. Both trails were thin and sooty, crooking away in opposite directions. Neither looked more hopeful than the other, but from reading storybooks, the girls knew.

Only one was correct.

"Which way?" Sophie rasped.

Agatha could see just how weak and shaken her friend was. She had to get her to safety. Hearing the skimming of arrows again, Agatha swung her head between the paths, burning trees growing nearer . . . nearer. . . .

"Aggie, which *way*?" Sophie pressed.

Agatha's eyes darted uselessly back and forth, waiting for a sign—

Sophie gasped. "Look!"

Agatha swiveled to the east path. A glowing blue butterfly flapped in darkness, high above the trail. It beat its wings faster and nosed forward, as if urging them to follow.

"Come on," Sophie said, suddenly strong again, and surged forward.

"We're following a *butterfly*?" Agatha retorted as she chased Sophie past WANTED signs on trees ahead.

"Don't worry. It's leading us out of here!"

"How do you know?"

"Hurry! We'll lose it!"

"You don't know what I've been through—" Agatha heaved, puffing behind.

"Let's not play who's had it worse, shall we!"

The butterfly sped up as if nearing its destination and veered around a bend, wings brightening to blinding blue. Sophie grabbed Agatha by the wrist, dragged her faster around the curve—

Into a dead end of fallen trees.

The butterfly was gone.

"No!" Sophie squeaked. "But I thought—I thought—"

"It was a *special* butterfly?"

Sophie shook her head, eyes welling, as if her friend couldn't understand. Then, over Agatha's shoulder, she saw a torch-lit shadow inch across the trees, then two more . . .

The hoods had found their path.

"We had our happy ending—" Sophie backed against a trunk. "This is all my fault—"

"No . . . ," Agatha said, looking down. "It's mine."

Sophie's heart clamped. It was the same feeling she had alone in the church, thinking about how her friend had changed. A feeling that told her none of the last month was an accident.

"Agatha . . . why is this all happening?"

Agatha watched the shadows grow closer around the bend. Her eyes stung with tears. "Sophie . . . I—I—I—made a—mistake—"

"Aggie, slow down."

Agatha couldn't look at her. "I opened it—I opened our fairy tale—"

"I don't understand—"

"A w-w-wish!" Agatha stammered, reddening. "I made a wish—"

Sophie shook her head. "A wish?"

"I didn't mean it—it happened so fast—"

"A wish for what?"

Agatha took a deep breath. She looked into her friend's scared eyes.

"Sophie, I wished I was with—"

"Tickets," a voice said.

Both girls turned to see an alarmingly thin caterpillar with a top hat, curled mustache, and purple tuxedo poking out of a tree hollow.

"Thank you for calling the Flowerground. No spitting, sneezing, singing, sniffling, swinging, swearing, slapping, sleeping, or urinating in the flowertrains. Violations will result in the removal of your clothes. Tickets?"

Sophie and Agatha gaped at each other. Neither had the faintest idea how to call the Flowerground.

"Look, mister," Agatha pressured, glancing back at shadows nearing the dead-end turn, "we need to ride right now and we don't have—"

"Leave it to me," Sophie whispered, and twirled. "Such a pleasure to see you again, conductor! Remember me? We met when you graciously escorted our class to the Garden of Good and Evil. And look at that lovely mustache! I just *love* a good mustache—"

"No ticket, no ride," the caterpillar crabbed, and withdrew.

"But they'll kill us!" Agatha cried, seeing red hoods turn into view—

"Special circumstances can be presented in writing on Form Code 77 at the Flowerground Registry Office, open on alternate Mondays from 3:00 p.m. until 3:30 p.m.—"

Agatha grabbed him from the tree. "Let us in or I *eat* you."

The caterpillar bleached in her grip. "NEVERS!" he

called. Vines shot out and sucked Agatha and Sophie into the hollow as arrows set the tree aflame.

The two girls fell through a pit of swirling pastel colors until vines flung them over a snapping Venus flytrap into a tunnel of blinding-hot mist. Shielding their eyes, the girls felt their vines cinch around their chests like straitjackets and hook on to something above them. Both peeked through their hands to see that they were dangling in midair from a luminescent green tree trunk stenciled:

ARBOREA LINE

"The butterfly called the train somehow!" Sophie yelled from her tight harness as the track propelled them ahead. "See! The butterfly was trying to help us!"

Coming out of the mist, Agatha gaped at the Flowerground for the first time, speechless. Before her was a spectacular underground transport system, big as half of Gavaldon, made entirely of plants. Color-coded tree trunks crisscrossed like rail tracks in a bottomless cavern, whisking passengers dangling from vine straps to their respective destinations in the Endless Woods. The conductor, perched in a glass-windowed compartment inside ARBOREA's green trunk, grumpily called stops into a willow microphone as flowertrains flitted by: "Maidenvale!" "Avalon Towers!" "Runyon Lane!" "Ginnymill!"

Whenever passengers heard their stop, they pulled hard on their vine strap; the strap fastened around their wrist, unfurled off their track, and ferried them high to one of many wind-wheel exits that churned them out of the Flowerground and up onto land.

Agatha noticed their green line's trunk was jam-packed with women in twittering conversation, some well dressed and cheerful, others oddly haglike and unattractive for Evers, while the red ROSALINDA LINE running perpendicular had only a few glum, scraggly-looking men. Under those two tree tracks, the yellow DAHLIA LINE buzzed with groups of beautiful and homely women, while its crisscrossing pink PEONY LINE had only three rumpled, dirty male dwarfs. Agatha didn't remember the caterpillar saying anything about women and men sitting apart, but then again she couldn't remember half his stupid rules.

She was distracted by two parakeets, feathers the color of a rain forest, who fluttered up with glasses of celery-cucumber juice and pistachio muffins. On the illuminated tree trunk above her head, an orchestra of well-dressed lizards struck up a baroque waltz on violins and flutes, accompanied by a chorus of caroling green frogs. For the first time in weeks, Agatha managed a smile. She inhaled the sweet, nutty muffin in one bite and washed it down with the tart green juice.

In the harness next to her, Sophie sniffed and poked at her muffin.

"You going to eat that?" Agatha said.

Sophie shoved it at her, mumbling something about butter and the devil's work. "It's easy to get home," she said, watching

Agatha scarf it. "All we have to do is ride this line in the opposite direct—"

Agatha had stopped chewing. Slowly Sophie followed her friend's eyes to her own punctured palms . . . to the raw marks around her wrists left by the Elders' reins . . . to the scarlet letters faint on her chest. . . .

"We can't go home, can we?" Sophie breathed.

"Even if we prove the Elders lied, the School Master will still hunt you," said Agatha miserably.

"He can't be alive. We saw him die, Aggie." Sophie looked up at her friend. "Didn't we?"

Agatha didn't have an answer.

"How did we lose it, Aggie?" Sophie said, looking so confused. "How did we lose our happy ending?"

Agatha knew this was the time to finish what she'd started at the hollow. But gazing into Sophie's big doe eyes, she couldn't bear to break her heart. Somehow there had to be a way to fix this without her friend ever knowing what she'd wished for. Her wish was just a mistake. A mistake she'd never ever have to face.

"There has to be a way to get our ending back," Agatha said, determined. "We just need to seal the gates—"

But Sophie was staring past her, head cocked. Agatha turned around.

The Flowerground was empty behind them. All its passengers had disappeared.

"Aggie . . . ," Sophie wheezed, squinting into the distant mist—

Agatha saw them now too. Red hoods swinging across the tracks, straight for their train.

Both girls tore at their harnesses, but the vines yoked them tighter. Agatha tried to make her finger glow, but it wouldn't light—

"Aggie, they're coming!" Sophie yelled, seeing the hoods leap onto the red line two tracks above.

"Pull on your vine!" Agatha shouted, for that's how she'd seen the others get off the ride. But no matter how hard she or Sophie tugged, the track just whisked them along.

Agatha fumbled for Radley's dagger and cut herself free, eyeing the red hoods getting closer. "Stay there!" she screamed at Sophie, measuring the distance to her friend's vine. Dangling from her strap, Agatha winced at the giant flytraps snapping out of the bottomless pastel pit below. With a cry, she kicked and swung herself into the tunnel wind for her friend—

Agatha's hands missed the strap and she crashed into Sophie, grappling her like a tree.

The green tree trunk turned bright orange and started flashing. "VIOLATION," a crabby voice boomed over a speaker. "NO SWINGING. VIOLATION. NO SWINGING. VIOLATION—"

A flock of green parakeets flew in and started pecking at Agatha's dress, trying to pull it off. She dropped her knife. "What the—"

"Get off her!" Sophie shrieked, slapping the birds away.

"VIOLATION," the crabby voice blared. "NO SLAPPING. VIOLATION. NO SLAPPING."

The lizards and frogs atop their track skittered down the green-flowered vines and started tugging at Sophie's clothes. Aghast, Sophie smacked at them, sending lizards and flowers flying. Agatha inhaled the pollen and sneezed.

"VIOLATION. NO SNEEZING. VIOLATION." Birds, lizards, and frogs from other lines descended to denude both girls as punishment—

"We need to get off!" Agatha cried.

"I know! I only have two buttons left!" Sophie squealed, slapping the frog away.

"No! We need to get off *now*!"

Agatha pointed at the red hoods swinging onto their track—

"Follow me!" she cried to Sophie, shaking off a rainbow of lizards, and swung to the next strap. She glanced back to see Sophie still grappling a canary on her collar. "Shoo! This is handmade!"

"NOW!" Agatha roared—

Sophie gasped and swung for the next vine. She missed and plunged screaming towards a gnashing flytrap. Agatha blanched in horror—

Sophie belly flopped onto the blue HIBISCUS LINE below, running parallel at high speed. Hands and legs wrapped around the glowing trunk, she looked up at Agatha, who heaved with relief.

"Aggie, watch out!" Sophie yelled—

Agatha wheeled to a hood on her vine. He grabbed her throat.

Hearing Agatha's choked gurgles above her, Sophie tried to stand on her trunk, then saw a thorn tunnel ahead about to decapitate her and plastered down just as her train whooshed through. Suddenly she heard a twinkly sound and swerved her head down the tunnel to see the glowing blue butterfly, hovering in place above the track.

"Help us!" Sophie begged—

The butterfly beat its wings and whizzed forward. As her train came out of the tunnel, Sophie scooted down the tree trunk to follow it, shadows of the hood strangling Agatha darkening the track ahead. Frantic, Sophie tried to keep up with the butterfly, but two red hoods landed in front of her, bows and arrows in hand. Just as they aimed, she looked back with terror and saw the hood about to snap Agatha's neck—

The butterfly dove and yanked the vine under Sophie's hand. In an instant, the vine snared Sophie's wrist, ripped her off the track, and lassoed Agatha's hand on the way up. The hoods whirled in shock, spewing their knives and arrows at them, but the vine coiled like a whip and launched both girls upwards into a blue windwheel of light. The rush of air sucked them towards the light portal in a storm of loose petals, pulling up, up, up—

And into a lush field.

Kneeling in a bed of tall red and yellow lilies, Agatha and Sophie heaved for breath, faces scratched, petals in hair, and dresses barely still on. Both looked down at the dirt-plugged hole they'd just spouted from, broiled with arrows from below.

"Where are we?" Sophie said, searching for the blue butterfly.

Agatha shook her head. "I don't—"

Then she saw a red lily and a yellow lily whispering to each other, giving her strange looks.

She'd seen flowers talking about her once before, she thought. In a field just like this, until they'd tugged her by the wrist and yanked her up to . . .

Agatha lurched to her feet.

The School for Good soared above them, shimmering in red-orange sunrise over the crystal-clear side of Halfway Bay. Its four glass towers, once divided between pink and blue, were now only blue, with flags bearing butterflies of the same color billowing from sharp minarets.

"We're back," Sophie gasped.

Agatha went white as snow.

Back to the one place she'd tried to forget. Back to the one place that could ruin everything.

Ahead, the closed doors to the Good castle lay atop a hill. Golden spiked gates barred the path up the Great Lawn, mirrored words arching over them:

THE SCHOOL FOR GIRL
EDUCATION AND ENLIGHTENMENT

Agatha closed and reopened her bleary eyes, for she had seen wrong.

It still said "GIRL."

"Huh?"

Sophie stood up beside her. "That's strange."

"Well, 'Good' and 'Girl' aren't so far apart," Agatha said. "Maybe one of the nymphs got confused."

But then she saw what Sophie was looking at. At the half-way point across the bay, Good's lake slimed into Evil's moat. Only the moat wasn't black, like it used to be. It was rusted red, the color of the cesspool in the Woods and guarded by the spiny white crocodiles she had seen eat the female deer—at least twenty of them, lurking in the sludge, black shark teeth glinting.

Slowly Agatha looked up at the School for Evil looming above the moat. Three bloodred towers, jagged with spikes, flanked a smooth silver tower, twice as tall as the others. Atop the four towers, black flags crackled in the fog, emblazoned with scarlet snakes.

"There used to be *three* Evil towers," Sophie said, squinting. "Not four . . ."

Voices rose across the bay and the two girls ducked into the lilies.

Out of the Woods stormed men in black through Evil's castle gates.

They were wearing red leather hoods.

"The School Master's men!" Sophie cried as they faded into the fog.

Agatha whitened. "But that means—"

She whirled back to the bay.

"It's . . . *gone*," breathed Agatha, for the School Master's sky-high silver tower, once guarding the halfway point between moat and lake, had simply . . . disappeared.

"No, it's not," Sophie said, still eyeing the School for Evil.

Now Agatha saw why there were four towers there instead of three.

The School Master's tower had moved to Evil.

"He's *alive*!" Agatha cried, gaping at his silver spire. "But how—"

Sophie pointed. "Look!"

In the tower's single window, veiled by fog, a shadow stared down at them. All they could see of its face was a gleaming silver mask.

"It's him!" Sophie hissed. "He's leading Evil!"

"Agatha! Sophie!"

The girls swiveled from the lilies to see Professor Dovey running from Good castle in her green high-necked gown.

"Come quickly!"

As the two girls hurried behind her through Good's golden gates, Agatha glanced back at the School Master's tower and the masked shadow in the window. All they had to do was kill him again, and her mistake would be hidden forever. They'd go home safe, her promise to Stefan kept, and Sophie would never know what she'd wished for. Looking up at that shadow lording over Evil, Agatha waited for her heart to rage with purpose, to propel her into battle . . . but instead her heart did something else.

It fluttered.

The way a princess's did in storybooks.

When she saw her prince.

5

The Other School

As she and Sophie sprinted behind Professor Dovey into the mirrored corridor, Agatha tried to find her breath. Professor Dovey was a famous fairy godmother, who'd always looked out for her. She had to give them answers.

"Who are those red hoods?" Agatha asked.

"How did the School Master survive?" said Sophie.

"Why are the Nevers on his side?" said Agatha.

"Quiet!" Professor Dovey snapped, erasing their footsteps with her magic wand. "We don't have much time!"

"You don't seem surprised to see us," Agatha whispered, but her fairy godmother didn't respond as she rushed them

into Good's deserted foyer, magically bolting doors behind them.

Only months ago, Sophie had eviscerated the hall in her witch's revenge on Agatha and Tedros, blasting its stained glass windows, spiral staircases, and marble floors to shards. But now the two friends drew breaths at its redone facade. Where there used to be two pink staircases and two blue, all four stairwells were now the same royal blue as the castle. Lit by high stained glass windows, the staircases spiraled up to the dormitory towers, names tattooed on richly decorated balusters: HONOR, VALOR, PURITY, and CHARITY. Agatha had loathed the prissy princess pink of the Purity and Charity towers, but seeing them turned the same color as the prince towers gave her an unsettled feeling.

Sophie nudged her, and Agatha turned to see her peering curiously at the Legends Obelisk in the center of the foyer, a soaring crystal column blanketed with portrait frames. Inside each of the frames was a painting of a past student, next to a storybook illustration of what the child became upon graduation. But looking up at the gold-framed Evers on top who became princesses and queens, the silver-framed ones in the middle who became helpers and sidekicks, and the bottom-rung lot who became cinder sweeps and servants, the two girls noticed something peculiar. . . .

"Where are the boys?" Sophie said, for all their portraits had been removed.

Agatha swung her head to the Honor staircase: the frieze of knights and kings had been replaced with a frieze of sword-brandishing, chain-mailed princesses. Sophie swiveled to the Valor staircase, once decorated with burly hunters and their trusty hounds—now huntresses in houndskins and decidedly female dogs. Both girls twirled to the lettered murals across the walls that once spelled E-V-E-R . . . and now spelled G-I-R-L.

"It *is* a School for Girls!" said Agatha, thunderstruck. "What happened to Good?"

"We can't fight the School Master without *boys*!" cried Sophie.

"Shhhh!" Professor Dovey hissed, rushing them up the Valor staircase. "No one must know you're here!"

As the girls chased her elegant silver-haired bun through Valor's princely blue arches and murals, they gawked at the once virile visions of princes destroying demons and saving helpless princesses, now flaunting different endings: Snow White smashing out of her glass coffin with her fists, Red Riding Hood slitting the wolf's throat, Sleeping Beauty setting her spindle on fire. . . . The red-blooded princes, hunters, men who rescued them, who saved their lives . . . gone.

"It's like Everboys never existed!" whispered Agatha.

"Maybe the School Master killed them all!" whispered Sophie.

She suddenly heard soft tinkling and twirled to see three glowing blue butterflies peeking from behind a wall. They caught her looking and with a high-pitched *meep!* ducked and disappeared.

"What is it?" Agatha said, glancing back.

"Hurry!" Professor Dovey scolded, and the two girls

scampered to follow, stooping past the Laundry, where two seven-foot, floating nymphs scrubbed sudsy blue bodices, through the Supper Hall, where enchanted pots stewed saffron rice and lentil soup, and past the Valor Common Room to the rear stairwell. Exhausted and aching from their torments in the Woods, Sophie and Agatha tried to keep up, but Professor Dovey was sprier than she looked.

"Where are we *going*?" Agatha panted.

"To the only other person who can keep you alive," her fairy godmother shot back, bustling up the stairs.

Sophie and Agatha instantly ran faster, up five long flights to the lone white door on the sixth floor—

"Professor Sader's office?" Agatha puffed. "But he's dead!"

Professor Dovey ran her fingers over the raised blue dots on the former History teacher's door. It swung open without a sound, and Sophie and Agatha scrambled in behind her.

A thin woman stood at the window, long black braid dangling over the back of her pointy-shouldered purple gown. "Did anyone see you?"

"No," said Professor Dovey.

Lady Lesso spun to Sophie and Agatha, violet eyes flashing. "Then it's time they learned what they've done."

"*We* did this?" Agatha blurted.

"But we weren't even here!" said Sophie, turning between the Dean of Evil at the window and the Dean of Good at Professor Sader's old desk, overflowing with open books.

Lady Lesso glowered at their dirt-smudged faces. "In this

world, actions have consequences. *Endings* have consequences."

"But our fairy tale ended happily!" Sophie said.

Professor Dovey let out a groan.

"Why don't you tell us how it ended?" Lady Lesso sneered, blue veins throbbing.

"We killed the School Master and solved his riddle!" Sophie said.

"That's how Sophie and I went home!" said Agatha.

"Clarissa, show them how it really ends," Lady Lesso growled.

Professor Dovey flung a book across the desk. It was heavy and thick, bound with brown sheepskin and spattered with mud. Agatha opened to the first soggy page. Black calligraphy, slightly smeared, spilled across fresh parchment.

The Tale of Sophie & Agatha

Sophie turned the page to a richly colored painting of her and Agatha, standing before the School Master.

Once upon a time, the script below read, *there were two girls.*

Agatha remembered the line. The Storian had written it to start their fairy tale when they broke into the School Master's tower. Flipping the book's pages, Agatha saw her and Sophie's story unfold in a brilliant sweep of paintings: Sophie trying to win Tedros' kiss . . . Agatha saving Tedros' life in a brutal attack . . . Agatha and Tedros falling in love . . . Sophie transforming into a vengeful witch . . . the School Master stabbing Sophie . . . Agatha reviving her with love's kiss . . . and then the very last page . . . a dazzling vision of Tedros desperately reaching for Agatha as she and Sophie disappeared, three words beneath to close their story. . . .

They were gone.

Agatha felt tears rise, soaking in all the pain and love she and Sophie had shared to get home.

"It's the perfect fairy tale," Sophie said, meeting Agatha's eyes with a choked-up smile.

They turned to the teachers, who looked deathly grim. "It's not over," said Lady Lesso.

The girls peered down at the book, confused. Their grimy hands lifted the last page, and they saw there was something on the other side.

A painting of Tedros, back turned, walking into dark fog, all alone.

And Sophie and Agatha lived happy ever after, for girls don't need princes for love to call. . . .

No, they don't need princes in their fairy tales at all.

"This one's from Maidenvale. But you can find it anywhere, really. They're even telling it in Netherwood."

Sophie and Agatha raised their heads to Professor Dovey, frowning over the messy desk.

"It's the only story anyone wants to hear."

Now the girls saw that all the open books weren't there by accident. Each book on the desk was spread to its last page. Some were in oil paints, some in watercolor, some in charcoal and ink; some were in a language the girls knew, others in scripts they didn't. But all ended their version of *The Tale of Sophie and Agatha* the same way: Tedros alone and unneeded, slumping into darkness.

"Goodness, all this gloom because we're *popular*?" Sophie said. "You can't be surprised. Snow White and Cinderella are sweet and all. But who wants them when they can have *me*?"

She turned to Agatha for support, but her friend was staring out the window. "Aggie?"

Agatha didn't answer. Slowly she approached the window, and Lady Lesso stepped aside without a word. At Sader's desk, Professor Dovey held her breath.

From the steep window, Agatha looked down at the Blue Forest, the enchanted training ground for Good and Evil, sprawled in an array of hues behind the school. It was as it always was, quiet and thriving despite the autumn chill, neatly fenced in by spiked golden gates.

The sounds were coming from beyond the gates.

At first she thought they were dead leaves, swathing the Endless Forest in tawny brown and orange beneath stripped, crooked trees. Then she looked closer and saw they were men.

Thousands of them were crammed against the Blue Forest gates in a filthy homeless camp, hunched around fires like miserable peasants. She couldn't see faces, but she glimpsed scraggly beards and blackened cheeks, mottled breeches and bony legs, ripped coats and sashes with gleaming . . .

Crests.

These weren't peasants. They were—

"Princes," Sophie gasped, looking out beside her.

"It's her!" a voice screamed from the crowd. Heads swung to the tower window.

"It's the witch!"

All at once, a savage mob rushed the Forest gates—

"Death to Sophie!"

"Kill her!"

"Kill the witch!"

The men fired arrows and catapulted stones at the tower, but the weapons instantly vanished into an enchanted shield, bubbly and violet tinged, that appeared over the school gates. As the crowd roared and swung pickets, mounted with the same WANTED signs the girls had seen in the woods, an intrepid prince leapt onto the spiked gates. The gold metal magically sizzled and he let go in shock, impaling on spikes below. Sophie spun in horror—

"How can those be princes?" she cried.

"How can those be princes?" Lady Lesso mimicked. "Those princes are there because of *you*."

Agatha and Sophie gaped at each other. "We don't understand—" Agatha spluttered.

Professor Dovey ground her teeth. The only time Agatha had seen her fairy godmother this furious was when she had disobeyed a teacher her first year and almost burned down the castle.

"*Think*, Agatha. Once upon a time, you believed yourself an ugly witch. But instead, your destiny was to become a *princess*.

To find Ever After with the most coveted prince in our land. It would have been Good's greatest victory! A restoration of all the values we'd lost! Kill the School Master, send your Evil friend home safe—and stay here with Tedros forever, as his future queen. All you had to do was take his hand before you disappeared. That would have been the *correct* fairy tale. But instead . . ."

She looked daggers at Sophie. "You chose her."

"And rightly so," Sophie riposted. "If you knew Agatha at all, you'd know she could never give me up for a *boy*." She whirled to her friend, knowing this time Agatha would defend her. But again, Agatha didn't. She just gulped hard and stared at her muddy clumps.

"What happened after we left?" Agatha said.

"The Eviction."

The girls turned to Lady Lesso, who shuddered at the memory.

"After your kiss, students tried to return to their schools, but the Evil towers ejected the Nevergirls. Sixty girls flung through windows into the bay—from stairs, classrooms, beds, toilets, common rooms. . . . They tried to go back, but the Evil gates barred their entry. All the Nevergirls fled to Good for sanctuary, and the Evergirls welcomed them, inspired by your happy ending."

"As soon as they arrived, the Good towers evicted the Everboys just as rudely," Professor Dovey went on. "The moment the boys were all gone, the castle magically changed to what it is now—their portraits removed, murals repainted, friezes recarved, as if mirroring your tale. The School for Good had become the School for *Girls*."

And indeed, the glittering crests over her and Lady Lesso's hearts, once silver swans, were now sparkling blue butterflies. Agatha shook her head, confused.

"But those aren't Everboys from school!" She pointed out the window. "Those are real princes!"

"What happened here happened everywhere in the Endless Woods," Professor Dovey said gravely. "As your story spread like a plague and princesses imagined a world without princes, the men were magically ejected from their castles and left homeless. They appealed to witches to break the curse, but they too had heard *The Tale of Sophie and Agatha*. Stirred by the power of your bond, witches joined forces with princesses and took control of the kingdoms."

"Witches and princesses are *friends*?" Sophie said in disbelief.

"No one thought it possible until your fairy tale," said Professor Dovey. "And now it is men and women who are enemies."

Agatha thought back to the Flowerground—the twittering women in groups, some pretty and cheerful, some homely and queer . . . the few scraggly, lonely males. . . .

"But we don't want the princes homeless!" Agatha cried. "We don't want them to be enemies!"

"We certainly don't want them to smell," murmured Sophie.

"You made princes irrelevant," Lady Lesso retorted. "You

made them impotent. You made them *obsolete*. And now you've made them turn to a new leader for revenge."

The girls followed her eyes to the sea of WANTED signs hoisted outside the gates, demanding Sophie's head at the orders of this leader.

"The School Master!" Sophie broke in. "We saw him—"

"Did you now?" Lady Lesso sneered.

"He's in the Evil castle! We have to kill him!" Sophie swiveled to Agatha. "Tell her!"

Agatha ignored the fluttering in her stomach. "But he *couldn't* have lived," she said, almost to herself. She looked up. "You were there too, professors. All of us saw him die."

"Indeed," said Professor Dovey. "But that doesn't mean he isn't replaced."

"Replaced?" the girls blurted.

"Naturally Lady Lesso and I believed ourselves the best candidates," Professor Dovey said, smoothing her gown's beetle wings. "Homeless and hated, the princes needed leaders they could trust. We assured them *The Tale of Sophie and Agatha* was closed forever. Under our protection, the Storian would restore boys and girls to balance, as it does Good and Evil. But just as we tried to bridge this peace between boys and girls . . ." Her face dimmed. "Something odd happened."

She thrust out the last page of their fairy tale and waited for the girls to say something.

"They drew Tedros taller than he is," Sophie suggested.

"Isn't something *missing*?" the Dean moaned.

Agatha remembered the storybook under her bed . . . the

wedded princess and prince. . . .

"'The End,'" she said. "Why doesn't it say 'The End'?"

Professor Dovey glared at her and slowly lifted the book to the light. Beneath the last line of their fairy tale, the two girls could see faded ink spelling those very two words . . .

Before they had been erased.

"What happened?" Sophie breathed.

"It seems your book has reopened," Professor Dovey said, guiding their eyes to all the other versions of their story splayed across the desk. 'The End' had disappeared off each of them too.

Sophie rifled through the pile. "But how can we lose a happy ending!"

"Because one of you wished for a *different* one," Lady Lesso lashed, not looking at her. "One of you wanted a *new* Ever After. And now, one of you has put our school on the brink of *war*."

"That's ludicrous," Sophie huffed. "I know I wanted to be a princess—but I can't, can I? I saw what this place did to me and have no desire to spend more time in it, even if Gavaldon smells like horse bottom and has no endurable men. So if I didn't make the wish, then surely it's a mista—"

But now she saw who Lady Lesso was staring at, and her cheeks lost all blood.

Sophie slowly turned to her friend, shadowed in the corner. "Aggie, at the hollow, you said . . . you said you made a . . . That's not what you meant, right?"

Agatha couldn't look at her.

Sophie's hands were trembling. "Aggie, tell me it's not what you meant."

Agatha tried to find words—something to redeem herself—

"All of this . . . ," Sophie gasped. "Everything that happened . . . is because of *you*?"

Agatha burned scarlet. She spun to Lady Lesso. "How do I fix it? How do I get Sophie home safe?"

The Evil teacher let the question dangle while she inspected her sharp red nails.

"It's simple," she said finally, lifting her eyes. "You must wish to end with each other, at the same time. Wish for each other and only each other, and the Storian will write 'The End' once more."

"And we'll leave the Woods?" Agatha pressed.

"Never to be hunted again—as long as your wish is *true*."

Agatha let out a rush of air. "We can fix it." She turned to Sophie. "We can get our ending back! The village won't hurt us!"

Sophie backed away. "What ending did you want?"

"Don't do this," Agatha said.

"What else could you possibly want?" Sophie demanded.

"It was a mistake, Sophie—"

"Answer me."

"Sophie, please—"

Sophie locked her gaze. "What did you wish for?"

"We can fix this *now*," Agatha begged.

"I'm afraid you can't."

Both girls turned.

"The Storian must write 'The End' to seal your wish," said Professor Dovey. "And at the moment, it is unable."

"What do you mean?" Agatha flushed angrily. "Where is it?"

"Where it always is," said Lady Lesso, scowling back. "With the *School Master*."

"Huh?" Agatha said. "But you said he was replace—"

The flutter in her heart.

The face she couldn't see.

Agatha slowly looked up.

"Who *doesn't* want your ending sealed?" Lady Lesso purred. "Who wants a *new* ending to your fairy tale?"

She held up their story's last page . . . a boy walking into fog all alone . . .

"Who heard his princess's *wish*?"

Agatha whirled to the window. Lightning exploded over the School Master's tower across the bay with a whip crack of thunder, and she saw the silver-masked shadow in its flash—

Golden hair, a body of muscle, a glinting sword sheathed . . .

The sky went dark, and he was gone.

Agatha felt faint. All the attacks . . . all the destruction . . .

"Him," Sophie whispered, crumpling against the wall. "You wished for . . . *him*."

Agatha searched for something to say, but one look at Sophie, curled up in a grubby pink heap, and she knew. There was nothing to say.

"How?" Agatha whispered. "How could he hear it?"

"Because you *wanted* him to," Lady Lesso slashed, prowling towards Agatha. "From the day you left, Tedros believed one day you'd call for him. From the day you left, he and his boys hunted your village, trying to cross into Woods Beyond—until your wish finally opened the gates."

Agatha paled, watching Lady Lesso circle her. "But your prince has to make sure his princess chooses *him* this time. He needs insurance you won't repeat your mistakes. So Tedros stole the Storian from under our noses, knowing the School Master's tower follows the pen wherever it goes. Now he'll stop the Storian from writing 'The End' to your tale—until he has his *new* ending."

Agatha's stomach went cold. "What's the new ending?" she rasped.

Lady Lesso stared through her. "Killing Sophie."

Sophie slowly lifted her eyes, red and raw.

"Tedros believes killing Sophie will fix your fairy tale as it should have been," said Professor Dovey. "The witch dies. The princess free to her prince. Your ending rewritten, just like Agatha wished."

Agatha couldn't breathe under Sophie's scorching stare.

"Why don't you save Tedros the trouble?" Sophie hissed. "Kill this witch yourself."

"That would solve everything," sighed Professor Dovey.

Both girls turned.

"Oh dear," said their teacher. "Did I say that out loud?"

"She'll die soon enough," Lady Lesso snarled. "Tedros counted on Sophie coming here for protection. Now he and his army will come to kill her."

"Army?" Agatha blanched. "He has an army?"

"You've forgotten about *his* school," said Lady Lesso.

Agatha swung her head to the window. Through the sheets of rain, she could see the red hoods skulking around Evil's towers, in black leather uniforms crested with scarlet snakes and shiny black boots. Slowly she lowered her eyes to the gate on the castle shores, rusted iron words arched over it:

**THE SCHOOL FOR BOY
VENGEANCE AND RESTITUTION**

"One wish has so many consequences, doesn't it?" Lady Lesso said, leering at Agatha. "Tedros has promised whoever kills Sophie half his father's treasure as a reward. Needless to say, both the Ever- and Neverboys took up the challenge."

"As did all those princes outside," Professor Dovey said, watching the filthy masses swarming the gates. "Tedros knows he can't attack us with just his school. Our teachers wouldn't give up Sophie without a fight."

"So he's using the princes to force our hand," Lady Lesso groused. "I cast a shield around the perimeter of both schools to keep them out. But if the princes get through, Tedros will have enough men to storm our castle and kill Sophie."

Agatha stared out at the red fortress, still numb. "The Storian's in a *boys' school*?"

"Either free it and get Sophie home alive . . . or kiss Tedros before he kills her." Professor Dovey met Agatha's shocked eyes. "Kiss your prince and mean it, and you'll stay here with *him* Ever After. Sophie will be gone from your story forever . . . and vanish home alone."

"Home *alone*?" Sophie gasped as if she'd been shot. "Gavaldon *alone*? While she gets . . . *him*?"

"These are the only two endings that can prevent war," Professor Dovey said.

The only sound in the room was the echo of murderous princes.

Sophie gave Agatha a horrible look and curled back into her ball.

Tedros, Agatha gritted. How could she wish for a boy who'd take love this far? How could she wish for a boy who'd kill her best friend? Her old witchy self would never have let this happen.

"Third option," she said, storming to the door. "Tell Tedros he's a delusional ass."

"No."

Agatha turned.

"You wished for him," Sophie spat, blotched with rage. "And you want me to trust you two *alone*?"

Agatha cowered. Sophie looked even more a witch than she did in the graveyard.

"I won't intervene in your lovers' quarrel, but I suggest Agatha make her choice soon," Lady Lesso snapped. "Once Tedros breaks the princes through my shield, all our lives will be in danger."

"We'll hide you and Sophie in the Blue Forest until you

have a plan," Professor Dovey said to Agatha, pulling out a ring of keys. "None of the girls can know you've come."

Agatha looked up, dazed. "Why not?"

"Because unlike your two teachers, they think this is the best thing that's ever happened," said a honey-smooth voice.

The two professors and two girls turned to see a tall, ravishing woman push through the door, milky smooth and full-bosomed in a teacher's electric-blue dress decorated with a pattern of butterflies. She had a waterfall of chestnut hair to her midback, forest-green eyes under thick dark brows, a luscious pink mouth, and a gap between her two shiny front teeth.

"My brother's office?" she said, biting her bee-stung lips. "I wasn't aware it was where we held secret meetings."

"It's the only place we can't be overheard," Lady Lesso returned, her voice oddly tentative.

"Well I do believe I should have been alerted to our honored guests," the woman said breathily, turning to Sophie and Agatha. "After all, they are the reason this magnificent school exists."

The two girls gawped at her.

"We've been meticulously preparing for your arrival," said the stranger, knitting her arched brows. "And we nearly may have missed it." She flashed a glare at the two teachers.

Agatha shook her head. "But how did you know we were com—"

"Goodness, you two look frightful," the woman said, magically restoring their faces and dresses with her finger. Only

Sophie's dress magically lost its pink color too and drained blank white.

Sophie grabbed her hem. "What happened to my—"

"Come, girls." The woman sashayed for the door. "We've put your books and schedules in your room."

"Schedules!" Professor Dovey launched to her feet. "You're not thinking of them going to class, Evelyn!"

The woman twirled. "As long as they are at *my* school, they will attend class and abide by the rules. Which includes *staying* in their school at all times. Surely you don't object to the *rules*?"

Sophie and Agatha waited for the professors to indeed object, but Dovey and Lesso were curiously quiet, eyes on a pair of blue butterflies that had settled on the tips of their noses.

"I see our *former* deans neglected to inform you about the most important change at your new school," the stranger said, smiling at the two girls. "Evelyn Sader. Dean of the School for Girls. Sorry for the hurry. I don't want to keep everyone waiting. Follow me, please."

As she turned and swept through the door, Sophie saw the two butterflies land on her matching dress and vanish magically into its pattern. She let out a breath of surprise. "Keep who waiting?"

As more butterflies fell into her dress, the beautiful woman didn't look back.

"*Your* army," she said, as if she'd just listened to their entire conversation.

6

Her Name Is Yara

"An army dedicated to producing stories just like *yours*," said Dean Sader, clacking through the sun-washed breezeway from Valor to Honor in her blue-glass heels. "Your tale was just a taste of what princesses and witches can do together. Here you will lead an entire school!"

"A school—" Agatha choked, chasing her down the Honor stairs. "We need to go home!"

"You see, the *former* deans and I have a difference of opinion," said Dean Sader as butterflies flew in from every direction and vanished into her dress. "They think you must leave our world to find your happy ending together. And I think you must *stay*."

"But the boys are going to kill me!" Sophie said, bumping Agatha hard as she passed.

"Mmmm, let's say you do break into a castle full of bloodthirsty males," the Dean said, sweeping her buxom behind through the foyer. "Let's say you free the Storian against all odds." She stopped outside the frosted doors of the Gallery of Good. "The wish won't work unless you mean it."

She gazed at Sophie. "How can you wish for Agatha if you know she wants her prince?"

The Dean turned to Agatha. "How can you wish for Sophie if you fear the witch inside?"

She leaned in so close the girls could smell her flawless honeycream skin.

"How can you wish for someone you *do not trust*?"

Sophie's and Agatha's eyes met dartingly, hoping the other would argue. Neither did.

"Your friendship must be fixed before you can go home. And here you will fix what is broken," Dean Sader said, a last butterfly fluttering into her dress. "Fairy tales have trained us to believe a beautiful bond like yours cannot last. Why? Because a boy must come between you. A boy so threatened by your story that he's willing to *kill* to destroy it. But at my school, we teach you the truth." She opened the door to pitch darkness.

"That a girl without a boy is the *greatest happy ending of all*."

Her finger magically lit a torch, and the flame roared red to a burst of drums. Agatha and Sophie leapt back—

Twenty rows of girls stood frozen, heads bowed, each wearing a white veil, royal-blue harem pants, and a light blue bodice stitched with a butterfly crest over the heart. There were more than 100 of them, stretching through the exhibits of the museum, past its open rear doors, and into the vast ballroom of Good Hall. Faces obscured, they stood eerily still, arms raised with hands to opposite elbows as if summoning genies. Hovering above them, just beneath the ceiling, two more veiled girls on magic carpets beat snare drums faster and faster.

At the front of this parade was a lone girl without anyone else in her row. Her veil was blue instead of white, her hair ginger red, and the pallid skin on her thin arms dotted with strawberry freckles. Slowly she raised her arms. . . .

The drums stopped.

With an untamed screech, the girl blew a blast of fire that singed the magic carpets and sent Agatha and Sophie quailing from flames. As the drums beat once more, the girl whipped into a whirling belly dance, punctuating each move with a wild whistle or trill.

"One look at her, and Tedros will forget all about his wish maker," said Sophie coldly.

"Sophie, I'm sorry." Agatha shifted closer to her friend. "I really am."

Sophie shifted away.

"I'd never lose you for a boy," Agatha prodded. But eyeing the dancing girl, she suddenly felt a twinge of jealousy. . . . Had Tedros seen her?

She crushed the thought. Tedros wanted to kill her best friend and she was still thinking of him? *He's the enemy, you idiot!*

Stefan's face haunted her, begging her to return Sophie

home safe. Where was the Agatha who'd do anything to protect her best friend? The one who had control over her feelings? The one who was Good?

By now, the rows behind started to echo the leader's dance, flowing with crisp hand movements. Then, with a sudden flourish, the girls all turned to each other and danced in pairs. Hands brushed and clasped as they touched backs before lifting arms and switching places, never losing the touch of their palms. In their glinting blue harem pants and white veils, they looked like swaying sea anemones. Despite the storm in her heart, Sophie managed a smile. She had never seen something so beautiful. Then again, she'd never seen girls dance without boys.

Agatha didn't like Sophie's expression. "Sophie, I need to talk to Tedros."

"No."

"I said I'm sorry. You have to let me fix it—"

"No."

"The fool thinks I want you killed!" Agatha said, smacking away a blue butterfly on her shoulder. "I'm the only one who can make him see reason."

"A prince who thinks he's School Master, bet half his fortune on my head, and you think he'll see reason," Sophie said, letting the butterfly perch on her. "I'm surprised Good ever wins if it's this naive."

Agatha glanced at the Dean's back to them. She couldn't possibly eavesdrop with the drums pounding and the dancing girl hooting like a hyena, but Agatha had the strange feeling she could hear everything.

"Sophie, I lost myself for a moment," she whispered. "It was a mistake."

Sophie watched the lead girl spew another jet of fire. "Maybe the Dean is right," she said, not whispering at all. "Maybe I should stay here."

"*What?* We don't even know where she *came* from, let alone how she's Dean! You saw the look on Professor Dovey's face. You can't trust her—"

"Right now, I trust her more than I trust you."

Agatha could have sworn she saw the Dean grin. "You're not safe here, Sophie! Tedros will come for you!"

"Let him. That's what you want, isn't it?"

"I want you home alive!" Agatha begged. "I want us to forget ever coming to the School for Good and Evil! I don't *want* Tedros!"

Sophie whirled, snarling. "Then why did you *wish for him*?"

Agatha froze.

"Let the gifts begin!" the Dean decreed.

"Gifts!" Sophie spun from Agatha, beaming. "At last, some good news." She sidled up to the Dean as the veiled girls fanned to the walls like a clamshell opening, leaving a wide aisle down the middle.

Agatha followed warily, remembering what this world had once done to her and her best friend. The longer they stayed here, the longer they were in danger. She had to get Sophie home *now*.

Moving into the sunlight of a small window, she noticed the museum exhibits had changed. Evidence of boys' achievements had all been stripped and replaced with relics from her and Sophie's fairy tale: Agatha's Evergirl uniform, Sophie's Lunchtime Lectures sign, Agatha's note to Sophie during the Trial by Tale, the slashed lock of hair from Sophie's Doom Room punishment, and dozens of others, each enshrined in a blue-tinted glass case. On the main wall, the Ever After mural, which once celebrated the marriage of prince and princess, was now covered with a navy canvas, embroidered with butterflies. Indeed, the only holdover was Professor Sader's old nook of paintings off the far corner. As a seer who could glimpse the future, the former History teacher had once drawn paintings of every Reader who had come from Gavaldon to the School for Good and Evil. Whenever Agatha needed answers, she always drifted back to these paintings, finding new clues. All she wanted was to study them again now, but there were two veiled girls marching towards her down the aisle, carrying an enormous purple vase.

"From Maidenvale," said Dean Sader, honeyed voice now deep and commanding. "An urn from Princess Riselda, who like hundreds of others heard your story and realized she'd be happier without her prince. She had his throne burned and offers the ashes to you."

The girls held up the urn to Sophie and Agatha, who peered at its carving of a prince magically ejected out a castle window to crocodiles below.

"We don't want it," Agatha crabbed.

"Shall we put it in my room?" smiled Sophie, turning to the Dean.

"Room?" Agatha blurted. "Sophie, you're *not* staying—"

But now two girls were marching down the aisle with oriental, bamboo drapes.

"From Pifflepaff Hills," the Dean boomed. "A hand-painted tree curtain from Princess Sayuri, who read your tale and realized that without princes, princesses and witches are happier."

Its exquisitely painted bamboo reeds depicted a princess and witch embracing in one panel, while in the other, a prince who looked a lot like Tedros was flogged to a pulp by a beast.

"This is horrible," Agatha snapped.

"Hang them by my bed," Sophie chimed to the two veiled girls. "What's next?"

The Dean pointed a gold-lacquered nail down the aisle. "From Netherwood, a tapestry of homeless princes . . ."

"I wish Professor Dovey and Lady Lesso could appreciate someone as *chic* as you," Sophie fawned to the Dean, as the procession of prince-abusing gifts continued, including prince voodoo dolls, looted prince swords, and a carpet made out of prince hair. "Do classes start today?"

The Dean grinned as she glided away. "Including *mine.*"

"You're not serious," Agatha hissed to Sophie. "Now you want to go to *class?*"

"Let's hope they renovated those rooms made of candy." Sophie's hand combed her hair, readying for the day. "I'm allergic to the smell."

"Sophie, there is a bounty on your head—"

"And lastly, a gift from me," declared Dean Sader, standing in front of the covered Ever After mural. "Students, your old school taught you balance was about vanquishing Good or Evil. But how can there be balance between Evers and Nevers until there is balance between Boys and Girls? It is no mistake our Readers have returned to join our school, for their fairy tale remains unfinished."

She looked right at the two girls. "And the battle for its ending just begun."

She let the canvas fall. Agatha and Sophie drew breaths.

The words EVER AFTER, giant and glimmering, still peeked from painted clouds at the top of the mural in gold block letters. Everything else had been redone.

Now the scene depicted two sprawling blue-glass castles around a lake, as girls in azure uniforms gathered on tower balconies, basked on the lakeshores, and strolled the gated grounds. Some of these girls were beautiful, some were ugly, but they worked, lived, and idled together without division, as if witches and princesses were always meant to be friends.

There were boys in the painting too, if one could call them that. With black peasant rags and ogrishly distorted faces, they scooped manure, raked a blue forest behind the castle, and built up the towers in miserable chain gangs before retreating to filthy prison slums at the fringes of the gates. Female overseers drove them like chattel and the boys put up no fight, slaves resigned to eternal servitude. Agatha's eyes rose to the top of the painting, where haloed in sun two women with crystal diadems surveyed their kingdom from the highest balcony. . . .

"It's us," Sophie gasped.

"It's . . . this school," scowled Agatha.

"Your true Ever After," the Dean said, stepping between them. "Captains of these hallowed halls, leading girls to a princeless future."

Agatha grimaced at the vision of Everboys and Neverboys hated and enslaved. "This school *isn't* our ending," she said, turning to Sophie. "Tell her we have to leave!"

But Sophie was gazing at the painting, eyes wide. "How do we make it come true?"

Agatha stiffened.

"How all heroes win their happy ending, dear," the Dean said, touching both their shoulders. "By facing the enemy." She grinned out the window at Tedros' tower. "And *slaying* him."

Agatha and Sophie locked eyes in surprise.

"My cherished students!" The Dean swept her hand over the crowd. "Welcome our Readers back to school!"

With a roar, the mob tore off their veils and rushed the two girls.

"You're home!" gushed Reena, embracing Agatha with freckly Millicent, while green-skinned Mona and one-eyed Arachne smooshed Sophie into a hug—

"Didn't know we were friends—" Sophie croaked, suffocated—

"We're on your side against Tedros," Arachne cheered, Millicent on her arm as if Evers and Nevers were suddenly bosom buddies. "All of us!"

"You're our heroes," Reena said to Agatha, who noticed the Arabian princess looked a bit bigger in the bottom. "You and Sophie taught us the truth about boys!"

Agatha fumbled for words before a shrieking blur bear-hugged her and Sophie. "My roommates!" Beatrix yipped. "Aren't you excited? The Dean put you both with *me*!"

Neither Sophie nor Agatha had time to process this cataclysm, because they were goggling at something more alarming— "Your hair!" Sophie cried.

"No boys means no need to look like stupid princesses," Beatrix said, rubbing her shaved head proudly. "Think about how much time I wasted last year on Tedros and Balls and beautifying all day. And for what? Now I read, I study, I learned to speak Elf. . . . I finally know what's going on in our world!"

"But what about Beautification?" Sophie fretted.

"That's long gone. There *is* no beauty or ugliness at the School for Girls!" said Reena, who, Sophie saw with horror, wasn't wearing a shred of makeup. "We wear pants, we don't do our nails . . . we even eat cheese!"

Sophie gagged and looked for the Dean, but butterflies were trailing her out of the gallery. "But surely some lipstick is allowed—"

"You can do whatever you want!" Arachne said, showing off a smatter of hideous blush on both cheeks. "Nevers can groom, Evers don't have to. It's all your choice!"

Millicent leaned in with a grin. "I haven't washed my hair for a *month*."

Sophie and Agatha both recoiled, only for the latter to be tackled by a yelping heap—

"*Eeeeeeyiiiiiii!* You're here! My best friend in the whole world!" Kiko gave Sophie a phony smile. "And you too." Then Kiko hugged Agatha again, her brown, almond-shaped eyes tearing up. "You don't know how much I prayed for you to come back! It's like heaven here! Wait until you take History—the Dean teaches it and we go into the stories—and there's dance lessons and a school newspaper and a book club and we put on a play instead of a Ball and we can sleep in each other's rooms and—"

Kiko couldn't finish because there were flocks of girls besieging Sophie and Agatha now, each girl acting as if she was their best friend too.

Agatha tried to fend off her horde and lunged to Sophie across the masses. "We have to get out of here right no—" She tripped and landed face-first. "Will you sign my storybook?" Giselle asked, black hair sheared into a blue mohawk. Agatha crawled back like a crab into more clamoring fans.

As girls thrust books, cards, body parts for Sophie to sign, Beatrix forced the girls into a receiving line and let them pay tribute one by one. Sophie could hardly tell who was from Good and who from Evil anymore, since more of the Evergirls had hacked their hair and let their figures go, while a large number of Nevergirls were experimenting with makeup and diets.

Meanwhile, Agatha finally extricated herself from her

gaggle. But just as she grabbed Sophie's arm to end this idiocy, she froze still.

The dancing girl shuffled towards them in her sky-blue veil. Gangly as an egret, she didn't so much walk as tiptoe, the heels of her white slippers never touching the ground. She pattered down the aisle, past gaping girls, until she stopped sharply in front of the two Readers. The girl raised her head of flowing, red hair and lifted the veil from her face.

Sophie and Agatha were both very confused.

She didn't look like any girl they'd ever seen, and yet she seemed almost familiar. She had a long, pointy nose, a strong jaw, and close-set blue eyes. Her neck was strangely long, and her cropped blouse revealed perfect stomach muscles that rippled beneath her pale, freckled skin. The girl smiled ethereally, looked into their eyes, and unleashed a low squawk that made Sophie and Agatha jump. Then she blew them a kiss, replaced her veil, and shuffled out of the hall.

All the girls watched her in dumb silence until the mob started pushing towards Sophie and Agatha again and Beatrix blew her whistle.

"What was *that*?" Agatha said to Kiko as she crankily signed an autograph.

"Her name is Yara," Kiko whispered. "No one knows how she got in! Doesn't speak, doesn't eat, far as we can tell, and disappears all the time. Probably has nowhere to live, poor thing. But the Dean lets her stay out of the goodness of her heart. Some people think she's half stymph."

Agatha frowned, thinking of the bony, carnivorous birds that hated Nevers. "How can someone be half stym—"

She lost her train of thought, because Sophie had culled the girls all to herself, smiling imperiously, signing autographs, and kissing cheeks, as if she'd finally found her way home.

"Can I help you fight boys?" Arachne hollered.

"Can I be your Vice Captain?" yelled Giselle.

"Can I be your Vice-Vice Captain?" echoed Flavia.

"Sit with my group for lunch!" Millicent called.

"No, sit with us!" Mona countered—

"How glorious it is to have *fans* again," Sophie said, ignoring Agatha's horrified look and dotting an autograph with hearts. "Here I am trying to get home where no one wants me, and instead stumble upon paradise, where *everyone* does."

"If you're miserable with Beatrix, don't worry," Kiko said, noticing Agatha's glum face. "You can always stay with me."

Agatha turned to her, and Kiko suddenly understood. "You aren't staying, are you?" Kiko rasped.

The crowd went silent around her.

"Now tell me about this school play," Sophie said loudly to Reena. "Have you cast the lead par—"

She stopped, for all the students had followed Agatha's gaze out the window. Across the bay, fog brewed thicker around the grisly red castle.

"If we stay, we're starting war," Agatha said to the girls. "All of you would be in danger."

She turned to Sophie. "You heard the professors. We can

fix what I've done without anyone dying. Not you. Not Tedros. Not anyone here. We wish for each other, and we can forget this school ever happened." She touched her friend's shoulder. "It's Evil if we stay, Sophie. And you're not Evil."

Sophie slowly gazed up at a sea of blameless girls, who would no doubt die at the hands of Tedros and his red hoods. Only Agatha had forgotten the Dean's warning. They could go home as long as both of them *meant* their wish. But Sophie knew Agatha couldn't mean a wish for her friend. Agatha couldn't forget this school.

Because a friend wasn't enough for Agatha anymore.

Agatha wanted a prince.

"We'll hide in the Blue Forest and come up with a plan," Agatha said to her quietly, anxious to escape before the Dean returned. "Maybe we can mogrify into the Boys' school."

Crestfallen, Sophie said nothing—

Until she met her own eyes in the painting on the wall.

Atop the castle in her crystal crown, she looked just like someone she knew, with the same goldspun blond hair, emerald eyes, and ivory skin. Someone who too had lost her happy ending to a boy. Someone who had died all alone because of it.

"You are too beautiful for this world, Sophie."

It was the last thing her mother had ever said.

She wanted me to find it, Sophie thought, this world where she wouldn't end like her mother.

A world where she and Agatha would be happy forever.

A world where a boy could never come between them.

A world without princes.

And only one prince stood in her way, Sophie gritted, tears glistening.

A prince that Agatha would surely forget once he was dead.

"It isn't Evil, Aggie," Sophie vowed. "This school is our only hope."

Agatha tightened. "Sophie, what are you—"

"He says he *wants me*?" Sophie bellowed to her waiting army. She bared teeth at Tedros' castle.

"Then let him *come for me.*"

The girls let out a raucous cheer and mobbed their new leader.

"Death to Tedros!"

"Death to Boys!"

Agatha drained of color as Sophie met her eyes and vanished into the swarm.

One wish, and she'd set a war in motion. A war between two sides fighting for her heart. A war between two people she loved. A war between her best friend and a prince.

Agatha's soul scorched with guilt, a promise to a father gone up in flames.

I need help, she prayed, watching Sophie blow kisses to her soldiers. Someone who could see through all this. Someone to tell her who was Good this time and who was Evil.

As she retreated from the horde, she noticed an odd glint from the corner, hovering near the floor in Sader's dark nook of paintings. Slowly two tiny yellow eyes floated towards her, like suspended marbles. Two more suddenly glowed next to them, then two more, as hunched shadows pattered from behind a marble column.

The three black rats glowered at Agatha as if she'd said the magic words. Then they skittered through the back doors to lead her to their master.

7

The Witches Brew a Plan

"So let me get this straight," Hester glared, straddling a gilded sink next to Anadil, both in their saggy black Nevers' tunics. "Tedros wants to kill Sophie. Sophie wants to kill Tedros. And unless you find an ending with one of them *now*, everyone in this school dies."

Agatha nodded weakly, leaning against one of Honor Tower's ivory bathroom stalls, fitted with a sapphire toilet and tub. She never thought she'd be so happy to see two witches in her life. Unlike the rest of the girls, neither of them had changed. Hester's red-and-black-streaked hair was greasier than ever, and the buckhorned red demon tattoo around her neck back to full color after a failed spell had weakened it the year before. Anadil, meanwhile, looked even paler than she did before, if that was possible for an albino with ghostly white skin and hair. Straddling the sink next to Hester, she dangled a live lizard to her three black rats that looked just like the ones slain in last year's Good-Evil war.

"A prince and a witch, willing to kill each other for you," she rasped in her scratchy voice. "If it was me, I'd feel flattered." She watched the rodents disembowel the lizard and lifted her hooded red eyes. "Thankfully I don't have feelings."

"Questionable. Who replaces dead pets with ones exactly alike?" Hester murmured.

"Look, I'm hungry, dirty, haven't slept, and an army of boys is trying to kill my best friend," Agatha said, voice cracking with stress. "I just want us to go home alive."

"And yet you wished for Tedros," Hester said in her usual sharp sneer. "Which seems to suggest you don't want to go *home* at all."

Agatha didn't say anything for a moment. "Listen, just tell me what to do so no one gets hurt."

"As if we're fairy godmothers, Ani," Hester snorted, blowing smoke rings off her glowing red fingertip.

Anadil graffitied a skull in the sink with her glowing green finger. "Only not as ancient or menial."

"Please," Agatha begged. "You're witches. You have to know another way to take back a wish—"

"So earnest!" Hester whirled and carved a box around

Agatha's face in the mirror with her lit finger. "Just look at that helpless, lost little soul. Still wearing black and searching for the *old* Agatha . . . the Agatha who threw headless birds, farted in Evergirls' faces, and loved her precious Sophie more than life." Hester met Agatha's reflected eyes and grinned. "But she's gone, princess."

"That's not true," Agatha retorted, but Reaper's scratches seared her hand as if they were fresh.

"To think we once wanted you in our coven," Anadil said. "And now here you are, afraid of hurting your best friend over a *boy*."

"Nice to see you two haven't changed," Agatha muttered, trundling for the door. "Reminds me why we weren't friends."

"In the end, only one can make you happy," Hester purred behind her. "The question is, *who*?"

Agatha turned to see the witches slide off their sinks and circle her like sharks.

"Sophie or Tedros?" Hester mulled.

"Tedros or Sophie?" Anadil stewed.

The two witches leaned against the sinks side by side. "This requires plenty of thought," said Hester, peering at Anadil. Their heads whipped back to Agatha.

"TEDROS," they chorused.

Agatha's heart skipped and she squelched it in shock. "But that's wrong! I don't want a prince!"

Hester slid off the sink in one move. "Listen to me, you bug-eyed tramp. Unless you kiss Tedros, the schools stay the way they are," she hissed, suddenly looking like the dangerous witch Agatha knew. "Kiss him, and everything is fixed. Prince with his Princess, Witch gone forever. Evers over here, Nevers over there. The School for Good and Evil back in time for me to be third-year Captain."

Agatha crossed her arms. "I see. I'm worried about my best friend's life, and you're worried about *school.*"

"Do you know what you've done to this place, you waffling wench?" Hester snarled, black eyes storming. "Do you know what you've put us through?"

She flung a wad of crumpled parchment from her pocket. Agatha unwrinkled a schedule, barely readable under all the graffiti.

HESTER OF [illegible]

GIRL, 2nd YEAR

HONOR, 42

Session	Faculty
1: DEBEAUTIFICATION	Prof. Emma Anemone & Pollux
2: PRINCELESS POWER	Prof. Clarissa Dovey
3: DEFENSE AGAINST BOYS	Lady Lesso
4: HISTORY OF HEROINES	Prof. Evelyn Sader
5: LUNCH	
6: FEMALE TALENTS	Prof. Shee[illegible]
7: SURVIVING FAIRY TALES (FOREST GROUP #[illegible])	Helga the Gnome

Agatha gaped at it. "But—these are about—"

"Girls, you stupid idiot! *Everything* at this school is about being a girl!" Hester screeched. "Do you know how hard I've tried to prove I'm more than a girl and now I have to live in a castle full of them! You can't have a school without boys! Even *we* know that, and we'd rather kill ourselves than touch one!"

"We did dance with them at Evil's Ball," Anadil corrected—

"Shut up," Hester boomed, spinning back to Agatha. "No one likes boys! Even girls who *like* boys can't stand boys! They smell, they talk too much, they mess up everything, and they always have their hands in their pants, but that doesn't mean we can go to school without them! It's like stymphs without bones! It's like witches without warts! Without boys, LIFE HAS NO POINT!"

Echoes shivered the mirror.

Agatha held up the schedule. "Um, and the teachers are *okay* with this?"

"Why do you think they weren't at your Welcoming?" Hester grouched, settling a bit. "They're as happy about this as we are. But they have no choice. Resist, and they'll suffer the same fate as Princess Uma."

Agatha saw the Animal Communication teacher wasn't on the schedule. "Where is she?"

"The Dean changed her class to Animal Hunting, since girls have to be self-sufficient and can't depend on boys for food. Part of the Five *Rules*," Anadil puffed, turning the sink faucet on to terrorize her rats. "Uma refused to teach the class, of course, on the grounds she wasn't going to kill animals she'd spent her whole life befriending." She stroked her quivering wet rats and looked up. "The next morning, a staircase evicted her into the Woods."

"She's probably better off," Agatha said, slightly relieved that she wouldn't have to learn more owl hoots and dog calls from the prissy pink princess. Then she saw Anadil still glaring at her.

"Do you remember what's *in* the Woods?"

Agatha's chest clamped. *Princes.* Vengeful, bloodthirsty princes.

"Why didn't the Dean rescue her?" Agatha croaked. "They'll kill her—"

"You think that's bad?" Hester barked, blood engorging again. "Do you know how much Nevers hate bathrooms? Do you know how much our bile boils just being near one, let alone hiding in one with *sapphire toilets*? That's how much we don't want to go to the classes here."

She glowered so hatefully Agatha swallowed her defense of Uma's fate as the worse.

"You want Sophie to stay alive? You want to avoid war between boys and girls? You want your happy ending?" Hester's eyes burned into Agatha. "Kiss Tedros."

Agatha could feel her heart rebelling from its clamps. *The correct ending,* Professor Dovey had said.

Agatha's cheeks splotched red. Betray her best friend? Abandon Sophie *forever*? After all they'd been through?

"I can't," she rasped, and slumped against the stall door. A cough suddenly came from behind it.

Hester bared sharp teeth. *"What."*

"Can I come out now?" peeped a familiar voice.

"You'll stay in there until you admit you're a traitor who no one likes and who is better off stabbing her own throat than ever showing her face *again*," Hester lashed.

Silence.

"Agatha, can I come out?"

Agatha sighed. "Hello, Dot."

The stall door slowly opened, and an Evergirl she'd never seen, with a slender waist and auburn curls, crept through first. Agatha gave her a baffled look and peeked in the stall for Dot.

The stall was empty.

Agatha slowly turned back to the stranger. "But you're—you're—"

"Hungry *all* the time," Dot said, and pulled her into a long hug before Agatha drew away and gaped at her. Dot was thirty pounds lighter, with a light sheen of makeup, red lipstick, and sparkled mascara. Her hair, brown with blond highlights, was tightly curled and clipped with glittery yellow barrettes. She'd even rolled up her uniform's light blue bodice so it showed off her taut belly.

"You're not going to get rid of this school, are you?" Dot fretted, nibbling on what looked like a clump of dried kale.

"Here we go," Anadil moaned.

"Daddy always told me I'd end up a fat, lonely villain like him," said Dot, eyes wet. "But this place lets me be who I want to be, Agatha. I feel good here for the first time in my life. And these two make me feel so bad for it. They made so much fun of me for being fat, and now they insult me for being thin."

"So you might as well *die*," said Hester.

"You're just jealous because I have new friends," Dot snapped.

The tattooed demon peeled off Hester's neck, inflated to life, and hurled a lightning bolt at Dot's head. Dot dove into a bathtub and the bolt blasted a hole in the marble wall. A tiny girl on her bed, reading *Why Men Don't Matter*, gawped through the hole and fled her room.

Grumbling, Hester summoned her demon back into her neck. Dot peeked at Agatha from the tub, now snacking on what looked like a star-shaped carrot. "She's mad because everyone else likes the Dean."

"I like that she can't make us wear that buffoonery," Hester said, scowling at Dot's blue bodice. "Professor Sheeks secretly taught us a charm that made us erupt in contagious boils any time we put on the uniform. After two days of screaming girls, the Dean gave up."

"How could she just take over?" Agatha said, bewildered.

"You have to remember how bad things were between boys and girls when you left," said Hester. "The most eligible prince in school lost his princess to a bald, toothless *witch*. Boys suddenly saw girls as the enemy—and girls saw the boys as bullies. When the schools changed to Boys and Girls, it already felt as divided as Good and Evil. The Dean just made things worse."

"But where did she *come* from?" asked Agatha. "She says she's Sader's sister—"

"All we know is, the night the schools changed to Boys

and Girls, Professor Dovey couldn't get back into her office," said Anadil. "She and Lesso tried to get it open for hours, and when they finally did . . . Dean Sader was sitting at the desk."

"But how'd she get in?" Agatha said, frowning. "And why don't they fight her?"

"For one thing, the male teachers tried," said Anadil. "And they haven't been seen since."

Agatha stared at her.

"As long as Dovey and Lesso had the Storian, we had a chance at peace," Hester pressed. "But now you kissing Tedros is the only hope. Because there *is* no way to fight the Dean."

She glared into Agatha's eyes.

"The castle's on *her* side."

As Sophie followed the Dean through the blue breezeway from Honor Tower to Valor Tower, girls kept popping up in their path, saluting Sophie like a ship captain.

"Death to the prince!" a pimply girl squeaked.

"Long live Sophie and Agatha!" chimed an elfish Evergirl.

Sophie forced a fraught smile as she tried to keep up with Dean Sader through the glass tunnel over the lake. As she walked, the Dean squinted out at distant princes clamoring outside the school gates, testing Lady Lesso's shield with rocks and sticks. Her thick red mouth pursed slightly and she walked faster, hips swishing in a dress that seemed so much tighter than all the other teachers'. Hustling behind, Sophie peered at the Dean's reflection in the breezeway. She'd never seen anyone so beautiful—even her own mother. Proportions exactly out of a storybook, rose-petal lips, hair so lustrous and full, as if the Dean had been drawn to a page and brought to life. What did she use on her skin? *Even thistleroot can't get pores that small,* Sophie thought, comparing them in the polished glass to her own—

Her bald, toothless reflection snarled back at her, covered in warts.

Sophie choked with terror and closed her eyes. *No . . . I'm Good . . . I'm Good now. . . .*

She opened her eyes to see her creamy smooth face once more.

"Sophie?"

Heart racing, Sophie turned to see the Dean frowning at the end of the breezeway. Quickly, Sophie hastened to keep up, legs quavering, as more girls passed and saluted her.

"Death to Tedros!"

"Death to the prince!"

"Um, when you said slay Tedros," Sophie fumbled anxiously, "you didn't mean *I—I—I'd* slay him . . . or that I'd be involved in anything . . . *Evil—*"

"Given your past history, I thought you'd be looking forward to it," the Dean mused.

Sophie wiped sweat. "It's just, um . . . I know I have a rather fearsome reputation. . . . But I've changed, you see. . . ."

"Have you?" The Dean gave her a pointed look. "In the gallery, you seemed quite ready to lead a war."

"Well, one must project the carriage of leadership," Sophie said, dripping sweat now. "But in truth, my witch days are long past, so perhaps it's best if someone *currently* Evil kills Tedros—might I suggest Hester or Anadil, both rather loathsome villains—"

"The boy who wants to *steal* your only friend, and you're afraid of a fight?"

Sophie slowly looked up at the Dean, grinning outside the entrance to Valor Tower.

"Perhaps because you don't know what it is you're fighting for."

The doors magically opened, and Sophie gasped.

The walls on both sides of the crowded stairwell, stretching all the way up the five floors, were painted with colossal, stylized stencil murals of her and Agatha's smiling faces, haloed with wreaths of stars, above the glittering blue headline:

HOPE FOR A BETTER WORLD

Instead of the musky leather, cologne smells, and animal skins of the old Valor Tower, now there were lush hanging gardens draped over the blue glass stairwell and marble columns, with azure-colored roses that showered the mob of students with petals as they headed to class, before lower-hanging vines swept them up. As Sophie followed the Dean up the stairs, girls immediately moved to the left in single file, clearing a path and greeting them with warm smiles as they passed. Through the spiral banister, Sophie saw a pack of blue butterflies zooming from floor to floor, rearranging into pictures to amuse the descending girls—a stymph, a nymph, a swan. . . . The Dean gave them a look, and with squeaky *meeps!* they zipped back into her dress.

She turned off onto the third floor and Sophie followed into a hall flurrying with activity. Against the walls, Evergirls and Nevergirls huddled side by side, watching a ghostly scene unfold atop the pages of *A Student's Revised History of the Woods* to finish an assignment. Above their heads, murals of an idyllic school of girls presiding over enslaved boys, watermarked with Sophie's and Agatha's deified faces, stretched down the long dormitory walls.

Reena darted to each of them with plates of poached eggs and pumpernickel toast, while Arachne passed mugs of chocolate buttermilk. In a corner, a group of girls practiced oboes, fiddles, and trumpets, though Sophie couldn't tell which were Evers or Nevers, since they all had ragged hair and no traces of makeup. Standing on ladders over the stairwell, Mona and Millicent finished painting pink roses on banisters a rich shade of blue, dripping paint on two girls sparring with wooden swords, while Kiko hopped past, flinging sheets of parchment—"Book Club meeting tonight! Come to Book Club!"—before she was drowned out by Giselle and Flavia practicing a loud song from sheet music. All around, doors chorused open and shut as girls scurried to their rooms from the Welcoming and rushed right back out with their books for class, unfussed by sweaty faces and armpits.

Sophie thought of the old schools—Nevers bashing each other to get to class, Evers primping for hours and hours, everyone in such terrible competition between schools, within schools, *all the time*. And now here they were, despite the sweatiness and raggedness and satanic smell of buttercream, thriving together, happy together . . . without a boy in sight.

"How can Agatha not want this?" she breathed.

"Some will always resist change," the Dean said next to her. "Agatha is a princess and still believes she needs a prince. Surely you know the power of that fantasy."

Sophie thought of all the hope, all the energy, all the time she had put into her princely dreams. The conviction that a gorgeous boy of noble blood would sweep her to his white castle and eternal bliss. Agatha had taunted her ruthlessly for it before the School Master kidnapped them. "As if this muscle-bound god would even *understand* you," Agatha scoffed. "We'd be better off together." She'd given her usual pig snort to make sure it sounded like a joke. But Sophie knew she meant it. Agatha always thought the two of them were enough for Ever After.

But had her friend fallen under the spell? Had Agatha started to believe in the same fantasy she once mocked?

Sophie's stomach sank. Had she and Agatha *switched places*?

"She wants to see him," Sophie said softly.

The Dean's face hardened, and she shunted Sophie behind the stairwell as girls streamed by. "If she kisses him, all is lost."

"She'd never kiss him—not if it means losing me—"

"She *wished* for him, Sophie," the Dean pressed, gripping Sophie close. "Wishes are borne of the soul. Deny them, and they only grow stronger."

Sophie's insides went cold.

Leaning in, the Dean took her cheeks into her gilded nails. "She's not the girl you knew, Sophie. There is a thorn in her heart. And it has to be *cut out*."

Sophie nestled into the Dean's shoulder. "I just want my friend back," she whispered.

"And you will, when her prince is dead." The Dean stroked her hair. "You'll stay together always. No boy between you, ever again."

Sophie's eyes misted. She wanted to hide in the Dean's arms forever. "Tell me what to do."

"Keep them apart," the Dean said, pulling away sharply. "Make Tedros fight us. When he does, you and your army will be ready."

"But I—I don't want to fight—" Sophie stammered, feeling warts burn as if they were there. "I—I want to be Good now—"

"And let your friend kiss her prince?" the Dean said, glaring at her. "Let her banish you to an ordinary life in a world of no consequence?" She edged closer. "Friendless . . . loveless . . . forgotten?"

Sophie's voice left her.

"Wasn't that your mother's ending?" the Dean asked, closer still. Her lips grazed Sophie's ear. "And what became of *her*?"

Sophie lost all color.

A hand grabbed hers and she shrieked in surprise—

"Don't worry!" Beatrix chimed to the Dean, dragging Sophie away. "I'll show her the room and her uniform and her schedule!" She put her arm around Sophie and yanked her down the hall. "Can you believe we once fought over a *boy*?"

Speechless, Sophie glanced back at the Dean against the wall mural, smiling at her like a mother to child. As the Dean receded into the hall's darkness, the last Sophie saw was her glowing green eyes, blending into those of her own muraled face, crowned above a princeless world.

A world where her best friend would never betray her again.

Sophie gritted her teeth.

As long as Agatha didn't kiss Tedros, they had a chance.

Agatha sat on the edge of the tub in dazed silence, knocking a soap bar to the floor. All she could think about was where she would be right now if she hadn't made the wish.

Her mother would be stewing lunch . . . garlic and liver, and the smell from the cauldron would mix with the ashy wind's, seeping through broken windows. On her bed, she'd be rushing to finish her grammar homework, due at afternoon lesson. Curled in a corner, Reaper would hiss at her, but a little less than yesterday. As she slurped up the last of the stew, she'd hear the weeds crackle, the soft humming . . . the glass heels on the porch. . . . "Walk to school?" Sophie'd say. They'd amble down the hill in their black and pink winter coats, cracking jokes about the barn-smelling boys in their class. "Let them try to marry us," Sophie would say, and she would laugh, because once upon a time, it was true. They had each other and would never need more.

"How could I ruin it?" she said, voice breaking. She looked up at the three girls. "How could I wish for him?"

"Because you're a princess, Agatha." Hester's face softened for the first time. "And no matter how much you fight it . . . you want a prince."

Agatha swallowed the knot in her throat. She looked up at Anadil, who nodded next to Hester and waited for Dot to concur.

She didn't.

The two witches shot her with sparks.

"Ow! Okay, *fine*!" Dot moped, munching on star-shaped celery. "Even if it means I go back to Evil and be fat and have no friends again!"

Agatha shook her head. "Look, Sophie just has to forgive me and everything will be—"

"*Forgive* you?" Hester cackled. "Her faithful Agatha, soiled by the boy once *hers* . . . and you expect the Witch of Woods Beyond to *forgive*? Oh please. Inside, Sophie wants you cut up in little pieces."

"You don't get it," Agatha said hotly. "Sophie's changed—she's Good—"

Even Anadil's rats snickered. "She's a Never, Agatha," Dot said. "No matter how much you love her, no matter how much you try to change her, Sophie will end Evil and alone."

"And not Class Captain," Hester mumbled.

Anadil kneeled in front of Agatha. "You will never mean your wish for Sophie, Agatha. Because you and Sophie will never be happy in your world." For once, Anadil's red eyes looked human. "You'll always end up back here again, wishing for your prince. And Sophie will always be the witch, keeping you and him apart . . . until you kiss Tedros." Her cold, white hand took Agatha's wrist. "Don't you see? Your wish was *right*."

Agatha sat on the tub in silence. It was as if she was caught in another riddle. And once again, only a School Master had the answer. This time, Sophie couldn't come with her.

"I have to see Tedros alone," she said quietly.

Dot nodded. "It's the only way you'll know if you're meant to be with him."

"And what if I'm not?" asked Agatha, thinking of all the reasons she hated her prince right now. "What if I still want to go home with Sophie?"

"Then we'll help you," Anadil groused.

Agatha thought of Sophie's face in Sader's office, lethal and ice-cold. "But how do I see him without her knowing? We're in the same *room*."

"Leave it to us," said Hester, gnawing on the ends of her red-and-black hair. "But it has to be tonight. I can't survive another day of class."

Agatha felt an odd relief, as if caught in a ferocious storm and suddenly given a glimpse of the eye. After all this, she would see Tedros. No matter what happened, there'd be hope after. A road to happiness. A choice made.

Hunched on the tub, she suddenly focused on the star-shaped bar of soap on the floor. She lifted her gaze to the star-shaped cucumber in Dot's hand.

"You'd think it'd be easier than chocolate," Dot sighed, turning another soap into a turnip. "But for a while, everything just turned to gouda chees—" Anadil covered her mouth.

The girls tracked her wide eyes to a blue butterfly fluttering in through the smashed hole in the wall.

Agatha snorted. "It's just a butterf—"

Hester shot her with sparks from her finger and Agatha gasped in pain. The tattooed witch glowered at her, and with her red-lit finger, drew smoky words in the air . . .

"She's listening."

Agatha shook her head, confused.

Hester and Anadil counted down on their fingers . . . 5 . . . 4 . . . 3 . . . 2 . . .

The bathroom door creaked open and a head poked through.

"There you are, Agatha," the Dean said as the butterfly drifted back into her dress pattern. "Class starts in five minutes and you're not in uniform? Not the best way to start your first day."

She flashed a black look at Hester and Anadil, as if this included their company. Her eyes drifted down to the hole in the wall behind them, which instantly filled in and repaired itself.

"Destruction of property is a rather *masculine* trait," she said to the two witches, her tone glacial. Then she smiled approvingly at Dot. "I suggest you two learn from your roommate how to behave like women. Or you never know. The castle might teach you the same lesson it taught the *boys*."

Hester and Anadil bowed their heads nervously, which made Agatha even more wary of the Dean. She remembered the odd feeling that she was eavesdropping during the Welcoming . . .

As a blue butterfly perched on Sophie's shoulder.

Agatha drew a breath. The butterfly in the Woods . . . the one in the Flowerground . . .

The Dean had been there all along, leading them here.

And she'd heard every word.

"Shall we, dear?" The Dean held open the door with long, sharp nails.

Muscles tensed, Agatha followed her out but kept her eyes pinned on the mirror, just in time to see Hester's reflection raise furious black eyes and mouth a last command.

"Tonight."

8

Unforgiven

"We'll be late for your first challenge!" Beatrix frowned from the door, two satchels of books in hand.

Sophie didn't move, glaring at Agatha.

"Now you want to *stay?*" she said leerily, perched on the middle bed in her school uniform, a crystal diadem glittering on her head. "You said it was *Evil* to stay."

Back turned, Agatha stared at the painting splashed across the wall, once a pink vision of dashing princes kissing their princesses—now a life-size mural of her kissing Sophie back to life in a starburst of blue light. *I'm just seeing him. I'm not choosing him. I'm just . . .* seeing *him.*

"What about seeing Tedros?" Sophie lashed, remembering the Dean's warning. "What about seeing your *prince*?"

Agatha didn't answer.

"Well?" Sophie pushed.

Agatha turned, pale limbs jutting from her uniform, diadem slipping down her hair. "I'm still here, aren't I?"

Sophie exhaled, the Dean's echo trickling away. Like the School Master, the Dean couldn't fathom the strength of their friendship. Agatha would never go to Tedros. They'd been through too much.

"You forgive me?" Agatha asked, surprised by Sophie's silence.

Sophie looked up, smiling to answer. But suddenly Sophie wasn't seeing Agatha anymore.

Suddenly all Sophie saw was the girl who'd wished for a boy. The girl who'd stabbed her in the back. The girl who'd ruined their Ever After.

An old fire of suspicion kindled inside.

Forgive her, Sophie thought, fighting it.

But her muscles were clenching . . . her fists curling . . .

The Good forgive!

But now her heart swelled to a witch's rage—

With a gasp, Sophie flung off the bed and hugged Agatha, jostling her friend's tiara. "Oh Aggie, I forgive you! I forgive you for everything! I know you'd never go to him!"

Agatha reddened, averting her eyes. "What *is* this cursed

thing?" she murmured, diadem now somehow in her mouth.

"Duh. Your Captain crowns," Beatrix crabbed, foot tapping impatiently. "You were the top Ever when you left, and Sophie was the top Never."

"Well, we're on the same side now," Sophie beamed and gripped Agatha's hand.

Agatha felt her palm sweat and let go to grab a satchel of books from Beatrix.

"Your rankings start over today, though," Beatrix said. "If we ever *get* to your first challenge."

As Sophie followed Beatrix's bald head out, she glanced back at Agatha, who was frowning at the book spines in her satchel:

Men: The Savage Race

Happiness Without Boys

The Princess's Guide to Princelessness

"Ready for our new school?" Sophie said, holding open the door.

Agatha looked up and did her best to smile back.

Professor Anemone gave Agatha a loaded glare as she trudged into her blue taffy-coated classroom for Debeautification without any of her usual manic flounce. Twenty girls straightened to attention in neat rows.

"This week we continue to debeautify everything a prince *expects* of his princess," Professor Anemone huffed, bright-yellow gown devoid of the brassy jewels, feathered bustiers, soaring headdresses, and fur regalia she used to parade. The classroom too had been stripped of all her old Beautification flourishes, including her antique mirrored stations from Putzi, before-and-after portraits of her most improved students, and shelves upon shelves of grooming equipment. Now all that was left were the white-fudge desks, a licorice chalkboard, and blue-taffy walls watermarked with Sophie's smiling face and a marshmallow speech bubble: *Beauty Is a State of Mind!*

"To review," Professor Anemone grouched, flashing Agatha another blameful scowl, "first we debeautified diets as insidious plagues and encouraged a girl to eat anything her heart desires . . . even candy."

Agatha coughed. Professor Anemone reviled candy so much she'd once punished her with two weeks of scrubbing dishes for eating it. Yet the Evergirls didn't seem at all fazed by this about-face. Indeed, Agatha noticed a few holes in Reena's fudge desk, and suddenly her plumper appearance was no longer a mystery.

"Second, we debeautified hair and a prince's preference for long, lustrous locks," the teacher continued, "instead advocating that each girl experiment and find a style that *feels* right."

Agatha saw her grimace as she took in Giselle's blue mohawk, Beatrix's hairless pate, and Millicent's dirty red mop—hair that Professor Anemone's old class had once spent months grooming to perfection.

"Third, we debeautified makeup as a pawn of patriarchy designed entirely to attract men," the teacher went on, wincing at the sea of unwashed faces, proudly worn blemishes, and Nevers who'd applied it curiously, like two-year-olds left to face paint. "And today, we move on to our fourth unit—" She turned to the chalkboard, words appearing as she moodily slashed her finger across it—

DEBEAUTIFYING PINK

The last letter appeared with a nails-on-board squeak and girls shielded their ears. "From last night's reading," the teacher grumped, "what are three reasons why pink must be exterminated?"

Agatha frowned. Professor Anemone *worshipped* pink.

"Yes, Beatrix," her teacher said, for Beatrix was waving her arm like she needed to pee.

"Because pink is a color associated with weakness, helplessness, and anxiety. But Professor Anemone—."

"Another reason, Dot?"

"Because pink is the opposite of blue, a color of strength and serenity, which boys have appropriated for themselves without giving girls a choice," Dot preened, earning high fives from her Evergirl coterie. Hester slingshot her with a shard of taffy and Dot yelped.

"Professor Anemone—" Beatrix interrupted—

"You had a turn, Beatrix! Arachne, the last reason?"

"Because pink is a sign of infection around a cut. And pinkeye means you have fungus in your eye—"

"Take this as a reminder to *do* your reading before you answer, Arachne," Professor Anemone snapped, adding under her breath, "and a reminder why Evers and Nevers should be in different schoo— WHAT IS IT, BEATRIX!"

"Professor Anemone, why are *you* wearing pink?"

Professor Anemone tracked her eyes to a heart-shaped pink barrette clipped in her own wild blond hair. Her cheeks ballooned red, about to blow—

Then she saw a butterfly on the windowsill.

"Oh dear! Am I?" She magically turned the barrette blue with her finger. "Turning a bit color-blind in middle age. Now please hand in your homework diaries on what steps *you've* taken to debeautify."

She stomped through the rows of girls to collect them, giving the butterfly a dirty look as it flew away, presumably because it could only hear and not see. Agatha scanned the loamy blue walls, once the same color as Sophie's favorite pink dress before the Dean had her way with it. Agatha never liked pink (it reminded her of baby vomit), but why shouldn't Professor Anemone decorate her classroom how she liked?

She glanced at Sophie in the next desk, ogling her watermarked face on the taffy walls. Allergies to candy were cured by celebrity, it seemed.

"Aggie, I've been thinking," Sophie said, turning to her. "Why do you think Tedros hasn't tried to see you?"

"What?"

"You've been here all morning. No Romeo sneaking through your window. No lovers' embrace . . . he hasn't even sent you a *note*."

Agatha stiffened. "Doesn't matter, does it?" she said, and feigned listening to the teacher.

"Well, it's even more reason not to try and see *him*," Sophie sighed, polishing her Captain's crown. "Who knows if he even wants you to? In any case, we have our first three classes together, then we have different schedules. Wonder why the Dean separated us. Don't think we're even in the same Forest Group . . ."

Her voice trailed off as Agatha gazed out the window at Halfway Bridge, obscured by swirling gray fog. She was still thinking about what Sophie had just said.

Why hasn't Tedros tried to see me?

A blue barrette dropped on her desk and clinked to the floor. As she reached for it, a hand seized hers—"Clarissa is livid," Professor Anemone hissed in her ear. "You must seal your ending with Sophie or Tedros immediate—"

She silenced, because the door swung open and Pollux the dog staggered through—or rather, his *head* staggered through, wobbling atop an antelope's body he clearly didn't know how to use.

"Sorry I'm late," he said, raising his nose snootily. "I had private counsel with the Dean about the need for more aggressive pink removal. Indeed, I found a thread of it in the fourth-floor carpet and had it exterminated at once."

Agatha and Sophie exchanged startled looks, for both were undoubtedly thinking the same thing. As one-half of a two-headed dog, Pollux frequently lost the battle to use their body to his brother, Castor, who taught in Evil. Since Castor was a vicious male dog, Agatha wasn't surprised he was evicted from the castle with the boys. But up until now, she'd been quite sure Pollux was . . .

"Male too?" she whispered to Hester behind her.

Hester eyed Pollux's weak jaw, scanty fur, and rosy nostrils. "I'd say he has about as much male in him as there is pink left in that carpet."

"My dear Professor Anemone," Pollux said in his strident voice. "I believe there was an unfortunate incident involving a pink barrette this morning. Perhaps *I* should administer today's challenge, if you're not up to your best?"

Professor Anemone glared blackly. "What about your pink *nose*?"

Pollux looked like he'd been slapped. "It's—it's an inherited condition—"

"Since choosing a challenge is the *one* freedom I am still allowed," Professor Anemone said to the students, "today's competition will be—"

The door opened again. "WHAT NOW?"

The Dean slipped in with a warm smile. "Since it's our Captains' first day, Emma, perhaps it might be more appropriate if *I* choose the challenge?"

Professor Anemone muttered grimly and dumped herself at her sour-candy desk.

"Pollux dear," said the Dean, sashaying in front of Professor Anemone's desk, "might we remind our Captains how rankings are awarded?"

"Certainly, Dean," Pollux sniffed. "All students in the School for Girls are ranked in class challenges from first to last. Given there are 20 students in each class, the best performer in a given challenge will receive a rank of 1, with the most feeble student receiving a 20. These ranks will determine whether you are tracked as a Leader, a Follower, or a Mogrif, the last referring to those girls who will undergo transformation into animals or plants."

Students murmured, perhaps having forgotten that in this world free of Good and Evil, some of them would still end up newts or ferns.

"Given our new and improved school," Pollux continued, "the Dean has chosen to wait until the start of third year to award tracks. So I suggest you continue to mind your ranks with urgency—"

"And perhaps, Pollux," the Dean cooed as she sat on the desk, backside in Professor Anemone's face, "there is another reason why now is a good time for the girls to mind their ranks?"

"Groom Room," Agatha mumbled, remembering the medieval makeover spa that once rewarded the highest-ranked girls.

Hester shook her head. "Incinerated. Part of Debeautification."

"Of course, Dean," Pollux said. "As you know, odorous and poorly dressed princes have been gathering in force at the Woods gate, ready to kill one of our own. With our Captains' arrival today, they will no doubt redouble their efforts. Though our castle enchantments have kept the princes out thus far, we must be alerted if they fail. Thus, beginning tonight, the two students with the lowest rankings at day's end will stand guard at the Woods gate from dusk until dawn."

Agatha grimaced as girls buzzed around her. Last year, failing in Good and Evil meant being turned into a guard for the opposite side. This year, girls who failed in their lessons against boys would get slaughtered by them first. So much for "new and improved."

"The first challenge is called Unforgiven," the Dean said. "In order to protect each other in the war to come, you must learn to resist the attraction of men. Each of you will face a phantom boy from your past for whom you've had feelings. Slay him ruthlessly, even if you want to forgive. He is the *enemy* now and sees you as the same. The more savagely you kill him, the higher your rank."

Agatha tensed. She and Sophie would face the same boy.

Beatrix went first. The Dean pointed a sharp nail at her heart and, as if carving with a knife, drew out a wisp of blue-lit smoke that congealed into a phantom and stepped from Beatrix's body like a shadowed self. Chaddick, the burly gray-eyed Everboy who had once asked her to the Ball, bent to one knee before her in a haloed blue haze and held forth a rose with a dashing smile—

Beatrix stabbed her glowing finger and blasted him to dust.

"Come a long way, hasn't she?" Anadil mused to her spooked rats, peeking from her pocket.

Professor Anemone was hopping with fury. "Evelyn, this challenge is cruel, nefarious, and hasn't the slightest to do with Debeautification," she fired, standing at her desk, "so I suggest you—"

She stopped because candy claws had magically grown out of the desk and gripped her by both shoulders, preparing to evict her.

"Suggest I what?" the Dean asked.

"Continue," Professor Anemone rasped, and the candy claws vanished back into the desk.

The girls resumed buzzing for their turn, clearly siding with the Dean. Meanwhile, Hester glowered at Agatha with a told-you look.

As more students took turns against their heart's blue phantoms—Kiko struggled to dispatch red-haired Tristan, Giselle made tan Nicholas grow braids that strangled him, Dot bombed when she could only give weasel-faced Hort a pimple—Agatha's thoughts drifted back to Tedros. She could barely admit it, but Sophie was right. Her prince would have come somehow if he wanted to see her. Suppose she'd missed his note? Or the Dean had intercepted it? Should she still go through with the witches' plan tonight—

Agatha swallowed a scream. *Have I gone mad?* Risking her best friend's life for a boy she barely knew? She thought about Sophie's lit-up face in their room, so relieved that they'd made peace. This wasn't about Evers and Nevers. This wasn't a battle between a prince and a witch. This was about her and Sophie, striving to forgive each other's mistakes, fighting to save a friendship.

Agatha winced at the irony. She had forgotten the lesson Sophie had almost died learning.

Her prince was a fantasy. Her best friend was the real thing.

Agatha took a deep breath. "Sophie?"

"Mmmm?" Sophie said, stealthily signing autographs for two Evergirls.

"You sure you forgive me?"

Sophie glanced up, focused and sincere. "Aggie, you took back your wish. That's all I wanted." She reached over and squeezed her friend's wrist. "Just give this place a chance, all right?"

Agatha looked into Sophie's hopeful eyes, the same hope she saw in all the other girls at this school. "There's life after boys," Sophie said, with a smile as bright as her diadem. "You'll see."

For the first time, Agatha let the thought in.

"Sophie is next," Pollux sniffed behind her.

Sophie turned to see the whole class goggling at her.

"We're doing a challenge?" Sophie asked, bewildered. "When does the Groom Room open?"

She barely gleaned the rules before Pollux shoved her forward with his antelope hoof—

"Just kill him fast!" Agatha hissed at her. "You can't be anywhere near those princes tonight!"

"But I don't want to kill anyone!" Sophie whimpered as Pollux trotted her past Professor Anemone, steaming at her desk.

Sophie took her place in front of the Dean, trying to calm down. All she had to do was slay a ghost and she'd be safe with Agatha, at least for the night.

The witch is gone.

Sophie nodded, ready to face the boy her friend had wished for over her.

The witch is gone.

The Dean raised her long, gold-lacquered nail and pulled trails of blue smoke from Sophie, slowly, luxuriously, until they began to take shape . . . and dissipated into thin air.

Sophie beamed proudly. "Like I said, I'm 100% Goo—"

Pain ripped through her chest and Sophie buckled. "Oh my God."

Agatha bolted to her feet. "Are you okay?"

But now bloodred smoke was leaking from her friend's chest, as Sophie clutched it tighter, choking in agony. She raised scared eyes to Agatha, smoke spilling from inside her. "Aggie—help—me—"

Agatha lunged over her desk too late—

Sophie screamed a cry and a rip of red light exploded from her heart.

The class slammed back against their chairs in shock. Agatha froze.

Protruding out of Sophie's body was a phantom's head.

Only it wasn't Tedros'.

A massive black Beast, half man, half wolf, with devil-red eyes, dripped smoking drool as it jutted its jaws from Sophie's chest. Sophie couldn't breathe, staring down at the Beast who'd cursed her dreams since she killed it a year ago—the Beast now birthed from her own soul.

Step by step, the phantom crawled out of Sophie's body, landing on knife-sharp claws, and grew erect on two hairy legs, head bowed, nostrils flaring.

Then it raised red eyes to the class and snarled.

Smashing through rows, the Beast inspected the face of each petrified girl, hunting for someone. It growled rejection again, again, snapping and seething, slobbering angrier, angrier . . . until it stopped cold.

Slowly the Beast turned to Agatha and smiled bloodstained teeth.

"No!" Sophie screamed—

The Beast launched across the room onto Agatha's desk and slashed claws across her with a hateful roar. Then it leapt back into Sophie's heart in a single bound, snuffing its infernal light.

Sophie fainted and crumpled to the floor.

No one moved. Agatha's chest pounded so loud, whiting out her vision until it ebbed just long enough for her to see what the Beast had magically slashed on her in gruesome pink scars.

UNFORGIVEN

With an ugly, slurping sound, the scars shriveled and vanished into her skin.

Agatha touched shaking fingers to her healed chest and slowly looked up.

On her knees, Professor Anemone had Sophie in her arms and gently revived her with a glowing fingertip. As her teacher shepherded her to her seat, Sophie panted and shivered in her grip. "I didn't do it—" she choked as she sat, barely audible. "It wasn't me—"

"Shhh, Agatha knows you'd never attack her, dear. In the heat of a moment, your soul just mistook her for a boy," the Dean soothed, caressing her and Agatha's shoulders. "Still, a model performance, despite its carelessness." She paused and smiled at the class. "Who's next?"

Professor Anemone gave the Dean a rancid glare and left the room.

At her desk, Sophie was quaking just as much as Agatha, neither able to look at the other. As unnerved students took turns, barely killing their phantoms, Agatha saw the rest of the class give her darting glances, as if they trusted the Dean's explanation and she should too.

Sophie looked up through tears. "Aggie, you believe her, don't you? I forgive you—I swear—"

But Agatha was staring at Hester, who had the same ominous face she'd worn in the bathroom, warning her wish wouldn't go unpunished.

"Please let's get the Storian," Sophie said, voice breaking.

Agatha slowly turned to her.

"We'll both mean our wish now, won't we?" Sophie begged. "You said you wanted to go home."

Agatha felt no relief. Only the deepening dread that it was too late to go home.

"Agatha," said a voice.

Agatha's eyes lifted over Sophie to see the Dean against the window.

"You're last, dear."

Agatha lost time in those moments, unsure how she made it from one point to another, until she stood before the Dean at the front of the room, listless and scared. Her chest simmered with heat, as if the slashed message had drawn under her skin and tattooed inside her. For the first time, she didn't hear the voices of Good, telling her to believe her friend. Instead, she heard the witches' voices, telling her that for the second year, there'd been no Great Mistake in why she'd come to school.

Because she'd wished for the right ending after all.

The Dean thrust her finger at Agatha and yanked smoke from her with so much force that Agatha toppled backwards. Billowing high, the blue wisps pooled in the air like a suspended cloud, about to reveal its phantom. . . .

Then the mist turned black.

The Dean's eyes widened. Thick as thunderclouds, the smoke began to swirl, faster, faster, funneling to deathly black fog. Agatha scrambled back. "What's happeni—"

Lightning exploded from the cyclone and black wind ripped from its vortex, knocking girls to the ground and smashing the Dean into the sour-candy desk. The wind tore across the taffy before it blew all the butterflies off the Dean's dress and blasted them like a cannon through the window. Swirling and howling with vengeance, the black gale snatched the door off its hinges and pinned girls against the wall, leaving only Agatha untouched. Sophie tried to crawl towards Agatha to save her, but the wind threw Sophie across the room into a cabinet. Then with a last burst of force, it picked Agatha up and sucked her screaming into its cloud.

Gasping, spinning, Agatha felt and saw nothing but black walls of wind, rising higher on all sides, shielding her view of the room. The wind bashed her from wall to wall with hellacious force, shredding and swallowing her Captain's crown, the roars growing louder, louder, splitting her ears—until all at once the winds died away, leaving her in a quiet eye of darkness.

The black walls around her started to thicken with dimension and light, morphing into the same ghostly shadow on all four sides . . . masks . . . giant silver masks . . .

Tedros' searing blue eyes gleamed through each, glaring down from every direction.

"Tonight," he boomed, voice resounding. "Cross the Bridge."

Dwarfed beneath him, Agatha faltered for voice. "But—but—"

Tedros vanished. The black winds ripped into her heart with a thunderclap, leaving Agatha back in the silent classroom without a hair out of place.

Girls slowly looked up from their disheveled heaps to see the room blown to smithereens, except for Professor Anemone, Professor Dovey, and Lady Lesso gawping through the doorway. The door magically slammed in their faces.

"Who was it?" The Dean staggered up, a windswept mess. "Who'd you see?"

Agatha's eyes lowered to the Dean's blank dress, emptied of butterflies. She couldn't hear everything, it turned out. Agatha glowered back at her, defiant.

The Dean's face melted into a slow, cryptic smile and a "20" burst into smoky maggots above Agatha's head. "For failing the challenge completely," the Dean declared, magically restoring her own looks as she awarded the rest of the ranks (Dot wrestled a putrid-smelling "19"). A thousand blue butterflies hatched from the Dean's dress seams like cocoons and flew into a new pattern.

Agatha sat down, catching girls' suspicious looks at their crownless Captain. Meanwhile, Hester and Anadil both had the same anxious expressions, demanding she answer their questions after class.

"It was Tedros, wasn't it?" a trembling voice said next to her.

Agatha didn't move.

"Aggie?" Sophie's voice squeaked. "What did Tedros say?"

Agatha hesitated, then lifted her eyes to her friend's bloodless face—

Her heart stopped.

There was something on Sophie's neck. Just under her collar.

A black wart.

"Aggie?" Sophie shifted and her collar obscured it. "What'd you see?"

Agatha wheezed for voice.

"Well?" Sophie said, face darkening.

Agatha hid her shaking hands—"You were r-r-right," she stuttered, trying to look ashamed. "He—he said he'd never c-c-come for me."

Sophie gaped at her in disbelief. "He . . . did?"

Slowly her emerald eyes hardened into suspicious, knife-edged disks. Agatha held her breath, feeling them cut into her soul and hang a noose around her lie, about to pull tight. . . .

"What did I tell you, Agatha?" Sophie breathed with quiet fury. She clasped her friend's hand. "I told you boys are Evil."

Agatha stared at her, stunned.

"Don't worry, Aggie. Nothing can stop us if we work together," Sophie vowed, her Captain's crown sparkling. "We'll get the pen from him. We'll get our happy ending back. Just like last time."

Heart hammering, Agatha gazed past her at Halfway Bridge, leading into fog.

This time, she knew it wouldn't be together.

"Tonight?" Sophie smiled at her hopefully.

Agatha smiled back in terror, hearing her prince's voice as her own.

"Tonight."

9

Symptoms Returned

"How big was the wart?" Anadil kneeled in the nook behind the Honor stairwell, lined with blue rosebushes. "You *sure* you saw it?"

Agatha nodded, biting her nails to stop their shaking. "She says she forgives me. She says she wants to go home—"

"It's too late." Crouched next to her, Hester crushed a rose. "Don't you remember? Once the symptoms start, she can't control her Evil. You have to kiss Tedros before she transforms into a witch or we're *all* dead."

Agatha shook harder, flooded by memories of Sophie's bald, murderous hag—slaying wolves, annihilating towers, and unleashing hell upon students. Back then there were warnings that preceded her transformation: bad dreams, bursts of anger . . . then the first wart. This time, Agatha hadn't noticed them, but they'd been there again. The nightmare scars under Sophie's eyes at the wedding. Her punishing glare in Sader's office. Her dark smile at the Welcoming. She'd denied it all, thinking her friend had changed. But Sophie hadn't forgiven her wish for a prince, and she never could.

Now that prince was her only hope.

"How long?" Agatha looked up at Hester. "How long until she turns?"

"The Beast was just a warning," Hester said, thinking hard. "She hasn't hurt anything real yet."

"There'll be more symptoms first," Anadil agreed. "But Hester's right. We're safe until she hurts something."

Dot swooped in, chomping on rose-shaped yams. "Does that mean Agatha can come to Book Club tonight?"

"It means Agatha can still kiss Tedros tonight," Hester growled, yanking Agatha towards the crowded hall. "But we have to act normal. No one can know she's seeing him—"

"Wait a second—" said Agatha.

"Hester, one kiss and we're back to Good and Evil," grinned Anadil, cozying up to her friend as they wove through girls. "Henchmen Training, Death Traps, and maggoty gruel . . ."

"Hold on—" Agatha started.

"Never be so happy to see a Doom Room reopen," Hester smirked to Anadil.

"Both of you, listen—"

"Book Club's discussing *Princeless but Fabulous*," Dot said, clacking behind, mouth full of yams. "I'd hate for her to miss it—"

Agatha whirled. "Is it ever possible to get in a word with you three?"

"That's why a coven isn't four," said Hester. "Another reason why you need to kiss Tedros."

"That's what I'm trying to tell you! He didn't say *how* to see him!" Agatha barked before scanning for eavesdropping butterflies. She lowered her voice. "Only that I should cross the Bridge."

"Halfway Bridge?" Anadil said. "Are you sure you didn't mishear?"

"Maybe he said 'fridge,'" said Dot, returning the waves of two passing Evergirls. "Is there a magic fridge in the kitc—*eeeyiii*!" She grabbed her blue harem pants, which Hester had just ripped. "What was that for?"

"For trying to be an Ever and Never at the same time, you underfed twit," Hester hissed, and turned to Agatha. "Dot's right. He couldn't have said 'Bridge.'"

Agatha grimaced. "But that's what he—"

"Suppose it's a trap?" Dot asked, turning the torn piece of pants to spinach.

Hester and Anadil both stared at her.

"Listen," Dot said, whipping back her hair. "I have self-esteem now, so if you act like cretins, I'll move in with Reena and—"

"Glimmers of intelligence, hasn't she," muttered Anadil.

"Inspired and fleeting," Hester grumped, and turned back

to Agatha. "It *could* be the Dean's ploy. Can't exactly forge a princeless school if her Captain's longing for a prince, can she? For all you know, she conjured Tedros to catch you trying to see him."

"Mmmm, imagine if they found out their Great Girl Hope tried to abandon them for a *boy*," Anadil purred, eyeing girls streaming by. "You'd be served at supper with a nice béarnaise sauce."

Agatha's blood chilled. "Do I still go to Tedros tonight?"

"You don't have a choice, do you?" Hester said softer, squinting over her shoulder. "You certainly can't sleep next to *her*."

Agatha swiveled to see Sophie hurrying towards her with a nervous look, as if scared to be alone after the last class. Three butterflies whooshed past her towards Agatha and the witches—

"But I'm in her room!" Agatha gasped, turning back. "How do I get out without her or Beatrix see—"

Hester and Anadil were already retreating, glowing fingers to lips. With naughty grins, they blew smoke off their fingertips, red and green wisps, which danced towards Agatha and coalesced into four bold letters . . .

Butterflies smashed through the letters, zigzagging in vain, searching for something to hear.

"Are the witches going to help us get the Storian?" Sophie

puffed, bounding up behind her.

Agatha turned and almost screamed. Sophie had covered her neck with a puppy-patterned shawl.

"It's Kiko's," Sophie sighed morosely. "But it's glacial in this place, and you know how I catch colds, low body fat and all. Neck's itching like mad, though—fabric must be ogrishly cheap—"

She saw Agatha gaping at the scarf, dead pale. "As if you're the Empress of Haute Couture," Sophie frowned. "*So?* What's our plan for tonight?"

Legs shaking, Agatha clung to her own plan. The witches were right. Fail the rest of the day's challenges, and she'd be safe with her prince before any more symptoms arrived.

With Hester and Anadil in different classes for second session, Agatha felt even more terrified sitting next to Sophie, who kept scratching under her shawl.

Like Professor Anemone, Professor Dovey was supervised by the Dean, whose presence prevented the former Good Deeds instructor from accosting Agatha. But Professor Dovey seemed to know exactly what was on Agatha's mind, because she kept giving her forceful stares as she rehashed the rankings system.

"And perhaps that bears repeating," she said loudly at her sugarplum desk, "failing students will guard the Woods gate on their *own* without teachers—"

"They *know* all this, Clarissa," the Dean moaned.

"Meaning they are completely *unsupervised* in the Forest—"

"Clarissa!"

Professor Dovey moved on, throwing Agatha a last urgent look.

Princeless Power was just a disguised version of Professor Dovey's old course on Good Deeds, with the only difference the jelly-bean painting on a pumpkin candy wall, depicting Agatha's face with a speech bubble: *Boys Are Born Slaves!*

Agatha held herself back from smashing it. It wasn't enough that her best friend was turning into a deadly witch? Now she was a poster girl for male *slavery*? Professor Dovey seemed to share the same revulsion, for she ignored the Dean's tightening jaw as she spoke.

"A boy is no more meant to be subjugated than a girl. True, girls have compassion and sensitivity that most boys do not. It is why, at times, boys and girls appear completely incompatible—"

In her caramel chair, Agatha threw Sophie quick glances to make sure more warts hadn't popped up or her teeth hadn't fallen out. But other than still looking itchy, Sophie was fair and lovely as ever. Agatha craned to see if there were more warts under the shawl. . . . Sophie caught her and Agatha pretended to be picking her nose.

Sophie slid a note over. *Should we use the Bridge tonight?*

Agatha smiled vaguely. To get to Tedros, she had to somehow bomb this challenge without arousing Sophie's suspicions.

"In order to survive, boys learn to project strength over emotion," Professor Dovey went on. "It is the reason they desire softness in a girl. By staying soft, you let them be vulnerable for the only time in their lives. Understanding a boy is your greatest hope to tame him."

"And make him a slave," the Dean interrupted, crossing her legs. "As we all know, boys respond best to beatings and the withholding of food."

"Boys respond to encouragement and common sense, Evelyn," Professor Dovey retorted. "And a faith in the love between princess and prince."

The Dean's creamy cheeks colored and the classroom walls shook. "Clarissa, what girls need is the right to be happy without savage, execrable pigs—"

"What girls need is the right to know what makes boys worthy of love. What girls need is the right to choose their own endings, not their Dean's," Professor Dovey seethed, voice rising. "What girls need is the right to know why that Dean shouldn't *be* here at all!"

The Dean launched to her feet. Candied arms magically surged from the walls behind Professor Dovey and flung her out of the classroom with such force the door blew shut behind her, spraying pumpkin flakes all over the desks.

Agatha went white, forcing herself to stay in her chair. Girls goggled in shock around her.

"Now then," the Dean said, turning to the class. "Shall we proceed with the challenge?"

Murmuring, the girls settled in, as if Professor Dovey had it coming for such blatant disrespect. Agatha struggled to look dismissive too, knowing her fairy godmother would want her to get to her prince at all costs. But what had her teacher meant? Did she know Dean Sader from the *past*?

She suddenly noticed Sophie next to her, whole hand up her shawl now, scratching vociferously, having missed the entire incident.

Agatha went a shade whiter and refocused on failing.

Magically conjuring dozens of green beanstalks from the treacle ceiling, Dean Sader explained that for the Faith Flying test, each student, blindfolded and abandoned high on a stalk, would use the directions shouted out by her classmates to swing across the other trunks and return to her desk. Whoever swung back to their desk the fastest would receive top rank.

Beatrix had every girl in class cheering her to her desk. Arachne and Reena loudly directed each other to the finish, as did Millicent and Mona. Terrified of another Evil episode, Sophie carefully obeyed the shouts of her classmates eager to stay on Sophie's good side after the Beast incident, and won the challenge in record time.

As she sat down, Sophie swept clumps of fallen hair off her dress. She glanced up and saw Agatha staring and shuddering as if she were ill. "Oh it's easy as *cake*, Aggie," Sophie said, combing out more loose hair. "Just listen to my directions and you'll be fine."

With her mind on balding scalps, hidden warts, and more witch symptoms to come, Agatha could barely focus on failing her turn. Still, she managed to feign confusion, deafness, and dyslexia and made sure the Dean saw her disappointed pout when she earned second-to-last place. (Dot accidentally swung out the window, beating her to the bottom.)

"But I shouted so loudly!" moaned Sophie, scratching her neck as she walked Agatha down the hall. "Aggie, you have to do well in the next one or you'll be on guard tonight!"

Agatha nodded, forcing a dejected look. When Sophie turned, she stooped and tried to peek under her shawl—

Sophie turned back and Agatha hunched over. "Sorry, fart coming."

"At least let's leave with our dignity!" Sophie gasped.

They were late to Defense Against Boys, meaning Agatha had to sit far across the room from Hester and Anadil, who looked desperate to talk to her. But Lady Lesso seemed to read Agatha's thoughts, for as Sophie walked in, the former Curses & Death Traps professor stood at the door with narrowed violet eyes, scouring every inch of her—

"Do I have a pimple?" Sophie murmured, biting her quill pen as she sat, only to jump up from her frozen chair. Frowning, she sat back down and scanned the chilled rock-candy room that replicated Lady Lesso's old Evil classroom, down to sugared icicles dangling from the ceiling. Then she saw Agatha gawking at her, looking as if she'd been stabbed. "Aggie, you're acting very strange," Sophie said, discarding her bitten pen.

Agatha heaved for air.

Sophie's front teeth had gone *black*.

"Just c-c-c-old in here—" Agatha stammered—

"And here you gave me such goonish looks over this shawl," Sophie humphed, turning away.

Agatha waved frantically at Hester and Anadil, mouthing "Symptoms! Symptoms!" until she saw Sophie peering and pretended to be swatting at flies. *Warts, falling hair, rotting teeth* . . . Would she even make it to Tedros before the witch came?

Perhaps the Dean knew she'd made her point with Professor Dovey, for she wasn't in the room to supervise Lady Lesso's class. Instead she sent Pollux, who sat in back, butterfly on shoulder, making odd sniffing sounds, as if waiting to be acknowledged.

"Boys are vile, dirty creatures, which is why Nevergirls do not *marry* them," Lady Lesso said, giving Evergirls repellent looks as she clacked through the aisle. "But that is no reason to kill them."

"Unless they attack, of course," Pollux said.

Lady Lesso raised her eyes as if she smelled a skunk, then lowered them. "Killing stains your soul permanently, whether you are an Ever or a Never. You may kill only for the purest self-defense or to slay your Nemesis and find peace. Neither are conditions you will experience in this *school.*"

"Unless there's a war, you mean," Pollux huffed.

"Perhaps it is time for another extermination," Lady Lesso said to no one in particular.

The dog didn't interrupt again. Still, Lady Lesso gave Agatha a concerned frown as she passed and put her near the end of the challenge order, as if to ensure she'd know what she needed to fail.

"For your challenge, you'll be defending against rogue Mogrifs. The boys may no doubt rely on shape-shifting in order to invade, so you must be prepared to do the same," said the teacher, tightening her braid. "But be warned, transformation lets us access our deepest instincts in order to survive. If you are stained by unforgivable Evil, the process can be corrupted." Her purple eyes sliced into Pollux. "Let this be a warning to all of you who speak so casually of *war*."

To defeat the phantom Mogrifs, each girl had to morph into an animal herself. A year ago, their Forest Group leaders had taught them how to mogrify into an animal of their choice using visualization. It was a relatively easy spell, hence taught in the first year, along with Water and Weather spells (though mogrifying involved the extra wrinkle of bursting out of one's clothes). Now the challenge seemed to be to find the *right* Mogrif to subdue their male opponents.

Pitted against a viper, Hester took nasty bites as a crab before her nimbler mongoose subdued it; Beatrix's ungainly pelican abandoned its fight against a piranha; Dot's piglet fled the moment she saw the ram charging for her. ("I thought boys like cute things," she oinked, scurrying back to her heaped clothes.)

Agatha was baffled as to how to do any worse. So when Lady Lesso conjured a breast-beating bear in front of her, she just stood and scratched her head. "I—I've forgotten—"

"*Forgotten* how to mogrify?" Pollux said suspiciously. "The girl who spent a significant portion of her first year as a cockroach?"

"Readers have minds like sieves," sighed Lady Lesso, trying not to look pleased. "Surely no one can match such incompetence."

"Guess I'm on guard tonight," Agatha said, plopping next to Sophie.

"B-b-but that means we can't get the Storian!" Sophie paled, revealing even blacker teeth.

Agatha gripped her seat.

"It doesn't make sense," Sophie said, sagging. "You're usually so good at challen—" Her face lit up. "Wait! What if I fail too, Aggie! Then I could guard with you! We could break into the boys' school and get home!"

"No!" Agatha cried. "Sophie, that's a terri—"

But Sophie was already bouncing to the front of the room, determined to lose her battle. Seeing Agatha's face, Lady Lesso likely guessed Sophie's plan, for she produced an obese pigeon as her opponent. Sophie turned into a plushy pink cat and shirked from its weak pecks.

"O mighty beast," Sophie mewled, as if auditioning for the school play. "I am no match for thee!"

Agatha caught Hester's jumpy look across the room. If Sophie was on guard with her tonight, how could she escape to her prince?

"Mercy, you brute!" Sophie's cat cried to the waddling pigeon. Dramatically flinging her paw to her head, Sophie stepped into her piled clothes and visualized herself human, ready to claim last place—

Only nothing happened.

Sophie's cat frowned and tried the spell again, but if anything, now her paws were furrier. The pigeon flew up and alighted on her head. Girls giggled, except for Agatha, who knew just how capable Sophie was of putting on a show.

"I can't—" Sophie gasped to Lady Lesso. "I can't change back—"

"Just concentrate!" Lady Lesso snapped, giggles around her turning to howls.

But whether eyes open or eyes closed, Sophie couldn't turn herself human. "It's not me—" she choked. "Something's stopping it—" The pigeon peed on her. "Helpppppp!" Sophie yowled, drowned out by the class's roars. Even Agatha had to snort.

"Enough idiocy!" Lady Lesso groaned, shooting a spell at her to end this charade.

Sophie's cat gaped back at her, unchanged. This time when Sophie tried to talk, all that came out was a meow.

The laughter stopped.

Red faced, Lady Lesso stabbed her finger again to turn Sophie back. Sophie meowed louder. Lady Lesso's eyes widened, and she swiveled to the butterfly on Pollux. "Find Evely—"

But the door was already open and the Dean surging in, finger outstretched. Muttering a strange incantation, she pointed at Sophie, who started to morph back to human. But before Agatha and the rest of the class could unclench, the process stopped short, leaving Sophie trapped somewhere between cat and human, hissing with pain.

Lady Lesso blanched. "Something's wrong—"

Finger thrusting, the Dean muttered faster, but Sophie's body ricocheted from human to cat, cat to human, in a violent tug of war, as she wheezed alternate wails and meows.

"Evelyn, it's getting worse—" Lady Lesso pressed—

The Dean pointed harder at Sophie, but every time Sophie's body tried to grow, it shrank back down. Sparks flew around her as Sophie morphed faster and faster, soul caught between forces, into a fiery, formless blur. The curious pigeon fluttered too close and vanished into the haze.

Agatha's head went light, her friend shape-shifting wildly, past human, past animal . . . until at last Agatha saw something inside Sophie win. In the blur of flames, a shadow grew clearer . . . skin shriveled and decayed . . . warts black and swollen . . . bald head gleaming . . . rising from fire reborn. . . .

Agatha closed her eyes in shock—

The Dean flung forth both hands and shot a blast of light. Sophie flew against the wall and crashed behind the desk.

Slowly Agatha opened her eyes to eerie silence. As curls of smoke rose over the frozen countertop, she and the rest of the girls slowly peered over it.

"I—I must have blacked out," Sophie said, blinking long lashes and back in her clothes. "All I remember is trying to change back—and something stopping me—" She glanced around for the unseen pigeon. "But I didn't hurt it! Surely that means I'm on guard now!"

Lady Lesso looked as if she'd swallowed her own tongue. "It means—it means your soul i-i-is—"

"Rusty with counterspells," the Dean said. "Wouldn't you agree, Lady Lesso?"

Lady Lesso stiffened, a strange weakness distilling

her usually cold eyes. She looked scared, Agatha thought, almost . . . *sad*. "Yes, of course," she mumbled to the Dean.

Agatha noticed her teacher's eyes dart to her and dart away.

"But I still . . . failed?" Sophie said hopefully.

"On the contrary, first rank," the Dean said, swishing out.

Sophie opened her mouth to protest, but Lady Lesso quickly awarded the rest of the rankings and jetted from the room when butterflies zoomed through to signal class's end.

Agatha didn't budge as girls exited, buzzing how lucky it was the Dean rescued Sophie from Lesso's incompetence. "The teachers are just jealous of the Dean," Beatrix sighed dismissively.

As the girls left the room, Agatha nervously watched Sophie, back turned to her, gathering her things. The Dean's arrival had been lucky indeed. For the girls hadn't seen what she had: the witch reborn, her symptoms complete. If the Dean hadn't intervened in time . . .

Tedros, Agatha thought, sneaking for the door. *Just make it to Tedros—*

"Aggie, I won't be on guard with you," Sophie said behind her. "You wouldn't go to Tedros, would you?"

Agatha stopped dead. "What? Why would you say that?"

"Because you keep looking at me like I'm a witch."

Agatha turned to see Sophie stalking towards her, eyes cold. Agatha felt her chest sweating, her legs jellying, symptoms that told her she was about to faint, the way she once did in Tedros' arms. But just as she collapsed into a deadly witch's arms instead of her prince . . .

"Your—your teeth—" she spluttered at Sophie, recovering. "They're—they're normal—"

Sophie gaped dumbly. "My teeth? What are you—" Her face hardened. "Agatha, that was *ink*. My pen must have leaked—had it in my mouth—"

"But your hair—" Agatha insisted. "I saw it falling out—"

"A piece got caught on a stupid beanstalk!" Sophie barked. "And you believed *I* was turning into a witch again? That I'd attack *you*? After everything we've been through!"

All Agatha managed was a croak.

"I trust you tonight, Aggie," Sophie said, face filled with hurt. "Even if you don't trust me."

Watching Sophie go, yanking at her disheveled shawl, Agatha sagged guiltily.

But then she remembered the *wart* . . . the wart she definitely saw . . . the wart that couldn't be explained away. . . . As Sophie trailed away, tearing off the shawl, Agatha chased to see under it—

A hand yanked her back.

"Lesso's lying," Hester said, closing the door and sealing them alone. "You heard her. Sophie's soul's corrupted by unforgivable Evil! That's why she couldn't change back! That's why the Beast came out of her! It explains everything!"

"But—but what does that mean?" Agatha rasped—

"It means this time the change is permanent!" Hester pressed. "When Sophie turns into a witch, she'll never turn back! I told you she wanted revenge!"

"But you said it yourself! She hasn't hurt anything! And

the symptoms *aren't* getting worse at all—"

"Oh they're getting worse, all right. The Dean just isn't seeing it," Hester said, looking away. "You have to kiss Tedros tonight!"

Agatha shook her head, still picturing Sophie's hurt face. "I can't. I can't go to him, Hester. I have to trust my best friend." She slumped, exhaling. "Probably wasn't even a wart. Just being paranoid, like I was with her hair and teeth. We're *all* just being paranoi—"

But now Agatha saw where Hester was looking.

Behind the desk, the phantom pigeon lay against the wall.

Only it wasn't a phantom anymore.

Blood spilled towards them from its mangled corpse, across the candy floor.

10

Doubt

"She's turning into a witch! She's turning and she doesn't know it!" Agatha choked, rushing with Dot into the Charity breezeway.

"Oh, she knows," Dot snapped. "She's just playing innocent. Why do you think she's wearing that stupid shawl!"

"We have to tell Lady Lesso—she'll know what to do—"

"No! You saw what happened with Professor Dovey. We can't put the teachers in danger!"

"Sophie was Good at home, Dot!" Agatha cried. "She was *happy*—"

"You want to see her happy? Wait until she does to you what she did to that pigeon!"

Thankfully, Agatha wouldn't see

Sophie the rest of the afternoon. With challenges complete for the day, their classes diverged until Forest Groups, so while Sophie had Female Talents with Anadil and Hester, Agatha hurried to History of Heroines with Dot.

"You can't be alone with her again!" Dot said as they neared the mass of girls filing into Good Hall. "Hide in Hester's room after classes!"

All Agatha could see was the pigeon's gaping eye . . . its blood seeping towards her. . . . She stopped against a sapphire column, gulping for air. "This is all because of my wish."

"No, this is all because you chose the wrong ending last time."

Agatha looked up at Dot's reflection in the polished glass.

"You heard Hester. Tonight's your last chance to do what your heart really wants," Dot said. "Or Sophie will be a witch forever."

Agatha's throat tightened, afraid to let the words out. "And if . . . if I kiss him?"

"She'll go home to her father safe, like you promised. The witch locked inside."

Agatha said nothing for a moment. Finally she turned. "How do I escape guard duty tonight? The other girl will tell the Dean—"

"Will she?" Dot took her arm. "Just 'cause I'm popular and wear glitter doesn't mean I'm a better student."

"We're on guard . . . together?"

"If you haven't noticed, I've been failing every challenge worse than you. And I've been trying!"

Agatha looked at her, scared. "But even if I do escape . . . what if I can't get into the boys' castle?"

"You will."

Agatha felt the unspoken ending in Dot's grip.

Because our lives depend on it.

Good Hall had the same briny smell and humid haze as last year, its marble ballroom swathed in emerald algae and blue rust, like a cathedral that had been sunken in seawater. Chipped marble murals on the wall depicted the history of the Great War, ending in the triumph of the Evil School Master over his own Good brother. As Agatha sat down in the pews, she found it odd that the Dean hadn't changed the murals to reflect either the School Master's death or the Boy Eviction. Surely she'd want history revised in her own image?

Odder still, though History was the Dean's class to teach, she failed to appear at all, leaving Pollux fumbling before half the school.

"Our Dean had urgent business, so I offered to present a comprehensive review of Male Brutality through the ages, with pointed emphasis on the persecution of those who do not display conventionally masculine traits."

He pursed his lips. "But the Dean preferred you each introduce your lineage instead."

Agatha tried to focus on paths into the Boys' school, but found herself tuning in to the girls' introductions. All the students at the School for Good and Evil came from fairy-tale families, except her and Sophie, the two unenchanted Readers kidnapped from Gavaldon. Agatha remembered that Hester's mother was the now-deceased witch who tried to kill Hansel and Gretel, while Anadil's grandmother was the notorious White Witch, who wore little boys' bones. But now Agatha also learned Beatrix's grandmother was the maiden who outwitted Rumplestiltskin, Millicent was the great-granddaughter of Sleeping Beauty and her prince, and Kiko was the child of one of Neverland's Lost Boys and a mermaid.

While Evergirls usually mentioned both parents, the Nevers proferred only one or none at all, whether Arachne's father, a robber of queens; Mona's green-skinned mother, who had famously terrorized Oz; or Dot's father, Nottingham's sheriff who never caught his Nemesis, Robin Hood.

"Why don't Nevers mention both parents?" Agatha asked after Dot sat down.

"'Cause villains aren't born out of love," Dot said, watching Reena rhapsodize about how her royal parents met. "We're made for all the wrong reasons, none of which keep a family together. Lady Lesso used to say villain families are like dandelions—'fleeting and toxic.' Sounded like it came from personal experience. Bet Sophie's is worse than any of ours."

"But Sophie had loving parents—" Agatha's voice trailed off.

"Stefan suffered most of all," her mother had said about Stefan's marriage to Sophie's mother. Had his marriage been unhappy from the start? Had Sophie too been born "for all the wrong reasons"? Agatha looked at Dot, who seemed to intuit her thoughts.

"The School Master wanted to marry her for a reason," Dot warned.

Agatha remembered his parting vow . . . his red-rimmed eyes claiming Sophie as his bride . . .

"You can never be good, Sophie. That's why you're mine."

Now, as Agatha thought of her best friend returning to being a witch, she wondered anxiously: Was the School Master right? And why couldn't the Dean see it?

"I mean, how can anyone even believe the Dean's hogwash," Agatha crabbed, trying to distract herself. "Kingdoms of women can't last without men. How would they, um . . . grow?"

"That's what we like about it." Dot grinned. *"Slaves."*

The only other memorable moment of class came when Yara, the dancing girl from the Welcoming, sashayed in halfway through, with her gangly walk and rippling muscles, acting as if it was perfectly routine to skip class all morning and flounce in at will.

"Care to present your lineage, Yara?" Pollux asked thinly.

Yara twirled with a squawk and sat down.

"Gypsies, no doubt," Pollux murmured.

As Agatha stared at Yara's beakish face, ginger hair, and strawberry freckles, she felt like she'd never encountered a girl so alien . . . and yet faintly familiar.

"Wanders in and out like the school pet," Dot whispered. "It's 'cause she can't speak. Dean feels sorry for her."

Agatha skipped lunch in the Supper Hall to meet Hester and Anadil atop the drizzly Honor Tower rooftop. (Dot declined to join them, citing a myriad of social obligations.) Where the open-air roof had once housed a topiary garden dedicated to scenes from King Arthur's story, the sculpted hedges had been remade in tribute to Queen Guinevere—Arthur's wife and Tedros' mother, who had abandoned them both and never been seen again.

"No wonder Tedros wants to attack us," Hester said, slurping homemade gruel as she eyed scenes of the sculpted, slim queen.

"How can the Dean think she's a hero?" Agatha said. "She deserted her son!"

"On the contrary, the Dean says Guinevere liberated herself from male oppression," Anadil quipped, watching her rats stab each other with stone shards, remnants of a gargoyle Tedros once killed. "She conveniently ignores that she left to shack up with a scrawny knight."

Agatha stared at the menagerie hedges making Guinevere out to be a saint. *"You don't expect me to tell the story as it happened, do you?"* Sophie had teased back home. Every fairy tale could be twisted to serve a purpose. Good could turn into Evil, Evil into Good, back and forth, back and forth, just like it had in the war between the schools a year ago. Even now, Sophie was vowing she was Good, while everything in their story was telling Agatha she was Evil.

"There's no shield *between* the two schools, only around the perimeter gates," Hester was saying to Anadil. "But even so, she can't swim to Tedros, with those crogs in the moat—"

"Crogs?" Agatha asked, turning to them.

"Those spiny white crocodiles. They only attack girls," Anadil said impatiently.

Agatha thought back to the cesspool in the Woods—the female deer dragged under by the crogs, while the male stag swam untouched. She felt doubly relieved she hadn't tried to cross.

"And she can't use the sewers since they're blocked," Hester was saying. "She can't even use the west Forest gate—"

"Is the Bridge portal still up here?'" Agatha said, scanning the roof.

Hester frowned. "I told you, Tedros *couldn't* have said 'bridge'—"

The door opened behind them and butterflies flapped in, just in time to hear the girls ramble cheerfully about how much they enjoyed rooftop picnics, while rain soaked their clothes and ruined their food.

With the glass castle falling into shadows, Agatha headed to Female Talents, increasingly edgy for the night. But unlike the rest of the faculty, Professor Sheeba Sheeks didn't even bother trying to teach. Once a fearsome teacher of villain talents, now she stood at the fore of a rainbow-lollipop room in her busty red velvet gown, boils on both dark-skinned cheeks, clutching a letter on sparkled, butterfly-themed stationery.

"The Dean has put me in charge of the s-s-school—" She choked. *"Play."* She collapsed against the wall. "Auditions begin on the 15th evening in the Supper Hall."

"What's the show?" Beatrix asked.

But Professor Sheeks was too shaken to answer. Blinking pallidly, she took in the bright swirl of lollipops, the Nevers sitting with Evers, and the sparkly edict to direct an all-female play. . . . "Devil's School!" she gasped, and made the girls read from *The Art of Feminine Wiles* for the rest of class.

As the other girls flipped pages, Agatha gazed out at the fortress of fog over Halfway Bay, so thick she could barely see the splashes of lightning behind it. A few more hours and she'd have her chance to rewrite her fairy tale once and for all. But could she actually go through with it? Even with Sophie turning deadly, could she kiss Tedros knowing it was forever?

Agatha suddenly noticed a scrap of parchment caught under Arachne's chair. Two girls had exchanged notes in the previous session. Agatha slid it over with her clump and scooped it into her hands. She recognized both scripts.

SOPHIE: Is there a way for a girl to get to the Boys' school?

BEATRIX: No, course not. Why?

SOPHIE: Just making sure.

Agatha's hands crumpled it. Sophie was on to her.

As she hustled to the Blue Forest for her last class, Agatha could feel her head throbbing, at a loss how to both get to a school with no route and ensure Sophie didn't see her. Scurrying past the Gallery of Good, she noticed two silhouettes through the cracked-open door. Agatha caught a flash of ginger hair—

"I've given you two weeks," the Dean's voice snapped.

"But I've tried!" said a low voice.

"If you want to stay here, you have to find a wa—"

The Dean paused suddenly and spun. The doorway was empty.

Strange, Agatha thought, stealing out of the hall. For she was quite sure the voice talking to the Dean belonged to the same girl no one thought could speak.

Once a lively gathering place for lunch between Good and Evil, the Clearing had overgrown to dead, crackling weeds. As Agatha came through Good's Tunnel of Trees, she saw a squirrel corpse rotting in the empty field and a faded pink bow near it, matching the one Princess Uma used to wear in her hair. The Evil tunnel, now the passage to the Boys' school, had been sealed with rocks—whether by the boys or girls, Agatha didn't know. Still, the teachers felt scared enough to confine the girls inside for meals, which made Agatha uneasy about crossing into the Blue Forest, sprawling directly beneath the boys' jagged towers.

A year before, the Blue Forest was a quiet, gated paradise, with every leaf, flower, and blade of grass a different hue of blue, meant to remind the students it was only a simulation of the more dangerous Woods. But now, as Agatha hurried through the gate, a winter breeze swirling, she could hear the chants of warmongering princes from those Woods: *"Death to Girls! Death to Girls!"*

In the cobalt Fernfield, girls sorted into their Forest Groups for Surviving Fairy Tales. Kiko and Beatrix followed Group 9's tree nymph to the Blue Brook, Anadil and Hester trailed Group 4's water siren to the Turquoise Thicket, while Agatha tried to glimpse Group 3's flag through the tall ferns. Sensing the girls' arrivals, the princes' chants from the Woods turned cruel and obscene, prompting Mona, Arachne, and the rest of Group 12 to lob blue pumpkins over the gate at them. The savage princes fired arrows back, only to find them consumed by the enchanted shield over the perimeter gate.

Under dark clouds, Agatha felt war about to break. Kissing Tedros wouldn't just save the girls from Sophie's witch. It would save them from a massacre if the princes found a way through the shield.

But how could she leave Dot on her own to guard bloodhungry princes? And yet, abandoning her post tonight was the only way to meet Tedros without Sophie knowing—

"Guess what?"

Agatha turned to see Sophie bounding towards her, wrapped in a thick blue cape. "I can watch you on guard!"

Agatha staggered back. There were no other girls nearby. "W-w-what?"

"Couldn't wear that ghastly shawl anymore. All those puppies—thought it'd start barking any moment," Sophie sighed. "Beatrix graciously lent me her cape from the room, and I happened to glance out our window and see where you'll be guarding! Speaking of which, did you know Beatrix's great-grandfather made Snow White's wedding gown? That girl might be mental, but her fabrics are exquisi—" She saw Agatha's face and cleared her throat. "In any case, now I can make sure you're safe from princes all night." Sophie nudged her. "A *witch* wouldn't do that, would she?"

"But—but—" Agatha stared at the cape that covered almost all of Sophie's skin, and knew the real reason she'd traded the shawl for it. "W-w-what about beauty sleep—"

"You would watch *me* on guard, Aggie." Sophie squeezed her shoulder. "What's a friend for?"

Agatha chilled to Sophie's touch. Somewhere a pigeon squawked.

"Uh—sorry—friend calling—" Agatha gasped, sprinting away from her.

Thankfully, Sophie wasn't in her Forest Group, so when Agatha found Kiko, Dot, and the rest of Group 3 at the Fern-field's edge, she grabbed Dot. "Warts—cape—turning—" Agatha stuttered, gulping breaths. "You were right! She *knows*!"

"I thought I told you to stay away from her!" Dot hissed.

"She's watching us tonight! From our room!"

"What!"

"We have to block her view somehow—"

"And here I thought you failed by accident," a voice lashed.

Agatha turned to see Sophie staring at her with shock.

Agatha floundered for words, but Sophie's stare turned ice-cold as she backed into the ferns and ran away.

"You're so dead," Dot croaked.

Agatha's gut twisted, watching Sophie disappear. "But she—she seems so hurt—"

"How many times will you make the same mistake, Agatha? She's a good *actress*."

Agatha's stomach wrenched deeper, knowing Dot was right.

"Ahem."

Both girls turned to see a frowning old gnome with long white hair and tanned, wrinkly skin in a hideous dress, pointy lavender hat, and wobbly heeled shoes. Agatha coughed. It was as if Yuba, her once crotchety, male gnome teacher, had turned into a frumpy housewife.

"I see our Reader has decided this is Surviving Chitchat," the gnome grouched in a hoary voice that sounded just like Yuba's, only higher. "My name is Professor Helga, and I'm afraid we'll have to do proper introductions later. Can't be holding back the whole group for a new arrival. Now as for today's lesson—"

Agatha frowned and nudged Kiko. "Um, isn't that . . ."

"We thought that too," Kiko whispered. "But any male would have been evicted, so it can't be Yuba! Plus the girls dared me to double-check."

"Double-*check*?"

"Don't ask. But trust me when I say she's a woman," Kiko said.

"Come, girls," said Helga, guiding the students into the Forest with her long white staff. "Last year you learned to tell an ordinary plant from a mogrified human! Today we'll be learning how to tell if it's a boy Mogrif or a girl Mogrif! Extremely useful in these times . . ."

Agatha followed, knowing there was only one thing useful

to boys *or* girls right now.

How many warts Sophie was hiding beneath that cape.

Eight hours later, at the stroke of ten, Agatha was back in the Blue Forest with Dot, being fitted with steel guard armor by Lady Lesso and Professor Dovey. Agatha tried repeatedly to whisper to them, but both shushed her, eyeing the blue butterflies circling overhead like drones, lit up by the torches over the north entrance gate. Still, the girls could feel their teachers' frustration, for they brusquely slapped on their breastplates and pauldrons as if harnessing horses.

"I don't know how boys wear this," Dot grumped as Lady Lesso shoved a helmet on her. "It's heavy, itchy, and it *smells*."

Agatha couldn't bear it anymore. "Professors, Sophie knows I'm seeing Tedr—"

Lady Lesso stomped on her foot and Agatha clammed up. Dot couldn't possibly be right about this woman having a family. If Lady Lesso ever had a child, it would have murdered her in her sleep.

Agatha's jaw clenched tighter as Professor Dovey fastened her musty helmet. What good was a fairy godmother if you couldn't *talk* to her? Irritated, Agatha's thoughts drifted to what had happened after classes. When the girls returned from Forest Groups, she'd laid down in Hester's room. It'd been almost two days since she'd closed her eyes . . . weeks since she felt safe, if even for a moment. She couldn't remember falling asleep, only blurring thoughts of capes and warts . . . the sensation of a boiling red rain . . . the prickle of thorns . . . a taste of blood. . . .

Agatha's body seized. *Wake up!*

Pain screamed through her stomach, dragging her back under, and something inside her was born. A pure white seed, then a blurry, milky face, bigger, bigger, until she saw a boy's blue eyes cut right through her—

"NO!" She thrashed awake into Hester's arms.

"Shhhh . . . just a dream . . . ," Hester soothed. Anadil looked worried beside her.

"B-b-but—it was a Nemesis Dream—" Agatha stammered. "It was Tedros—his face—"

"Evers can't have Nemesis Dreams, Agatha," Hester sighed, putting a tray of braised beef and potatoes in front of her.

"But I tasted blood—and I saw him—"

"Only villains dream of their one true enemy." Anadil poured her a mug of ginger beer, which one of her rats promptly jumped in. "Princesses like you dream of your true love, remember? That's why you saw his face."

"But—suppose it's a trap—" Agatha said manically. "Suppose Tedros isn't my happy ending—"

"The only other ending is we all die!" Hester roared, demon tattoo twitching. "Sophie's about to be a witch again, Agatha! You said it yourself! She's probably covered in warts by now!"

Frightened, Agatha refocused as Hester and Anadil explained the plan to break into the School for Boys.

"There's no guarantee it will get you to Tedros," Hester warned at the end, "but it's our best hope. So remember, first wait until—"

"Are you sure I shouldn't use the Bridge?" Agatha prodded.

Hester's demon exploded off her neck at her and Anadil had to strike it down.

Now, as her teachers snapped on the last of her and Dot's armor, Agatha tried to remember every step of her friends' plan.

Professor Dovey watched the hovering butterflies. "The night is long," she said to Agatha vaguely. "Be *careful*."

"Cast your glow into the sky if the enchanted shield breaks," Lady Lesso ordered Dot as she strapped on her sword. "Don't dare take on the princes yourself."

"Why would she be by herself?" the Dean's voice cooed as she sauntered up behind them. "Agatha will be by her side all night."

"Of course she will," Lady Lesso stiffened quickly, not looking at the Dean. "But Dot has a reputation for rash decisions and idiotic behavior."

"I do," Dot chimed, munching a codpiece turned to cabbage.

The Dean smiled. "Shall we move to your posts?"

Agatha saw Lady Lesso and Professor Dovey give her the same scared but hopeful nods, as if sending her on a quest from which she might not return.

"Bet boys pee in this. That's why it smells," Dot grumbled through her helmet as she and Agatha waddled in full armor behind the Dean, towards the south gate, leaving the teachers behind. Agatha could hear the buzz of the princes get louder, drowned out by her thumping heart.

"Dean Sader?"

"Yes, Agatha?"

"What if Sophie's turning into a witch again?"

"I see no reason to worry," the Dean answered without turning.

"But suppose you can't see it?" Agatha pressed her. "Suppose we can see what you can't?"

"Well, dear." The Dean glanced back. "Sometimes we see what we *want* to see."

She smiled and swept ahead towards the princes' chants.

Agatha froze cold in the thicket, her last hope for help gone.

Only she could stop the witch now.

"Agatha, look!"

Agatha spun to Dot, stopped behind her. Slowly Agatha followed her gaze up to the moonlit towers shimmering over the Forest, windows all dark, except for one.

Sophie's emerald eyes glared down at her through its shadows, glowing like tainted stars.

Agatha forced a smile, holding in tears.

One day Sophie would understand why she'd done it.

There, in a blue forest, far away from home, Agatha silently said good-bye to her best friend.

Then she turned her back and moved on.

Her prince was waiting.

11

Double Crossings

"You two are very codependent," Beatrix yawned from bed, squinting at Sophie perched on the blue-glass windowsill.

"Just want to make sure she's safe." Sophie peered down at the two armored knights, one short, one tall, standing in the blue pumpkin patch near the Woods gate.

"You sound . . . like . . . a . . . prince . . . ," Beatrix babbled before her breaths turned heavy, untroubled by the angry chants echoing outside.

Sophie could barely see the source of these chants over the spiked gates, just snatches of the princes' shadowed, distorted faces and shredded clothes. Nothing in this world was ever certain. Princes could become as frightening as ogres. Princesses could become villains. Best friends could become enemies.

Sophie's eyes watered. After returning home, all she had wanted was to be Good. She wasn't perfect, of course—her father could attest to that—but she'd been a true friend to Agatha and tried to live by her example. Every day she'd fought to keep her Evil thoughts at bay, the rages and storms that swelled in her heart. And what had she earned in return? *Betrayed for a prince. Branded a witch. Avoided like a plague.* And now Agatha was one kiss away from abandoning her forever. Sophie wiped her eyes, sniffling. Who was the Evil one now?

But hours passed, and neither Dot nor Agatha budged from the pumpkins, enduring the princes' blind threats and their weapons fired and absorbed into the enchanted shield over the gates. Midnight came and went, then two o'clock . . . four o'clock . . .

Agatha made no move towards Tedros' castle.

Finally, as the moon sank into the glow of a new sun, Agatha still in place, Sophie colored with shame. This school had turned both of them distrustful. After what happened during Forest Groups, Agatha must have come to her senses. It was natural for both of them to have doubts about the other, Sophie consoled herself. But their friendship was stronger than doubt. Soon they'd wish for each other and mean it, ready to leave this place behind. Soon they'd be back home like Agatha promised, Tedros gone forever.

Resting her head against the glass, Sophie realized how exhausted she was. Adrenaline had kept her up for two days straight, but now her thoughts thinned to fragments and flowed into dream. . . .

Her mittened hand picking moss from a neglected grave . . . a butterfly, carved into its stone . . . two swans etched into the graves beside it . . . one swan white . . . one swan black . . . black like a shadow torn apart by his Good twin . . . black like dead feathers strewn across the ground . . . black like the unnatural sky . . .

Sophie's eyes flared open. The sky over the Woods gate had gone pitch-dark—torches extinguished, moonlight snuffed. The princes howled with confusion before the torch and moon suddenly returned, leaving them dumbstruck at the passing eclipse. But Sophie knew it wasn't an eclipse at all. It was a Lights-Out Jinx. She'd seen one used in last year's Trial. . . .

It was Agatha's favorite spell.

Sophie leapt to her feet—but neither of the knights had shifted from their post. Sophie groaned and plopped down on her bed. Enough paranoia. Time to sleep. She pulled back her bedcovers but felt herself hesitate. Slowly she turned to the window again.

The taller knight had lost an armored shoe. The orphaned shoe was clearly visible a few feet away, but neither the taller nor the shorter knight made an effort to retrieve it.

Sophie squinted closer and saw that shoeless Agatha was having trouble standing, while Dot tried to prop her up. But the more Dot tried to help, the more Agatha flailed and flubbered, until finally the two knights fell to the ground, Dot's sword slipping from its sheath as she squealed in horror. Dot lunged to grab it, but it was too late—Agatha crashed face-first on the sword in a terrible heap and impaled on the blade, severing her neck.

Sophie opened her mouth to scream, watching Agatha's head roll out of its helmet—

Agatha's big, blue pumpkin head.

Sophie froze. Dot slowly looked up from the Forest, covered in pulp and seeds.

Blood roared through Sophie's veins.

She'd been tricked.

"By the time Dot restores the light, you should be at the Turquoise Thicket," Hester had drilled Agatha again and again. "Sophie won't be able to see you through the trees. Just mogrify into something small and get to Tedros as fast as you can."

Yet when the light returned over the princes, Agatha was sprinting back to the girls' castle instead. For one thing, Agatha still didn't trust her magic enough to mogrify, given what happened at Stefan's wedding. For another, surely the boys protected their school against magical entry, given they'd spent an entire unit in Chivalry last year on Castle Defense.

But most of all, she knew what she'd heard. No matter what the witches said, her heart put its faith in Tedros.

Stealing back into the girls' castle on bare feet, Agatha knew there was only one way to Halfway Bridge. A stream of patrolling butterflies zoomed out of the foyer before Agatha skittered from behind the obelisk of girl's portraits and slipped up the Honor steps, past darkened dorm rooms, candied classrooms, and the two-floor Library of Virtue, and through the frosted door onto the roof.

The hedges of Guinevere's menagerie had a cold green glow under the moon, which lit up the queen's sleek frame in each scene. Though she'd been young when Sophie's mother died, Agatha remembered she had the same slender hips and bony build, so different from Callis, Honora, or the other mothers of Gavaldon, who lived on meat and mash. Together, she and paunchy Honora must have made an odd sight as best friends, Agatha thought.

Just like her and Sophie.

Agatha squashed her guilt. *How many times will you make the same mistake?*

Pushing forward, she kept her eyes peeled for water. That was the secret portal last year to the bridge between schools. *Find the scene with water . . .*

Across the roof, a torch suddenly sparked in the highest floor of Charity's glass tower. The Dean's office. Did the Dean know she'd escaped guard?

Agatha stifled her panic and quickly wove through the hedges—Guinevere ruling from her throne, Guinevere with the Knights of the Round Table, Guinevere beheading a giant with her sword. . . . *As if she'd ruled Camelot all by herself,* Agatha thought, feeling strangely defensive of Tedros' father. Keeping an eye on the Dean's office, Agatha didn't catch any hint of water as she neared a high wall of sharp purple thorns at the end of the menagerie. But just as she lost hope and set to turn back, she heard shallow burbling behind the thorned wall.

In a pond shimmering with reflected stars, Guinevere bathed baby Tedros in his baptismal robes. Agatha felt touched by the sight of her prince, helpless in his mother's arms . . . until she saw his mother's face. For even though the hedge leaves softened the details of it, it was crystal clear what Arthur's once-queen thought of her new son. Glaring at Tedros, Guinevere's mouth snarled with hate.

She wasn't bathing him. She was drowning him.

Agatha blanched. Whatever happened tonight, whatever happened in her story from here, Tedros couldn't ever see this.

She wheeled to see torch flare spilling through the Dean's office, the door swinging open. . . . With a prayer, Agatha jumped into Guinevere's pond and instantly felt a blast of white-hot light—

A moment later, she stood dry in a crystal-blue archway on Halfway Bridge, panting with relief. But as she looked out at the long, narrow stone span into the School for Boys, Agatha's relief vanished.

Now she saw why the witches said not to use it.

Sophie's pink feathers shivered in gusty wind as her hawk flew across the sky towards the School for Boys. She'd been scared to mogrify again after the cat incident, but rage blasted away any fear. She had to get to Tedros before Agatha kissed him.

Angry tears dripped onto Sophie's wings. She'd lost her mother. She'd lost her prince. She couldn't lose her only friend too. Why did everything she love try to leave her?

I can't lose Agatha, she prayed. Not the one person who kept her Good. Not the one person who kept the witch dead.

Not Agatha.

With an anguished caw, she ripped towards the boys' jagged red towers—

CRACK!

An electric shock stabbed through her and she plummeted out of the sky. Sophie tried to flap her wings, but every inch of her body was paralyzed. *Mogrif shield,* Sophie gasped. Hurtling towards Evil's shore, her feathers violently sloughed to skin, her beak to lips, her body to human, preventing any return to bird—before she belly-flopped into mulch, fifty feet from Evil's entrance tunnel. Sophie's groans snuffled against wet earth, her legs sticky and cold. For a moment, she was grateful the shield had reverted her without any trouble, given what happened in Lesso's class. Then reality set in.

She was splayed bare in dirt, outside the School for Boys.

How could she be so stupid! Of course they enchanted the school against Mogrifs! Tedros wouldn't just leave his tower unprotected! She was too scared to move or look up. How long until the boys came for her? How could she stop Agatha and Tedros now? And how would she find *clothes*?

Sophie willed herself not to faint or throw up. All she needed to find was a few leafy vines or ferns; she'd made wearable ensembles out of far less. She looked up determinedly to the boggy field and froze.

On the ground under her face was a crinkly blackish sheath of scales . . . like a snake's shed skin, only twice as long and thick. Sophie's eyes slowly moved to another shed sheath a few feet in front of her. Then two more . . .

Sophie raised her head. She was surrounded by snakeskins. More than she could count.

Through darkness, she saw their makers rise from the mulch. Acid-green eyes glowed under misshapen, flattened black heads, their thick, eel-like trunks speared with needles through every scale. Sophie scrambled back, only to see more rising behind her. They curled higher, in a perfect circle, trapping her right and left, front and rear, high and low. With identical grins, they silently flicked tongues and glared down at the intruder, waiting for her move.

There was only one to make.

Sophie flung out her glowing finger—the snakes lunged instantly and pinned her body to the ground, spread-eagled to sacrifice. Needles slashed into her wrists and ankles as the snakes unleashed ugly, screeching hisses, drowning out her cries. Sophie heard boys' voices echo through the entrance tunnel, following the alarm, and knew she was doomed.

"Why can't I kill her!" a weaselly voice said.

"Get back to your guard," retorted a harsh deeper voice.

"But I heard the spiricks first!" the weaselly voice mewled. "Suppose it's her—"

"Shut up!" barked the deep voice. "Boys, weapons ready!"

Sophie's nails clawed at dirt. *Please . . . I don't want to die. . . .*

But now she could see the glint of swords and hooded shadows down the tunnel. They were seconds away.

Then suddenly out of pain, a memory came back like a song. . . .

Snakeskin under her hands as Professor Manley spoke of its magical properties in an Uglification class . . . sounds of her Evil cackles high in a tower as she pulled that same snakeskin over her body . . . the cries of Evers and Nevers all around . . . *"Where'd she go!" "Where's the witch?"*

"But I want to kill Sophie!" the weaselly voice said, eliciting a chorus of snickers.

"As if you could kill a toad," said the deep-voiced boy. "Or a girl you're soft for."

"I'm not soft for anyone!"

Sophie's fingerglow flickered as snake needles stabbed into her palm. She gasped in agony, trying to visualize the spell.

"Shhh! I hear her!"

Snakeskins shivered on the ground around her—

"Ready . . . set . . ."

Hundreds of skins rose into air over the snakes—

"Charge!"

Four enormous boys in red hoods and black uniforms dashed from the tunnel, swords aimed—

"Holy hell," growled their strapping, deep-voiced leader, a gold badge over his snake crest. In the dirt pit, confused snakes hissed at each other—nothing pinned beneath. The leader shot a spell at them and the snakes fled, shrieking. He ripped off his hood, revealing spiked black hair, ghostly pale cheekbones, throbbing blue veins, and lethal, violet eyes. "Stupid spiricks."

Needle cuts burning, Sophie endured the pain, invisible under the mound of sheathed skins.

A last scrawny hood bumbled from the tunnel. "You think I'm soft?" the weaselly boy cried, tearing off his mask. "Wait until I win the treasure! Just wait!"

Sophie held in a gasp. Hort had grown in her time away, now sporting whiskers on his chin, wilder black hair, and beady brown eyes that no longer looked like a little boy's. "I'll buy Dad a gold coffin. Two years he's waited for a grave. Killed by Peter Pan himself, my dad." He glowered at the empty pit. "You'll see, Aric! I'll be the one to kill Sophie. You don't know my villain talent!"

"Turnin' to a man-wolf for three seconds at a time?" said Aric, and his henchmen chuckled.

"That's not true!" Hort howled, chasing them towards the tunnel. "I can last long now! You'll see!"

Watching them go, Sophie sighed with relief—

Aric whirled, sword thrust out. Sophie stiffened like a corpse as he stared at the spot where she lay naked, his violet eyes narrowed.

"What is it, captain?" his henchman asked.

Aric listened to the silence.

"Come on," he grunted at last, and led his troops into the boys' castle, Hort runting at the rear.

None of them saw the flash of pink glow in the bog behind, turning invisible skins into an invisible cape.

Halfway Bridge had been blown up.

From the towers, all Agatha had seen was the swirling fog cloaking its midpoint. But now, standing in the cold, thick haze, she gazed down at the splintered rock around a gaping hole. The Bridge had been shattered with such force that the stone on either side drooped limply towards the rusted red moat below. Jagged slivers shed off both ends into the white crogs' thrashing snouts, sensing a girl above.

How stupid she was to ignore the witches, Agatha gritted, dashing blindly back into fog towards the portal. She glanced up at the lightening sky. She had an hour at most to find another route that wasn't the sewers, moat, or—

A butterfly exploded towards her out of fog and squawked with discovery. Agatha gasped and shot it with her lit-up finger but missed, and it surged yelping through the portal, back to the Dean.

Agatha froze in terror. If she was caught here, Tedros' and her story would be over before it began. Sophie's witch would kill them both.

Hands shaking, she slowly looked back at the boys' castle across the broken Bridge.

"Cross the Bridge," Tedros had ordered.

There's no way, Agatha thought, panicked—

Cross the Bridge.

Cross *it*.

Agatha stared down at the blown-up hole. Last year, against all odds, she'd done what no one else had been able to do: move between Good and Evil. Tedros had faith she could do it again.

Cross the Bridge.

Heart rattling, Agatha charged towards the broken gap. As her bare feet curled over the stone's cliff edge, she thrust out her hand, praying she was right—

Nothing but cold, empty breeze.

Jaw clenching, Agatha reached her fingertips farther, right foot leaving stone, only to feel more air skim uselessly through fingers. Sweat streamed down her ribs. Reach any more, and she'd fall into the moat. The spiny crogs snapped and splashed in red waves below, jostling for first feed.

Agatha welled frantic tears, knowing the Dean would be here any moment. She only had one choice left. . . .

Trust Tedros with her life.

Agatha exhaled slowly. Her left foot skated over the edge as she tilted forward on her right, surrendering to faith. Her right toes slid farther across the pockmarked stone, then her arch, then her heel, hands grasping at nothing . . . nothing. . . . Her foot lost the edge, and with a cry she toppled towards the moat, hands blindly flailing—

Something.

Agatha's palms smashed into a hard, invisible barrier and she ricocheted back, falling to the girls' side of the Bridge.

In the hidden barrier, a reflection fogged into place. Her own face glared down at her, crystal clear.

"Girls with Girls
Boys with Boys

Back to your castle
Before you're destroyed."

Agatha paled with surprise. Why was everything in this school so much worse than before?

"Told you last year, didn't I? Good with Good, Evil with Evil," her reflection grinned. "But you thought you were better than the rules. Now look what you've gotten yourself into."

"Let me pass," Agatha demanded, glancing back anxiously for the Dean.

"We'll be happier on this side," said her reflection. "Boys ruin *everything*."

"And a witch will ruin even more," Agatha retorted. "I'm saving both schools—"

"So this is all about Good now, is it?" her face smirked. "Not about a Girl who wants a *Boy*."

"I said let me *pass*."

"Try all you want. You won't trick me again," her reflection said. "You're obviously a Girl."

"And what makes a Girl?" Agatha asked.

"All the things a Boy is not."

Agatha frowned. "And what makes a Boy?"

"All the things a Girl is not."

"But you still haven't told me what a Boy or Girl *is*."

"I know someone who wishes for a Boy must be a Girl," her reflection said confidently.

"And why's that?"

"Because Girls wish for Boys and Boys wish for Girls and

you *wished* for a Boy so that makes you a Girl. Now back to your castle or—"

"And what would that make someone who kissed a Girl?"

"*Kissed* a Girl?" her reflection said, suddenly wary.

"Kissed a Girl to life like all the best princes," Agatha glowered.

Her reflection glowered back. "*Definitely* a Boy."

Agatha's lips curled. "Exactly."

Her image gasped, deceived once again—and vanished into thin air.

Agatha glanced down at the red moat churning beneath the deadly high gap. Trembling, she reached her pale, naked foot over thin air and this time felt it land on an invisible step.

Agatha looked down at herself, floating magically over the crogs gnashing in fury. In disbelief, she took another step forward over the gap, then another, until she crossed back onto the other side of the stone bridge, Tedros' call answered.

Sophie would never catch them now.

Fear leeched out of Agatha's chest, giving way to hope. Tedros had saved her from the witch, and now she would save him.

Stomach filling with butterflies for their meeting to come, Agatha sprinted towards the boys' castle, armed with the deepest faith in her prince.

Far behind, in the shadows of the Girls' blue archway, Dean Sader's green eyes pierced the fog. But watching her student vanish into the rotted towers, she made no move.

Sophie chasing Agatha. Agatha chasing her prince.

Two friends once unbreakable and now torn apart.

The Dean turned and sauntered back to her castle.

Be careful what you wish for, girls.

Her gap-toothed grin gleamed through darkness.

Be careful what you wish for, indeed.

12

The Uninvited Guest

"Wait!" Hort yelped, chasing Aric and his men through the serrated tunnel shaped like a crocodile snout. "Shouldn't we search the shore?"

He scrambled to keep up as the tunnel grew narrower and narrower.

"Mogrif shield wouldn't activate for nothing! Spiricks must have caught somethi—"

But Aric and the boys had already vanished into the foyer. Hort peered back down the dark tunnel, tempted to go searching himself, but his hair was itchy with lice and his stomach rumbly. "Bet the girls have decent meals," he moped, turning for the castle—

A pink blast of light sizzled his skull and he crashed to the floor, head slamming on stone.

When Hort's eyes fluttered open, he found himself splayed in his underpants and nothing else. Given he tended to lose his clothes quite often, Hort didn't think much of this until he looked up. "What in the . . ."

His black-and-red uniform magically floated away from him, towards the swarthy torchlight of the boys' castle, before it swallowed into thin air and disappeared.

As she entered the boys' rotted foyer, Sophie made sure the invisible cape covered every sliver of Hort's suffocatingly snug uniform. (For a moment, she panicked that she'd swelled in size—then remembered Hort's meager chest and flat bottom.) Under the cape, she'd stay undetected, provided she didn't puke from the castle's stench.

Worse than Evil's, she thought, like sweaty socks doused in vinegar. She knew it must be the unwashed Neverboys, for the Everboys of Good were almost fussier about hygiene than the girls. Even after double Swordplay sessions last year, they'd come to lunch, hair wet, smelling minty clean, as if they'd collectively made a trip to the bath post-class. How were they possibly surviving in this rathole?

Besides an extra coat of grime and a few more leaks, the Evil foyer looked much the same. Through the sunken anteroom, she saw the three black, crooked staircases twist up to the three towers, carved MALICE, MISCHIEF, and VICE.

Demonic gargoyles glared down from the rafters, torches flaring in their mouths. But as Sophie stepped into the light, she saw the boys had left their mark.

Crumbly columns decorated with swinging trolls and imps that once spelled N-E-V-E-R now spelled B-O-Y-S, while the iron statue of a bald, toothless witch had been decapitated. At the rear of the stair room, the door to the Theater of Tales had been sealed with a neurotic number of bars and locks, preventing any access to the Tunnel of Trees behind the theater. Sophie's eyes drifted up the scorched walls, where thousands of crammed alumni portraits flaunted only boys' faces, both Evers and Nevers. A year ago, her portrait had stood out among the villains on this very wall. Now Tedros' took its place, with its halo of gold hair and cocksure smile. Sophie's heart twinged at their resemblance. *We'd have looked so perfect together.*

Faint shouts echoed high above, with the sounds of tramping boots. Sophie tore eyes from Tedros, remembering everything he'd taken from her . . . her dreams, her innocence, her dignity. He wouldn't take Agatha too.

Pulling her vanishing cape tight, Sophie followed the echoes up the Malice staircase—but not before shooting a spell behind her, setting the prince's face aflame.

Agatha expected Tedros to be waiting for her once she slogged up the decaying thirty-flight staircase from the Bridge to the open-air belfry. After all, she'd crossed the Bridge as ordered and come to him at risk to her life and others'. But the belfry's round cloister was deserted, shadowed by the School Master's sky-high tower rising above it. *What's he waiting for?* Agatha thought, glaring up at its distant window.

With less than an hour before Sophie woke up, Agatha didn't have time for a prince's poor planning. If Tedros wasn't going to come to her, she knew who would take her to him.

A castle full of boys can end one of two ways. Either its inhabitants channel aggression into order, discipline, and productivity. Or they degenerate into hormonal apes. As Sophie stepped onto the fifth floor of Malice Hall, she saw Tedros' school had gone the latter.

Hooting, half-naked boys in black breeches hung from the rafters and crammed into every inch of the sweltering hall, as if spending time in each other's sweat was preferable to being in their rooms. The scorched stone floor was smeared with rotted banana, breadcrumbs, egg yolks, ham bones, chicken feathers, and milky stains, while the gray brick walls were graffitied with infantile warmongering against girls—WHO NEEDS GIRLS, I HATE GIRLS, and caricatures of Evergirls and Nevergirls being eaten by wolves, pitched from towers, and cast off a ship plank. Hidden against the wall, Sophie inched closer, expecting nothing less from smelly, villainous Neverboys . . . until she saw it wasn't the Neverboys at all.

Hairy, burly Chaddick swung from the ceiling, whooping and kicking open rooms, while handsome, dark-skinned Nicholas fired stun spells at a cornered mouse. Regal-nosed Tarquin and muscled Oliver took turns punching each other's flat stomachs; baby-faced Hiro led a burping contest; and quiet

Bastian beat bongos, all pausing to join Chaddick's fist-raising chant of "We Are Men, Mighty and Free."

Sophie blinked, aghast. What happened to beautiful, chivalrous Everboys? What happened to princes-to-be?

"*Bonded by strength and fraternity*," the boys bellowed, "*Gods beyond authority*—"

A door slammed open. "If we're not back to Good and Evil soon, I'm going to kill all of you," Ravan hissed in his pajamas, matted black hair and brown skin oilier than ever. "It's enough we're out of food, we've lost our teachers, and we're down to the only floor in this stinking castle with bathrooms that ain't flooded. All you have to do is slay one witch—*one measly witch*—and you're too busy havin' a house party!"

Pointy-eared Vex blearily poked out next to him. "Isn't killing witches Good's *job*?" he yawned.

"There is no Good as long as there's Girls!" Chaddick barked back. "We're men first!"

"Men first!" Everboys chorused.

"We want to stay up all night and never bathe? We want to raise hell and never clean? We want to mark our territory like dogs?" Chaddick thundered. "Who's gonna stop us!"

No wonder it smells, Sophie thought, invisible in the corner. She squinted out the window at the School Master's soaring spire. How would she get up *there*? And how would she get to Tedros in time? Her stomach plunged. Suppose Agatha was already with him!

Sophie slowly unclenched. She was still here, wasn't she? Which meant Agatha hadn't kissed her prince yet. Her pulse quickened with hope. Perhaps Agatha hadn't made it to the boys' school at all.

She shielded her ears from Everboys' deafening stomps and monkey hoots, as more and more Neverboys jabbed sleepy heads out.

"You hear me!" Chaddick howled, pounding his chest. "Who's gonna stop u—"

A purple spell slammed into him, zipping his mouth shut. Sophie twirled and saw Aric stomp by, violet eyes glowing, followed by his four chiseled henchmen. Spooked boys straightened in front of their doors, hands to head in salute, as Aric paced through the hall, inspecting each. Only Chaddick didn't raise his hand. Aric leaned in and glared into his gray eyes.

"May I remind you that given your failure to kill Sophie in the Woods, Master Tedros has *replaced* you as captain," Aric said, gold badge glinting. "And unfortunately, neither I nor my henchmen have the same tolerance for idiocy as our predecessor."

Screams echoed from the dungeon below.

"My boys relish any chance to punish an Ever. But a former Ever captain?" Aric smiled at Chaddick. "The Doom Room would have a proper reopening, indeed."

Red faced, Chaddick forced a desultory salute. "That's better," Aric said, unzipping his rival's mouth.

"How'd you and your henchmen break through Lady Lesso's shield if none of the princes can?" Chaddick spat. "Why should we trust you?"

"Because I have an investment in this war, greater than anyone else's," Aric said coldly, walking away.

"If you broke through the shield, then why haven't you broken the princes in too?" Nicholas shouted. "We could have killed Sophie by now!"

"Yeah," hollered Vex, "why hasn't Tedros kissed Agatha?"

"Why aren't we back to Good and Evil?" Ravan yelled.

All the Nevers jumped in with *"Evil! Evil! Evil!"* until Aric roared and they shut up.

"How do we know it's just Sophie who's our enemy . . . ," he snarled. *"And not Agatha too?"*

The Neverboys gaped at him. "B-b-b-but Agatha wished for Tedros," Ravan said anxiously. "She wants to fix her fairy tale—she wants to fix our schools—"

"And how do we know her wish isn't a trap?" Aric said. "These are two girls who said their fairy tale doesn't *need* a prince. Two girls whose kiss *evicted* men from kingdoms. Two girls who now want to make all of you boys *slaves*."

The boys went dead quiet.

Their captain's eyes slowly raised to the corner. "They could be in our castle right *now* . . ."

Sophie's heart stopped, sweat crawling down her leg.

"Plotting their attack . . ."

Aric's violet pupils zeroed in on her. . . . A drop of sweat beaded off Sophie's invisible cape. "Listening to these very words . . ."

His eyes traced down, just as her sweat hit the floor—

"I GOT HER! I GOT SOPHIE!"

The boys whipped around to see Hort in his underpants dragging a girl in a blue uniform down the hall, her head masked by his red hood. Yet his prisoner showed surprisingly little resistance and, in fact, seemed to be dragging him, leaving Hort huffing and puffing—

"I told you! I told you someone was out there! She took my clothes and burnt Tedros' portrait and I saw her in the dark and I get the treasure 'cause I caught—" He tore off the hood, revealing Agatha.

"Not Sophie," Hort gulped.

Sophie stifled a cry.

Aric skulked towards Agatha, baring ragged teeth. "How did you get *in*."

Agatha glimpsed his captain's badge and stood her ground. "Take me to Tedros *now*."

"And why should I listen to an *intruder*?" Aric growled, finger glowing purple. "Why should I trust a friend of the *witch*?"

"Because I'm here to save you from her," Agatha said, knife-sharp.

Aric's face changed, and the hall silenced.

"Sophie is turning into a witch again. Forever, this time." Agatha's mouth started to dry out, her voice fading. She hesitated a long moment, then finally looked up.

"All your lives are in danger unless I see Tedros."

Sophie froze behind Agatha, shell-shocked by what she was hearing.

"How long do we have?" said Chaddick, stepping out behind Aric.

"Until she finds out I'm here," Agatha answered, a red rash spreading across her neck.

The boys murmured as Sophie stayed trapped in the corner, eyes filling with tears.

Aric stared at Agatha, studying her face. His fingerglow extinguished and he stalked from the hall. "Follow me."

Agatha trailed after him, darkened by his shadow.

Sophie followed close behind, noticing her friend's legs shaking. She knew they were thinking the same thing.

Agatha may not have kissed her prince yet. But her and Sophie's happy ending was already gone forever.

Agatha kept up with Aric across a craggy red-stone catwalk to the School Master's tower, clutching her arms in the wind. "Tedros knew I was coming," she said, nodding towards the skyscraping spire. "Why wasn't he waiting for me?"

Aric didn't reply. With his cruel violet eyes and deep, eloquent voice, he reminded Agatha of the best villains. *How did he break through Lesso's shield?* she wondered, her mind flooding more questions. With a ways to the tower, she saw the chance to have them answered.

"What happened to your teachers?"

"After the castles changed and Dean Sader appeared, our teachers charged the Bridge to fight her." Aric paused. "They never made it across."

"Why? Where'd they go—"

A loud thunk echoed behind Agatha, and she and Aric turned. A loose stone had fallen off the castle railing a few steps behind.

"Must have brushed it," Agatha said, sheepish.

Aric studied the stone carefully and resumed walking.

"What happened to the Bridge?" Agatha pressed. "And the stymphs—"

"One of the many reasons I hate princesses is they don't find answers for themselves," Aric groused.

Agatha quietly dropped behind. Against the dawning sky, the boys' castle glowed angry red, while across the bay, the girls' castle shone sapphire, like a vision of heaven and hell. Agatha looked over the railing at the boys' shores below, where the white crogs feasted on scraps of skeletons, littered all over the banks. Agatha wondered what creatures could possibly create so much bony carnage . . . then saw a skull intact far off the shore. So much for her question about the stymphs.

A squeal flew behind her.

Agatha whipped around. No one was there.

"What is it?" Aric called back.

Agatha squinted down the empty catwalk. "Probably a rat," she said, eager to move on.

As they neared the School Master's tower, Agatha peered up at its pea-sized window, cloaked by cloud mist. "How are we going to get up ther—"

Aric unleashed a whistle, and a massive rope of braided blond hair flung out the window and tumbled to the Bridge below. The captain leered at Agatha and grabbed on to it. "Hope princesses can climb."

Scowling, Agatha jumped on, bare feet scratchy against the dried-out hair. Pulling herself towards the faraway window, Agatha didn't flag, even with the crogs gnashing in the moat below, even with the strange sensation of something under her weighing down the rope. Farther and farther she rose, into lashing winds, determined to stop a witch. . . . But with each pull upwards, thoughts of Sophie receded, something deeper propelling her. Her reflection had seen what she couldn't admit. This wasn't for Good anymore. This was for a boy.

The old graveyard girl sloughed away as Agatha surged into fog, her heart cracking open to a new ending. Her fingers sprouted blisters as sweat soaked her back, but still Agatha climbed. She was so close now, so close to the end . . . grasping higher, higher, like Rapunzel's prince . . . finding more and more strength . . . until at last she saw the pointed spire prick through clouds.

Above her, Aric smoothly swung off the braid anchored to the window and vanished through the opening into the School Master's chamber. Agatha waited for the rope to settle, then dragged up the last few lengths and raised her head enough to peek inside—

Two shirtless boys clashed swords in spirited fight, one pale in a red hood, one tan in a silver mask. Dodging and recoiling, they bashed into bookshelves lining the ashy walls, spilling colorful storybooks all over the stone floor. The pale boy nicked the tan one's chest, the tan boy nicked the pale one's calf, leaving twin welts as their swords slammed once more.

Now the pale boy turned aggressor, driving the tan boy towards a stone table against the far wall, where a thick storybook lay open to its last page. Iron chains strung down from both sides of the ceiling, restraining something in place over the storybook . . . a long sliver of steel like a knitting needle, sloping to a deadly sharp nib . . . an enchanted pen, flailing to break free. . . .

Agatha's eyes widened.

The Storian.

Agatha watched the pale hooded boy battle the tan boy back, the hooded one's eyes dead set on the chained pen. Fending off the pale boy's blows, the tan one tripped on a book and faltered. The pale boy bucked past him, lunging straight for the pen—

"Aric," smiled the tan boy, seeing the captain. Spooked, the pale one whirled around.

"Says he wants to guard the Storian with me," the tan one said. He pulled off the pale boy's hood to reveal Tristan, hair bright red, long-nosed face dotted with freckles. "Thought I'd put his skills to the test."

"Shouldn't even be up here, master," Aric lashed, glowering at Tristan, who anxiously stared at his shoes. "Comes and goes, does as he pleases. Deserves punishment—"

"Leave him be. Doesn't fit in with the other boys, does he?" said the tan boy, pulling off the School Master's silver mask. Tedros shook the sweat off his thick gold hair and sheathed his sword, Excalibur. He caught a glimpse of himself in the reflective hilt—his body bigger, harder than a year ago, his cheeks glazed with glistening stubble, his jaw steel tight. He turned back to Aric. "Need to make sure we end things right this time and an extra guard can't hurt. Besides, until Sophie's dead, I might as well have some company. How the School Master stayed up here without slitting his throat out of boredom, I haven't the faintest ide—"

His voice petered off. A shadow stood in front of the window, its two big brown eyes staring through darkness like a cat's.

Aric cleared his throat. "Master, we found her trespass—"

The coldness of Tedros' gaze stopped him. Bare chested, Tedros moved past him towards the window. With each step, he slowly watched the shadows recede . . . over short black hair . . . skin white as snow . . . thin, pink lips, in a terrified smile. . . .

Standing at the window, Agatha held her breath, neck burning even redder than before. Tedros' face was harsher than she remembered, his presence darker, the innocent, boyish glow . . . gone. But deep inside his eyes, she could still see him. The boy she'd fought to forget. The boy who came in her sleep. The boy her soul couldn't live without.

"Take Tristan and go," Tedros said finally, not looking at Aric.

Aric frowned. "Master, I must insist on—"

"It's an *order.*"

Aric grabbed Tristan by the throat and shoved him down the rope, leaving the prince alone with his princess.

Or so he thought.

Invisible under her cape, Sophie was still puffing from her climb up the hair. She crouched deeper beneath the stone table, the Storian struggling to break free over her and Agatha's storybook. Despite her squeal on the Bridge—she'd gashed her leg on a broken brick—somehow she'd made it to Tedros alive and unfound. But as Tedros moved towards Agatha, Sophie's relief flushed to panic. For as she looked at a prince and princess deep in each other's eyes, she knew her story was already over.

Agatha had chosen a boy.

And there was nothing she could do to stop it.

"You're . . . here," Tedros said, touching Agatha's arm as if unsure she was real.

Feeling his hand, Agatha's neck went violent red. She couldn't get the words to form—he needed to move back—he needed a—

"Shirt," she croaked.

"What? Oh—" Tedros reddened and grabbed a sleeveless black shirt off the floor, pulling it on. "I just—I didn't think that—" His eyes scanned the room. "You're here . . . alone?"

Agatha frowned. "Of course—"

"*She*'s not here with you?" Tedros craned out the window, squinting down the rope.

"I came here like you asked," Agatha said, thrown. "I came for you."

Tedros stared at her oddly. "But that's . . . How could . . ." His eyes hardened as if a door inside had closed. "*You.* You put me through *hell.*"

Agatha exhaled, prepared for this. "Tedros . . ."

"You kissed her, Agatha. You kissed her instead of me. Do you know what that *did* to me? Do you know what that did to *everything?*"

"She saved my life, Tedros."

"And ruined mine," he said furiously. "My whole life, girls only liked me for my crown, my fortune, my looks, none of which I've earned. You were the first girl who saw through all of it . . . who saw something inside me worth liking, however stupid and impetuous and prat headed I can be." Tedros paused, hearing his voice crack. When he looked back up, his face was cold. "But every night, I had to sleep knowing I'm not enough. I had to sleep knowing my princess chose a *girl.*"

"I didn't have a choice!" Agatha insisted.

Tedros scowled and turned away. "You could have taken my hand. You could have stayed here and let her go home." He looked down at the last page of the book beneath the Storian—his own shadow slumping into darkness alone. "Don't say you didn't have a choice. You *had* a choice."

"A choice a boy could never understand." Agatha looked at his back turned to her. "All my life, I was a freak, Tedros. No one let their pets near me, let alone their kids. As I got older, I holed up in a graveyard because I could forget the things I didn't have. Like someone to talk to. Or someone who wanted to talk to me. I started to tell myself that being alone was real power. That we all die eventually and rot to maggots, so what's the point anyway . . ." She paused. "But then Sophie came. Four o'clock on the dot after school. I'd wait for her by the door every day, 'like a dog' my mother said, longing for that hour before sunset we'd have together. I'd watch her as the sky went dark . . . the way she fidgeted, like she didn't want me to go home either, even if she pretended I was a Good Deed. She made me feel loved for the first time in my life." Agatha smiled, hearing the lightness in her voice. "And I knew everything would be okay in the end, no matter how our stories turned out. We'd have each other in our trapped, pointless little village, always each other, and that was the happiest ending I could imagine. Because she was my friend, Tedros. The only friend I'd ever known. And I couldn't imagine a life without her."

Tedros didn't move, his back still to her. Slowly, he turned, his face soft.

"Then why did you wish for me?"

Agatha looked down. She held the words as long as she could, afraid to say them out loud.

"Because now I need more than a friend."

Silence fell, broken only by soft sniffles that Agatha knew must be hers, even though they sounded far away.

She felt Tedros' arm on hers and looked up into his luminous blue eyes.

"I'm here, Agatha," he breathed. "Right here."

Agatha felt tears stinging. "She'll never forgive me for it," she rasped, shaking under his warm touch. "Sophie's becoming a witch again. She'll kill us both."

Tedros' eyes flashed. He charged for the window, drawing his sword—"We need the princes—"

"No!" Agatha said, grabbing him by the shirt.

"But you said—"

"We can end this. We can . . . rewrite our story." Agatha's mouth parched. Her face went pink. "S-s-she'll go home. Like you wanted her to. No one has to die."

Tedros' face slowly calmed, understanding.

Holding his gaze, Agatha pried Excalibur from his calloused fingers, its golden hilt sinking into her hand. She saw the fear in Tedros' eyes, felt the sweat of his palm, and let her hand stay against his a moment longer. Their eyes stayed locked as Agatha stepped back, blade pointed towards him. Tedros watched her, nostrils flaring, neck veins pulsing, like a tiger on edge. "Trust me," she whispered, gripping the sword tighter. . . .

Then she swiveled to the Storian over the table and slashed it free from its chains. Tedros lunged towards it in surprise—

The enchanted pen plunged with relief to the storybook, conjuring a new last page. From its nib spilled a brilliant painting, a vision of prince and princess in their tower chamber, hands on each other, poised to seal "The End" with their kiss.

Tedros froze, gazing at the painting. He heard the sword clink to the ground behind him. Slowly he turned to see Agatha's cheeks burning fiery pink.

"You'd stay here forever?" Tedros' throat bobbed. "With . . . me?"

Agatha reached out a shaking hand and touched him,

mirroring the storybook painting.

"The Storian will only write 'The End' if I mean it," she said quietly. "And everything in my heart tells me it's with you."

Tedros' eyes misted. "It's always the princess who gets her fairy-tale ending," he said, taking in Agatha's face. "This time, it feels like it's mine."

The silence thickened as Agatha pulled him in by the waist, the sound of the Storian grazing the page behind them. He could see their two shadows coalesce in the Storian's shining steel . . . feel her shallow breaths as she drew him against her. Tedros' muscles softened as his princess gripped him tighter . . . tighter . . . bringing his lips to hers—

He jolted back. There was a black shadow in the pen's steel.

Tedros whirled around—

Nothing but the pen.

"She's here," he breathed, backing away. "She's here somewhere."

"Tedros?" Agatha frowned, confused—

Tedros hunted behind bookshelves. "Where is she! Where's Sophie!"

"She's not here!" Agatha pressed, reaching for him—

He drew away sharply. "I c-c-can't—not if that witch is alive—"

Agatha's eyes flared. "But she'll be gone forever!"

"She's a *witch*," Tedros seethed. "As long as Sophie's on this earth, she'll find a way to tear us apart!"

"No! You can't hurt her! Tedros, this is the only way—"

"I let her live last time because of you, and she *took* you," Tedros retorted. "I can't make the same mistake, Agatha. I can't lose you again!"

"Listen to me!" Agatha said, glowing crimson. "I'm willing to give up everything I know for you! Never see my home again! Never see my mother again!" Agatha clasped his shoulders. "She's not part of our story anymore. That's why you told me to come tonight. Because you don't want to hurt her. Because you know *I'm* enough." She held him tighter, staring into his eyes. "Let her go home. Please, Tedros. Because I won't let you touch her."

Tedros peered at her oddly again. "I forgot how strange you are."

Agatha tackled him in a hug, tearing with relief. "A strange princess," she whispered against his chest. "About time we had one of those."

"Who tells strange stories."

"Like what," Agatha smiled, tilting up to his kiss. . . .

"That I told you to come tonight," said the prince.

Agatha lurched back from him, smile gone.

The only sound in the chamber was the sound of an invisible girl's sniffles suddenly stopping.

Aric stormed down the catwalk. *Females can't be trusted.* He'd learned that lesson young. In the distance, he could see Tristan's pale legs fleeing into the castle. *What a waste of a man. Shouldn't even be called a ma—*

He stopped.

Slowly Aric kneeled down to the ground and looked at a broken brick on the catwalk railing, dripping with fresh blood.

Aric's finger lit up, and he blasted a flare into the castle to call his men.

He didn't remember Agatha bleeding.

Hidden under the table, Sophie watched Agatha retreat from Tedros, his blue eyes dimming.

"You *t-t-told* me to come," Agatha stammered. "You told me to cross the Bridge—"

"We blew *up* the Bridge, so you can't have crossed it," Tedros shot back. "Only a *witch's* magic could have gotten you here."

"But I—I saw you, Tedros! In the classroom—in the wind—"

"What?" Tedros scoffed.

"I saw—your—your—" Agatha's voice faded away, replaced by the Dean's echo.

"Sometimes we see what we want to see."

A phantom. Her heart had birthed a phantom, just like all the other girls'.

Only she'd believed her phantom was real.

Slowly Agatha looked up at her prince, his finger raised at her, glowing gold.

"You never came," she whispered.

"How did you get here, Agatha?" Tedros said, blocking the Storian from her with his body. His lit finger stayed pointed at her, visibly shaking. "How did you cross the Bridge?"

Agatha backed up, her own finger glowing to defend. "By

trusting you," she breathed, head spinning. *The arrows. The Wanted signs. The princes at the gate.*

"This was never about me . . . ," she said. "This was about revenge on Sophie . . ."

"Don't you see? You thought you knew your heart last time too," Tedros pleaded. "I'm doing this for you, Agatha. For *us*."

"Why can't you trust me?" Agatha choked. "Why does she have to die?"

Tedros gazed at their lit fingers, each pointed at the other.

"Because one day you might change your mind again," he said softly.

His eyes lifted, racked with pain.

"One day you might wish for her instead of me."

"Please, Tedros," Agatha begged. "Please let her go—"

"What if I tried to hurt you right now?" Her prince's eyes were wide, scared. "Would she show herself? Would she save you?"

"She's not *here*! I choose you, Tedros!"

"Choosing me isn't enough this time, Agatha."

Tedros looked right through her, like he did in her dream.

"This time I'm making sure of it."

Agatha gasped.

In a flash, Sophie saw her chance and blasted a pink spell between them—Agatha lunged, thinking it was Tedros'; Tedros dodged, thinking it was Agatha's. Instantly, ten red hoods launched through the window, arrows drawn at Agatha. Agatha retreated in shock, surrounded on all sides. She glowered at Tedros, cheeks blotched with fury—

"You're an *animal*," she hissed. "I'll never choose you. You hear me? *Never!*"

She shot a spell and the window's dawn light magically went out, plunging the tower into darkness. A moment later, the light came back—but Agatha was gone.

Tedros swiveled to the window, but the rope and catwalk were deserted, his princess lost. Rage cooled in his blood. He could have had happiness right then and there. He could have had The End. But he'd let his obsession with a witch poison it once more. Now he was alone with the pen, his Ever After ruined by his own hand.

"She told the truth," he whispered. "I'm—I'm a fool—"

"Not quite."

Tedros turned. Aric looked down at the Storian as it finished a rich-hued painting in the storybook: a vision of Tedros and Agatha shooting spells at each other, surrounded by armed henchmen. Only as Tedros stepped closer, he saw there was someone else in the painting . . . someone else beneath the table, smiling gleefully under her invisible cape. . . .

Tedros' and Aric's eyes slowly moved beneath the table, Sophie long gone.

"Agatha was lying all along, master," Aric said. "They were both here to kill you."

Tedros fell silent, staring at the painting, mouth open with shock. He saw his ashen face reflected in the Storian, waiting for his next move. He looked away.

"The princes," he rasped. "It's—it's time you let them in, isn't it?"

Aric grinned. "I'd say it is."

Tedros listened to him and his henchmen go.

"Aric."

He heard his captain stop behind him.

"Tell them the bounty isn't just for one head anymore."

Tedros turned, scarlet red.

"It's for *two*."

As the sun broke, a frantic, big-eyed fly squeezed under the locked Theater of Tales door in the boys' castle and to their Tunnel of Trees, blocked entirely by rocks. Wheezing with panic, the fly sputtered and skirted around rock after rock until it made it back to the Clearing.

Dripping tears, Agatha's fly flew up the girls' towers, towards her room atop Honor's blue turret, terrified of what she'd find. Grazing the open window and chipping her wing, she crashed to her friend's bed . . . the friend she'd betrayed to boys, the friend she'd traded for a prince, the friend she'd vowed was a deadly witch . . .

But racing up the sheets, Agatha froze in horror. For she'd seen what she'd wanted to see, from finish to start.

Sophie smiled as she slept, like the most peaceful of nights.

Her neck creamy and bare, not a wart in sight.

PART II

13

The Supper Hall Book Club

Sunlight glinted off the glass clock painted with a waltzing princess and witch. It was well past seven now, dawn come and gone, replaced by a cold December morning.

Lying in bed, fully dressed, Sophie watched Agatha sleep. Beatrix had gone down to breakfast. The two of them were alone.

Sophie's ankles and wrists still stung where the spiricks had pinned her; her calves throbbed from her invisible race out of the boys' school: to the teachers' old balcony over the

Clearing, past the two Everboy guards and down its buttress, into the girls' Tunnel of Trees, and back to her room while Agatha's fly still struggled in the boys' rock-packed tunnel. She'd shoved the cape with Hort's uniform under Beatrix's bed and slid beneath her sheets just as she heard Agatha buzzing through the window . . .

And now they were here, quietly human, side by side, like so many times before.

Only everything had changed.

Sophie scoured Agatha's face, looking for the graveyard girl she had once known. But all she saw was a princess nose . . . snow-white skin . . . delicate lips that reached for a prince. . . .

A prince who hadn't kissed her.

Because of me.

Sophie sickened with shame. She'd stopped Agatha's wish from coming true. She'd broken her best friend's heart.

Sophie bit back tears. She'd tried so hard to be Good, but that moment of losing Agatha—that unbearably real moment—had made her Evil again. Now she'd ruined a happy ending, like the witch she once was.

And yet, just as guilt swallowed her, Sophie suddenly felt a glimmer of hope. . . .

I need more than a friend, Agatha had said.

But what if she could make Agatha happy again? What if she showed Agatha she didn't need Tedros? That their friendship was greater than any Ever After with a prince?

What if I teach Agatha what she once taught me?

Then keeping Agatha from Tedros would be worth it,

Sophie thought, hope deepening. Everything she'd done last night would be worth it. Because Agatha would wish for The End with her, and mean it.

If I can just get Agatha back.

Agatha opened her eyes. She saw Sophie staring and visibly recoiled.

"How was last night?" Sophie asked, clearing her throat.

"Oh. L-l-last night?" Agatha turned away and started grabbing pieces of her uniform off the floor. "It was long—you know—Dot talks a lot—" She hesitated. "You didn't, um, watch us, did you?"

"Fell asleep," Sophie said, watching Agatha carefully. "But there was nothing to worry about, was there?"

Agatha's whole body went rigid.

"Eesh, smells like a furnace in here," Sophie rambled as she buttoned one of Beatrix's long cloaks over her uniform. "Kitchen fumes, no doubt. For all we know, Evergirls eat *bacon* now—"

"Sophie?"

"Mmm?"

"I have to tell you something."

Sophie slowly raised her eyes.

Bloodcurdling screeches exploded in the hall, sending both girls cowering. Agatha whirled to the door and yanked it open. Thick smoke flooded into the room as shadows of fleeing girls and butterflies ripped past, neon-haired nymphs floating behind them, shrieking alarm like banshees.

"What's happening!" Sophie gasped, grabbing Mona's arm.

"The princes! They broke the shield!"

Sophie and Agatha spun to each other, stunned.

Pollux's voice blared from a distant bullhorn—"All girls to the gallery! Use the breezeways, not the foyer! I repeat—do *not* use the foyer!"

Agatha and Sophie sprinted after Mona towards the breezeway from Honor to Valor, choking on acrid smoke.

"Where is it coming from?" Sophie wheezed, waving it away. The blue breezeway in front of her was clogged with bodies, butterflies swarming above them.

"Come on!" Agatha said, dragging her back towards the stairs. "We'll get there through the foyer—"

"But Pollux said not to use it!"

"Since when do we listen to *Pollux*?"

As they staggered through smoke down the Honor stairs, Agatha caught a glimpse of Halfway Bay through the glass walls. In the far distance, filthy, armed princes flooded through a hole in the shield over the Woods gate and onto the shores of the School for Boys. Agatha froze, dread rising. After last night, the timing couldn't be coincidental. Sophie bumped her from behind and Agatha struggled blindly down the last flight into the foyer.

All the smoke was seeping into the towers from here. The domed sunroof had been shot through and shattered, each of the G-I-R-L walls impaled with hundreds of fire-tipped arrows. Nymphs floated in a circle around the four tower staircases, shooting water spells to extinguish the small fires, while a scattering of dead butterflies smoldered on the ground, caught in the crossfire.

"Doesn't make sense," Sophie said, gripping the glass

railing. "Why would they shoot the foy—"

But as the fires cleared, the girls saw that each of the dripping-wet arrows had been speared to something: paper scrolls that had been taken away, leaving parchment scraps under the arrow tips.

"Sophie, look."

Sophie followed Agatha's eyes to a shadowed patch of floor behind the stairs. There was a fallen scroll, thoroughly singed, but still intact. As the nymphs swept up the ashes and pulled out arrows around the foyer, Agatha quickly hopped over the banister and grabbed it. The scroll was sealed with a wax snake, the color of blood. Sophie landed beside her and looked over her shoulder as Agatha unrolled the scroll's scorched edges, the two girls hidden behind the stairs.

TEN DAYS from today,
the Trial by Tale will take place
in the Blue Forest at sundown.
Your best 10 girls will compete against our best 10 boys.
The side with the most remaining at dawn wins.

If the GIRLS win, we surrender
to your school as SLAVES.

If the BOYS win, you surrender
Sophie and Agatha for PUBLIC EXECUTION.

You are in no position to negotiate participation or terms.

Tedros

Sophie clutched the page so tightly her knuckles blued.

"Agatha?" she breathed, looking up. "What were you going to tell me?"

But Agatha was still staring at the scroll.

The dark cast in her eyes returned. The blush faded from her cheeks. The graveyard girl was back, a wish forgotten. She looked up at Sophie, sad and empty.

"I should have listened to you," she said, voice cracking.

Sophie paused carefully. "You went to him?"

Agatha smeared away tears, unable to look at her.

"And he attacked you, didn't he," Sophie said.

Agatha cried harder. "How'd you kn-kn-kn—"

"I warned you," Sophie whispered. "I warned you what boys do."

Agatha collapsed into her arms, sobbing. "I'm sorry . . . I'm so sorry. . . ."

Sophie hugged her tight, shoving away her guilt.

It wasn't Evil, stopping their kiss last night. No, it was all for Good.

Her friend had come back to her.

From the School Master's window, Tedros watched Aric's red-hooded henchmen police the mob of princes at the rip in the bubbly, purple-tinged shield, letting in only the biggest or best armed. Standing beside him, Aric clenched his jaw.

"With all due respect, master, this Trial is a coward's game," he sneered. "With our numbers, we should storm their castle—"

"Not after last night. Those girls are far too cunning for us to fight on their turf," said Tedros. "Besides, the girls would have their teachers fighting with them. A Trial puts us on even ground."

"Even ground!" Aric snarled. "I broke the princes through the shield because you assured me a *war*."

"This is about saving our school from two girls intent on destroying it. Not cheap, villainous carnage."

"When our teachers return, they will punish you for all you've done," Aric spat—

Tedros slammed him against the windowsill, Aric's head dangling over it. "Remember your place, you savage. I let you into this school. And I can show you out."

Aric stared at him, eyes wide.

Tedros pulled him up and looked away. In silence, the two boys watched more feral princes climb through the hole in the broken shield.

"You must be quite the magician to crack it," said Tedros finally. "Lady Lesso cast that shield herself."

Aric didn't reply.

"Aric, I want only the best fighting with you and me," Tedros said, turning to him. "Whoever wins can have my treasure, as promised."

Aric gave him a simpering smile. "As you wish, master."

A shadow moved on the wall and Aric swiveled to see Tristan hovering near the chained Storian. Aric bared jagged teeth like a dog and Tristan cowered.

"Oh leave him alone," Tedros sighed. "I need his help on

guard. Especially after last night."

His eyes drifted across the bay to the girls' school, glittering like a sapphire city. He could see the last of the smoke plumes dissipating from its four towers. The Trial announcements had been delivered.

"She was lying about Sophie being there the whole time?" Tedros asked.

"There is doubt in your voice, master."

"It's just the way she looked at me . . . touched me . . . like she meant it. . . ."

"She attacked *you*. And her witch was there to finish the job," growled Aric. "Why do you think she freed the pen? Your death would seal their story and spread its lesson far and wide. A world without princes. A world with girls as masters—and boys as slaves. The End." The captain glared at Tedros. "If I hadn't arrived to save you . . ."

Tedros looked down. "I am aware."

"It is a difficult thing to admit. A son reliving the mistakes of his father. Both your loves . . . lost to another."

Tedros slowly raised his head.

"What would he have done?" Aric said, violet eyes searching him.

Tedros turned away, rage ripping through his chest once more. He looked down at the barbarous princes marching into his castle.

"She attacked *me*," he whispered, as if finally believing the words were true.

"He attacked *you*?" Hester said to Agatha, sitting with Anadil, Dot, and the rest of the girls on the gallery floor, waiting for the Dean and teachers to arrive.

"Convinced I'd brought Sophie to kill him," Agatha said sourly. "Tried some strange spell—swear it looked pink, but it came too fast to see. Barely missed me before his henchmen came."

"Henchmen?" Dot gawked. *"Tedros?"*

"And a *pink* spell?" Anadil said, her three rats looking just as befuddled. "You definitely saw wrong. If a boy's using a pink curse, it'd be serious black magic."

"I wouldn't put it past him," Agatha shuddered.

Rumors of the Trial had spread fast, with girls heatedly debating who would be picked to compete against the boys. With Sophie in the bathroom washing ash off her face ("Death threat or no death threat, I'm not getting blackheads"), Agatha took the chance to tell the witches everything that happened since nightfall.

"He's the Evil one, not Sophie," Agatha said, thinking of her prince's searing eyes, his hunt for vengeance. "That dream was warning me."

"So Sophie isn't turning?" Hester asked, dumbfounded.

Agatha shook her head.

"And there's no wart?" said Anadil.

Agatha looked down, ashamed.

"But you swore you saw one!" Hester hissed. "And what about the Beast? What about the cat—"

"For the last time, none of that was me!" Sophie scowled,

plopping down between them. "And this is the first time I'm hearing of a wart. Our heads on the chopping block over a . . . *wart*?"

The girls gaped at her—except Agatha, who couldn't meet her eyes.

"We almost lost each other last night, Aggie," Sophie said, softening. "But you have to believe me. As long as we're friends, I'm *happy*. As long as we're friends, there *is* no witch."

"Should have stolen the Storian for us when I had a chance," Agatha mumbled, picking at her clumps. "No doubt I'd mean my wish now. You and I'd be long gone."

Sophie blushed with surprise.

"Look, this doesn't make sense," Hester snapped. "We saw that pigeon *dead*—"

"I don't care what ooga booga you saw," Sophie shot back. "Someone obviously wanted you to think I was Evil. Someone who wants Agatha against me."

"But *who*?" Agatha asked, relieved there might be someone else to blame for her betraying her best friend. "The Dean needs us to be friends to fight the boys—"

"Maybe it was Lesso or Dovey who conjured her symptoms," Dot said, turning an exhibit plaque to avocado. "They always thought Agatha should be with Tedros."

"Maybe it was Anemone or Sheeks," Anadil said, tying her rats' tails together. "They want back to Good and Evil even more than us."

"Or maybe it was someone who wants me gone," Sophie

said, eyes veering to Hester. "Someone who wants to be Class *Captain*."

Hester answered with a violent fart, refusing to dignify the charge with words.

"Look, it doesn't matter who it was. We're all on the same side now. Against *Tedros*," Agatha said, taking Sophie's hand. "And we're not going into his Trial."

Sophie warmed inside. It'd been so long since they felt like friends. "Aggie's right," she said. "We have to stop the Trial from happening."

"We?" Hester leaned against a glass case. "I think a Trial against boys sounds delicious."

"About time we had a little bloodshed," said Anadil, entangled rats yipping agreement.

"I'd quite like a slave," Dot chimed.

"This isn't a game, you idiots! If we lose, Agatha and I *die*!" Sophie barked. "The Dean has to refuse—"

Butterflies skimmed under the gallery door, which swung open as the Dean arrived, groomed and coiffed as ever, followed by disheveled, grim-looking teachers. Professor Dovey and Lady Lesso looked grimmest of all.

"As you've heard, the boys demand a Trial," the Dean proclaimed, the torches magically spotlighting her. "And though the teachers see otherwise, I see no reason to deny their terms."

Sophie and Agatha choked.

Agatha whirled to Lady Lesso and Professor Dovey, who both looked at her equally scared, as if they knew last night had gone all wrong, even if the ever-present butterflies would preclude them from knowing how.

"Class challenges will continue until the Trial, with the eight highest-ranked students chosen for the team." The Dean's shiny eyes fell upon Sophie and Agatha. "Our Captains' two spots are *guaranteed*, of course, given it is their lives that are in the balance."

Both girls went a shade whiter. "But there's no way to beat boys, Aggie! They're faster, stronger, *meaner*," Sophie whispered. "We have to get home now or we're dead!"

"There is no way home!" Aggie hissed back. "Tedros still has the Storian!"

Sophie moaned and slumped against her.

Then slowly Sophie straightened, eyes wide.

Agatha saw her face and recoiled in horror. "Sophie, you can't possibly be thinking—"

"You said it yourself! Our wish will work now!" Sophie whispered. "We can write 'The End'—forever this time! All we need is that pen!"

"Are you insane! There's an army of boys thirsting to kill us! And even if by dumb luck we get past them, Tedros will never let us near that tower! There's no way—"

"There has to be, Agatha," Sophie pressed her. "Or we both die before a very big audience."

Agatha felt sick to her stomach. Around her, she saw the other girls whispering to each other, absorbing the reality of a lethal contest against boys.

"For those of you plotting poor ranks to *avoid* selection for the team, you should rethink," the Dean said as a few butterflies floated back into her dress. "After all, your rankings will determine your third-year tracks, with the lowliest of you poised to become animals or plants." Girls stopped chattering, as if the Dean had overheard their schemes. "Finally, given the unfortunate *failure* of Lady Lesso's shield, nymphs will take over nighttime guard duties at the perimeter."

Lady Lesso stared at her pointy steel shoe tips, pale cheeks pinking.

"All classes and events will proceed normally," the Dean continued, "including our school play, to be unveiled on Trial eve." She smiled at Professor Sheeks, who didn't smile back. "Clubs and extracurricular activities should go on as usual—"

"Book Club tonight!" Dot chirped loudly, waving at her friends. "Book Club in the Supper Hall—"

Anadil's shoe rammed her bottom, and Dot yelped.

"Given the current state of the castle, classes will resume tomorrow," the Dean finished, the torches dimming behind her. "I encourage you to rest for the difficult weeks ahead. The boys will not go down without a fight."

Murmuring girls followed the teachers out. Professor Dovey and Lady Lesso hovered behind for Agatha, clearly desperate to speak to her, but the Dean ushered them away with the rest.

Agatha slouched miserably as she watched Lesso and her fairy godmother go, just as desperate for their help. She heard the witches chattering ahead.

"I bet Yara could beat the boys," said Dot. "Seen her muscles?"

"Yara?" Hester scoffed, batting away a butterfly. "No one's seen her for days. For all we know, a crog ate her."

"You really think she's half stymph?"

"She's half *something*," Anadil murmured, rats following her through the frosted door.

Agatha shambled ahead as Sophie sidled up beside her.

"Look, we still have ten days to get the pen, Aggie," Sophie prodded, seeing her friend's morose face. "One wish, and we're safe from boys forever."

Agatha frowned deeper, and Sophie knew why.

After last night, the chance of getting that pen was as slim as their chance to win a Trial.

"They'll never get it now," Tedros grunted, holding down the floundering Storian with his foot. Tristan replaced the missing brick, sealing the pen beneath the tower's floor.

They could still hear the Storian thrashing.

"Help me move the table," Tedros said, and Tristan eagerly pulled his side of the heavy stone table over the loose brick, muffling the pen. As Tedros adjusted the table, Tristan stealthily dug his boot tip into the brick, leaving a scratch mark.

"There." Tedros glowered at Sophie and Agatha's open storybook on the table. "Let them try to write 'The End' now."

"SLAVES?" Ravan's voice echoed outside. "IF WE LOSE, WE END UP *SLAVES*?"

Tedros leaned out the window and watched Everboys, Neverboys, and scores of new princes mobbing the catwalks between towers as Aric's henchmen confronted them with clubs.

"CAN'T BARTER AWAY OUR LIVES IN SOME COCKAMAMIE TRIAL!" Chaddick bellowed, hurling stones uselessly at the School Master's tower.

"You promised war!" yelled a new prince, stabbing his finger up at Tedros.

"War! War! War!" boys and princes howled as they battered the henchmen back into the towers.

Tedros chewed on his lip. "Take away Good and Evil, and boys just want treasure and blood."

"Look, they need you down there," Tristan offered. "You have to make it a real school again. Like the girls did." He sneaked a glance at the marked brick. "Plus you might want a nap—or a bath, even—"

"Do I smell that bad?" Tedros said, sniffing himself.

Tristan's cheeks glowed as red as his hair. "N-n-no—"

Yowls echoed below as they watched a henchman flee from Hort, who chased him with fistfuls of flaming rat poo, hissing like a weasel. Tedros sagged, discouraged.

Suddenly the prince's eyes flared wide. "Tristan, you're right! They do need me!"

Tristan lit up with relief, practically shoving the prince towards the window—until Tedros shot his gold glow into the castle to call Aric.

"But I can guard alone!" Tristan insisted.

"Let Aric do it." The prince heaved the heavy coils of blond hair off the floor and flung them out the window. "You and I have a job to do."

"A j-j-j-job?" Tristan sputtered.

"Come on." Tedros shoved him towards the rope. "We're bringing the teachers back."

Located on the first floor of Charity Tower, the girls' Supper Hall was circular like a bull ring and brightly lit, crammed with glass tables of different shapes. Dot had chosen it specifically for Book Club meetings because the enchanted pots in the kitchen provided punch and sandwiches, while the Dean's eavesdropping butterflies stayed away, put off by the clattering plates, assaulting aromas, and overlapping conversations.

At precisely half past eight, Dot hustled down the stairs, expecting a healthy crowd after *Shame: The Secret Life of Prince Charming* brought in a bevy of new members the week before. Hester had mentioned a meeting with Agatha and Sophie after supper, but Dot couldn't be bothered. With her teeth brushed, makeup retouched, and discussion questions prepared, Dot cleared her throat and grabbed the door—only to notice a sign posted on it.

BOOK CLUB
CANCELED
INDEFINITELY
DUE TO STRUGGLES WITH MALNUTRITION,
EVER-WANNABE DISORDER,
AND IRRITABLE BOWEL SYNDROME
LOVE, DOT

Dot screeched, throwing open the door. "What in the—"

Bunched against the wall of the deserted room, Anadil, Hester, Agatha, and Sophie huddled near one another.

"Will you help us or not?" Sophie said, glaring at Hester.

"Fine," Hester grouched. "But only because I'd rather not see Agatha die. You, I'd pay to see publicly executed."

Sophie gasped.

"Look, Sophie's right. This is our only hope to escape alive," Agatha said, though still sounding unsure whether a public beheading was worse than going back to the boys' castle. "Tedros has probably hidden the Storian by now. We need a spell that can let us stay in that school long enough to find it."

"Invisibility?" offered Anadil.

"Two of us? Way too easy to get caught," said Sophie, knowing Aric had surely found her trail.

"How about crossing the Bridge barrier again?" Hester said to Agatha.

"They'll surely have guards there after last night," Agatha said—

All at once, the girls noticed Dot at the door, red faced and glaring. "Irritable *Bowel* Syndrome?"

"Seemed fitting, given your predilection for hiding in toilets," said Anadil.

"But you can't cancel Book Club!" Dot mewled, tearing up. "It's how I made friends!"

"And we need privacy, so this is your Book Club now, which is appropriate, given we're your *real* friends. Now sit down and shut it," Hester lashed. Dot obeyed, still sniffling.

"There has to be a way to talk to Dovey or Lesso," Sophie urged, "or even Professor Sheeks—"

"It's too dangerous," said Agatha, for she had yet to see any teacher free of the Dean's minions. "The Dean even suspects what we're up to, and she'll trap us here. You heard her. She thinks we can *win* this Trial!"

"Can't you just Mogrify?" Dot moaned—

"No," Sophie and Agatha said at the same time.

Agatha stared at her friend.

"I mean, I know nothing about their school since I've never been there, but it's obvious, right?" Sophie babbled, beading with sweat. "Boys would protect against it."

Agatha peered harder at her. Sophie could feel her cheeks turning cranberry red. . . .

Agatha turned back to the witches. "See, Sophie gets it. We need something unexpected."

Sophie exhaled, smiling guiltily. One day she'd tell Agatha where she'd been last night. One day when they were safe at home, stronger and happier than ever.

"Let's meet here every night until we have a plan," Hester said, then noticed Dot shaking her head. "If you're still sulking about your idiotic Book Club—"

"It's not that," Dot said, furrowing. "Don't you think it's strange that Tedros *attacked* Agatha?"

Sophie bristled. "He tried to kill her last year—"

"Because *you* were there last year, ruining things," Dot shot back. "Tedros loves Agatha! He'd never attack her with magic." Dot turned a stray fork into bok choy, thinking hard.

"Feels like there's a piece missing."

Dot looked up and saw Agatha gazing at her.

"Only piece missing is how to sneak into the boys' school," Sophie snapped, and steered the conversation back to the plan. "We need to search the library for spells—"

Agatha tried to pay attention, but her eyes kept drifting back to Dot. . . .

"Agatha?" Sophie frowned. "Can you come then?"

Agatha jolted to attention. "Sure—of course—"

All of a sudden, she noticed something on Sophie's wrist, peeking from under her cloak . . . tiny patterned cuts, thinly scabbed over. Struck by a familiar feeling, Agatha tried to squint closer, but a flurry of noise rose outside and the girls turned—just in time to see the doors fly open and Pollux stumble in, head atop a dead ostrich, scowling with suspicion at a book club that didn't seem to have any books.

14

Merlin's Lost Spell

With Christmastime coming, the butterflies used the night to pull tinsel and starry lights around the tallest pine tree in the Blue Forest, as if a deadly Trial shouldn't deter from festive traditions.

By dawn, the boys had urinated on it from their windows and set it aflame.

As Lady Lesso awarded ranks, Sophie passed notes with Anadil and Hester about paths into the boys' school. In the next aisle, Agatha leaned her frozen chair back, squinting at the faint marks on Sophie's wrist.

It was only noon, but Trial Tryouts were in full swing. Each of the class challenges involved slaying phantom princes that the teachers conjured to be as vile as possible, lunging at the girls with zombified faces and sickening screams. Indeed, the teachers seemed to have lost all reluctance, with even Professor Anemone sanctioning the most vicious deaths. Lives were at stake now, and the teachers fully invested in finding the best possible team.

Sophie and Agatha resolved to act enthused through all of it so the Dean wouldn't suspect their impending plans to escape. And indeed, Sophie played her part well, dispatching boy phantoms with alarming vengeance, cheering on her fellow classmates, and remaining immune from the frightening witch symptoms that had plagued her days before. Even more, Agatha noticed Sophie back to her jaunty old self now, chummily grabbing her arm between classes, romanticizing their coming return to Gavaldon, and acting as if Agatha's visit to Tedros had simply never happened.

"Elders won't hurt us if there're no more attacks . . . and I'll just spend time at your house instead of mine . . . ," Sophie considered as they'd walked to Lesso's. "Maybe I'll even get my own show after all!"

"As long as you don't put me in it," Agatha grouched before Sophie's grin made her crack up.

Agatha wanted to be suspicious of it, to ask how Sophie could forgive her so easily—but Sophie just seemed so relieved and happy to have her best friend again.

Given all she'd caused with her wish, Agatha had even

more motivation than Sophie to get out of this school. She racked her brain for ways into Tedros' tower but always came up empty. Her frustration leaked into Tryouts, where she lashed out at boys like the witch-girl of old, stabbing phantoms through, setting them on fire, watching coldly as they shattered to dust. By the third challenge, all the reasons she'd once hated Tedros came roaring back—his arrogance, his recklessness, his hotheaded immaturity—

And yet . . . why did Dot's question still nag at her?

There was no missing piece, Agatha assured herself. *Tedros* had attacked her. *Tedros* ruined their fairy tale.

Her soul's wish for him had been wrong.

And yet . . . Agatha found herself tilting farther in her chair, Sophie's hand still too far away to see. She reclined even more, teetering on one chair leg, until Hester's iced desktop was in front of Sophie's wrist, magnifying it like a lens. Agatha's eyes widened, recognizing the faint wounds in her friend's creamy skin, patterned with deep needle pricks.

Spirick cuts.

Where had Sophie encountered spiricks?

In the Woods, of course, Agatha reminded herself. That's where they'd attacked *her*, hadn't they? And yet, Sophie's wounds still looked fresh . . .

Sophie turned to her, and Agatha's chair nearly toppled. "Come to the library with me?" Sophie smiled, helping her up. "Ten minutes before fourth session. We can look at spying spells!"

Agatha smiled back and grabbed her bag, shoving spiricks from her mind.

No more doubts. No more distrust, she thought, following her best friend upstairs.

She'd learned her lesson with the wart.

Melting black candles lined the walls of Evil Hall, with yellow-green flames the color of snake eyes.

In the center of the room, twelve white coffin beds lay in a row, each with the body of a male teacher from Good or Evil. Tanned, mustached Professor Espada, who taught Swordplay to Everboys; pimpled, bald Professor Manley, who taught Uglification to Neverboys; wizened, doddering Professor Lukas, who taught Chivalry; Castor, who led Henchmen Training, his brother Pollux's head missing from their two-headed dog body; Beezle, Evil's red-skinned dwarf, next to a pack of Forest Group leaders—an ogre, a centaur, and a sprite among them; even Albemarle, the spectacled woodpecker who'd once tallied Good's rankings . . . all breathing in sync, their sleeping faces peaceful.

On the floor in front of them, Tristan slouched, surrounded by open spellbooks from the Library of Vice. "We've been up all night," he yawned, pawing his red hair. "The Dean's magic is too strong."

"Well, we'll all be slaves unless we break it," Tedros mumbled, rifling pages of *Sleep No More.* "You don't know what they're like together, those two girls. They'll make mincemeat of us if the boys don't get behind this Trial and start Tryouts now." He grabbed another book. "But we need our teachers back if we're to have any chance of winning."

"How about I go and check on the Storian?" Tristan said quickly. "Just to make sure—"

"Look, it's a sleeping curse. It has to have a cure."

"Not unless you have a man-wolf handy," Tristan snorted, tossing aside *Spells for Sleeping Beauties.*

Tedros closed his last book a moment later. He saw the dark circles under Tristan's eyes, obscuring his freckles. "All right," the prince caved, standing up. "Let's go back—"

He suddenly noticed the book Tristan had tossed, open to a cobwebbed page. Tedros slid it closer with his foot.

Chapter 14
Sleep Spell Counter-Curses

*Author's Note: The sleep curse remedies in this and most books are applicable exclusively to slumbering maidens, since they are the most likely victims. Males, of course, can be roused only by a man-wolf's scream. (In absence of a live man-wolf, you may puree the lungs of a dead one and pour the draft into the sleeping man's ear.)

The Waking Princess Elixir
Ingredients

2 cat claws

1 bushel of fresh mint

"Hate to tell you," said Tristan impatiently, "but Sader told us last year. Man-wolves only live in Bloodbrook—"

"Funny." Tedros looked up, eyes twinkling. "Isn't that where Hort's from?"

Sophie flung *The Sneak and Spy Handbook* onto a heap of discarded books and squinted up at the Library of Virtue's two-floor gold coliseum, dominated by a sundial clock. "It will take us months to go through all these!"

"They're all the same spells," Agatha frowned, sitting at her table and paging through *Snoop Spells, Volume 2*. "Invisibility, disguise, advanced Mogrifications—nothing they wouldn't expect. We need to be in the boys' school long enough to break into Tedros' tower. Could take us days."

"*Days?* With those dirty princes? We'll die of fumes," Sophie moaned. She squinted at the leathery tortoise behind the reception desk, asleep on a massive library log. "Is that thing ever awake?"

She turned and saw Agatha frowning at a few butterflies that had fluttered in. "Don't fret," Sophie whispered. "We're the perfect team, remember? Think of how you sneaked into the Trial last year."

"This is different, Sophie. We need *help*," Agatha said quickly. "And as long as the Dean's listening, we can't get it."

With their schedules separating, Sophie headed to Female Talents with Hester and Anadil, while Agatha caught up with Dot in History of Heroines.

"Still nothing?" Dot said, seeing Agatha's face as she settled next to her in Good Hall's calcified pews. "Daddy would know what to do, but he's on the run from Maid Marian. She's enslaving all the men in Sherwood Forest after she found out Robin has a wandering eye." Dot sighed. "Coulda told her that myself."

Kiko's head poked beside Agatha's from the pew behind. "Eeee! You finally get to see the best class! Wish you were here the first week. We went inside Cinderella's story—did you know she just married her prince until he signed his kingdom over to her? Then she had him thrown in the dungeons and ruled herself, pretending their marriage was happy. Turns out boys have been covering up the truth about fairy tales for ages, just to make girls seem weak and stupid. Then we went inside Goldilocks' story and watched her tame the three bears and turn them into fur coats, and then we went inside Snow White's, when she poisoned those sexist dwarfs with apples—"

"Huh?" Agatha said, confounded. "First off, nothing you just said sounds anything like the 'truth.' Second of all, how do you go *inside* stories?"

Kiko smiled mischievously. "You'll see."

The Dean clacked in through the double doors, heels echoing on stone. "In addition to attacking our team, the boys will no doubt lace the Blue Forest with deadly traps—as will *we*," she said, hips swishing up the aisle to the wooden lectern. "But a boy's mind is perhaps the deadliest trap, girls. When their dignity is on the line, they will resort to desperate tactics, perverse and unimaginable. You must be prepared."

From inside the lectern, she pulled a massively thick text—*A Student's Revised History of the Woods*, by August Sader—and opened to a page in the middle. The Dean's disembodied voice boomed over the hall, as if coming out of the book:

"'Chapter 26: The Rise and Fall of King Arthur.'"

In a tiny cloud of mist, a ghostly three-dimensional scene melted into view atop the book page . . . a silent living diorama of King Arthur in his gold crown and night robe, stalking through the halls of Camelot.

Agatha could hardly see it from the back of the pews. "It's so small—"

"Wait," Kiko said behind her.

The Dean raised up the book and, with a gap-toothed grin, blew on the phantom scene. With a fizzling *whoosh*, the scene shattered into a million glittered shards and crashed over the students like a glass sandstorm. Agatha shielded her eyes and felt her body floating through space, until her feet touched ground. She slowly peeked through her fingers. . . .

Good Hall had disappeared, along with the pews and the rest of the girls. She was standing in a dark-wood chamber hall, the air thick and hazy around her, giving the room a vaporous feel, as if it wasn't quite real. She squinted and saw a bearded, powerfully built gray-haired man in a wolf-fur night robe and gold crown tiptoeing towards her. . . .

Agatha gasped. Kiko was right. She was *inside* the book's scene.

Her hand reached through the smoky air towards a wall painted with paisley bronze patterns, and her fingers went straight through like a ghost's. King Arthur slipped past her, flickering and distorting slightly like a phantom, bare feet pattering across the rose-colored carpet towards the end of the hall.

Agatha recognized him from the square jaw and crystal-blue eyes he'd passed on, as well as the gold-hilted sword tucked into his robe. The same sword she'd taken from his son's hands two nights before.

"Arthur met Guinevere at the School for Good and Evil before he became king," the Dean's voice narrated. "From the day they met, he knew she despised him. Still he forced her into marriage, for boys are brutal, ruthless creatures—and none more than Arthur."

Agatha squinted hard at the phantom king. Was any of this the truth? Or just another of the Dean's twisted tales?

She watched Arthur approach the last door in the hall, the king careful not to make a sound. . . .

"Guinevere had one condition, however: that each night, she and the king sleep in separate chambers," the Dean continued. "Arthur could not deny the request, for Guinevere behaved the perfect wife and birthed him the wretched son he'd always wanted. Yet still the king couldn't sleep. Night after night, Arthur tried to see inside his queen's room, but her door was always locked. Until one night . . ."

Now Agatha saw what the king had. Tonight, the queen's door was cracked open. Following behind Arthur, Agatha leaned over him and peeked through it. . . .

Just in time to see Guinevere sneak out her window, slide down its curtain, and disappear into the night.

"The next morning, the queen was at breakfast, smiling and agreeable as always," the Dean's voice said. "Arthur said nothing of what he'd seen."

The scene vanished around Agatha, instantly replaced by a dusty cave, littered with burbling laboratory vessels, shelves of murky vials and jars, and dozens of half-filled notebooks. Now Arthur was arguing with an ancient, scrawny man, a stark white beard down to his stomach.

"Arthur tried invisibility, trail tracking, Mogrification—everything he'd learned at the School for Good—but still couldn't find where Guinevere disappeared to each night. His lifelong adviser, Merlin, refused to help, insisting matters of the heart were beyond magic. . . ."

Merlin stormed out of his cave. Arthur pursued him but stopped suddenly. He peered closer at one of Merlin's open notebooks and took it into his hands. . . .

"Then Arthur saw something Merlin had been brewing down in his lair. . . ."

Arthur's eyes flared wider . . .

"Something so daring, so dangerous he knew it was his only chance. . . ."

Hands trembling, Arthur ripped out the page.

The scene flashed to a hooded figure in a forest, galloping past Agatha on a black horse, camouflaged by the night.

"That evening, Arthur had guards seal Guinevere's windows. Cloaked in a hood, he climbed out from the adjacent room to find a horse waiting. . . ."

The horse came to a stop in a pitch-dark clearing. Agatha watched a thin, shadowed man creep out from behind a far tree and slowly approach the horse's rider. But shrouded completely in his cloak and hood, King Arthur didn't dismount. He just waited as the shadowy man grew closer . . . closer . . . each unable to see the other . . . until Agatha finally saw moonlight spill on the shadowed man's light-brown skin, hooked nose, and knight's uniform.

"It was Lancelot. The friend Arthur loved so much he called him a brother. The man Guinevere had come to every night."

Lancelot drew nearer to the horse, the hooded cloak still drawn over the rider's face. Lancelot hesitated, sensing something wrong . . . but then saw delicate white slippered feet peeking from beneath the rider's cloak. Agatha stared at these girlish feet, confused, as Lancelot smiled lovingly and moved closer to the horse. Agatha watched as Lancelot reached up . . . gently pulled back the rider's hood . . . revealing King Arthur's crystal-blue eyes. . . .

Agatha choked.

His eyes weren't a man's anymore.

In a flash, Arthur drew a blade, stabbing Lancelot's stomach. The horse sprinted away, returning the king back to the castle.

The scene melted to vapors and Agatha was back in Good Hall with the silent, stunned class.

"The spell made King Arthur a girl?" Beatrix cried, aghast. "A boy—became—a *girl?*"

"Just long enough for the king to see his queen had made a fool of him," the Dean said. "But by the time Arthur reverted from the spell and returned to Camelot, Guinevere was gone. He sent his men to finish off Lancelot, but the knight too had vanished. Neither he nor the queen was ever seen again."

Agatha couldn't breathe, still questioning everything she'd just seen. And yet she needed this story to be true—she needed it to save her and Sophie's life—she needed—

"The spell!" she blurted, lurching to her feet. "Where's Merlin's spell!"

"Lost, like all of his spells, of course," the Dean replied, closing the book. "But the spell is hardly the point, dear." She looked up at Agatha with a daring smile. "It's that a boy was clever and disciplined enough to find it."

As Agatha sank down, girls buzzed feverishly around her, dissecting every moment of their trip through time.

"Told you it was a good class," Kiko whispered behind her.

But Agatha slumped deeper, for all it'd given her was more dead ends. Her and Sophie's only hope was that the baboonish boys she'd seen across the bay, lacking in cleverness or discipline, had hit a dead end of their own.

"I want to be on the Trial team," said Hort, still in underpants, voice resounding in Evil Hall. "That's my condition."

"Sorry, Hort, but we need the strongest boys," said Tedros, after he'd sent Tristan away for this negotiation. "That's why we brought in the princes. Only Aric and I don't have to try out—"

"You need a man-wolf scream? You need my villain talent? Then give me a spot on the team," Hort snapped. He looked down at his underpants. "And a new uniform."

"Look, it's just one scream—"

"No, you look! My dad said villains can't love, and I tried to love," Hort said, beady eyes gluing to the floor. "Chasing after Sophie like I was an Ever when I'm just . . . well, look at me." He rubbed at his whiskery cheeks. "Made a fool of myself . . . and my dad. Least I can do is win the treasure and bury him. You understand that, don't you?" He looked up at Tedros. "Trying to make him proud, even if he's dead?"

Tedros' jaw softened. He could see the flush across Hort's chest, his bottom lip trembling. The boy had been born with none of his good fortune, and yet they were so much the same.

"No one will fight like me," Hort pleaded, looking like a shivering squirrel. "No one."

The prince folded his arms, trying valiantly to ignore him. "Hort, these girls want me *dead*. This isn't like last year. This is a real Trial, with all our lives at stake, and I'm the leader of this school and responsible for the boys' safety and they're already revolting over the fact they might end up slaves—"

Hort was whimpering like a homeless puppy. Tedros gritted his teeth.

"So what would it look like if I just—if I—if—if—"

The prince slumped, exhaling. "Aric will shoot me."

Hort beamed sharp yellow teeth. He whirled to the sleeping teachers, unleashing a scream so primal his body jerked into contortions and so loud that Tedros quailed against the wall, covering his ears. By the time the prince looked up, Hort wasn't human anymore. He was swathed in a man-wolf's dark fur over bulging muscles, erect on two legs, roaring and roaring until he finally ran out of breath.

"Told you I last longer," Hort growled as he listened proudly to boys' terrified shouts upstairs, torn from their sleep.

They weren't the only ones woken.

Slowly the teachers stirred in their coffins, one by one. Manley was the first to rise, jowly, pockmarked face flickering in torchlight.

Tedros grinned and extended his hand. "Professor, welcome back to the School for Boy—"

"Fine mess you've gotten yourself into. A castle full of filthy strangers. A Trial with ludicrous terms. Terms you *trapped* us into once the girls agreed," Manley sneered, tramping for the door. "Slaves to *girls*? Imagine what the stories would look like with the Storian in Dean Sader's hands. Men dying at the end of every tale. Men on a losing streak worse than Evil's."

"And yet a silver lining if we *win*," Professor Espada said, glowering at the two boys as his pointy black boots hit the ground. "Win this Trial, and those two cursed Readers die. Their fairy tale instantly undone . . . our schools back to Good and Evil, like they always were."

"Ten days to right this ship, then," Albemarle the woodpecker said, trailing after them with the rest of the Forest Group leaders. "I'll prepare the schedules."

"I'll ready the classrooms," said Chivalry's Professor Lukas.

"AND I'LL WAKE THE SORRY LOSERS UP," Castor roared, shaking out his fur.

Beezle burped with glee and ran after him.

"But—but what about *me*?" Tedros called behind them—

"You can compete for the Trial team like everyone else," Manley spat back.

"Compete?" Tedros blurted.

"How about me!" Hort spluttered, shrinking to human. "He s-s-s-said—"

"*He* ain't in charge anymore." Manley's voice echoed as he vanished down the hall's stairs.

Hort glowered at Tedros, betrayed. The prince went red, straining for voice. "But how—how did they know—"

Castor swiveled from the door, rabid and bloodshot.

"JUST 'CAUSE WE'RE ASLEEP DON'T MEAN WE CAN'T HEAR."

For five nights, Sophie, Agatha, and the witches met in the Supper Hall for Book Club, debating possible schemes to get the Storian and wish themselves home. And yet none seemed without serious risk. With each passing day, Agatha grew more and more doubtful of every new spell, Sophie more and more sharp with her, and both more and more convinced the Trial would happen as planned. Together they decided that come the 6th night, they'd pick a plan, for their time was running short.

At half past eight, Agatha and Dot swept down to the Supper Hall, frantically comparing spells, only to find Sophie, Hester, and Anadil standing outside the door.

"We have a problem." Hester stepped aside, revealing the sign pasted over their book club's.

PLAY AUDITIONS TONIGHT

A Pageant History of Female Accomplishment

Note: If no one shows, there will be no play.

* Challenge exemptions for all those who do not show.
Professor Sheeks, Play Director

* Challenge exemptions are prohibited, per the Dean.
Pollux, Play Director's Supervisor and Creative Consultant

"Can't we move somewhere else?" Dot asked.

"It's the only place butterflies don't come," worried Sophie. "We've already lost a week. We need a plan tonight."

The girls fell quiet.

"Guess we're all auditioning for *A Pageant History of Female Accomplishment*," Agatha crabbed. Then she caught Sophie's excited look and frowned. "You're not getting a *part*."

Ten minutes later, Sophie was cavorting in front of the curtain on a makeshift stage in the Supper Hall, delivering an inexplicable monologue in an inexplicable accent. "Hear me, Prrrrrince Humperdink! Do naht be fooled bah mah beauhty and charrrm. I ahm a simple woman. Simple in mahnd, simple in hearrrt—but do naht take thaht for simple in spirrrit."

She looked down at Professor Sheeks and Pollux's head, perched on the table, both blinking at her.

"I thought it was quite good," Pollux wisped.

A hand yanked her behind the curtain.

"Was it too subtle?" Sophie said, eyeing the paltry line of girls waiting their turns.

"The only thing subtle is your chance to live," Hester seethed. "We're deciding on a plan and we're deciding on a plan now. Everyone give their best idea."

"I found a Spyder Sling Spell that sticks you to ceilings," Anadil offered, leaning against the window. "You could hide in the vents for days."

"And where do I bathe?" said Sophie. "Where do I eat?"

"You eat?" Anadil said, gaping.

"We could send my demon to steal the pen," Hester mulled. "Surely he'll get past the shield."

"And if he gets caught? Your demon dies and so do you," Sophie returned. "And now that I think about it, it's a lovely idea."

"What if I turn you into vegetables?" Dot offered. "Boys don't eat vegetables."

Everyone stared at her.

"Aggie?" Sophie said. "Surely you found something?"

Agatha had been quietly shifting in her clumps during all this, for she had been counting on the witches to find something foolproof. But now she had to face what she'd suspected all along.

"There isn't anything safe, no matter what we choose," she said. She looked up at Sophie, tearing. "This is my fault—we're going to end up in that Trial, and it's my fault—"

"But—but—we can't die, Aggie," Sophie rasped. "Not when we're finally friends again."

Agatha shook her head. "They'll find us, Sophie. Any of these spells—they'll find us. . . ."

She stopped, because her eyes had caught something out the window.

"Aggie?" Sophie asked.

Agatha put her hands on the window as the witches crowded around her.

"Oh, it's just Helga," Sophie huffed, watching the frumpy, lavender-dressed gnome scurrying through the Blue Forest to her burrow by the brook. "Strange, though. She looks skinnier. . . . I didn't know gnomes go on diets. And her hair is different too! Looks like . . . like a . . ."

Now all the girls pressed their noses to the glass in shock.

"It can't be," Hester gasped.

For as the gnome slid back into Helga's burrow in Helga's dress and Helga's hat, a face that *wasn't* Helga's peeked up through the hole to make sure no one saw it.

"It was a girl during class—it's been a girl every day," Dot said. "It's impossible!"

But it wasn't, Agatha thought, mirroring a Dean's daring smile. For she'd seen the spell that had made it possible, lost and now found.

The spell that had hidden Yuba in the enemy's castle all this time.

And the spell that would now help her and Sophie do the same.

15

The Five Rules

"I don't understand," Sophie whispered to Agatha. "What does all this have to do with getting into the boys' *school*?"

Agatha ignored her, glaring at Helga the Gnome, bound to a frilly rocking chair, long white hair covered in kale flakes. "Either tell us how you do it, Yuba, or we give you to the Dean."

"I find your charges deeply offensive," Helga retorted, her voice tight and pitchy. "All males have been *evicted*—"

"We saw you, Yuba," said Hester, arms crossed next to

Dot. "We saw your *face*."

"Yuba? *Me?* Preposterous," Helga scowled, struggling for the white staff out of reach. "Now leave at once, before I call the Dean myself."

"Please! We need your help," Agatha begged—

"But how can she help us with *boys*? And why do you keep calling her Yuba?" Sophie badgered, pointing at the dowdy gnome. "I feel like I'm missing something—"

"A brain," Hester murmured.

With the butterflies generally dormant at night, the girls had waited until after midnight before each took a turn sneaking into the Blue Forest (Anadil was caught by Pollux and had to abort the plan). There was no way to squeeze through the tiny gnome hole they'd seen, but Dot had turned the ground around it to kale and the rest stomped through, stunning Helga in her lair. While the witches tied the gnome to the chair, Agatha poked around the tiny furniture and bookshelves for signs of a male inhabitant, but the doily linens, abundance of flowerpots, and lavender wallpaper all had a decidedly female touch.

Sophie frowned as she sniffed a flowerpot. "Strange, though . . . ," she said airily. "Never met a girl who likes *hydrangeas*."

Agatha humphed at Helga, as if this idiocy would have to suffice as proof. "We know about Merlin's spell, Yuba. We saw it in our book. We know you *used* it."

"The Dean has revised all her brother's texts to reflect her own agenda," Helga shot back, reddening. "Besides, what do I know of Merlin's spells?"

"Only what you taught Merlin yourself," a voice said.

They all swiveled to Dot, in front of a bookshelf, peering at *My Life in Magic* by Merlin of Camelot. She held open the first page, eyeing the gnome.

To Helga and Yuba
My greatest teacher

"Should be teacher*s*, shouldn't it?" said Dot.

The den was quiet.

Agatha kneeled down in front of the old gnome. "Surviving Fairy Tales. That's what you teach." She took Helga's wrinkled hand. "And we can't survive ours without you."

Helga's gray pupils glued to the ground, unable to look at her student for a long time. Slowly, her long white hair retracted into her skull, growing scratchy and short. The grooves of her face magically deepened and the skin hardened to a leathery tan beneath a growing white beard. Her cheeks hollowed, her nose fattened, her eyebrows bushied, her body burlying to a barrel shape . . . until at last Yuba the Gnome gazed up at his former students, in the same lavender dress and wobbly heels.

"Do you mind if I change?" he asked quietly.

Sophie gawped at her old Forest Group teacher, morphed from a girl into a boy. She twirled to Agatha, appalled.

"That's how you want us to get in the boys' school? By turning us into . . . *gnomes*?"

Agatha banged her head against the wall.

On a dusty wool couch, Agatha, Sophie, Hester, and Dot held mugs of turnip-root tea, eyes flicking back and forth as Yuba paced the room in his belted green coat and orange cone hat.

"The irony of teaching is we often teach what we can no longer do. Though I have been teaching students for 115 years how to survive in the Endless Woods, I could hardly survive a day outside these gates anymore," the gnome said, no longer straining to disguise his voice. "When the Eviction happened, I needed to remain here safely until the balance was restored. Disguising as Helga was the only way. No one would ever find me out. No one would have a clue." He glowered at Sophie and Agatha, squished next to each other. "But given what you've done to the rules of Good and Evil, I'm not surprised you're back to ruin the rules of Boys and Girls."

Sophie leaned to Agatha. "I really don't see how turning into gnomes ruins any—"

Agatha elbowed her and Sophie shut up.

Yuba slurped from his teacup and sat back in his rocking chair. "Gnomes are different from other creatures in the Woods for two reasons," he said. "From your classwork, Hester can surely tell us the first."

"They're always neutral in war," Hester answered confidently.

"Indeed. Gnomes have never once been drawn into a conflict, in over 2,000 years. We've maintained peace between ourselves and others, without exception."

Sophie yawned and started pouring more tea.

"The second reason we're different is less known and won't be found in your books," said Yuba. "Gnomes are born with the ability to change sex."

Sophie missed her cup and poured tea into Hester's lap.

"Temporarily, of course," the gnome continued, ignoring Hester's loud curses. "Boy gnomes can turn into girl gnomes and girls into boys at will until they come of age, when they revert permanently to the sex that they were born."

Now Sophie dropped the whole pot on Hester.

"No wonder Daddy never let us near young gnomes in Sherwood Forest," Dot marveled as Hester beat Sophie with a pillow. "Probably thought they were contagious."

"The sheriff is not alone in his thinking," Yuba sighed. "And yet, these two properties of gnomes were of deep interest to Merlin, the greatest student to ever attend the School for Good and Evil. In his free time, and often in this very cave, he probed and studied gnome biology so relentlessly his ranks suffered. It is why he was ultimately tracked as a Helper to Arthur's father, instead of as a hero of his own tale."

"But why would Merlin care whether gnomes were peaceful or changed sexes?" Agatha asked.

"Because be believed the two *linked*," said Yuba. "He believed the brief period of playful transformation allowed gnomes to be more sensitive and aware than other creatures. If there was a way for humans to have that experience, even for a *moment,* you too would be as peace loving as the gnomes. All wars preempted, all notions of Good and Evil dissolved . . . mankind perfected." Yuba paused. "He was such a passionate fellow I couldn't help but believe him."

Now Sophie and Hester were both paying attention.

"So you helped him find a spell?" Agatha asked. "A spell to turn human boys into girls and girls into boys?"

"A highly fleeting spell that would work on *any* species," said Yuba. "Better to do it under my supervision than attempt such a dangerous spell on his own." The gnome swallowed ruefully. "Long after he left the School for Good and Evil, he'd return to work with me on the formula. Indeed, it is why I still had the recipe, for I often spent free moments fine-tuning and testing it on myself before his next visit. It took us 20 years to perfect the spell—until Arthur used it to attack Lancelot for all the wrong reasons. Sabotage, subterfuge, revenge . . . Instead of Merlin's spell bringing peace, now word spread of a curse that could bring down kingdoms and destroy men for all time." Tears glistened in Yuba's eyes.

"Merlin fled just before the armies came for him, but they incinerated the lifetime of work he'd left behind. Without his wife and his beloved adviser, Arthur succumbed to drunkenness and heartbreak. Neither I nor anyone else ever saw Merlin again."

Yuba put down his rattling cup. "Professor Sader later effaced the episode from his histories, afraid of the embarrassment it would cause Arthur's son. But the Dean has no such consideration for a boy."

"Nor do we," Sophie lashed, standing up. "That *boy* is planning our execution as we speak—"

"And Merlin's spell is our only way into his castle," Agatha insisted.

"So if you'll please hand it over," said Sophie, huffing towards Yuba, "my friend and I can go hom—"

She paused midstride, blinking.

"Aggie, darling? Not to be gauche, but how exactly would Merlin's spell help us? I don't mean to imply that our night has been a complete goose chase or that you've poorly thought this out, but what could we possibly do with some ludicrous spell that turns boys into girls and girls into . . ."

Sophie's eyes suddenly popped.

"Here it comes," Dot mumbled.

Sophie swiveled to Agatha. "But—but you don't want us to—you weren't talking about—"

"And if you find the Storian . . . ," the gnome said to Agatha, "there will be peace?"

Agatha gave him a sad smile. "A wish started this war, Yuba. Now a wish can end it."

"A *BOY*?" Sophie screeched, clutching her stomach. "AGGIE, YOU WANT ME TO BE A . . . *BOY*?"

"It's the only way to wish for each other without Tedros discovering us," Agatha said, finally looking at her.

"But . . . b-b-b-b-boys? Two . . . *b-b-b-boys*?"

Yuba cleared his throat behind them. "I'm afraid only one can go."

"What?" Agatha said, spinning—

"I left my notes in Sheeba's classroom, when the butterflies heard me collecting ingredients," said Yuba, hunching over the flowerpot with the hydrangeas. He dug his fist into the dirt and withdrew a small glass vial, shaped like a teardrop, filled with a fluorescing violet brew. "When I returned later, the recipe was gone. I am old and dodgy of memory and cannot reconstruct it, no matter how hard I try. This is my last dose of the potion." He looked up at the two girls. "Enough for one of you to last three days in the boys' castle."

Agatha whitened. "But how will you teach class—how will you stay at this school—"

"I'm willing to risk my life if it means peace," Yuba replied.

Neither Sophie nor Agatha said anything for a moment, staring at the smoky potion in his hand.

"I'll go," said Agatha, lurching for the vial.

"No! They'll kill you!" cried Sophie, grabbing her. "We can't be apart now—not after everything—"

"Someone has to bring the pen back—" Agatha said, wresting free.

"Send Hester!" Sophie shrieked, shoving the tattooed witch forward.

"Me?" Hester roared, shoving her back. "Now I'm being dragged into this?"

"Look, this is my idea, so I'll go," Agatha snapped—

"Or Dot!" Sophie said, goosing Dot forward. "She's always trying to be useful—"

"I don't want to be a boy!" Dot screeched, and ran around the sofa while Sophie chased her.

"We'll draw lots!" Sophie gasped, grabbing one of Yuba's notebooks, desperately ripping up pages—

Yuba stayed her hand. "Lives at stake, two schools at war . . . and you expect to draw *lots*? No no no," he said, tucking the vial into his coat. "It should be *me* who goes, of course—but boys will surely suspect a gnome in their midst, given our penchant for peace. And if I can't go, there's only one way to settle this indeed. A proper *challenge*, just as this school requires. And there's certainly no reason it shouldn't be Hester or Dot who goes, or even Anadil, since you'll no doubt betray everything to her that happened here tonight."

The girls goggled at him.

"Tomorrow we choose our boy," Yuba said, shunting them all out. "Forest Groups exist precisely to winnow those who can survive in the bleakest circumstances versus those destined to fail."

As the girls scrambled from his kale-crusted burrow and towards the tunnel, Sophie brightened with relief. "See? Hester will get the pen! Hester wins everything—"

"Never making friends with Evers again," Hester boiled, shoving Agatha hard as she tramped into the trees.

Agatha watched her trail away, stiffening with guilt. "I should be the one to go," she said to Sophie. "How can he leave this up to a *challenge*? It doesn't make any sense—"

Dot butted between them, licking kale off her fingers. "That's 'cause you haven't heard the Five Rules."

"I say we fail on purpose," Anadil harrumphed.

"And end up a newt during tracking? No thank you," Hester grumped, the two witches in black traipsing behind Sophie, Agatha, and blue-uniformed girls flooding through the gates for Forest Groups. "What I don't understand is how you or I bring the Storian *back*. The School Master's tower follows wherever the pen goes. If we steal it, the tower will chase us—"

"Suppose *I* win?" Dot fretted, catching up. "I beat everyone in the poisoned-apple-making tryout this morning!"

"That's because it involved food," Anadil muttered.

Humming a cheerful tune, Sophie noticed Agatha still looking glum after last night. "Aggie, it really is the best solution," Sophie whispered to her, once a few butterflies flew over. "Hester will get the pen in no time. We'll write 'The End' before the Dean suspects a thing!"

Despite her unease over dragging the witches into this, Agatha knew Sophie had a point. If there was one person who could be trusted to accomplish a mission quickly, it was Hester.

"But it's Yuba's last dose," worried Agatha. "How will he survive here?"

"Think he'll be just fine," Sophie snorted.

Agatha followed her eyes to the sea of girls, seated in front of the Blue Brook's bridge, once made of stone, now replaced with rickety planks, suspended by two thick ropes. The girls gaped in silence at the old gnome standing atop the rope bridge, in a lavender dress and wobbly heels, his face completely obscured by bulbous red blisters, his hair hidden beneath a hideous babushka.

"A highly contagious disease of indeterminate duration, so I encourage you to keep your distance," Yuba huffed in his best Helga voice. "Now, given you may soon need to survive *among* boys, perhaps it is time to remind us all of the Five Rules." He flashed a loaded look at Agatha, Sophie, and the witches as he wrote in the air with his smoking staff:

1. Girls soften. Boys harden.

2. Girls reflect. Boys react.

3. Girls express. Boys suppress.

4. Girls desire. Boys hunt.

5. Girls caution. Boys ignore.

Agatha grimaced. "These are sexist and reductive—"

"Says the girl ignored, suppressed, and hunted by her prince," Sophie replied.

Agatha went quiet.

"As you all know from your history classes last year, Ingertrolls are lady trolls, most often found beneath bridges in Netherwood and Runyon Mills," Yuba declared. "And just for today, beneath our very own."

The girls all peered under the bridge to see the other female group leaders uncage a bony, blindfolded troll, with saggy skin scaled pink like a salmon's. It sat in a child's squat, tongue lolling idiotically, scratching hairy armpits and swallowing flies.

"Ingertrolls are quite fond of young men and will do anything to separate them from their beloveds," Yuba continued, frowning at Yara as she ambled in and plopped in the front row. "If a couple steps foot on their bridge, an Ingertroll will throw the girl off and let the boy pass unharmed. For today's challenge, then, each of you will try to cross our bridge without being ejected—a feat no Evergirl or Nevergirl has *ever* managed at this school." He eyed Hester confidently. "But the truly exceptional student will succeed."

As all the girls lined up at the bridge, Agatha questioned how 120 girls could each take a turn by the time class ended—and got her answer when Yara took her first step and was flung squawking into the trees before she took another. Girl after girl barely made it past the first plank, hurled left and right by the hopping Ingertroll, smacking her gums and wagging her bottom.

"Use the rules!" Yuba berated, tightening his babushka.

But they were no use either. Dot was pitched into the Periwinkle Pines, Anadil into the Blue Brook, and Hester into the Fernfield before Agatha was thrown off, fastest of all, into the Turquoise Thicket.

"At least you got to the second plank," Agatha sighed to Hester, picking thorns out of her backside. "Looks like it's you after all."

"EYYYIIIIIIII!"

They glanced up to see Sophie screeching and holding on for dear life to the rope bridge like a bull rider, while the Ingertroll tried to fling her off. Sophie would have happily allowed this, except for a minor problem.

"MY SHOEEEEEEE!" she bellowed, tugging frantically at her glass heel, trapped in a plank. "IT'S

S-S-T-T-UCCCCCKKK—"

"And you say she's *changed*?" Hester frowned.

"The old Sophie would have stopped Tedros from kissing me," said Agatha, wincing as Sophie unleashed a torrent of rather unfeminine words.

"And you believe her? That someone *else* caused her symptoms? That she's Good now?"

"Doubting Sophie is the worst mistake I ever made. It put all of our lives at risk," Agatha said as the troll flipped the bridge and Sophie continued her wailing upside down. "I believe what I see now, Hester. And that's a friend willing to do anything to get me home safe."

Hester paused, taking this in. "Look, I'll endure this hideous spell and get you two home. But only if it's what you really want this time."

Agatha turned, surprised. For a moment, she forgot about the howling girl behind her.

"Will keeping Sophie make you happier than a prince?" Hester said.

Agatha looked away, tense. "Once upon a time, all I needed was a friend to be happy, Hester. Then I thought I needed more. It's the problem with fairy tales. From far away, they seem so perfect. But up close, they're just as complicated as real life."

Hester glared at her. "Will you be happier with her, or a prince."

"Tedros never loved me. If he loved me, he would have trusted me."

"*Her* or a *prince*."

"I don't belong here. I don't belong with a prince—"

"Agatha—"

"There is no choice anymore, Hester!" Agatha cried, voice cracking. "There is no Tedros!"

Hester was speechless.

Agatha recovered, managing a smile. "Besides, who could ever love me as much as Sophie?"

"AGATHHHHHAAAA, HEELLLPPP!" Sophie's voice mewled, and the two girls turned back to see her straddling the bridge ropes like a demented ballerina.

"How that girl gets out of bed in the morning, I have no idea," Agatha sighed.

Finally the Ingertroll stopped shaking the bridge and tried to dislodge Sophie's foot from the shoe—only to receive a firm slap.

"How rude!" Sophie scolded the stunned troll. "Even Cinderella's prince asked permission!" Sophie pried her shoe loose and smacked the troll with it. "And that's for causing trouble between perfectly happy pairs," she said, smiling at Agatha as the troll swelled furious red, about to smite her. Sophie peered down at it. "You know, I used to be just like you."

The troll deflated, confused.

"But now I have my friend back," Sophie whispered. "A friend who makes me Good." She patted the troll's head. "One day I hope you'll find a friend too."

She left the gaping creature behind and moseyed forward, settling on a rock to replace her shoe. "Now I see why Agatha wears those odious clump—"

Sophie realized where she was and bolted to her feet.

Yuba was wide-eyed on the other side of the rope bridge.

"No no no—" Sophie yelped, waving him off—

"Each of the girls' rules disobeyed so skillfully that you've managed to convince the most discerning of monsters you're not a girl at all!" Yuba pipped.

A gold "1" rank exploded over Sophie's head like a crown. "It—it was an accident!" she cried, batting it away as all the other girls' ranks appeared—

But the gnome was giddily waddling towards his hole. "Looks like a girl, acts like a girl . . . who knew!" he babbled, grinning back at Sophie as smoke rose subtly from his staff into the air . . .

9 o'clock

Sophie turned green. Slowly she looked down and saw Agatha and the witches even more gobsmacked than the rest of the class.

Because the one girl who they could never, ever imagine surviving as a boy was about to become one.

16

A Boy by Any Other Name

"It's what you always wanted, isn't it? A part big enough to hold you!" Agatha prattled, slipping with Sophie through the Tunnel of Trees. "And who better to play a part than you?"

Pulling her cloak tighter, Sophie raced ahead into the snow-sprinkled Clearing, dimly lit by two torches on the Blue Forest gate. She'd insisted that the witches stay in the castle tonight. Having a gnome and her best friend there would be humiliation enough.

Yuba had picked 9 o'clock carefully, for most of the girls were bathing, at club meetings, or busy studying for the next Trial Tryouts, while the butterflies tended to settle on rafters or banisters.

in the foyer, dormant to everything but the most egregious noise. With Beatrix at Elf fluency lessons and the Dean in her office, they'd have enough time to go through with the plan. How Agatha would explain her friend's disappearance, Sophie asked repeatedly, but her friend shooed the questions away—no doubt because she didn't have the answers.

"You might even enjoy being a boy," Agatha gibbered on, clumps crunching onto snow. "Think of it as a costume—think of it as a show—"

"Only the audience is trying to kill me," Sophie growled.

She heard her friend's clump crunches slow behind her.

"How can I leave you alone with him?" Agatha whispered, shivering in her cloak.

Sophie stood still, listening to the Valor tower clock toll and fade, snowflakes smothering against her neck. "Everything Good in me is because of you, Agatha. Isn't it time I did something Good for you too?"

She turned to see Agatha, snow caked in torchlight and smiling crookedly like she had in those first days as friends, so surprised Sophie wanted to spend time with her.

"I'll owe you one, all right?" Agatha said, eyes glistening. "Even if I have to sing in your musical."

Sophie cracked a smile back.

They both noticed Yuba's white staff poking out of a hole in the distance, wagging impatiently.

"Listen, try to get on tower guard—that's how you'll get to the pen—" Agatha jabbered again as she gripped Sophie's hand and pulled her into the Forest. "And watch out for a strange spell—that's what Tedros used against me—"

But Sophie couldn't hear Agatha's voice anymore, only the frantic thumps of her own heart, knowing the time had come.

"Any questions about the plan once Sophie transforms?" Yuba whispered to Agatha, his face clear of the magical pox he'd given himself during class. He eyed Sophie, pumping herself a glass of water in the kitchen, and lowered his voice even more. "It is her surest way into the boys' castle."

"B-b-but are you *sure* it will work?" Agatha whispered back, appalled by what the gnome was proposing. "Suppose the crogs think she's a . . ."

She held her tongue, for Sophie had stopped pumping water and could hear them now.

"Sophie, we were just waiting for you," Agatha called quickly, hands shaking as she unfolded a bamboo curtain in the corner of the den. "Remember the spell only lasts three days—"

"Which gives Sophie only until the Trial begins," the gnome said. "Sophie must retrieve the pen *and* storybook before then." He stoked the fire with his staff, and his den swathed in hot glow. "Remember, the School Master's tower will chase Sophie once she takes the Storian, and the boys will know they've been tricked. Agatha, you must be waiting the instant she returns, ready to make your wish. The pen will write 'The End' in your book, and you'll both be gone before the boys attack."

Agatha's throat bobbed. "And Sophie can revert to a girl as soon as she escapes?"

"The same way she'd un-mogrify—without any residual effects."

"Hear that, Sophie?" Agatha said, hanging her friend's cloak on the curtain hook. "You can revert without any—"

But Sophie was still hunched in the kitchen, staring mournfully at her reflection in a glass flower vase.

Agatha came up behind her. "We have to get you there before curfew."

Sophie took one last long look at her face, then forced a smile and huffed past Agatha towards the curtain, blathering to herself. "Boys played girls all the time in old theater, didn't they? . . . A good old spot of make-believe . . . a *tour de force*, even. . . . *Brava! Brava!*"

Agatha waved at Yuba to give Sophie the potion as quickly as possible.

A few moments later, Sophie stood behind the bamboo curtain, clutching the vial. "Just a spot of make-believe," she cooed, starting to feel rather cocksure about all of this.

"Drink it in sips," Yuba's voice said on the other side. "It will ease the process."

With a deep breath, Sophie yanked the glass cork from the tear-shaped bottle. A blast of sandalwood, musk, and sweat blinded her, and she recorked it, hacking and wheezing. She held the vial far away from her and stared at the violet potion smoking dangerously. This wasn't make-believe.

Silence festered in the gnome's lair.

"I'll go if you can't," Agatha's voice said gently. "Just say the word."

Sophie thought of all the torments her friend had endured for her last year—flying through flames as a dove, surviving for weeks as a cockroach, risking her life in a sewer, facing the murderous School Master. . . .

"I need more than a friend," Agatha had told her prince.

Sophie pictured Agatha wrapped in his arms in that tower, so madly in love . . . Sophie banished the thought, panicked. Doing this would show Agatha just how much she needed her.

Doing this would make Agatha never doubt her again.

In a flash, Sophie ripped out the cork and chugged the potion in one gulp. A bitter, acid taste exploded through her and she grabbed her throat in shock, hearing the vial shatter against the floor. She could hear Agatha scream for her and Yuba holding her back, before their voices slowed to syllabic growls, drowned in her choking gasps. The skin over her face stretched tight, like warm putty, remolding itself over her bones as her hair turned coarser, slurping back into her head.

As the rancid potion flooded her chest, Sophie felt her whole body inflate like a cement-packed balloon, shoulders straining against her girls' uniform, shredding its seams. Her forearms bulged with tight blue veins; her feet swelled and arched, tiny hairs sprouting on her toes; her calves tightened like melons and she careened off-balance, onto her knees. Then came heat, hellish heat, scorching and smoking through every pore, incinerating softness to burn. Every time she thought it was over, the pain spread farther, every part of her demolished and reconstructed until Sophie curled up into a ball on the floor, praying this was all a dream, a dream she'd wake up from in an empty grave as her mother held her and wiped her tears, whispering it was all a mistake.

"Sophie?"

No answer came.

Agatha broke free of Yuba's grip. "Sophie, are you okay?"

When no reply came, Agatha gave the gnome a worried look and hustled for the curtain—

Something stirred behind it and Agatha froze.

Slowly a figure stepped out, hooded in Sophie's navy girls' cloak.

The cloak didn't fit anymore.

Agatha's eyes drifted down strong knees, muscular calves, hairy ankles . . . to two big, unsteady feet.

She inched towards the figure, holding her breath. She could feel Yuba clinging to the tail of her shirt, peeking behind her. Standing on tiptoes, Agatha slowly reached for the hood and pulled it back. She toppled with a gasp, taking the gnome with her. By the time she looked up, Sophie had already grabbed the glass vase off the table and collapsed against the wall, whimpering in fright at her reflection.

She'd morphed into a powerful, square-jawed version of herself, with short, fluffy blond hair, high cheekbones, straight brows, and deep-set emerald eyes. Long limbed but taut with muscle, she looked like an elfin prince, with big pulled-back ears, a sharp regal nose, and a dimpled chin. Her hands gripping the undersized cloak were hardy and big knuckled, her shoulders broad, narrowing down to a trim waist, and her golden-stubbled cheeks streaked with fiery blush.

Sophie wheezed like a punctured balloon. "I'm—I'm a boy—"

Only her voice didn't sound like a boy's at all.

"The spell's one shortcoming. Still have your old sound," Yuba sighed. "Breathe from your belly and speak in low tones, and it'll sound about right." He chewed his lip, studying her. "But strong face . . . solid trunk . . . jolly good work, I'd say. None of those lads will suspect a thing."

But Sophie's eyes stayed on her reflection, doubting the gnome. For as she touched her face and form beneath her cloak, she felt the boy on the outside, hard and toughened, like a rock shell. But inside . . . inside she was the soft, scared girl who didn't want to leave her friend. Look close, and the boys would find her. Look close, and she'd be dead before dawn.

She gazed up at Agatha, who stared speechless at the sculpted, sharp-jawed face in the vase's reflection.

"Even better looking as a boy, I have to say," Agatha marveled finally.

Sophie flung the flowers out of the vase at her and Agatha ducked. Sophie turned away, shaking.

"I don't know how to be a boy," Sophie said, voice high, tears streaking her stubbled cheeks. "I don't know how to walk or act or—"

"You won the challenge for a reason, Sophie," Agatha said behind her. "I know you can do this."

"Not without you there," Sophie rasped.

Agatha touched her friend's back, feeling unfamiliar

muscle beneath her fingers. "I need you to be a boy now," she said, her voice calm. "Just be a boy and get us home."

Sophie nodded in her alien body and tried to stop shivering. Agatha's faith slowly seeped into her, steadying her heart. They'd been through so much, trying to hold on to each other . . . but now only she could get them to The End. Her friend was right. She was a boy now, and she had to act like one.

With a deep breath, she braced herself and turned into the light.

"I need clothes," she said, voice sharp and low.

Agatha stared at the elfin boy's hardened face and, for the first time, saw a stranger.

Agatha smiled her old, crooked smile. "What you need is a name."

Hort hugged his pillow, still in underpants, tossing and turning in his smelly bed while a hulking prince snored like a gorilla across the room.

The last week had been miserable. With the Trial approaching, the teachers had taken over, determined that the boys win and restore the School for Good and Evil. Not that Hort cared about any of it anymore. Tomorrow was the first day of official Trial Tryouts, and he didn't have the faintest chance of making the team. He still hadn't gotten a new uniform, the new princes called him Wart, the big ones kept stealing his lunch pail, and without Dot here, he didn't have anyone to talk to.

Why was he at this horrible place? What had the School

Master possibly seen in him? He was a bad villain and an even worse son.

Hort rubbed his eyes, thinking of his dad's body, lying in the Garden of Good and Evil, with a mile-long line of corpses awaiting burial. Hort couldn't even afford a coffin, so his father lay to waste beneath circling vultures, the Crypt Keeper years away from reaching him.

Hort grated his teeth. If he won the Trial, he'd have the treasure to give his father the most beautiful coffin in the Woods. If he won the Trial, he'd have revenge on the girl who'd broken his heart. No one would ever question him being soft again . . .

A hacking snore snapped his trance and Hort shoved his pillow over his head, tempted to suffocate himself and die. There'd be no treasure. There'd be no revenge. Because that hairy, big-chested prince in the other bed was going to make the Trial team and his scrawny waste of a self wasn't.

If I could just have one friend here, Hort prayed. One friend who could make him feel like more than a loser. Sniffling, he balled his knees and huddled near the window, pulling the covers over his head—

Hort bolted back up, gaping through the window.

There was a body on the boy's shore, the tattered, wet clothes streaked with blood. Moonlight seeped from behind a cloud, trickling onto the boy's pale forearm, and for a second Hort saw his fingers twitch.

Gasping, he flung off his covers and raced out of bed.

Surely the best way to make a new friend was to start by saving his life.

"What's your name?" a familiar voice snarled.

Sophie's eyes flickered open to her hard stomach against the floor, her thick hands cuffed. Her abundance of new muscles ached, and a bleary haze clouded her vision. She remembered little of how she'd arrived—only fleeting images of her refashioning Yuba's ragged tablecloth into a tunic big enough to cover her bulky new frame ("I have shoulders like an elephant," she crabbed), lumbering awkwardly behind Agatha and the gnome onto the girls' shore ("Why is everything so stiff!"), and managing a histrionic good-bye ("Farewell, dignity! Farewell, femininity!") before Yuba knocked her out with a stun spell.

She'd pretended not to have heard the plan when he and Agatha had gone over it earlier—the plan where the gnome and her best friend would float her body through the girls' lake towards the crog-filled red moat, knowing the currents would drag her to the boy's shore. The gnome promised Agatha the crogs wouldn't do more than nip a boy, but both parties thought it wiser if Sophie wasn't awake for the experience, and Sophie certainly saw no reason to argue. She glanced down at the serrated tooth marks and drips of blood across her tunic and was thankful the first few hours of her life as a boy had been mostly spent unconscious.

"What's your *name*?"

Sophie slowly lifted her eyes to Castor, standing in front of the male faculty, all clad in black-and-red robes, glowering down at the new boy in front of them.

Sophie lurched to her knees, heart hammering. The return

of the teachers wasn't her only surprise.

The school around them had been completely cleaned up. Gone was the ape regime, with boys swinging from rafters, graffitied doors, and a putrid stench. Evil's foyer had been repainted blood crimson, the walls decorated with scarlet snake crests. The three staircases in the anteroom had been given fresh coats of black paint, the twisting banisters painted red, like red-bellied snakes. High on the stairs, more than two hundred boys leered down at the new arrival—dozens of familiar Ever- and Neverboys, together with handsome new princes, all showered, scrubbed, and dressed in clean black-and-red leather uniforms.

Sophie's mouth parched. She'd always dreamed that one day she'd be in a castle full of gorgeous, virile boys.

She should have been more specific.

"YOUR NAME, BOY," Castor roared, grabbing her throat with his paw.

Agatha thought it was a terrible idea. To give herself the name of the boy her father had always wanted. The unborn boy her father had loved more than he ever loved her.

But Sophie refused any others.

"Filip," she rasped in his grip.

Saying the name out loud stirred something inside her. She looked up at Castor, hardened.

"Filip of Mount Honora," she repeated, voice deep and strong. "Lost my kingdom to a hideous witch. I come for a chance at the treasure."

Murmurs rippled through the boys eyeing the elfish prince.

"Is that an Ever kingdom?" she heard Manley whisper to Espada.

"An enclave of Maidenvale, I believe," Espada said, mustache twitching.

"And how did you get here, Filip of Mount Honora?" Castor barked, releasing his grip on the boy.

"Through a crack in the shield," said Sophie.

"Impossible," said a voice high above.

Sophie peered up at Aric and his red-hooded henchmen on Malice's banister, looming over all the other boys. They had coiled whips at their belt, red soldier jackets over their shirts, and the rest of the boys looked even more scared of them than before. Clearly the teachers had found their replacement for last year's wolves.

"I'm the only one who can break through Lady Lesso's shield," Aric leered, glaring down at the prisoner. "The hole was sealed *tight* after I let the princes in."

Sophie met his violet eyes. "Perhaps you should have done a better job."

The staircase audience stiffened. Aric and his henchmen looked daggers at this new boy, shorter, skinnier, daring to challenge them in front of the whole school.

But Castor was smirking at the stranger, amused. "Welcome to the School for Boys, Filip."

Sophie exhaled relief. She saw Aric's glare burning colder.

"In three nights' time, we face a buffoonish Trial against girls that threatens to leave us all *slaves*," the dog declared, looking up at the boys on the staircases. "Win, and we rid ourselves of two Readers who've corrupted Good and Evil. Win, and the schools return to *tradition*."

Boys burst into bellowing cheers. Sophie swallowed, trying to look enthused at the prospect of her own execution.

"For the next three days, Trial Tryouts will determine who will fight against the girls," the dog continued. "Top nine boys after Tryouts will make the team. The tenth member of the team will be *chosen* by the first-place leader. Let this encourage you to make friends with the new princes around you and forge Ever-Never alliances."

Boys old and new scanned each other warily, sizing up the competition.

"As a further incentive," Castor said, "the highest-ranked student at the end of each day has the prestigious *honor* of guarding the School Master's tower for the night."

Boys grumbled on the stairs, as if this didn't sound like much of an honor at all. But Sophie was too busy buzzing with joy to notice. The dog had just unwittingly saved her and Agatha's lives. Win enough challenges today and she could steal the Storian tonight! She'd be home with Agatha by dawn!

"No bunks available for Filip, Castor," said Albemarle, the spectacled woodpecker, studying his ledger. "Castle's at full occupancy."

Castor peered down at the new boy. "Put him in with the runt. Whoever's ranked lowest between them at the end of each day gets punished."

Sophie's smile vanished. The boys on the stairs chortled as

Albemarle dutifully pecked into parchment. Aric was grinning at her now.

The runt? Sophie thought, tensing. *Who's the runt?*

Castor unlocked her cuffs. "Go get yourself settled before class, boy. Anyone want to show young Filip here his room?"

Fumbling bootsteps thundered down the stairs, and Sophie squinted up at Hort, crashing through boys like a loon in a new uniform two sizes too big. "That's me! That's me, Filip!" He snatched the schedule from Albemarle's beak and yanked the new boy to his feet—

"I'm Hort and I saved you so now we can be best friends even though you're an Ever," he gushed, shoving him his schedule. "I'll explain classes, rules, and you can sit with me at lunch and—"

But Sophie wasn't listening. All she could see was the top of the parchment page, freshly pecked in stiff, unmistakable letters.

FILIP OF MOUNT HONORA

BOY, 2ND YEAR

ROOMMATE: TEDROS

It answered her question about the runt.

17

Two Schools, Two Missions

"Agatha?"

Agatha stirred, snowflakes melting on her eyelids.

"Agatha, wake up."

Agatha opened her eyes to see Tedros, clean shaven in his blue Everboys' uniform, kneeling in front of her bed, hair dusted with snow. He gently brushed back her hair. "Come with me, Agatha," he whispered. "Before it's too late."

She looked into his eyes as he leaned over her, his soft and innocent eyes, just like they once were . . . his lips coming for hers. . . . She felt his warm breath, then his mouth's sweet taste—

Agatha bolted awake, burning with sweat and clutching her pillow.

For a moment, she wondered why Reaper wasn't curled next to her like he usually was. Then it all came flooding back. Agatha sprang up to the sight of morning snow blowing through the window on a wind, swirling across two empty, canopied beds before settling on hers. Agatha couldn't breathe, staring at Sophie's perfectly made sheets dotted with snow. Her best friend was in the enemy's castle, risking her life for them as a *boy* to get them home, and she'd just dreamed of . . . of . . .

Agatha gasped and scrambled out of bed, quashing the thought. It was nothing. Just a leftover, a residue, a phantom of a wish that would soon be corrected. What mattered now was Sophie.

She swiveled frantically to the clock as the hands ticked past 7:30. Fifteen hours before she'd know if Sophie had survived . . . 54,000 seconds. They'd arranged to each hang a lantern in their window at sunset to communicate with the other: green flamed if they were safe, red flamed if they weren't. Until then, all Agatha had was the image of her best friend, once an aspiring princess, now a hard-edged prince, dragged unconscious into the boys' castle by Hort.

Agatha flung around the room, pulling on pieces of her uniform, still a bit flustered by her dream. Getting rid of Beatrix last night had been easy enough—a few coughs at curfew check, splotches of beetroot on her face, and a reminder of Yuba's contagiousness sent her roommate dragging all her trunks into Reena's quarters. Still, someone would come checking on her and Sophie before long.

Agatha fumbled towards the door, jiggling her feet into her clumps. She had to find Professor Dovey and confess everything. Dovey was a famous fairy godmother, after all; she'd made her name solving people's problems! But where could they possibly meet without being overheard? The Dean's spies followed her teacher incessantly, and all the best spots had proved vulnerable—bathrooms, Supper Hall, Sader's office. If only there was a place where even if the butterflies did find her, they *still* wouldn't hear . . . Agatha waited for her mind to give her a solution, to propel her out the door. . . .

She slumped back down on Beatrix's bed, answerless. Agatha kicked her clump hard against the bedpost in frustration—

The back of her heel struck something wet.

She looked down and saw a tiny puddle under the bedskirt, where the melting snow had pooled behind something. She slid onto her stomach and extended her arm under the mattress, until it touched a thick, rubbery mass. Slowly Agatha pulled out a ball of clothes, which unraveled in her hands, revealing a black-and-red leather uniform, scrunched in with a thin snakeskin cape.

Agatha held up the uniform, speckled with blood and dirt. Why was Beatrix hiding a boys' uniform? Had she found one somewhere in the Blue Forest? Why hadn't she mentioned it? Agatha's fingers drifted to the cape's shimmering, black-hued scales. Last year, she'd learned that snakeskin capes were invariably used for one purpose: invisibility. But why would

Beatrix need to be invisible in her own castle?

A strong whiff of lavender came off the cape and Agatha sneezed. Beatrix may have given up her princess hair, but she'd certainly been borrowing Sophie's perfume.

Agatha shoved the clothes back under the bed, quite sure that Beatrix's oddities had nothing to do with her dilemma. What she and Sophie needed was a teacher's help . . .

A soft sound scratched behind her. Agatha turned to see an envelope peeking under the door. Taking it into her hands, she tore open Professor Dovey's pumpkin-sealed stationery and pulled out a small parchment card.

Sewers. Now.

The one place they couldn't be overheard.

Agatha saw then that she didn't need to confess what she and Sophie had done.

Her fairy godmother already knew.

"Yuba has told us everything," Professor Dovey said, huddling with Lady Lesso in the dark, misty sewer tunnels as water from the lake roared past, muffling her voice. "And we are appalled, revolted, and flabbergasted at the inanity of such a *ridiculous* plan—"

Agatha glued her eyes down, reddening.

"—but also quite impressed."

Agatha gawked up at her smiling teachers. *"What?"*

"Anything that involves tormenting that flower-scented

ninny earns a gold star in my book," Lady Lesso drawled.

Professor Dovey ignored her colleague. "Agatha, you could have sacrificed your friend to stay here forever with your prince. You could have kissed Tedros and protected your own life. Instead, you chose to protect Sophie's from him, even knowing her symptoms," she said. "Only when you write 'The End' with Sophie will Tedros see you meant him no harm. Only then will Tedros realize he should have trusted you."

Agatha felt wisps of her dream returning and squelched them, alarmed.

"The prince's humbling lesson will spread far and wide," Professor Dovey went on, "and Lady Lesso and I believe it a lesson powerful enough to bring Boys and Girls back together. The correct ending to your story, after all. And all we need is for Sophie to bring back that pen so you two can write it."

Agatha quickly nodded relief—only to remember a bigger problem. "But how will we cover for her!"

"Yuba's too good a teacher to leave that in doubt," Professor Dovey said, glancing back down the tunnel. "Seeing your places are both guaranteed for the Trial team, he sent word to the Dean as Helga, asking to personally train you in the Blue Forest for the remaining three days, assuring her it will increase your chances of victory over the boys."

Agatha's eyes bulged. "And?"

"She's rather surprisingly agreed, provided you're both ready to compete on Trial eve. She thinks you're both with Helga as of this morning."

"That solves everything!" Agatha gushed with relief.

"Not quite," Lady Lesso snapped, rushing sewer water flecking her gown. "There still remains the question of where Sophie's symptoms have gone."

"She said they were conjured by someone else—" Agatha defended.

"Indeed," said Lady Lesso. "But a witch's symptoms cannot be conjured, unless by magic far more formidable than ours. So there're two possibilities. First, that Sophie is *lying* about forgiving your wish for Tedros, and you've, in fact, sent a deadly witch to your prince."

"No," Agatha said forcefully. "Sophie's Good now. I know it."

"Are you sure she's Good, Agatha?" said Professor Dovey, exchanging looks with her colleague. "This is absolutely crucial."

"After what she just did to get me home?" Agatha shot back. "100% sure."

"Then the symptoms were surely conjured by a powerful force," said Professor Dovey, "a force that happened to be in each and every place that Sophie's symptoms appeared. A force Lady Lesso and I have been trying to *warn* you of since your arrival."

Agatha heard the answer in her scolding tone. "Dean *Sader*?" she blurted. "It can't be! She wants us friends—"

"Evelyn is a dangerous woman, Agatha," said Lady Lesso, tensing with that strange fear Agatha had seen before. "If she conjured Sophie's symptoms, there's no reason to believe she wants you and Sophie friends at all."

Agatha gaped at her. "But she'd never want me to think Sophie a *witch*—"

"You know *nothing* of Evelyn Sader and what she is capable of," Lady Lesso retorted, eyes suddenly wet.

"What? How would you—"

"Because Clarissa and I watched Evelyn Sader *evicted* from this school ten years ago!" spat Lady Lesso, red faced. "The same school that is now on her *side*."

Agatha stared at her, stunned.

"Who's there?" a voice echoed behind them. They twirled to see a shadow down the tunnel, creeping through the fog.

Professor Dovey stiffened and grabbed Agatha's shoulders. "Once you are banished, the school never lets you return! But your and Sophie's fairy tale somehow let her back *in*, Agatha. She's part of your story now, just like the School Master was a year ago. And if she conjured Sophie's symptoms, surely she too has an ending in mind."

Agatha shook her head. "But Sophie's getting the Storian—"

"You don't think Evelyn has *thought of that*?" Lady Lesso hissed. "Evelyn's always one step ahead, Agatha! For the next three days, she thinks you are in the Blue Forest. This is your chance to follow her undetected until Sophie returns. You must find out *why* Evelyn conjured Sophie's symptoms! You must succeed where Clarissa and I have failed. Spend your time wisely, understand? It is the only way to ensure you and Sophie escape alive! Now go!"

Agatha could barely speak. "I don't—I don't understand—"

Dovey and Lesso were already retreating. "We cannot meet again," Dovey ordered.

"I said who's there!" the voice bellowed.

Agatha whirled to the shadow breaking through fog. She spun back—"How do I—"

But Dovey and Lesso were gone.

Seconds later, Pollux poked through to a deserted sewer bank and huffed back upstairs, forgetting to check the sewer itself, where a terrified girl clung to the wall, neck deep in churning waters, wishing she could talk to her best friend.

"Never thought I'd have a prince as a best friend," Hort motor-mouthed, hustling through Evil's sewers.

"Where are we going? Said you were taking me to my room," Sophie said, steeling the nerves out of her voice as it echoed over the red mud roiling through the dank tunnels. She plodded behind him on the thin path in her sleeveless black-and-red leather uniform, bumping her bulky shoulders into the wall, still unused to all the extra weight. In the shiny mud, she caught a glimpse of her fluffy blond hair, chiseled jaw, and veiny biceps, and quickly averted her eyes.

"Tried to make 'em bunk us together, but they already put a prince from Ginnyvale in my room," Hort said, peeping back at the new boy. "School's strict now that the teachers are back. If you ask me, Aric and his henchmen make those old wolves look cuddly. But don't worry. I'll keep my best friend outta trouble."

Sophie frowned. How was it that even as a boy, she couldn't

escape this rodent? She saw the sewer midpoint in the distance, the division between sludge and lake sealed by giant rocks. "But I still don't understand. Why are we down her—"

"*Where* is it!" Manley's voice boomed ahead, over the churning red slime.

"I showed you where I buried it," Tedros' voice insisted—

"And it's not *there*. As long as you keep lying, there'll continue to be no food."

"It's those two girls! They're hiding in the castle!"

"Think we wouldn't know if a girl was in our castle?" Manley's voice sneered. "That pen is still *somewhere* in the School Master's tower, or the tower would have *moved* to follow it. Now tell me where you hid it, or I'll melt your father's sword and gild the toilets with it—"

"I told you! It was buried under the table!"

Sophie's heart stopped. *The Storian . . . missing?* How could she and Agatha write 'The End' now?

Suddenly, placing first in the day's challenges was even more crucial, she thought, panicked. If the pen was hidden in that tower, she'd need time to find it.

Stomach churning, she followed behind Hort, skirting the sewer wall as it turned to the rusted grating of a pitch-dark dungeon cell. In the corner, Manley's bald head and bulbous shadow obscured the figure beneath him.

"Please, professor, you have to let me into the Trial," Tedros' voice begged. "I'm the only one who can beat those girls!"

"You'll die of starvation long before the Trial if we don't find that pen," Manley said, turning for the cell door.

He saw the new boy gaping at him through the grating. "Boys don't like a liar, Filip. Tedros promises the boys he'll kiss Agatha. Promises he'll fix the schools to Good and Evil. And what do they get instead? A chance at *slavery*. Ain't it a wonder all the boys hate him now," Manley sneered, pulling the door open. He shoved the new boy into the cell as he left. "Whole school's on your side today, Filip. Teach this puffed-up cockerel a lesson."

Sophie swiveled. "W-w-wait—"

Hort slammed the cell door. "See you in class, Filip!"

"Hort! This can't be my *room*!" Sophie cried, gripping the grates.

But the weasel was already charging after Manley, chattering with excitement. "He'll beat Tedros so bad today, professor. You'll see. . . ."

Sophie slowly turned to the rotted dungeon lit by a single candle. A chilling collection of torture instruments hung on the walls in steel cages, over two metal bed frames without mattresses or pillows. She couldn't breathe, thinking of what happened here a year ago with the Beast. This place made her Evil. This place made her lose control. Sophie turned away, panicked—

Two bloodshot eyes glowed from the corner.

Sophie staggered back.

"Is it true?" said Tedros' voice out of darkness.

"What is?" Sophie breathed, keeping her tone low.

"The worst of us in Trial Tryouts gets punished each night."

"That's what the dog said."

Slowly Tedros rose from shadows. He was at least twenty pounds thinner, his boys' uniform crusted with dirt, his blue eyes inflamed.

"Then we ain't gonna be *friends*, are we?"

Sophie stepped back from the prince skulking towards her, teeth bared.

"I'm making that Trial. You hear me, boy?" he sneered, spit flying. "Those two girls took everything I have left in this world. My friends, my reputation, my honor—" He grabbed the new boy by the throat and jammed him against the grating. "I'm not going to let you or anyone else take my chance at fighting them."

Choking in his grip, Sophie held up her hands in surrender. She had to get out of here! She had to get out of this body! She couldn't last as a boy—

Suddenly a shot of unfamiliar anger tore through her blood, searing away the fear. Her mind went strangely clear, zeroing in like crosshairs on the boy pinning her . . . the boy who'd taken her princess dreams . . . the boy who'd almost taken her only friend . . . the boy now trying to take her and her friend's lives. Alien strength blasted through her new muscles with hormonal rage, and before she knew it, she'd shoved the prince back with a roar.

"Quite the bully, aren't you, for someone who lost his princess to a *girl*," she snarled, startled by the darkness in her voice.

Tedros loosened his grip, just as stunned, and watched his new cell mate seize him by the collar. "I see why she chose Sophie," the stranger lashed at him. "Sophie gives her friendship, loyalty, sacrifice, love. All the powers of Good. What do you have to give her? You're weak, empty, callow, and *boring*. All you have is your pretty face." The new boy pulled the prince closer and their noses touched. "And now I see what's under it."

Tedros turned beet red. "I see an overgrown elf with puffy hair who knows nothing about me—"

"You know what I see?" The stranger's emerald eyes cut into his. *"Nothing."*

The fight seeped out of Tedros' face. For a moment, he looked like a little boy.

"W-w-who are you?" he stammered.

"Name's Filip to you," said Sophie, ice-cold, and let go of him.

Tedros turned away, catching his breath. Sophie could see his rattled face in the metal bed's reflection and held in a grin.

Suddenly she liked being a boy.

Keys jangled outside. The two boys turned to see Aric's hooded henchman pull open the cell door.

"Time for class," he growled.

Two hundred boys competing for the day's first rank. Two hundred boys standing between her and the Storian. Sophie galumphed awkwardly to catch up with the herd of fellow uniformed boys, driving towards Evil's classrooms. The odds weren't good.

She wiped sweat from her armpits, irritated by how much her new body perspired. If she'd known boys were insufferably hot *all the time*, she'd have packed a fan or jug of cold water. Stomach rumbling, she distracted herself with thoughts of lunch. With the size of these boys, they must have a feast planned: roast turkey legs, streaky bacon, succulent ham, rare-cooked steak. . . . She could taste the juicy flank already, saliva foaming—

Sophie paled, smearing away drool. Since when did she think about meat! Since when did she think about *food*! She stumbled and knocked into Ravan. "Walking. It ain't *hard*," he scowled, shoving past her.

Sophie kept her eyes down, her fluffy hair flopping over them. Nothing in her body seemed to bend . . . like she was a wooden puppet, strings pulled too tight. She peeked ahead at Aric, chest puffed, swaggering like a stallion, and tried to imitate him as best she could.

Sophie glanced back at Tedros lagging behind the mob, all alone and friendless. Manley said the boys had turned on him for risking their freedom in the Trial's terms . . . but Sophie wondered if there was more to it. Boys loved to tear down the things they built up, whether a sand castle or a prince. And for most of the past two years, Tedros had been the rich, popular, preposterously handsome Ever captain who all the boys wanted to be. Now that Manley was punishing him for the missing Storian, they gleefully indulged in his fall, like a weakened lion left to hyenas. Sophie watched him shivering slightly in the cold breeze from the balcony, his thinner frame suffering from withheld meals. She didn't spare even a grain of pity for him.

"Filip! Filip, you forgot your schedule!" Hort shoved in, foisting crumpled parchment on her. "You're with me all day—"

Sophie blew her hair out of her eyes and peered down.

FILIP OF MOUNT HONORA

BOY, 2ND YEAR

ROOMMATE: TEDROS

SESSION	FACULTY
1: TRIAL TRYOUTS: WEAPONS FOR BOYS	Prof. Rumi Espada
2: TRIAL TRYOUTS: SURVIVAL OF THE FITTEST	Castor
3: TRIAL TRYOUTS: DEFENSE AGAINST GIRLS	Prof. Bilious Manley
4: LUNCH	
5: TRIAL TRYOUTS: FRATERNITY & TEAMWORK	Prof. Aleksander Lukas
6: TRIAL TRYOUTS: FOREST FITNESS (GROUP #2)	Mohsin the Giant

"They've been prepping the rest of us for Tryouts for weeks with workouts and lectures and reading, so you'll need a little luck," Hort said, with a sly wink. "Especially with the way you bumble around. It's like you've spent your whole life on giant heels or something."

Sophie broke into a dripping sweat. She still couldn't walk like a boy, and now she'd have to beat a school of them in warrior competition?

Ten minutes later, Professor Espada stood in Evil Hall with his class of forty boys, a long table in front of him, covered with a dark sheet.

"We have informed Dean Sader in the girls' school that the rules of the Trial by Tale will follow tradition," he said, his slicked hair as black as his curled mustache. His thin, self-righteous smile reminded Sophie of the youngest Elder—the one who'd streaked her with her own blood.

"Ten girls and ten boys will enter the Blue Forest at sundown. The teams must fend off not only each other, but the teachers' traps as well. Whichever side has the most players still in the Forest at sunrise will be declared the winner. If the boys win, Sophie and Agatha will be turned over for execution and the schools will remand to Good and Evil. If the girls win, we will surrender our castle to them and become their slaves."

As boys murmured to each other, Sophie felt her broad back slopped with sweat now.

"As is customary, each contestant will be given a flag of surrender," Professor Espada continued. "If you find yourself in mortal danger, drop it to the ground, and you will be rescued unharmed from the Blue Forest. To protect yourselves, each competitor is allowed one weapon for the Trial. Today's challenge will test the one most often used . . ."

He pulled the sheet off a table, revealing a row of different-sized swords and daggers, all of which looked much sharper than the usual training blades.

"In past years, swords were dulled for Trial competition. Given the stakes in this year's Trial, we see no reason to offer the courtesy," Espada said, beady eyes glinting. "A sword rewards quickness and strength, so you must use both to be effective. Aim your sword at a girl's heart, and she will drop her flag of surrender immediately."

He held up two kerchiefs, one red, one white. "Now let's see which of you drops *yours*."

Sophie tensed. She'd never held a sword in her life.

Professor Espada called forth pairs of boys, who picked their blades and faced off until one surrendered. With Ever-boys and the new princes well trained in deft swordplay and the Neverboys well trained in poor sportsmanship, the duels were feisty affairs: Chaddick over Hort with a sword tip to the throat, Ravan over an Avonlea prince with a knee to the groin, Aric over Vex with a simple glare. . . .

"Tedros and Filip. You're next," Espada declared.

Sophie slowly looked up at Tedros glowering at her, eyes blazing. He hadn't forgotten what she'd said to him in the dungeon.

"FIL-IP, FIL-IP, FIL-IP," chanted the boys raucously, as Espada handed the two boys their flags. "Pick your weapons."

Sophie's eyes blurred with sweat; her big hands tremored as she took a long, thin slab of metal off the table—

Hort elbowed her. "That's the sharpener, you idiot!"

Sophie grabbed the short blade next to it and whirled to Tedros, but the prince had seen the mistake. Tedros held up his enormous sword, teeth gnashed, nostrils flaring.

"Ready . . . and . . . go!" Espada barked—

"AAAAHHHHH!" Tedros bellowed, charging for Filip like a bull.

Sophie couldn't maneuver her boy body, let alone a sword, and capsized back against the wall, fumbling for her flag. Her long, thick fingers jammed into her pocket and she looked up frantically, Tedros thundering towards her, blade raised. With a cry, Sophie yanked her kerchief free to drop it—

Tedros tripped and landed splat at her feet.

Sophie gaped down at him, then lifted her eyes to Hort grinning proudly, boot in Tedros' path.

Tedros tried to grab his sword, but Chaddick kicked it away. The prince staggered up and Ravan shot a shock spell at him, knocking him down. As Tedros yelped in pain, Sophie saw Hort waving and pointing at Tedros' kerchief. Sophie calmly kneeled, pulled it out of the prince's pocket, and dropped it to the floor.

"Filip wins!" Espada decreed, and the boys erupted in roars as Sophie took princely bows.

"But—but that's unfair—" Tedros cried—

"A clever boy makes allies," Espada said, smirking back.

A "20" burst in black, poo-smelling smoke over Tedros' head. Sophie looked up at the crowning gold "1" over hers and beamed.

By the time the sun set, classes complete on the first day, Sophie swaggered back to the Doom Room, the top-ranked boy in the school. She hadn't won a single challenge on merit, but the entire school had conspired to help Filip beat Tedros again and again—tainting the prince's meerworms in Survival, scaring away his two Wish Fish in Defense Against Girls, refusing to partner with him in Fraternity, and sneaking a spider into his pants before the Forest Fitness test.

It was certainly odd that *all* the boys joined in to boost her rank, Sophie thought—even the new princes—as if no one wanted the top rank for themselves. But she wasn't about to look a gift horse in the mouth. As for the teachers, they turned blind eyes like Espada, intent on teaching Tedros a lesson for stealing the Storian in the first place. Indeed, Manley was so delighted that he publicly bestowed Filip with a key to the dungeon room, so he could come and go as he pleased—a privilege denied to the "runt."

Sophie unlocked the cell and entered, ruddy and freshly showered, belly full from a bean stew and stuffed goose supper, and eager to get to the School Master's tower for duty. *If only Agatha could see me now,* she grinned, for she'd not only eaten *beans*, of all things, but she'd passed her mission with flying colors. She'd have the whole night to find the Storian. Tedros would soon face punishment. And tomorrow, she and her best friend would be back home, safe from a deadly Trial. . . .

She kicked the cell door shut, humming a tune. Being Filip wasn't so bad after all. The walk was settling in, the voice growing more natural, the extra weight suddenly feeling strong and inspiring. . . . She was even getting used to her new face, Sophie thought, eyeing her square jaw, regal nose, and soft, full lips in a gleaming spear on the torture rack. Agatha was right. She was handsome, wasn't she. . . .

"You cheated."

Sophie turned to Tedros, sitting alone in the dank, dirty corner.

"I don't care that I have to be punished or that I can't eat supper or that everyone hates me," the prince said, staring at her. "I care that you cheated."

Sophie pulled the door open to leave. "A bit busy for chit-chat, unfortunately—"

"You're no better than Agatha."

Sophie stopped cold.

"I loved her so much," he mumbled behind her, almost to himself. "I tried to make her wish come true. I tried to fix the story like a prince is supposed to. Kill the witch, kiss his princess. That's how fairy tales work. That's what she asked for." His voice broke. "But I would have let Sophie live if it meant having Agatha forever. I would have kissed her right there and we would have had The End. But then she cheated. Agatha cheated. She had Sophie under the table the whole time . . . and she *lied* to me."

Sophie turned to see Tedros hunched over, head buried between his knees.

"How could anyone be so Evil?" he rasped.

Watching him, Sophie's face slowly softened.

A shadow washed over the prince.

Tedros lifted his eyes to Aric, smirking in the open doorway.

"Special occasion," the captain said, cracking his knuckles. "Think I'll do the punishing myself."

Tedros turned away, like a dog offering his neck.

Aric's eyes flicked to Filip. "Get *out*."

Sophie's heart chilled as she backed through the grated door and Aric slammed it in her face. She saw the captain creep towards the prince before she hurried away, leaving Tedros to his tormentor, trying desperately to convince herself that he deserved it, he deserved it, he deserved it.

Far across the bay, in a dark room window, Agatha looked out at the School for Boys, her blue bodice splotched with blood, her arms and legs scraped and bruised.

Hurry, Sophie, Agatha prayed.

For if what she'd learned today about the Dean was true, they were already out of time.

18

Sader's Secret History

Eight hours earlier, three witches had perched on Agatha's bed. "Tell us everything Dovey and Lesso said," ordered Dot.

"In detail," said Hester.

"In as few words as possible," said Anadil, nodding at her three black rats guarding the gap under the door with gnashed teeth and ready claws. "They can only kill so many butterflies before one gets through."

Agatha stared back at them, head swimming. After her secret meeting with Professor Dovey and Lady Lesso, she waited until all the girls were in their first sessions. Then she delivered identical notes to the witches' room and hid in her own's closet, avoiding patrol butterflies zooming through and Beatrix swinging in and out between classes, until the notes were opened and obeyed. Now Agatha told the witches what the teachers had said in the sewers, her heart thumping faster and faster, reliving every word—

"They *know* the Dean?" Dot blurted finally, spewing a mouthful of artichoke.

Hester scrunched her fists. "I knew Dovey and Lesso were acting funny that first month of school. Lesso looks like a wounded puppy every time the Dean's around."

Agatha couldn't think of a better description herself. Something about Evelyn Sader managed to turn the most terrifying teacher in school . . . human.

"And remember when you said the Dean punished Dovey for questioning her?" Hester added. "Sounded like she was settling an old score."

"Lesso said Evelyn Sader was evicted ten years ago," Agatha went on. "And that if you're evicted, you can't ever come back."

"That's because only the School Master can admit students or teachers to the School for Good and Evil," said Hester. "If he banished her, it's irrevocable—unless he let her back in himself. And that would be difficult, considering he's *dead*."

"If a boy broke the princes through the shield, why couldn't Evelyn break through too?" Agatha countered.

"Even if she did, the castle would have evicted her the moment she stepped inside," said Anadil. "Besides, I still find it hard to believe a boy cracked that shield open. Someone surely helped him who knew Lady Lesso's spells."

"But if Evelyn Sader isn't allowed in the castle, how is she *here*?" Agatha asked, still baffled.

"The question isn't how—it's *why*. Remember what Dovey and Lesso told you. She's part of your fairy tale somehow," said Hester. "So what do we know for sure about Evelyn Sader? First, she's Professor Sader's sister. Second, she hears things. Third, your and Sophie's kiss let her back in this school. Somewhere in there is the answer to why she's in *your* story."

Agatha saw Dot thinking hard, nibbling on an artichoke leaf. "Dot?"

"When I wrote Daddy last year about History of Villains and how boring Professor Sader was, I remember him writing back that he thought 'she' was long gone," said Dot. "Been ages since Daddy was at school, so I figured he got mixed up. But now I wonder . . ." She turned to the girls. "Do you think Evelyn used to be a *teacher* here?"

Hester was already ripping a textbook out of her bag. "Chapter 28 on Notable Seers in our history book—it mentions August Sader and his family. I remember thinking it odd a teacher wrote about his own relatives. . . ."

"Only *you* would be looking at chapters that weren't assigned," Anadil murmured.

"Because I don't want to end up in an oven like my mother or impaled in a barrel like yours!" Hester fired back, flipping pages until she finally reached the one she wanted—

"Of course. '*Chapter 28: Notable* Female *Seers*,'" Hester growled, and snapped the cover shut on *A Student's Revised*

History of the Woods. "Yuba was right about her tampering with the books." She peered up at Agatha. "Best way to avoid someone finding out your history is to rewrite it, don't you think?"

"Here's what I don't get," Anadil proffered. "Dovey and Lesso say *she* caused Sophie's witch symptoms?"

"They said either it's her or Sophie, and we know it's not Sophie," Agatha answered, equally puzzled. "But why would the Dean want me to think my friend was a witch?"

"Unless she wanted you to go to Tedros all along," mulled Hester, gnawing on her lip.

Even the rats went quiet.

Hester turned to Agatha. "Look, we're stuck in Trial Tryouts for the next three days. But the teachers are right. You have to follow Sader and find out what she's up to. Let's reconvene Book Club each night to go over what you've found."

"But how?" Agatha pressed. "How can I possibly follow the Dean without being . . ." Her voice suddenly petered away, her gaze drifting towards Beatrix's bed.

"What is it?" Hester said.

Screeching hisses and crackles erupted at the door, and all the girls swiveled to see rats gobbling up butterflies trying to slip into the room. "Hurry," Anadil snapped at the witches, "the Dean will know something's up!"

"Sorry we can't help you," Hester groused to Agatha, shoving Dot towards the door—

"You can help me use this," Agatha's voice said behind them.

The witches turned to see Agatha holding up a shimmering snakeskin cape.

"Seems like Beatrix has been keeping secrets," Agatha said, brows raised.

Hester's mouth curled into a wide grin.

Though the butterflies heard four people leaving the room, witnesses in the hall would later insist to Pollux they'd only seen three.

With the Dean teaching her version of History in Good Hall most of the day, Agatha detoured to the Library of Virtue, hoping to find out more about the history of Evelyn Sader.

Under her new invisible cape, still reeking of lavender perfume, Agatha slipped through Hansel's Haven—past Professor Sheek's class, undergoing a Sword Shrinking tryout to magically whittle down a boy's blade; past Professor Anemone, barking at Yara for traipsing in late to a Spell Sparring tryout; and past Professor Dovey, who seemed to glance in her direction while forcing girls in a Boy Diplomacy tryout to talk down blood-hungry phantoms with compassion and common sense.

Agatha hustled up the back stairs to the library's entrance, where the sundial clock glittered high over the two stories of fiery red and gold bookshelves in the early afternoon light. She rushed past the librarian's desk—and froze.

For the first time in her two years here, the tortoise was awake. Stooped over his giant library log, the reptile slowly spooned a runny salad of tomatoes and cucumbers into its mouth with the feathered end of his pen, spilling a fair bit into its lap. Between old age, arthritic limbs, and a tortoise's nature not to hurry, each bite took as long as a normal three-course dinner. Impatient, Agatha tiptoed past him, careful to time her steps with the tortoise's chomps, and hurried to the back of the first floor, where the history books were kept.

There had to be something here, Agatha thought as she scanned the shelves, a few butterflies circling overhead. Something about the school's history that Evelyn hadn't doctored or expunged. But as she read the books' spines, Agatha's stomach sank:

The History of Princely Failures
Rapunzel: The Real Giant Killer?
A Chronicle of Fraudulent Prince Rescues
The Fragile Male: The Decline of a Redundant Species
The Hidden History of Snow White's Divorce

Agatha slumped to the floor. The Dean had covered her tracks even better than she thought.

Agatha looked up, discouraged, and saw the tortoise glaring right where she was sitting. Agatha didn't budge, knowing it couldn't possibly see her under her cape—and yet its shiny black eyes stayed fixed on her very spot, blinking heavy lids, the reptile's body motionless. Still watching her, the tortoise slowly reached back with stubby arms and pulled off its mottled shell. From inside its body, it silently drew out a single thick book and slipped it onto the edge of the desk. Then it replaced its shell and resumed chewing, eyes on the remaining heap of his lunch.

Agatha gaped at the book, haloed by the sun streaming through the second-story windows.

Giggles echoed outside, along with nearing footsteps. Instantly Agatha flung up and raced towards the desk, scooping the book under her cape just as Arachne and Mona entered, too immersed in gossiping to notice the breeze that ruffled their hair.

Under her invisible snakeskin, Agatha sprinted upstairs to Honor's rooftop and closed the frosted door behind her. Braving the icy winds, she wove through Guinevere's hedges, peppered with idle doves, to find the last one, the pond scene near the balcony, secluded behind a wall of purple thorns. She sat on its shores and pulled the book from under her cape.

A Student's History of the Woods

AUGUST A. SADER

Agatha let out a rush of air and gripped her old history textbook to her chest. Leave it to a librarian to find the book she needed, she thought, silently thanking the tortoise. What did he want her to find in its pages? Agatha caressed the book's silver, silk-clothed cover, embossed with the glowing Storian clutched between black and white swans.

She thumbed open the thick textbook to see no words, but a familiar rainbow of raised dots in neat rows, small as pinheads. Though Professor Sader was blind and couldn't write history, he had *seen* it and found a way for his students to do the same. As Agatha ran her fingers across the rows of dots, ghostly scenes magically unfolded atop the book page in three dimensions, playing out to Sader's narration—the same scenes the Dean had revised in her new edition, so girls no longer knew what was true and what wasn't.

Agatha swept her fingers across pages, fast-forwarding scenes until she found the page she wanted:

"Chapter 28: Notable Seers," boomed Professor Sader's warm, deep voice.

A small, silent scene fogged into view atop the book page—a vision of three old men, beards to the floor, standing in the School Master's tower with hands united. Agatha hunched over to watch the scene as Sader's disembodied voice continued:

"As we learned in Chapter 1, with the Three Seers of the Endless Woods, seers commonly share three traits: they live double the life span of ordinary humans; they age ten years as punishment if they answer a question about the future; and their bodies can host spirits, with deadly effect. . . ."

Agatha's hands scanned through the chapter, past scene after scene, until her fingers stopped suddenly in the middle of the page, finding a few rows of polished dots that looked newer and shinier than the rest.

Curious, she touched the first new dot.

Instantly a man's handsome face sprung into the mist—a face Agatha recognized immediately, with silvery-gray hair and hazel eyes. Her throat tightened as she gazed at her old history professor from the School for Good, blinking back at her in phantom blue glow. Agatha swallowed and forced her fingers to keep moving. . . .

"The Saders are the longest and most successful line of seers. The most recently deceased member of the Sader family is the youngest son, August, who perished during The Tale of Sophie and Agatha.

"After the Great War between the two School Master brothers of Good and Evil, August Sader had long believed the Good brother created a spell against his twin before he died—a way to prove the balance of Good and Evil still intact—and hidden the spell in the uniform crests of the students. When the Evil brother destroyed this balance by killing a student under his protection, the spell unlocked, bringing the Good brother's ghost back to life. As a seer, Sader sacrificed his body to the ghost, allowing the Good brother to slay his Evil twin and restore the Woods to balance."

Agatha's hand stilled on the page, her heart sinking. That's why the dots were new. *He'd added his own death before it happened.* She watched Sader's ghostly face, frozen atop the book, smiling softly at her, the way he had when she first entered the School for Good. Perhaps he'd foreseen even before she'd arrived that he'd die for her. And still he'd smiled at her. Still he'd helped her.

Agatha could feel her chin quivering. She'd never regretted not having a father. She'd never let the thought in . . . not until this fleeting moment, when she realized what it must mean to have one.

A tear splashed through the misty vision, dissipating her dead professor's face.

Agatha wiped her eyes and forced her hand to keep moving along the rest of the new dots.

"In addition, August Sader is believed responsible for the arrival of unenchanted Readers into the Endless Woods. After the Evil School Master killed his Good brother in order to control the Storian, the magic pen instead responded by making Good win in every new story—an eternal reminder that Evil was incapable of true love. To find a weapon even stronger than love, the Evil School Master sought out every seer in the Woods until he found August Sader, who, in exchange for a faculty position at the School for Good and Evil, revealed that the weapon the School Master sought would come from beyond the Woods. Sader's prediction would come to be known as the Reader Prophecy, the most famous prophecy to emerge from the all-male Sader lineage of seers."

Agatha bolted straight. *A lineage of* boys? She reread the line, agape. *How could August Sader have a sister in a lineage of boys?*

She flipped pages anxiously, the dots no longer new, scanning dense Sader family trees and visions of Professor Sader's brothers and nephews . . . until she reached a blank page, signaling the end of the chapter and the end of the trail.

Apparently Sader didn't think his sister was worthy of mention, Agatha thought, grimacing. Frustrated, she was about to fling the book into the pond—when she suddenly noticed a row of teensy, shiny new dots, footnoted at the bottom of the blank page.

Squinting closer, her nose practically to the book, she

touched the first dot, and a small two-dimensional portrait melted into yellowing mist, small as a postage stamp. A ravishing, gap-toothed woman smiled through the portrait frame, with flowing chestnut hair, bee-stung lips, and forest-green eyes.

Agatha's pulse quickened and her fingers raced on.

"There is one more member of the Sader family that deserves mention. As a condition to the School Master for answering his question, August Sader asked that he teach history at the School for Good—and that his half sister, Evelyn, teach history at the School for Evil. However, as the illegitimate daughter of Constantin Sader, Evelyn Sader is not considered part of the Sader line, nor possessed seer powers.

"Evelyn Sader taught for two months before she was evicted from the school forever by the School Master for crimes against students.

"August Sader took over teaching her classes in the School for Evil until his death."

The Dean's portrait hovered in mist as Agatha's hand shook on the last dot of the page, her old professor's words ringing in her ears.

Crimes against students.

Crimes so terrible, so unforgivable that an Evil School Master had banished a teacher from *his own side.*

Agatha's heart stopped.

What had Evelyn Sader done?

Suddenly the Dean's phantom portrait glowed hot red over the book and her face spun sharply to Agatha—

"UNAUTHORIZED BOOK!" she hissed. "THIS BOOK IS UNAUTHORIZED—"

Instantly the page turned razor sharp and flew shrieking out of the book, slicing Agatha's chest with a vicious paper cut. Terrified, Agatha tried to make her finger glow, but more screeching pages sharpened and tore from the book, cutting her from every direction. Agatha backed against a hedge, batting pages away, trying to focus on her fingerglow, but there were dozens of pages now, slicing at her arms, belly, legs, until her whole body was on fire. Gasping, she tried to scream for help, only to see hundreds of pages rip from the book and fly at her face, turning knife-edged for the kill. With a cry, Agatha finally felt her finger burn gold and stabbed it at the pages—

A thousand white pages turned to white daisies in midair and fluttered down into the pond.

Panting, Agatha stared at the floating flowers, flecked with her own blood.

A booming crash exploded from the Library of Virtue below, sending the doves in the hedges scattering. Agatha's eyes flared wide. She swept on her invisible cape and staggered out the frosted door, stumbling down the stairs, and lurched into the library . . .

But its keeper was gone from the desk, his feathered pen left behind with a half-eaten lunch dripping off his log. In the center of the room, Mona and Arachne sat white-faced at a library table, parchment and books strewn in front of them, gaping up at the second-floor window.

Agatha slowly tracked their eyes to the giant smashed hole

in the glass . . . shaped like a tortoise.

Soft scratching sounds etched behind her, and Agatha turned to see the feathered pen magically writing in the log, dragging and sputtering with each stroke as if in pain, before collapsing to the desk, dead still.

Heart skittering, Agatha stepped closer, until she could read the tortoise's last words.

BEWARE THE TRIAL

Hurry, Sophie, Agatha prayed.

Sitting in her window, she looked out at the School for Boys as the sun set, her blue bodice splotched with blood, her arms and legs scraped and bruised. Next to her, a green flame glowed inside a circular lantern she'd made out of parchment.

Sophie would flash her lantern back any minute now, green if she was safe too, red if she wasn't.

Agatha watched the clock: 7:15 . . . 7:30 . . . But still no glow came from the Boys' school.

Agatha could still feel her heart beating, the tortoise's warning tattooed in her skull.

Two days until the Trial.

Two days.

She and Sophie had to get out of this school *now.*

Her eyes darted back to the clock . . . 7:45 . . . 7:50 . . .

No light from the boys' castle.

. . . 7:55 . . .

Sophie was alone in there with her prince. . . .

Her Evil prince . . .

Her Evil prince who she dream-kissed this morning, not looking Evil at all . . .

Shut up, Agatha berated herself, whipping back to the clock.

. . . 8:00 now . . .

She heard swelling buzz in the halls, girls returning from supper. . . .

Agatha broke into a sweat. Wherever Sophie was, she was in trouble! She lunged towards the door, panting with pain—she had to rescue her friend!—

Agatha froze. Slowly she turned back to the window, eyes wide.

High in the sky, across the bay, a green flare flashed behind thin clouds. Agatha stepped closer, squinting as the mist broke apart. The green glow wasn't coming from a balcony or a boy's castle spire.

It was coming from the School Master's tower.

Agatha's breath left her. She waved her hand in front of her lantern, flickering the flame.

Far away, Sophie did the same.

Agatha's eyes popped, relief crashing over her. Sophie was already in the tower! She'd free the Storian any minute!

Breathless, Agatha slung on her cape and raced out of the room, leaving symptoms, dream kisses, and Evelyn Sader behind. As she rushed down steps, she could feel the pen getting closer, "The End" spilling from its nib. She'd hover by the shore for Sophie's return, a wish waiting on the tips of their tongues. The tower would chase her, the boys mobbing behind for war, only to see two girls splinter to light and vanish hand in hand . . . a Trial thwarted, a happy ending restored, two friends home, stronger than before . . .

But the night came and went in gusts of cold, and Sophie didn't come back.

19

Two Days Left

The boys in line for breakfast gave Filip a wide berth when he shoved by, covered in dust and ash, eyes bloodshot and bruised, smelling like a barn in summer.

As the enchanted pots in Evil's Supper Hall slopped scrambled eggs and a mountain of bacon into her rusty pail, Sophie blinked back tears, reminding herself that boys don't cry. She should be home by now—back in her own skin, Agatha at her side, The End written and sealed. And yet here she was, with her elephant shoulders, hairy legs, and hormonal rages, letting pots heap greasy bacon that the boy hijacking her body couldn't wait to eat.

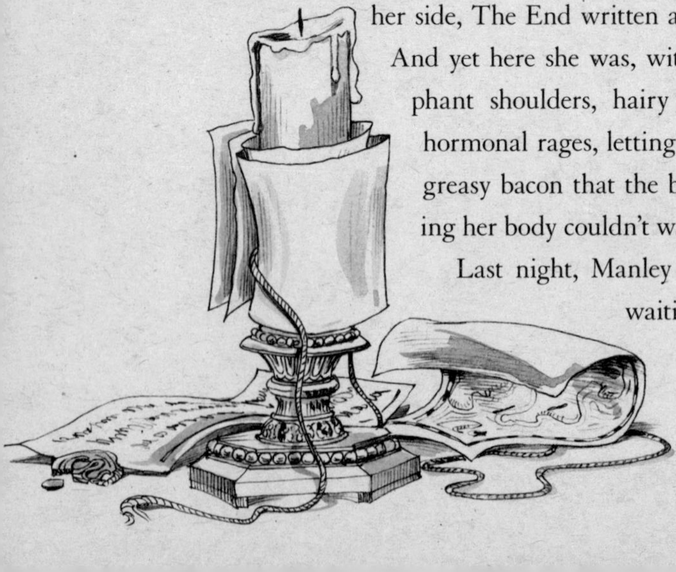

Last night, Manley had been waiting for her when she climbed in for Storian duty. "Already searched a thousand times," he scoffed. "Castor thinks we need young eyes."

Sophie grimaced at the plundered mess once he left, a heap of broken bricks, fallen fairy tales, dust and soot—but still had hope she'd succeed where they failed. She spent the entire night scouring the School Master's chamber, tearing up loose bricks, muscling behind bookshelves, shaking out fairy tale after fairy tale, while her and Agatha's storybook seemed to leer at her from atop the stone table. In the end, when Castor appeared at first light, she faced him empty-handed, like the rest.

"A useless prince. What a surprise," the dog snapped, kicking at a few loose silver bricks with his paw. "Pen *has* to be in this room, or the tower wouldn't still be here." He looked out the window at the glass castle across the bay. "Pollux would have loved a good game of hide-and-seek. Two heads better than one for this kind of thing." His big black eyes seemed to mist up. . . .

"Let me keep looking," said Sophie quickly, shaking out *The Ugly Duckling*—

"You had your chance, Filip," Castor growled, shoving her towards the window.

Sophie nodded and slumped onto the blond-haired rope, knowing she'd failed her mission.

"Tell Tedros he better pray we find it," Castor said behind her. "Storian falls into the Dean's hands and all of us are doomed."

Sophie slid quietly down the sunlit hair.

Now she dumped herself at a small round iron table, sore

from crouching and digging, and wolfed down fistfuls of bacon and eggs, no longer in control of either her hands or manners. Had Tedros lied to Manley and hidden the pen to keep it from her and Agatha? Or was he telling the truth—that someone else had found and hidden it? In which case, who? And *where*?

"Storian ain't your problem, mate," Chaddick said, plopping down at the table, his eggs doused in chili sauce. "Teachers tried for a week. Just using boys as slave labor now."

"Why'd you think the new princes helped you cheat too?" chimed Nicholas, chomping crispy bacon as he sat down. "No one wants Storian duty."

"Worth it though to see Aric's scowl when you won first day," Ravan smirked, squeezing in with Vex and Brone. "Lucky he'll be on your team. Already planning on murdering the girls in the Trial instead of making them surrender."

Sophie stiffened, seeing Aric at the head table with his henchmen, all eating triple portions. Two days until she and Agatha went into the Trial against those brutes. She had to find that pen tonight.

"Bet Tedros didn't expect a tag team yesterday," Vex said to her, pointy ears wagging. "All of us makin' sure you beat the stuffin' out of him."

"How about an encore today?" Sophie simpered anxiously—

Chaddick snorted. "First off, an *encore*? Never heard that out of a boy's mouth who wasn't an apple tart. Second, think it's about time you handled your own self. Don't want you in the Trial if you don't deserve to be there . . . *slavery* on the line and all."

Sophie reddened. How could she get back on Storian duty if she didn't have help? She shoveled eggs into her mouth, trying to avoid any further blunders—

"Hi Filip!"

She looked up to see Hort try to sit next to her.

"No room," said Chaddick, scooting over and blocking him.

Drowning in his oversized uniform, his pouty lip quivering, Hort looked like a child spurned from his own birthday party. He gave a weaselly whimper and trudged away.

Sophie's eyes flared. "Hort! Sit here!"

Hort turned, beaming, and plunked next to her, ignoring all the other boys' grumbles. "Do you want my bacon?" he yakked, sliding his pail to Filip. "Can't touch the stuff. Dad gave me a pet pig once and said I'd have to kill it someday—it's what most Evil parents do, make their kids eat their pets—"

"Tedros might beat me today, Hort," Sophie whispered, trying to sound guileless. "What do I do?"

"That's what best friends are for, Filip," Hort whispered back mischievously. "Um, and to tell you that you cross your legs like a girl—"

"You'll help me?" Sophie brightened, breathing relief.

"Just like you'll help *me* when the time comes," said Hort, suddenly looking very serious.

Sophie smiled tightly and dug into his bacon, praying she

and her real best friend would be long gone before she ever found out what this weenie expected in return.

I must have missed a corner last night, Sophie thought, hastening through the sewers as she bit into an apple. The Storian was so thin and sharp it could be stashed in the cracks between silver bricks or even in the cloth of a book spine. And yet, wouldn't she have heard it thrashing and struggling somewhere?

Temples throbbing, Sophie turned the corner past the churning red moat. Tonight she'd look harder. She pulled open the door to the Doom Room, desperate for a few minutes of sleep before class—

Tedros looked up from his bed, stopping her in her tracks.

His eyes were puffy and red, dark bags beneath them. His skin had gone from tan to ghostly pale, the veins showing through, and Sophie could see his shivering, starved muscles taut over jutting bones. There were no bruises on him. No wounds or welts. And yet, everything in his eyes said he'd been tortured beyond what a boy could handle.

"What did Aric do to you?" she said softly.

Tedros bent over, face in his hands.

Sophie walked up to him and held out her half-eaten fruit. "Please—"

Tedros smacked it out of her palm, and the apple skidded to a filthy corner. "Get away from me," he whispered.

"You have to eat someth—"

"GET AWAY FROM ME!" he screamed into her face, his cheeks red as blood.

Sophie fled the cell as fast as she could, his echoes chasing her all the way.

"I can't do it. I can't cheat," Sophie said to Hort as they headed into Evil Hall for Weapons Training. "Not if it means he's tortured again."

"Well, do you want Aric to torture *you*?" Hort snapped.

Sophie fell quiet, looking back at Tedros clutching his own arms, barely able to walk. Guilt rose into her throat—

What's wrong with me! she scolded, turning around. Why was she caring about *Tedros*? Why was she worrying about a boy who wanted her *dead*?

"Fine, stick with the plan," she gritted to Hort.

"There's my best friend," Hort beamed chummily. "We'll make a great pair in the Trial, won't we?"

Sophie frowned. "Hort, you're not even close to making the Trial tea—"

But the weasel was already whistling and motoring ahead.

For the first three Tryouts, Hort's deftness at cheating and Sophie's skills as an actress helped her win first rank each time, without any of the teachers or boys noticing. Hort magically moved her arrow to the phantom princess's heart in the Archery tryout, charaded answers during a Do You Know Your Monsters? oral quiz, and tasted her plant leaves during a Poisoned Or Palatable? survival challenge so she'd emerge unscathed. By lunch, Sophie caught all the boys eyeing Filip of Mount Honora with newfound respect, as if he surely deserved a spot on the Trial team. Even Aric's glares looked less baleful, as if a teammate like Filip was the reason he'd brought the new princes through the shield in the first place.

But Tedros knew Filip was still cheating. He didn't say a word to the boys or to the teachers, but Sophie saw him glowering darker at her after every new tryout, as if he'd never seen anyone so Evil. By the third Tryout, he wasn't even trying. And by the last, when Mohsin, the hairy giant leading Forest Groups, threw Tedros and Filip into a ring for a Magical Sparring Tryout, a one-on-one bare-knuckled brawl with no rules . . . Tedros simply dropped to his knees and conceded before they began, cutting into Filip with a withering glare.

The boys cheered raucously, anointing the new boy the winner for a second day. But as Sophie looked into Tedros' cold eyes, seeing right through her, she felt not even a shred of victory.

Why isn't Sophie back yet? Agatha thought, scuttling through the purple breezeway to Charity under her invisible cape. Last night, Sophie's lantern had glowed safely from the School Master's window—and yet she hadn't returned with the pen. Which could only mean one thing . . .

She couldn't find it.

Agatha's breath shallowed. Every second brought her and Sophie closer to the Trial. If Sophie couldn't find that pen . . . Agatha's gut twisted, remembering the tortoise's warning.

She had to find out what the Dean was planning.

She'd spent the morning hiding under her cape and waiting for Evelyn outside Good Hall, hoping to follow her between her History sessions. As each new class began, Agatha peeked through the doors to watch her take a group of girls inside *Bluebeard*—a gruesome tale of a husband who murdered all eight of his wives, which left the girls looking nauseous.

"I show you this story not to frighten you," the Dean said to close class each time, "but to remind you how vicious the boys will be during the Trial. Do not expect them to wait for you to drop your kerchief or to settle for your surrender." She smiled thinly. "Nor should you give them the same courtesies."

As the Dean sashayed out of the ballroom between sessions, Agatha tried to follow her, but maneuvering invisibly through crowded hallways required agility and grace, neither of which was a strength. After losing the Dean four times, Agatha slackened against the wall, discouraged.

"Really, Pollux, I'm fully capable of getting lunch by *myself*," huffed Professor Dovey's voice behind her—

Agatha looked up to see Pollux's furry head attached to a rickety old owl's body, flapping after the green-gowned professor.

"Strange business of late," Pollux panted. "Voices in sewers, butterflies eaten by rats, ghosts bumping girls in the halls . . . Dean's advised me to keep a close eye on both you and Lesso until the Trial."

"Perhaps if Evelyn hadn't taken my *office*, it would be easier to find me," Professor Dovey fired, and hurried down the steps, Pollux's owl sputtering behind her.

Agatha's eyes bulged wide.

With thirty minutes left in class, she scurried up Charity's spiral glass steps to Professor Dovey's old office, the lone white-marble door on the sixth floor, once inlaid with a single emerald beetle, now a blue butterfly. Agatha peered down the stair gap and made sure no one was coming up.

She tried the silver door handle, but it was bolted shut. She shot a shock spell at the keyhole with her glowing finger, then an even more useless melt spell, then a desperate freeze spell . . .

The lock caught.

Agog at her luck, Agatha grabbed the handle, only to see it opening from the *inside*. Panicked, she ducked against the stairway banister as the door flung wide.

A girl poked her long-nosed freckled face through, eyes darting right and left before she hurried out the closing door and nimbly slid down the banister to the floor below.

Crouched on the ground, Agatha gaped at the girl's red hair flowing out of sight.

What was Yara doing in the Dean's office?

Suddenly Agatha heard a creak behind her and whirled to see the door closing, about to bolt shut—

She stabbed out her foot, jamming it just in time.

Professor Manley came by the Doom Room twice before supper, promising to feed Tedros if he told him where the Storian was. Tedros begged and pleaded for mercy . . . but he had no new answers. Manley left the prince hungry once more.

Light used to come through the sewers at sunset, when the sinking sun's reflection over the bay fractured to slivers, spilling red-orange glow from the Good tunnels into Evil's. Now the prince sat on his metal bed frame in perpetual darkness, listening to the churning moat slap against the rocks that blocked the two sides from each other. It'd been six days since he'd eaten. His heartbeat puttered sluggishly, like a dying piston. His empty stomach hurt so much he couldn't stand. His teeth had started to chatter, even in the sweltering tunnels.

He wouldn't survive punishment tonight.

The cell door unlocked and creaked open, but the prince didn't look up. Not until he smelled the meat.

Filip slid a pail of braised lamb chops and mashed potatoes in front of him and stepped back.

"Told Manley it was for Castor," he said, in his strange, affectedly low voice. "Told Castor it was for Manley."

Tedros peered at the elfin prince, so strong and yet delicate, like a boy who wasn't sure how to be one. He smiled too much, stood too close to the other boys, played with his hair excessively, ate in oddly small bites, kept touching his face like he was checking for pimples. . . . And yet strangest of all were those eyes . . . Filip's big emerald eyes, sometimes ice-cold, sometimes deep and vulnerable, as if flickering between Good and Evil. Once upon a time, Tedros had been taken by eyes just like them.

He'd learned his lesson.

Tedros snatched the pail and flung the food against the stone wall, splattering Filip with grease. He dumped the pail to the floor with an ugly clang and sat back down on his bed, panting.

Filip said nothing and slouched down on the edge of his own bed.

The two cell mates hunched next to each other in dead silence . . . until the door creaked open once more and a dark shadow floated over them.

"No—" Filip gasped, looking up at Aric, a coiled whip on his belt. "You'll kill him!"

"Late for Storian duty, *aren't you*?" Aric sneered.

"Look at him!" Filip pressed, voice straining. "He can't survive—"

But Aric's violet eyes had drifted down to the empty pail near Tedros' bed. "Stealing food, I see." He leered at the prince, fingering his whip. "Perhaps we'll start with extra punishment tonight."

"No!" Filip cried. "It's my fault! Tedros, tell him!"

Tedros silenced him with a glare and turned away coldly.

Tedros heard Filip stop breathing behind him, realizing he wasn't wanted. Filip's shadow hovered on the wall a moment longer, then finally slumped out of the cell.

"Hands on the bricks," Aric ordered the prince.

Tedros turned and put his hands high on the rotted wall.

He heard the soft snap as Aric unhooked the whip from his belt and the panicked thumping of his own heart, telling him that one of these lashes would kill him. He didn't want to die—not like this. Not worse than his father. Tears rising, limbs shaking, he looked up at Aric's shadow on the wall, uncoiling the whip.

The shadowed hand rose with the handle and then swung full force, the first lash hissing towards his back—

Aric's shadow lurched on the wall, and the whip cracked

sickly against someone else's skin.

Tedros spun around.

Filip had Aric by the throat against the bricks, the whip coiled around Filip's bleeding forearm.

"Tell the teachers that if anyone tries to hurt him again, they'll have to get through me," Filip snarled.

Tedros blinked hard, unsure if he was alive or dead.

Under Filip's tightening grip, Aric looked nervous—before he managed a cruel smile and wrenched away. "Just what we need in the Trial. Someone who puts loyalty first," he said, leaving quickly. "I'll talk to the teachers about finding you a more suitable room."

"Fine right here!" Filip barked after him.

Tedros' eyes were the size of marbles now. Slowly he turned to Filip, who bared teeth at him, cheeks blushed furious red.

"Either you eat now, or I kill you myself," Filip lashed.

This time Tedros didn't argue.

Agatha gazed up at the grandmother clock in the corner of the study.

Ten minutes before the next class break.

She peered around at the Dean's office, which was strangely barren. Where Professor Dovey's desk had once teemed with broken quills, ranking ledgers, and scrolls under pumpkin paperweights, Evelyn Sader's desk was clean, empty mahogany, with only a tall, thin candle in its corner, the color of parchment.

Why had Yara been in here? Agatha wondered. She was

sure she'd heard Yara speak to the Dean that day in the Gallery. Something about letting Yara stay . . . Agatha brushed the thought away. She should be focused on the Dean, not some crackpot girl who might or might not speak.

Agatha hunched in the sturdy wooden chair behind the bare desk, each minute ticking by. She stared distractedly at the candlewick.

The Dean had arrived the day the School for Good and Evil became the School for Boys and Girls. Which meant her and Sophie's fairy tale had killed the School Master . . . and then let an Evil teacher he'd *banished* back in.

But *why*?

Agatha remembered what Dovey and Lesso had said. Sophie's symptoms had come either from Evelyn or Sophie herself. There were no other suspects. Evelyn had been convicted of crimes against students before. Evelyn had been in the room for all of Sophie's symptoms . . . the Beast . . . the wart . . . the corrupted Mogrif. . . . *Why am I thinking about this?* . . . Of course it had to be Evelyn. . . . It *was* Evelyn. . . .

And yet . . . if it *wasn't* Evelyn . . .

Agatha closed her eyes, letting a dream back in. . . . He'd looked so calm, so happy, his golden hair haloed in snow. . . . She could see his crooked smile, his shirt laces undone, as they were when he once asked her to a ball in this very same school . . . as if everything since had been a wrong turn in their story . . . as if all of this was a big mistake. . . . She tasted his lips again as he held her, her heart fluttering against his, fluttering more than ever before—

Agatha's eyes flashed open to the cold, empty office.

This time it was more than a dream.

Her heart was still wishing for Tedros.

Wishing even stronger.

Agatha scorched red. She was still wishing for her prince over her friend? Her loyal friend, who was risking her life to save them from the very same boy she was wishing for? Agatha pushed up angrily from the desk, hating the weak, foolish princess inside her, the princess she couldn't silence . . .

Then slowly Agatha sat back down.

There was an odd, jagged wrinkle in the candle's texture. She reached out and touched it, expecting to feel wax—only to feel paper instead. She pulled the candle closer and saw a camouflaged scroll bound tightly around it, tied with a small white string. Agatha tried to settle her emotions, knowing the Dean would be back any moment. She carefully untied the scroll, lifted it off the candle, and spread its parchment across the desk.

There were three pages.

The first was a map of the Blue Forest, the same map the students received every year in Forest Groups, with all the notable areas labeled: the Fernfield, Turquoise Thicket, Blue Brook . . .

Then Agatha noticed one of these areas circled in red ink, the lone marking on the page, strangely conspicuous. She stared at the circled label.

The Cyan Caves

The teachers never mentioned the caves nor took students there, presumably because there was no way up the jagged cliff face, nor any reason to explore empty caves. Why had the Dean marked them?

Agatha moved to the next sheet: a letter with a broken seal of a scarlet wax snake. It was dated today.

Dear Evelyn,
So that there is no room for ambiguity, here are the rules of the Trial.

1. Tomorrow at noon, I will meet you at the Blue Forest gate. As the acting Deans of our schools, each of us will have thirty minutes to lace traps into the arena. The Cyan Caves are off-limits, as you request.
2. Given the high stakes involved, the traditional pre-Trial scout of the Forest will be canceled for both sides.
3. Ten competitors will participate from each school, and each may have one weapon of their choice. No others may enter and the Forest will be veiled from spectator view. All magical spells and talents are allowed.
4. If both boys and girls are still in the Forest when the sun rises, the Trial will continue until only boys or girls are left.
5. Regardless of the outcome, Tedros' original terms will be obeyed. If the girls win, the boys will surrender to your school as slaves. If the boys win, the Readers will be turned

over to us for execution and the schools
returned to Good and Evil.

Any violation of these rules will void the terms of the Trial and precipitate war.

Best of luck.

Professor Bilious Manley
Acting Dean, School for Boys

Agatha frowned, questions churning. Why had Evelyn wanted the Trial scout canceled? And why had she circled the caves if they were off-limits? She flipped to the third page, still silently fuming for even thinking of Tedros, let alone wishing for—

Her heart stopped.

In her hands was a long, tinily scrawled list of potion ingredients, followed by an even longer series of precise directions for brewing them, filling up every inch of an old, tattered page.

A page Yuba said he'd lost in a classroom weeks ago.

Now as Agatha stared at it here in the Dean's office, a question burnt into her skull, searing away everything else.

Only the question wasn't how Evelyn Sader had found the gnome's recipe for Merlin's lost spell.

The question was what she had done with it.

20

One Step Ahead

On his knees, Tedros snatched another lamb chop off the floor and ripped into it like a lion, shredding off the meat and flinging the bone onto the heap of others. After devouring six more, he clutched his stomach, slightly green, trying to hold it all down.

The cell door squeaked open, and he looked up at Filip slicked with sweat, forearm streaked with dried blood, carrying two steaming mugs.

"Knew you'd overeat," Filip said, and put down a mug of frothy liquid in front of him. "Bit of rice stewed in hot water calms the stomach. Wish we had some peppermint or fresh ginger—brew a nice *digestif*—"

Sophie saw Tedros staring and she cleared her throat with a macho grunt. "Drink up."

Tedros stuck his tongue in the tea and put it down, frowning. "Late for Storian duty, aren't you, Filip?"

"Told Manley I should interrogate you first," Sophie said sternly as she sat facing him.

That's why I saved his life, she scolded herself, resting her bulky shoulders against the wall. Because Tedros would tell her where the Storian was. *That's why.* Not because she cared the slightest bit about him. She glared at him, muscles clenched, refocusing on the goal.

"Tell me where it is, Tedros."

"For the last time, Tristan and I buried it to keep it away from Sophie and Agatha," he snapped. "We hid it under a loose brick. I don't know how it could have moved." He saw Filip studying him and hung his head. "Look, I wouldn't lie to you, Filip. Not after what you've done for me."

"But who took it, then?" Sophie said, stomach turning. "Did they question Tristan?"

"Pfffft, he'd be the first one to hand it over to a teacher," Tedros groused, kicking off his boots. "Besides, no one's seen that mouse for days. Probably left before classes started. Never liked the other boys."

"But Castor said we're all doomed if we don't find—"

"Because the pen reflects the soul of its master," Tedros mumbled, slumping deeper. "If it gets into Dean Sader's hands, you can bet there'll be a lot of boys dying at the end of stories. Starting with mine."

Mine. The word hit Sophie harder than the prospect of Woods-wide death. She had always thought of it as *her* story, with Tedros the villain in her way. But now she realized: Tedros thought it was his fairy tale . . . and that he deserved a happy ending just as much as she did.

"Agatha's wish for you," Sophie said quietly. "How did you hear it?"

Tedros paused, jaw clenching. "I was nine when my mother left. It was the middle of the night, and I was asleep in the opposite wing. I remember bolting up in a pool of sweat and stumbling to the window without knowing why, my heart feeling like it was ripped open. The last thing I saw was my mother on my favorite horse, galloping into the Woods." He traced the space between bricks with his finger. "I woke up the same way when I felt Agatha's wish. She *wanted* me to hear it, Filip." His eyes watered. "And I believed it was true."

Sophie fidgeted with her grubby nails. "Maybe it was true," she said, almost to herself. "Maybe something just . . . got in the way."

Tedros rubbed his eyes and sat up straighter. "You're a good friend, Filip. You didn't have to help me."

Sophie shook her head. "I couldn't let you die," she breathed, unable to look at him. "I couldn't."

"Sophie said the same thing last year. Vowed to protect me in the Trial—then left me to die alone," Tedros said, picking at a hole in his dirty black sock. "Suppose that's the difference between a girl and a boy."

Sophie finally looked up, blinking wide.

Tedros nodded. "Trust me, I know, Filip. She was every bit as Evil as the storybook says."

Sophie swallowed. "Can you . . . tell me about her?"

"She was the most beautiful girl I'd ever seen—blond hair just like yours . . . and now that I think about it, green eyes a lot like yours too," Tedros said, peering at Filip. His cell mate glanced away, uncomfortable, and Tedros quickly looked down. "But there was nothing beneath it. Every time I gave her a new chance, I saw more and more deceit. It was like she wanted a prince only to have one, caring nothing about who I actually was. I never knew what Agatha saw in her worth saving."

"Perhaps you don't know Agatha the way Sophie knows her."

"I know Agatha used to be a Good soul who deserved happiness with a prince," Tedros retorted. "Now she gave up true love for something masking as it. Sophie did that to her. Sophie *ruined* her."

"Only because you made your princess *choose*," Sophie shot back, elfish face flushing. "You're responsible for your own fate, Tedros. Not Agatha. And not Sophie."

Tedros grimaced and said nothing.

"Why can't a girl have both?" Sophie asked softly. She looked at her boy face reflected in the bed frame. "Why can't she have the love of her prince and the love of her best friend?"

"Because we grow up, Filip," Tedros exhaled. "When you're young, you think your best friend is everything. But once you find real love . . . it changes. Your friendship can never be the same after that. Because no matter how much you try to keep both, your loyalty can only lie with one." He smiled sadly at his cell mate. "That's Agatha's greatest mistake. She can't see that she and Sophie were doomed the moment she let herself love me."

Sophie felt the wall of muscle encasing her new body slacken, as if Tedros had put words to the truth she'd been shutting out. That night, Agatha was supposed to kiss Tedros and live out her Ever After. That night, she herself was supposed to go home all alone, her only friend moved on to a boy.

But she'd rewritten their story. She'd held her best friend back.

At what cost?

"It's too late," Tedros breathed, resting his forehead on his clasped arms. "I won't love someone again."

"Maybe Sophie needs Agatha more than you need her," his cell mate pressed, tears in his eyes. "Maybe Agatha is the closest to love that Sophie will ever get. Maybe Sophie did the Good thing after all!"

Tedros raised his head, glowering.

"Don't you see, Tedros? You'll find someone else," Filip said, voice shaky. "Sophie won't."

"You're as bad as a Reader, Filip," said Tedros darkly. "There's only one true love. Only *one*."

The boys gazed hard at each other before they turned away and sat in silence, two silhouettes beneath a dying torch.

Filip lurched up for the door. "Come on."

"What?" Tedros blurted. "I'm not allowed to leave—"

"Difference between you and me." Filip glared down at him. "You're a prince who plays by rules. And I'm not."

Tedros stared at his new friend waiting impatiently.

"Takes quite the boy to boss me around," Tedros muttered, pulling himself up.

Filip held the door open. "You have no idea."

On the rehearsal stage in the Supper Hall, Pollux barked at his cast of five baffled-looking Nevergirls heaped with white clown makeup and poorly fitted cheongsams. "For the last time, you are a living *metaphor* for the Trial . . . an embodiment of eons of female submission and objectification . . . a monument to a deadly Trial that may cost us lives—"

"This play looks more deadly than a Trial," Dot murmured to Yara, who ignored her and cheerfully readied the burkas and swan headdresses for the next act. Dot eyed Hester and Anadil across the room, whispering while they painted one of the sets, an odd gap between them that Dot surmised must be Agatha. "If I'd known this was what Book Club would turn into, I'd have tried out for chorus," she sighed, turning a swan feather to arugula before traipsing over to join their conversation.

"What could the Dean possibly be doing with Merlin's spell?" Anadil was saying.

"Could she have used it herself?" Agatha said, slipping back her cape's hood so they could just see her big brown eyes.

"First of all, we would have noticed if the Dean had turned

herself into a man," Hester returned. "Second, either be invisible or not. Your eyes are too big and sentimental to be taken seriously."

"Well I didn't know we were all volunteering for *stage crew*," Agatha snapped as Anadil's rats took turns bathing in paint and rolling across the set.

"You didn't seem to have any better ideas of where we should meet—"

"Because I'm too busy trying not to *die*—"

"And you think we aren't?" Anadil shot back. "We've been killing ourselves to make the Trial team in case this all goes to hell—"

"Do you think the Dean sent a girl into the boys' castle?" Dot wondered airily, chomping salad greens.

The other girls turned to her.

"If she did, that might explain why Sophie hasn't found the Storian yet," Dot said. "The Dean might have had one of the girls turn into a boy and hide the pen so you can't make your wish. You know—to make sure the Trial goes on as planned."

Anadil blinked at her. "Maybe I should start eating vegetables."

"And who would this Storian-stashing girl be?" Hester leered, looking irritated she hadn't come up with the idea.

"Beatrix," Agatha returned, pulling the hood back to reveal her face. "This is her cape, isn't it? And she had that boys' uniform under her bed too! She loves the Dean! It has to be her!"

"Look, we'll see what we can get out of her," Anadil said, scooting to block Agatha's face from view. "But there's only two nights left, Agatha. Sophie has to find the Storian by tomorrow. Where was her lantern tonight?"

"Can't see a thing outside tonight. Completely fogged out," said Agatha miserably. "Left my lantern in my window, but can't see hers until it clears."

"She has to bring that pen back, Agatha," Hester pressured. "Or we're *all* going into that Trial."

If Agatha wasn't scared enough, the fear in Hester's face turned her stomach to jelly.

"The Dean had a Trial map too—" Agatha stammered. "She marked the Cyan Caves—"

"Cyan Caves?" Hester scoffed, exchanging looks with Anadil. "They're just a decoration by the south gate. Caves don't go deeper than fifty feet. What could possibly be in them?"

"Well, she canceled the pre-Trial scout, so we can't even look," Agatha griped, disappearing back under her hood.

"Unless she already gave you permission to."

Agatha looked up at Hester, peering slyly at her invisible friend.

"As far as the Dean knows, you're in the Blue Forest with a gnome."

As the clock tolled midnight, Agatha prowled through the foggy Blue Forest towards the south gate, concealed under her cape. She'd never seen fog like this, swirling white clouds of mist that obscured every last blade of navy grass. She squinted through the haze at the School for Boys but couldn't see a single brick.

It certainly was a coincidence, Agatha thought—that her only means of communication with Sophie had been severed by strange weather.

Lady Lesso's warning floated into Agatha's mind . . . *"Evelyn's always one step ahead."*

Agatha shook off the thought and snuck deeper into the Forest, moving slowly in case she collided with any trees or equally fog-blinded animals. In the eerie silence, she began to feel thoughts of Tedros rising faster than she could hold them down. The more she denied him, the stronger he seemed to become, like a monster at the door. Nerves shredding, she focused harder on the fog-covered path. As soon as she got home to the graveyard, she'd burn every last storybook she could find. Gavaldon would be a world without princes, indeed.

She felt the path begin to slope uphill, meaning she was beyond the pumpkin patch and nearing the south gate. Tomorrow night would be Trial eve, featuring Pollux's infernal play and the announcement of the team. By then, Dean Sader and Professor Manley would have laced the Forest with their traps. They'd agreed that the Cyan Caves were off-limits. . . . So what was the Dean hiding there?

A white rabbit scurried past her clumps, carrying its terrified baby in its mouth, and vanished into the white fog as if erased off a page. Agatha treaded carefully, step by step, until she glimpsed the wall of blue-green rock in front of her.

Buried high on a cliff at the southeast corner, cloaked by giant overhanging blue pines, the Cyan Caves were a bubbled arrangement of three circular, sea-green holes of different sizes. Agatha gazed up at the caves atop the ledge, unsure how to even get up to them. She couldn't mogrify and lose her magic cape, so her only option was to climb one of the blue pines and jump onto the cliff. Luckily, the pine branches were thick and sturdy, and Agatha made her way up quickly, thankful for the prickly needles to guide her hands through the fog. At last she reached the highest bough and with a deep breath leapt down invisible onto jagged rock, with only a small stutter in her landing.

Agatha peered at the row of caves in front of her: three circles of different sizes that looked like they belonged in Goldilocks' story—the first cave too big, the second cave too small, the third just right. She could feel her neck rashing red under the invisible cape collar. Something told her that whatever was in these caves would answer her question of why Evelyn Sader was in her fairy tale . . . and how she planned for it to end.

Legs shaking, Agatha headed into the first giant cave, feeling her fingertip glow gold like a torch. The cavernous walls were glassy aquamarine, dimly reflecting her fingerglow and tense face. Step by step, she moved through the mirrored den, scanning every inch, seeing nothing but a few scraggly meerworms and beetles, until she reached a dead end.

Frowning, Agatha retreated to try the second cave. But with its hole no bigger than a dinner plate, Agatha couldn't fit more than her head in. Worse still, this cave was even shallower than the first, with her fingerglow illuminating only bare walls and a few patches of mold. Agatha wrenched back out, irritated.

What am I doing here? she chastised herself as she stomped into the third cave. She should be waiting for Sophie in the castle, she thought, lighting up the midsized, deserted den. Her friend would be back with that pen any moment. . . . Last year, she herself had been the rock, the finisher, the one who would do anything to get them home. Now it was Sophie. That's why Sophie had won the challenge to be a boy instead of her. Sophie was the prince this time. Sophie wouldn't let her down. . . .

Extinguishing her glow, Agatha hurried back towards the mouth of the cave—and stopped cold. A strange hum echoed behind her, like a chorus of angry whispers.

Slowly Agatha turned around, hearing the whir grow louder and louder. She held up her lit finger, flickering with dread. . . .

A storm of blue butterflies crashed into her from darkness, swamping her invisible body like bees and ripping her invisible cape to threads. They moved with deliberate purpose and ruthless speed, eviscerating the snakeskin and bashing her back onto the cliff edge. Beneath their beating wings, Agatha could see her skin and clothes reappearing in moonlight, patch by patch, until they finally tore the last of the cape from her and swarmed away with a violent gust, blowing her off the ledge. Agatha fell down the cliff with a scream, flailing through fog, and landed on her tailbone in a tangled pine shrub. Bruised and aching, she looked up to see the cloud of butterflies vanish into fog, shedding the last black slivers of the cape over the Forest like ash.

Agatha couldn't breathe, feeling the relief of being alive

give way to the panic of what had just happened.

The Dean had planted that map in her office for her to find. Which meant the Dean knew she hadn't been with Yuba in the Blue Forest the past two days . . .

Or with Sophie.

An alarm roared in her brain and Agatha was already running.

She dashed down the fogged path, forgetting her pain, trying to remember where Yuba's den was. Branches and thorns ripped at her clothes as she crouched to the dirt, scanning the glen between the Fernfield and Thicket—until she saw wisps of black smoke rising from a hole in the ground ahead. She fell to her stomach and plunged her head through the tiny opening—

But it was too late.

Yuba's home had been incinerated, every inch burnt to a crisp, except a few hydrangea petals, scattered over cinders . . . the gnome nowhere in sight.

Stomach sinking, Agatha stood back up in the Blue Forest and watched the fog magically recede, as if its work was done. The mist thinned into a trail and slurped back towards the School for Girls, vanishing into its highest office.

Agatha looked up at Evelyn Sader in the window, circled by returning butterflies, her gap-toothed smile glowing through darkness like a Cheshire cat's.

A smile that said Evelyn knew exactly where Sophie was right now . . .

Because she'd been one step ahead all along.

Slowly Agatha turned to see the fog evaporate around the School for Boys, leaving it bare and clear in the night.

No green glow in any of its windows.

No sign from her friend at all.

"Shouldn't you be looking for the Storian?" Tedros asked in the dark hall, trying to track Filip's fluffy blond hair past the teacher dormitories. "Past midnight now—"

"Want to show you something first," Filip said, sliding through two narrow rock columns.

"Where are we going?" Tedros moaned, stomach still bloated from his dungeon feast. "All I want to do is take a bath and go to be—" He fell quiet.

They were standing on the teachers' balcony, perched over the Blue Forest, giving them a panoramic view of the terrain. A strange, icy haze broke apart in the air, as if a thick fog had just passed.

As the air grew clearer over the Forest, Tedros saw the leaves and grass fluorescing magically with an arctic-blue sheen. Wind raked across fronds and flowers in harplike waves, sounding steady, oceanic breaths. Close to the north gate, the electric-blue Fernfield, dotted with silver spores, fanned over the thin west path; over the east path, the willows lost more of their sapphire leaves with every sweeping gust, while the Cyan Caves to the south cast a bubbled shadow over the blue pumpkin patch.

Tedros had seen so much beauty traveling with his parents when he was little—the paradise grottos in the Murmuring

Mountains, the siren lakes in Avonlea, the Wish Fish oases in the Shazabah Deserts. . . . But from high above, the prince looked at this small, gated Forest, innocent to the dangers of the world, and knew what heaven could be. Two nights from now, he'd be the one who turned it to hell.

He suddenly noticed movement near the gate . . . a human shadow slipping out of the Forest. . . .

Tedros squinted closer—

"You going to join me?" Filip said behind him.

Tedros turned to see him sitting on the wide, flat marble ledge, kicking legs over the Forest.

"Or do you still want that bath?" his cell mate said archly.

Tedros climbed up onto the ledge and sat closer to Filip than he would under ordinary circumstances. He wasn't especially fond of heights.

"How's your arm?" Tedros said, inspecting his cell mate's gash, still raw and bloody. "I don't want it to get infected—"

Filip pulled it away, staring out at the Forest. "How can you sleep knowing you're sentencing two girls to death out there? Two girls who each loved you?"

Tedros said nothing for a moment. "There's always three in a fairy tale, Filip. The true loves and the villain. In the end, someone has to die. The moment Agatha hid Sophie in my tower, the moment Agatha attacked me, she made *me* the villain." He glared at Filip. "And I have no problem playing the part if it means saving my life."

Tedros saw his cell mate gaping at him, cheeks going redder, redder. . . . All of a sudden Filip started laughing so convulsively he started tearing up.

"What in God's name is wrong with you?" Tedros frowned.

"Everyone just wanted to find love, and now everyone wants to kill each other," Filip giggled, wiping his eyes. "No one knows the truth anymore."

"With all due respect, Filip, what the hell do you know?"

Filip laughed and cried louder, burying his face in his hands.

"You're worse than a girl," Tedros mumbled.

Now Filip was howling, but seeing Tedros' stony face, his laughs turned to pants and then to silence.

Somewhere below, crickets thrummed off rhythm. Tedros peered down at a stork wading through the Blue Brook, while two squirrels chased each other over the bridge's railing. Tomorrow Manley and the girls' Dean would lace the Forest with traps, and the animals would go into hiding until the Trial was over and its dangers passed.

"So what's your castle like, Filip?"

His cell mate blinked. "Castle?"

"You're a prince, aren't you? You don't live in a tiki hut, I presume."

"Oh, yes—it's a, um, small . . . castle. Shaped like a . . . cottage."

"Sounds cozy. Never liked living in a big castle. Spend most of the day trying to find people. Does your whole family live with you?"

"Just my father," said Filip sourly.

"Least you have a dad," sighed Tedros. "I have nothing to go home to when school's done. Just an empty castle, thieving servants, and a failing kingdom."

"Think you'll ever see your mother again?"

Tedros shook his head. "Don't want to, either. Dad put a death warrant out for her. Once I turn 16, I become king. I'd have to honor Dad's warrant if I found her."

Filip swiveled to him in shock, but Tedros quickly squinted up at the sky. "You should look for the Storian, Filip. It'll be light soon."

"How could you ever hurt your mother?" Filip asked, astonished. "I'd do anything to see mine again. Anything. That would be my real Ever After." He sighed and hunched over. "But I'm not like Agatha. No one hears my wishes."

"Tell me what she was like . . . your mother."

"Her name was Vanessa. Means 'butterfly.' I still remember her face when they used to fly through the lane every spring, in big blue swarms. . . . She used to say that one day I'd fly away just like them—find a life bigger than hers, somewhere where all my dreams came true. 'Don't let anyone stop you from your happy ending,' she used to say. 'Don't let anyone stop you from being loved,'" Filip said, voice cracking. "'Caterpillars can't know a butterfly.'"

Tedros touched his shoulder. Filip leaned against him and finally let himself cry.

"Her only friend took the only boy she ever loved, Tedros," Filip said. "I don't want to end up like her. All alone."

Silence thickened between the two boys.

"Never met a boy who wanted to be a butterfly," said Tedros softly.

Filip looked up. The two boys gazed into each other's eyes, legs touching on the ledge.

Tedros swallowed and jumped onto the balcony. "Heading back. Go find that pen."

"Tedros, wait for me—"

But the prince sprinted away, stumbling between columns, before he faded into shadow.

Sophie's hand slowly drifted to the place on the ledge where Tedros had been.

She told herself to hurry to the silver tower, to find the pen in the hours she had left and get Agatha home—to get up *now*—

But instead she just stayed there, alone over the Forest, until morning light shattered the dark.

21
Red Light

By now, the three witches considered Agatha a good friend, despite their generally poor abilities to make good friends. Thus one might expect Hester, Anadil, and Dot to grin, wave, or, at the very least, make room for Agatha as she entered Good Hall for History on the last day before the Trial. But as Agatha squeezed next to them in her school uniform, eyes red and sleepless, the witches acted as if seeing their new friend was the worst possible thing in the world.

"What are you *doing* here?" Hester hissed. "And why can we *see* you—"

"She *knows*," Agatha hissed back.

The witches spun to her. "Knows?" Dot blurted.

"How much?" breathed Hester.

The double doors flung open behind them and the Dean breezed in, revised textbook in hand, and gave Agatha a puckish smile as she ascended the stage.

"Pleasure to see our Captain has returned from her training. I'm sure it's been time well spent," she said smoothly. "I hear Sophie isn't *feeling herself*?"

Agatha withstood the sting and glared back at her. "She's *looking* for something as we speak."

All the girls in the hall swiveled to the Dean, befuddled by this exchange.

"Oh dear. Time is of the essence, with both your lives at stake tomorrow," replied Evelyn innocently. "Suppose it's something she *can't find*?"

"She'll find it," Agatha spat as girls whiplashed back to her. "You don't know Sophie."

"And you know her, of course," said the Dean, eyes twinkling. "*Warts* and all."

Agatha bleached white as confused girls in the hall gibbered around her.

"Everything," Hester gasped. "She knows . . . *everything.*"

"Tonight at supper, we'll have our Trial eve festivities, featuring our play pageant, announcement of the Trial team, and a proper feast to wish our combatants luck against the boys," the Dean declared from her brother's old wooden lectern. "But this morning, we still have one history lesson left to prepare us for the Trial—"

"She couldn't possibly know Sophie's a boy," Dot whispered to Agatha and the witches. She glimpsed two butterflies over

Anadil's shoulder and turned them to brussels sprouts. "For one thing, how could she know we used Merlin's spell?"

"She *taught* us about Merlin's spell, didn't she?" Agatha said, remembering the Dean's cryptic smile that day. "She practically dared us to find it."

"Maybe it was part of her plan all along," echoed Anadil. "Get Sophie and Agatha apart, then hide the Storian so they have to go in the Trial."

"She could have just locked them up somewhere," Hester said, shaking her head. "Why go through all this trouble to get Sophie into the boys' castle?" Her black eyes narrowed, clouding over. "Unless . . ."

"Did you talk to Beatrix?" Agatha pressured Anadil, seeing more butterflies fly off the Dean's dress towards them. "She has to tell us where the pen is!"

"Don't think she's the one who hid it," Dot piped up. "I pretended to be studying for Tryouts with a few Evergirls and asked her the properties of snakeskin. She hadn't the faintest clue it makes you invisible. None of the Evers did. Whoever used that cape in your room had to be a Never!"

Hester looked up at her as if suddenly interested in what she had to say, but Agatha waved Dot off. "Beatrix is lying," Agatha insisted. "It *has* to be her!"

"Well, Baldy's not telling us anything, and tonight's your and Sophie's last chance to escape," Anadil snapped.

"And you're 100% *sure* it's Evelyn who was responsible for Sophie's symptoms?" said Hester, frowning at Agatha.

"If you saw Sophie's face when she grew hairy legs and an

Adam's apple, you'd stop questioning whether she's Good," Agatha retorted.

Hester scratched her demon, grumbling.

"Look, we're arguing for nothing," Agatha exhaled. "Sophie was *in* the School Master's tower, remember? She flashed her lantern there two nights ago! She's probably close to finding the Storian as we speak."

"Then why didn't she light her lantern there *last* night?" Hester prodded. "Why didn't she light her lantern at *all*?"

Agatha ignored her as she watched the Dean open her book for the day's lesson. She'd barely slept a wink, asking herself the very same question.

"You're almost Trial team leader!" Hort beamed, hurrying Filip to their first class. "So remember. I help you and you help me. Deal?"

Sophie didn't answer, legs heavy, breath dodgy, and keenly aware of a pimple on her forehead. At sunrise, she'd wandered back to the dungeons, managing only an hour of sweaty sleep before Tedros woke her up, freshly bathed in a cut-off shirt and holding a hunk of buttered bread.

"Thought Aric would have my head for showing up at breakfast, but no one said a thing. Think they're all afraid of Filip the Barbarian after last night," the prince said, grinning at his cell mate. "Come on, butterfly boy, eat up."

Eyes coated with sleep, Sophie squinted at the bread's oily coat of butter. Her cavernous stomach was rumbling as usual, demanding anything edible, but even as a boy, she had her limits. She moaned and pulled the sheets back over her shorn, fluffy hair.

"Well don't whine later," Tedros said, biting into the loaf himself. "Better get moving if you want a bath, Fil. Only ten minutes before class."

Sophie groaned like a wounded ape.

"I know I was a bit of an ass when we first met, but I'm glad we're mates now," she heard Tedros say across the room. "And glad you won't be bunking my challenges anymore. Need to win today so I can get in that tower tonight. If I find the Storian myself, maybe Manley will give me a spot on the Trial team."

Beneath the covers, Sophie felt nauseous. "So you can kill Sophie."

"So I can protect *you* from her."

Sophie sat up, eyes wide.

"Along with everyone else," the prince said, as he slipped on his uniform shirt.

Sophie saw Tedros' bare back to her for a moment, the skin glowing healthily again, a bit more meat on him than yesterday. Suddenly she was aware of the muscles in his shoulders . . . the unfreckled, gold tan . . . his minty bath smell. . . .

"Filip!"

Hort's nasal voice snapped her out of her daze.

"Do we have a deal?" he goaded her as they turned towards Evil Hall.

Sophie's cheeks burned cherry red. Agatha was waiting for her, girls' lives were depending on her, and she was daydreaming about her would-be killer?

"Deal," Sophie said forcefully to Hort, picking at her uniform's snug breeches. "You need to help me get back on Storian duty tonight."

"That's my Filip. Boys spreading rumors you spared Tedros from punishment last night, and I knew it couldn't be true. Tedros wagered all of us on this Trial, including *you*. Least we can do is teach Prince Handsome a lesson—"

"No. This is about my ranks, not anyone else's. Leave him alone."

Hort stopped dead in the hall. "You *did* spare him last night!"

Sophie turned to Hort, her sharp-jawed, princely face ice-cold. "Don't think it's any of your business, frankly."

Hort gaped at Filip as if he'd been stabbed. Then he swallowed and forced a smile. "B-b-but—but we're still best friends though, right, Filip?"

Sophie simpered. "Of course," she said, not looking at him as she walked ahead.

"Good man," Hort gushed, skipping to catch up. "Just making sure you know who your *real* friend is."

Sophie nodded distractedly, trying to focus on Agatha, Agatha, Agatha, even though all she could think of was a prince.

"For our last lesson before the Trial, I thought perhaps I should give you a window into my *own* history," said Evelyn Sader, her voice resounding through Good Hall.

Agatha and Hester stopped whispering and looked up at the stage, surprised. The last person they expected to shed light on the Dean's past was the Dean herself.

"The Storian never chose to write my story, an omission it will no doubt correct in time. For it is my own survival over a savage boy that brought me back to lead all of you," Evelyn went on, lording over her audience of girls. "Now, for the first time, history will reflect the truth."

She ran her fingers over her textbook open on the lectern, and her sultry, disembodied voice echoed over the hall:

"'Chapter 28: Notable Female Seers.'"

A three-dimensional, ghostly vision of the old School for Good and Evil faded in over the book page, hovering in mist.

"Guess we should have kept reading," Hester murmured to Agatha.

The Dean smiled down at her students. "Welcome to *my* fairy tale."

She blew on the phantom scene, and it burst into shimmering shards, sweeping over the girls with a crackling swish. Agatha covered her eyes from the glare and again felt herself falling through air, before her feet gently hit the floor. She opened her eyes to find herself in Good Hall again, the three witches and all the other girls of her school gone. Now the air in the cathedral hall was gauzy and thick, like a hazy film over the scene; the walls were less briny and calcified, and the pews were packed with girls in pink pinafore dresses and boys in blue Everboy uniforms.

Agatha slowly looked up to see Evelyn at the wooden lectern, ten years younger, bright faced and warm. Only instead of the twitching, fluttering butterflies on her dress being blue, now they were scarlet red.

"Once upon a time, I taught here in the School for Good, while my brother, August, taught in the School for Evil," her present voice narrated over the scene.

Agatha furrowed, incredulous. Professor Sader had claimed exactly the opposite in his book—that Evelyn had taught in Evil, and only because he'd asked the School Master to let her.

"But my brother had long been envious of my powers," the Dean's voice decreed, "and plotted to take my school for himself."

Agatha frowned deeper. *This is lies,* she thought. And yet, as she looked at handsome, attentive princes-to-be and smiling, fair maidens absorbed in the lesson, the moment felt so . . . true.

"Soon enough, my brother spawned his attack . . ."

The hall windows shattered and a hazel-green fog swept in, blasting students out of the pews. Terrified Evers fled for the doors as the fog lassoed Evelyn and evicted her through the window, her red butterflies flurrying after her—

"And I vowed to return upon his death," Evelyn declared, "promising that one day girls would be safe from men's lies and brutality . . ."

Agatha's jaw tightened as screaming Good students crashed out of the hall, the scene feeling more and more visceral. She thought of the way Dovey and Lesso had each branded August Sader as delusional and dangerous during her first year at school. . . . Had he made those changes in the tortoise's textbook to cover his own history? Had *he* been the one lying all along?

As green plumes filled the conjured hall, phantom Evers fleeing past her, Agatha closed her eyes, head battering, blinded to what was real and what wasn't anymore—

Until something very real prickled the tip of her nose.

Agatha opened her eyes to see a single white swan feather floating past her through the smoke and stampeding Evers, towards the far muraled wall of Good Hall.

Agatha followed the white feather towards the mosaic painting of the silver-masked School Master, the Storian hovering over his outstretched hand. The swan feather drifted into the wall and pinned against the painted Storian, like a quill pen waiting to be used. Agatha reached up instinctively, her fingers grazing the feather. . . . The tile beneath the feather receded sharply into the wall and vanished. All at once the tiles in the column beneath vanished too, revealing a vacant strip in the wall, just large enough for her to slip through. Heart thumping, she squeezed her way into the hole . . .

. . . only to find a dimly lit chamber with a smaller white-marble door waiting for her. Agatha opened the door to see a dimmer passage and a smaller white door, then more dimmer passages and smaller doors, dimmer, smaller, smaller, dimmer . . . until at last she crawled on her knees through a tiny porthole into pitch-blackness.

Agatha staggered up in cold, infinite dark, clasping her goose-pimpling arms. She focused on her rising fear and felt her fingertip heat up, flickering to light.

"Where am I?" she gasped.

"In the part of her memory Evelyn wants no one to see,"

replied a voice she knew.

Slowly Agatha held up her fingerglow like a spotlight.

Professor August Sader smiled back at her.

With her last chance to find the Storian at stake, Sophie knew she'd have to win most of the day's five challenges.

She felt palpable relief after she won the first two, with Hort magically brittling her opponent's blade in Weapons' axe-chopping contest, then distracting people away from Sophie's hiding spot in Survival's massive game of hide-and-seek. But even with Hort's help, she'd barely beaten Tedros, who back at full strength managed the second rank in both.

As Sophie entered Professor Manley's charred classroom, focused on the next challenge, she felt the prince hang his arm over her broad shoulders.

"Cheating again, I see, Filip."

"Perhaps if *I* find the Storian, it'll stop your stupid Trial," Sophie shot back.

"You sure did a good job of finding the Storian last night," Tedros puffed.

"Kept you alive, didn't I?" Sophie retorted—

"Tedros, Filip, stop your flirting," Manley growled, entering behind them.

All the boys looked at Tedros and Filip, who stiffened awkwardly and separated.

Flustered, Sophie placed behind Tedros in the next two challenges, distracted by thoughts as to whether the prince was, in fact, flirting with her—

Of course he wasn't flirting with me, she harangued herself. *I'm a boy, you idiot. A boy!*

"He's taking your top ranks, Filip," Hort grouched as they headed to last class. "Whoever wins last Tryout wins the day. You might lose your team leader spot, Filip! We have to sabotage him—"

"I said *no*," Sophie lashed so sharply Hort jumped.

With the Blue Forest off-limits until the Trial the next night, the 80 boys in Forest Fitness converged inside Evil Hall and found Albemarle perched atop a rotting chandelier.

"A simple race around the castle," the woodpecker directed, peering down at them over his spectacles.

Sophie watched a fluorescent yellow line magically shoot across the brick floor, between her legs, out the hall, and down the stairs.

"First one to follow the yellow brick road all the way back to this hall wins first rank." Albemarle rustled a small ledger from under his wing and squinted hard at it. "Based on the tally, Filip has a slim lead over Aric and Chaddick for the team leader spot and the right to choose the tenth member of the Trial team. But it's still anyone's race."

Sophie eyed Aric, Chaddick, and the fleet of snarling boys, all crouched to a runner's lunge.

"Ready . . . ," Albemarle chirped. "Set . . ."

Sophie felt Hort's grip on her bicep and his wet breath in her ear. "Run, Filip. Run for your *life*—"

"Go!"

Seventy-nine boys thundered like bulls towards the door—

Sophie, however, remained in place, buffing her ragged nails until she heard the deafening crash. Nonchalant, she crawled over the mass of moaning bodies at the door, wondering how boys had ever survived this long in nature if they didn't even have the common sense to take turns going down stairs. By the time the first boys recovered, Sophie had already returned to the finish line, barely breaking a sweat.

"Seems Filip really wants Storian duty, doesn't he?" smirked Castor, tramping in behind the last groaning boy.

Sophie sighed with relief, blowing up her floppy hair. Somehow she'd find that pen tonight. She'd unearth each and every brick if she had to—

"And yet Filip didn't show *up* for his duties last night," the dog sneered rabidly at her. "If you think something else matters more than finding the pen that keeps our world *alive*, Filip, by all means, hop to it."

Sophie straightened. "No—I just—"

"Vex, you were closest to the door. *You'll* take Storian duty instead," Castor snapped.

"No, no, no!" Sophie cried, aghast. "I'll do it!"

"See, Filip will do it," Vex piped, clearly unenthusiastic about a sleepless night of searching—

"Not if Filip's Trial team *leader*, he won't," Castor grouched, peering at Albemarle's ledger. "Even more reason Filip needs his rest tonight, if we don't want this lot to be slaves." He glowered menacingly at his new, elf-faced team leader. "Try to leave your bed tonight, and I'll chain you to it."

Sophie stifled a scream, heart imploding. The Storian!

She'd just lost her chance at the Storian!

She spun away from the dog, hyperventilating. *How can we go home?*

Adrenaline blasted through her boy muscles. She had to call Agatha. Light a red lantern in her window and Agatha would know to get here *now.* Sophie wheezed for breath, sweat pouring down her ribs. *Don't panic!* Agatha would find a way. Agatha always saved her. They'd flee this castle together and hide in the Woods until it was safe to return—safe to find the Storian and get home—

"One more thing, Filip," said Castor. "As official Trial team leader, you earned the right to choose a friend to join you in fighting Sophie's team. . . ."

Sophie couldn't hear the dog anymore . . . just her pummeling heart, pleading for Agatha . . .

"All those boys who think they've been a good enough friend to Filip to deserve a spot in the Trial, step forward now," growled Castor.

Everboys, Neverboys, and foreign princes burbled and buzzed to each other, but only one boy stepped out from the mass.

Sophie ricocheted to attention, seeing Hort's stupid grin.

Of course. This was the deal the weasel wanted.

Sophie inhaled, trying to slow her heartbeat. Let the cretin in, for all she cared. She'd never go into that Trial. One red lantern and Agatha would be here to get them home. She started to nod at Hort, desperate to get out of this hall and light the alarm—

Until another boy stepped forward.

"I'd like to be considered too," said Tedros.

"Professor Sader?" Agatha rasped, finger glowing brighter as she stepped towards him in the pitch-black void.

Wearing his usual shamrock suit, her silver-maned, hazel-eyed history teacher gazed back at her as if he was still alive. "We only have a few minutes, Agatha, and I have much to show you."

"But how—how are you here—" Agatha breathed—

"Evelyn made the mistake of letting you into her tampered memories," said Professor Sader, seemingly floating in the darkness. "As soon as you doubted their truth, you opened the door to what lay behind them."

"So what I saw in the tortoise's book was right?"

"No history is the complete truth, Agatha. And after your time at this school, you should know far better than to trust what you find in any book. Even mine."

"But why did you make the School Master bring your sister to teach here ten years ago? And why did he banish her—"

"We don't have time for questions, Agatha," her teacher said sternly. "What you are about to see are Evelyn's own memories, untampered, undiluted, and buried so deep that she will surely know when they are accessed. But we must take that risk. For this is your only way to understand why she is in your fairy tale. And the only way to understand the truth about the enemy you face."

Agatha couldn't get words out, tears burning her eyes. She didn't want to see anything. She just wanted to stay here in darkness with him, where she felt so safe—

"I must leave you now, Agatha," said her teacher gently. "But know I am watching you, every step of your story. And there is a long way left before you find its end."

"No, please—" Agatha choked. "Don't leave!"

Professor Sader flashed to light in a silent blast, and Agatha shielded her face . . . before feeling herself tumbling through blinding white space until her feet touched ground.

Agatha opened her eyes to find herself facing a shelf crammed with books, the air clearer than in Evelyn's corrupted stories, the hues richer and more vibrant, as if the haze had finally been lifted from the truth. She peered at the colorful spines on the shelf—*Hansel and Gretel*, *The Princess and the Pea*, *The Juniper Tree*—and knew instantly where she was.

Agatha whirled to see the School Master hunched over the Storian as it magically painted the last page in a storybook atop the white stone table. Agatha watched the School Master frown deeper and deeper as the enchanted pen finished its ending, his billowing blue robes draped over his body, his gleaming silver mask covering all of his face except his shiny blue eyes, full lips, and thick, ghostly white hair. The sight of him so present, so alive, made the hair stand up on the back of Agatha's neck, but she knew he couldn't see her.

The School Master leered harder as the pen finished its last stroke, completing its vision of a giant gruesomely stabbed by a prince, clutching his fair princess—

"The End," he growled, and magically dashed the book against the wall.

With a puff of smoke, the Storian conjured a fresh storybook from its nib, flipped the green wooden cover to the blank first page, and the School Master watched it begin a new tale.

"Once upon a time, there was a girl named Thumbelina . . ."

Shadows of butterflies fell over the page, and he turned to see a red-winged swarm float through the window and magically congeal into Evelyn Sader, still ten years younger. Only unlike the kind-looking, bright-faced Evelyn in her false history, this Evelyn had the same mischief and malevolence in her eyes that Agatha recognized.

"You are forbidden here, Evelyn," the School Master hissed. He stabbed his finger, erasing the patch of floor beneath her in slashing white streaks—

"My brother is lying to you," Evelyn said calmly.

The School Master froze his spell, leaving Evelyn on a small stone patch of floor, surrounded by white oblivion.

"I know you're Evil, Master. Evil as your brother was Good," Evelyn said, unyielding under his glare. "And I come to tell you that you've chosen the wrong Professor Sader with whom to invest your future."

The School Master slowly lowered his finger, and the floor filled in around Evelyn, putting her back on solid ground.

"I know what it is you seek, Master," Evelyn continued, slinking towards him. "A heart that will reverse the curse on Evil . . . that will commit any sin in the name of your love . . . a heart that is worthy of Never After . . ."

She put her hand on his chest, her green eyes burning into his.

"And that heart is *mine*."

The School Master stared at her, frozen still . . . before his lips curled and he turned away. "Be gone, Evelyn. Before you make an even greater fool of yourself."

"August tells you the one you seek is from Woods Beyond. That is why you pollute our school with these vile Readers."

The School Master tightened, his back to her.

"It is a death trap, Master," said Evelyn. "I know my brother's heart. He leads you not to your true love—but to the one who will slay you."

The School Master spun to her. "You are only jealous of your brother's powers, like a third-rate henchman. You have no power to see the future—"

"I have the power to *hear* the present, and that is far stronger," Evelyn said, undaunted. "I can hear words, wishes, secrets—even yours, Master. I know what it is people seek, what they desire, what they would give their *lives* for. I can change the course of anyone's story and end it the way I wish."

"The laws of our world forbid interfering in the tales of the Storian without incurring our own destruction," the School Master said, grimacing at the pen. "It is a lesson I have no intention of learning *twice*."

"Because you still believe in the power of the pen. You try to end Evil's slaughter without taking action yourself. You try to control a pen that seeks only to punish you for killing your brother." Evelyn's face lost its hard edges. "But I know your heart, Master, and surely you know mine. For only you and I know what Evil is truly capable of—Evil far greater than any story has ever seen. Kiss me, and you'll have love on your side, love as hateful as Good's is true. A Never After so enduring, so poisonous that Good has no weapon to defeat us. Kiss me, and we shall destroy Good, one story at a time . . . until the pen has no power left at all."

The School Master lifted his shining blue eyes to her. "And you believe without doubt that *you're* my true love?" he said, slowly leaning in. . . . "That *you're* the one my soul seeks?"

Evelyn blushed in his grip, ready for his kiss.

"With every shred of my dark heart."

The School Master's lips stopped an inch from hers. He smiled wickedly. "Then prove it."

Agatha's heart chilled as the scene evaporated around her, replaced by the open, grassy field of the Clearing at lunchtime. But instead of its usual quiet decorum, with Evers sitting together on one side and Nevers on the other, now the Nevers gaped in astonishment as Evers assaulted each other in civil war—Everboys punching and beating one another with sticks, Evergirls in hair-pulling, nail-clawing catfights, teachers, wolves, fairies trying uselessly to pull them apart—as bloodred butterflies swarmed over the scene. Agatha saw a younger-looking Professor Dovey sprint past her, accosting Lady Lesso, who'd just come from Evil's Tunnel of Trees.

"It's Evelyn," Professor Dovey panted. "Her butterflies are eavesdropping on my students' conversations and whispering them back in the halls! Every minor grievance, insult, jealousy aired solely to incite chaos!"

"One of the lessons I teach Nevers is that they should insult each other to their faces. Avoids such dramatics," Lady Lesso purred.

"You are Evil's Dean! It is your responsibility to control her—"

"And Ever discipline is *your* responsibility, Clarissa," Lady Lesso yawned. "Perhaps you should speak to her brother. He's the one responsible for her placement here."

"August refuses to speak to her or answer my questions. Please, Lady Lesso!" begged Professor Dovey. "A teacher cannot interfere in students' stories! It's only a matter of time before Evelyn meddles with your students too!"

Lady Lesso frowned at her Good colleague, deliberating. . . .

The scene melted away, and Agatha found herself in Lady Lesso's old frozen classroom, with Evelyn Sader standing before Evil's Dean at her ice-carved desk.

"I will not ask you again," said Lady Lesso glacially. "You will cease spying on students, Good or Evil, or be removed from this school."

Evelyn smirked through gap teeth. "And you expect me to take orders from *you*? A Dean who sneaks into the Woods to see the son she hides?"

Lady Lesso blanched, violet eyes wide. "What did you say?"

"Misses you, does he?" said Evelyn, skulking towards her. "Perhaps he'll grow up to be as weak as his mother."

Lady Lesso looked stunned for a moment before recovering her icy snarl. "I *have* no son."

"That's what you told the School Master, didn't you?" Evelyn returned, prowling closer. "You know there's a curse on Evil in the Woods. You'd do anything to keep yourself safe here at school. But no teacher of Evil is allowed to retain attachments outside these gates—and certainly not its *Dean*. So you too vowed that you gave up your child and dedicated your soul to the pursuit of cold-blooded Evil." Evelyn loomed over Lady Lesso, gilded nails digging into her frozen desk. "But every night you still sneak to that cave where you keep him. Every night you pretend he'll always have a loving mother, instead of telling him the truth. But mark my words, Lady Lesso . . . one day your son will *hate* you even more because of it. Because soon you'll have to pick between yourself and him. And we both know who you'll choose."

"Get out!" Lady Lesso leapt up, spitting. "GET OUT!"

But Evelyn was already sashaying away, butterflies following her in a slash of red.

Lady Lesso sat alone in the cold, empty classroom. Her cheeks reddened as she began to shake uncontrollably, welling tears. She heard voices and quickly wiped them away before the next class of Nevers surged in. . . .

Agatha could barely breathe as the scene dissolved, returning her to the School Master's tower. This time, the School Master was alone with August Sader.

"Lady Lesso and Professor Dovey insist your sister be evicted immediately," said the School Master. "And given my Deans' usual inability to agree on anything at any time, I believe I must fulfill their wishes." He peered out the window at his schools. "I'll need you to take over Evelyn's classes in Evil as soon as she is gone."

"As you wish, Master," Professor Sader replied behind him.

The School Master turned. "And you offer no defense of your own sister? You are the one who insisted she teach here."

"Perhaps she's just here before her time," Professor Sader said with a mysterious smile. "Now if you'll please excuse me, I have a class to teach."

Eyeing him carefully, the School Master raised his finger. Professor Sader started to disappear in streaks of white—only to suddenly fill back in.

"One last thing, August," said the School Master, recalling him. "The one I seek . . . you swear on your own life she is not one of our world?"

Professor Sader didn't blink. "I swear on my life."

The School Master smiled and turned away. "By the way. Do let Lady Lesso know that her privileges to travel beyond the school gates have been revoked."

Professor Sader erased from his tower behind him in a brilliant flash of white.

Agatha covered her eyes until the white light dimmed and peeked through her fingers to see Evelyn back in front of the School Master.

Evelyn looked past him to see hundreds of students gathered in the windows of Good and Evil, along with the teachers of both schools, like an audience in wait of an execution.

"And you choose my brother over me?" she said, sneering at the spectating masses. "You choose a man who will destroy you over a woman who will save you?"

"Your brother does not lie," said the School Master quietly.

Evelyn twirled to him. "He would sacrifice more than truth to see you dead. He would sacrifice his *life*."

The School Master gazed at the Storian thoughtfully. "My brother put a piece of his soul into the students' crests, ensuring that they are protected from me," he said at last. "I too prefer not to take chances without insurance."

He turned back to Evelyn. "But I'm afraid your time at this school has come to an end for now."

Evelyn grabbed him by the shoulders. "And what if you're wrong? What if I am your true love?" she pleaded frantically. "What if you *die* for your mistake?"

The School Master looked down at her hands clawing him. "Such devotion . . ." He grinned into her forest-green eyes. "Surely I can't deny you *all* hope."

Slowly he reached towards his chest and drew out a ghostly wisp of bright-blue smoke, like a glowing sliver of his heart. Clasping it in his fist, he placed it against Evelyn's heart and watched it sucked inside. Evelyn looked down in shock as all the red butterflies on her dress magically turned blue.

"*My* insurance, Evelyn." The School Master caressed her cheek, amused. "For if I am wrong, then one day you may return to this school." He pulled away sharply. "And bring your true love *back with you*."

Evelyn gasped—

The School Master blasted her out of the tower in a comet of blue light, which raged high over the Woods and ebbed into the horizon.

Agatha stared into the School Master's lethal blue eyes as the scene suddenly evaporated in a cloud of smoke—

Agatha coughed, waving her hands from the noxious fog as screaming Evers fled past her. She was back in the phantom, hazy Good Hall . . . back in Evelyn's tampered history . . .

Which could only mean one thing.

Agatha spun to see Evelyn Sader storming towards her across Good Hall, her face flushed with wrath. Only this Evelyn was ten years older. This Evelyn's butterflies were blue instead of red. This Evelyn wasn't a phantom at all, charging lethally towards the girl who'd just invaded her memories. . . .

"That's why you're in our fairy tale—you're using us somehow—" Agatha cried, retreating. "You're—you're bringing him b-b-back—"

Evelyn shot her with a flash of blue light as the hall melted back to the present, the witches running towards Agatha as she collapsed to the floor, too late to save her.

Agatha.

Agatha.

Agatha.

Sophie gaped at Tedros and Hort, both asking to be her teammate in the Trial against *herself.*

I need Agatha now, Sophie thought, trembling. She couldn't get anywhere near that Trial.

Castor kicked Hort forward with his paw. "Each of you has one chance to tell Filip why *you* deserve to be his choice."

Hort glared at Tedros so horribly he looked like he might burst into flames. "I should fight with Filip because I'm not a fair-weather friend who was only nice to him when I didn't get whipped." He pouted at Sophie, pale lips quivering. "Plus I'm Filip's best friend. He said it himself."

Sophie stared at Hort, who'd lost all his fury and now just looked like a pitiful rat.

"Well, maybe I'm not Filip's best friend," a new voice said behind him. "But I'll keep him alive."

Sophie slowly looked up.

"What I had with Agatha was the deepest love I'd ever had," said Tedros, their eyes locking. "But Filip showed me something even deeper, like the bond of a brother I've always wanted. He isn't like us princes—rash and uptight and with our heads up our bums. He's honest and sensitive and thinks a lot and has real feelings. Boys never have real feelings . . . at least not ones that they don't toss off or hide. But he's a boy in the way a real boy's supposed to be, built of honor, valor, and heart. And maybe for the first time, he's made me understand why only death will separate Agatha from Sophie." Tedros gazed at Filip's stunned, elfish face. "Because I've never felt as loyal to someone, boy or girl, as I feel about him."

No one in Evil Hall made a sound.

Sophie teared up, staring at her once-prince. All her life, she'd just wanted a boy to want her. How could she ever know it'd be as a boy herself?

"Tedros or Hort, Filip?" Castor said, stepping between the boys.

Sophie tore eyes from Tedros. What was she doing! She had to call Agatha right now!

"TEDROS OR HORT?" Castor roared, scowling at her.

Sophie steadied her breaths, squelching Tedros' echoing words. Agatha would be on the way soon.

It doesn't matter what I say. It won't happen. The Trial won't happen.

But if it did . . . if somehow it did . . . the prince whose mission it was to kill her was now asking to be *let in*!

Hort.

HORT.

SAY HORT!

The name came smoothly, soundly off her tongue, and she heaved relief, raring to light a lantern and call her best friend—

But as she looked up at Hort, the weasel's smile disappeared, replaced with a look of such horror and betrayal that Sophie knew it wasn't Hort she'd named at all.

Slowly Sophie turned.

Tedros smiled back at his best friend, glowing with gratitude and affection—glowing with the promise to protect Sophie the Boy from Sophie the Girl.

Only it wasn't Tedros' glow that stopped Sophie's heart.

It was the glow over his shoulder . . .

. . . seeping through the window of the boys' hall . . .

. . . blaring far across the bay from the girls' tower . . .

. . . the glow of a red lantern, blazing with alarm . . .

And that's when Sophie knew she'd made a terrible, terrible mistake.

22

Last One In

"Feels like home."

Ripples of water strummed beneath the boy's words, like harp strings to a song.

Agatha opened her eyes to sun spilling across the surface of a familiar lake, the water shivering and spangling in a warm breeze. For a brief moment it stilled, reflecting her dumpy black dress and ghostly pale face, next to a golden-haired boy in a blue Evers' coat.

"H-h-how did we get here?" Agatha

breathed, looking up at him.

"There's my princess," Tedros said, gazing out at the water. "Old Agatha would have flushed like a tomato, asking 'Where's Sophie?'"

Agatha flushed like a tomato. "Where is she! Is she safe?" she blurted, swiveling to a blinding glare of gold light, erasing everything around the lake. "Is she here—"

"Been meaning to ask you," Tedros said, flicking a blade of grass into the water. "From the moment we met, you despised me . . . called me a murderer, a puffed-up windbag, a donkey's behind, and who knows what else. . . ." He flicked another blade, not looking at her. "What made you change your mind?"

"I don't understand—where are we—" said Agatha anxiously, scanning the fiery gold walls of light hemming them in, like the black walls of wind that had once hidden her prince's phantom. "What happened to our story—"

"That's what we're both trying to figure out, isn't it? It's why I need the answer, Agatha," Tedros said, still looking ahead. "I need to know what you saw in me."

The red seeped out of Agatha's cheeks. Once upon a time, she'd been here on this same shore, flicking matches instead of grass, asking Sophie what her friend saw in her.

"It was one moment," Agatha said softly. "That's all."

Her prince finally met her eyes.

"It was the way you looked at Sophie after she abandoned you in last year's Trial," she said. "The heartbreak in your face. As if all you'd ever wanted was for someone to protect you the way you protect them."

Tedros growled and turned away. "You make me sound like a girl."

Agatha smiled to herself. "It's what made me see a boy."

The prince's shoulders tensed.

"A boy as vulnerable as he is strong," Agatha said, watching him.

"And yet you think I'm weak enough to hurt you," he said quietly. "You, the only person who ever saw who I truly am."

Tedros turned with a piercing, pleading stare.

"Feels like there's a piece still missing, don't you think?"

The wall of gold behind him cracked open, swallowing him with light before Agatha could reach for him. The grass suddenly colored navy blue around her, the trees turned periwinkle, the lake scorched to fire, waves rising out of flame—

Agatha shot her eyes open in the dark, head hammering. Silver stars blinked back at her in a dead-clear sky. She jolted up, swaddled in puppy-patterned blankets, to the warmth of a small crackling fire beside her, two girls' shadowy faces gaping at her in the barren, deserted Clearing.

"You're awake," Kiko peeped. "She's awake!"

Reena choked on a chocolate lollipop. "I-I-I'll go get the Dean," she stammered, big backside wobbling into the dark.

Agatha felt words garbling and shriveling away in her dry mouth. Her limbs were ice-cold, her temples throbbing as her mind sloshed around panicked images . . . Tedros' beseeching, beautiful face by a lake . . . Sophie's petrified face as a boy . . . Evelyn's face charging towards her . . .

"The School Master—have to tell Dovey—" Agatha rasped frantically, her last moments awake blurring back. "She's bringing him to life—"

"Oh dear. Dean told us you'd be a bit batty when you woke," Kiko fussed, palm to Agatha's forehead. "Mmm, terrible fever, like you've baked near a fire."

"There's a fire right there," Agatha croaked—

"Dean said you had a reaction to the phantom smoke," Kiko motormouthed obliviously. "'Cause you're a Reader, sensitive immunity and all that. Hester, Anadil, and Dot kept raving the Dean did something to you, but everyone thinks they inhaled too much smoke too. Last I saw, Hester was waving some red lantern out a window like a loon. Only thing worse than a tattooed witch is a *deranged* tattooed witch. Still, to be out cold for a whole *day* is pathetic, Agatha, immunity or not. You missed everything: the team announcement, the big feast, the play—though it ended early because Mona's headdress tried to eat her. I say Hester cursed it, if you ask m—"

Agatha seized her collar. "Listen, you nutbrained canary!" she barked, still ragged and slow. "The Dean's *dangerous*! I have to tell Dovey and Lesso before the Trial—"

"Agatha." Kiko's voice was hard and firm. "The Trial started two hours ago."

"What?" Agatha let go of her in shock. "But that's—that's—" Dread clamped her voice.

Slowly she looked down and pulled away the puppied blankets, revealing her body clad in a sapphire-blue Trial tunic, made of thin armored mesh and a matching hooded wool cloak over it lined with silver brocade. Tucked into the cloak's front pocket, crested with a blue butterfly, was a white silk handkerchief, glinting at the seams with enchantment.

Agatha spun to the Blue Forest gates towering over her, magically aglow with flames, sealing those inside, while a fuzzy, enchanted gray haze veiled the trees through the gates, preventing a view into the Forest. Agatha craned up to the giant wooden board over the west gate, glowing fireflies spelling out each word:

TRIAL BY TALE: GIRLS

Sophie
Hester
Dot
Beatrix
Anadil
Mona
Arachne
Millicent
Yara

"That's who's in the Forest now," said Kiko. "They're sending pairs in every ten minutes: one girl, one boy. Nine pairs in, with one left to go. No one's dropped their flags, so no surrenders yet—"

But Agatha was still gaping at the board. "*Sophie?* Sophie's . . . *inside*?"

"Went in with the first pair, the Dean said. Thing is, no

one *saw* her go in. But the fireflies lit her name up, which means she *has* to be in the Forest! Thank God, 'cause we can't win without you two. Dean never doubted you'd wake up—"

"But how can Sophie be in the Trial!" Agatha sputtered, staggering back towards the gates. "When did she come back? Why didn't she help me? I need to see Dovey or Lesso or—"

A cheer exploded above her.

"AG-A-THA! AG-A-THA! AG-A-THA!"

Agatha gawked up at the blue castle balconies, teeming with students who now had a direct view of her through the Clearing's bare trees. They hollered her name as they rang noisemakers and rained confetti, waving colorful signs: Go Girls! Boys = Slaves! S&A Save the Day!

Agatha squinted at the highest Charity balcony, where all the teachers were cramped together, faces barely visible. But she could see Professor Dovey's and Lady Lesso's stiff silhouettes, their terrified gapes—and Pollux guarding the door behind them, head on a massive bear's body.

"See, Bilious, I told you she'd be ready," a voice chimed.

Agatha whirled to the Dean sweeping around the west gate corner with pockmarked, pear-headed Professor Manley, accompanied by two floating, green-haired nymphs. Professor Manley growled at Kiko, who fled like a lamb, before snarling even more menacingly at the sight of Agatha.

"Lucky you," he sneered. "Just in time."

"Lucky indeed," the Dean said, with a smirk that told Agatha it wasn't luck at all.

Manley tramped towards the east gate. "Evelyn, any more

funny business and it'll be open season on all of you," he spat back. "Sending in our last boy in two minutes whether the Reader's ready or not."

As soon as he vanished, Agatha spun to the Dean, scarlet red. "How'd you get Sophie into the Trial, you witch! Did you trap her when she came back for me? Did you stun her *too*?"

The Dean slunk towards her, lips curling into a grin. "You see, Agatha, in your version of the story, I'm the villain. In your version, *I* caused Sophie's symptoms . . . *I* put Sophie in the Trial . . . *I* can bring back a ghost . . . ," she cooed. "But haven't you learned by now?" She took Agatha's cheeks into her sharp, gilded nails. "Your version of the story is usually *wrong*."

Agatha bared teeth in her face. *"Really?* Pray tell, if it's not you doing all these things, who *is*?"

The Dean smiled darkly. "What's that my brother used to say? Sometimes the answer is too close to see. Sometimes the answer"—she pressed her cold lips to Agatha's ear—"is right *under your nose*."

"You're nothing but a pack of lies," Agatha seethed, shoving her away, but the Dean just grinned wider, as if savoring a secret.

"Take her to the gates," she declared.

Nymphs grabbed each of Agatha's arms, and together they pulled her off the ground, floating her towards the Forest's west gate—

"No! Sophie's coming out alive, you hear me!" Agatha yelled back. "We're coming out *alive*!"

But the Dean's Cheshire cat smile receded as the nymphs

flew Agatha around the corner, past the gate's flaming, criss-crossed bars, the girls' cheers amplifying above.

The nymphs dragged her towards a swarm of butterflies, hovering deliberately over a portion of the west gate beneath the girls' scoreboard. Writhing uselessly in the nymphs' grip, Agatha peered up at the boys' red castle, towering over the Forest from the east. She could see boys cramming the balconies in their red-and-black leather uniforms, waving signs and bellowing faraway chants that faded into the girls'. The boys' scoreboard angled towards their school over the east gate, lit up with fireflies. *That's where the boys must be going in,* she thought—

Suddenly the moment hit her dead-on. This was it. It was really happening.

She was going into the Trial against her own prince. Outlast him and all the other bloodthirsty boys and princes, and she and Sophie might escape alive. Lose, and she and her best friend would be executed together.

There is no missing piece, she gritted, cursing her weak, prince-filled dreams.

It was she and Sophie against Tedros in a Trial to the death.

But when did Sophie come back? Had she found the Storian? Agatha thought frantically, looking at her friend's name on the scoreboard. *Did she fight going into the Trial?*

And yet . . . none of the girls had *seen* Sophie go in, Kiko said. Agatha frowned, confused. Had the Dean not forced her friend in, after all?

"What happened to Sophie?" she appealed to the nymphs

as they flew her closer to the butterflies under the girl's scoreboard. "Did you see her—"

Her voice dropped off. Because now she could read the names on the boys' scoreboard across the Forest.

Tedros

Aric

Prince of Avonlea

Prince of Ginnymill

Ravan

Nicholas

Prince of Shazabah Desert

Prince of Foxwood

Only there was one more name, glowing at the top.

Filip.

Agatha held in a scream.

Filip.

Filip.

Filip.

Sophie was in the Trial as a boy.

Sophie was in the Trial fighting with the same boys who wanted to kill her.

Agatha's horror abated, all questions of how it had happened fading away. If Sophie was a boy, she'd be *safe* from Tedros, wouldn't she? *As long as Sophie stays Filip, Tedros can't find her,* Agatha thought, heartbeat slowing as the nymphs set her down in front of the circling butterflies. *And if he can't find her, he can't kill her.* Perhaps her friend had made an ingenious move after all. . . .

Agatha's stomach took a sharp twist.

Three days. Yuba had said Merlin's spell would only last three days . . . until the start of the Trial.

Sophie would revert back to a girl any second.

Right in a pack of boys who would kill her on the spot.

Blood shot through Agatha's legs, priming her to run.

She had to find Sophie *now*.

From the boys' and girls' scoreboards came a detonation of red and blue flares into the sky. AGATHA's name sparked in firefly glow onto the girls' board as their last combatant, VEX's onto the boys'—

The blue butterflies zoomed towards the gate, outlining a shape of a door against its flaming bars. Through this door, the flames instantly melted to water, opening a small rain-curtain into the Forest. Agatha squinted through the blurring downpour at a slim dirt path ahead, snaking through shimmering blue ferns.

A year ago, she and Sophie had fought this Trial together and come out alive.

This year, they'd have to find each other.

All Agatha could hope was that Tedros hadn't found Sophie first.

I'm coming, Sophie.

The nymphs shoved her through the gate and she felt a warm, embracing rain. Then Agatha heard the roar of flames behind her and she knew she was inside.

23

Death in the Forest

Every muscle in Sophie's boy body froze as she watched Agatha's name light up on the girls' board over the Blue Forest.

She's inside.

Agatha's inside.

All the fear and self-loathing Sophie had bottled up for the past day, since she'd seen her friend's red lantern blazing, since she'd trapped herself in this execrable Trial, rushed out of her like a wind, and she nearly buckled to her knees. Whatever

she'd done to bring them both here, at least they were both alive and in the same place.

How could I pick Tedros! Sophie abused herself. In that dundering moment of absolute stupidity, thinking he might actually like her again, she'd forgotten two things. First, Tedros wanted to kill her and her best friend. And second . . . he thinks *I'm a boy. A BOY!*

Sophie looked out at the dense Forest in front of her, lit up for the Trial with a snowy white-blue glow, like a psychotic winter wonderland. Everything in her wanted to scream out for Agatha, to run and hide with her—

"Hurry up, Filip," Tedros frowned, glancing back as he waded through the tangled Turquoise Thicket, round steel shield and sword Excalibur in hand, the sewn T on his black-and-red cloak collar spotted with blood. "You've almost killed us both already. Try to keep up."

Sophie rushed to follow him, sheathed sword banging against her hulking thigh, the F initial on her boys' uniform stained with even more blood. Twenty minutes into the Trial, they'd come across a wounded stymph, its fleshless body lying in the Blueberry Fields, one of its bony wings smashed. Tedros said to leave it be, for stymphs attacked Nevers, not princes—only to see it lunge screeching at Filip and swallow his shield whole. Tedros leapt to his friend's defense while Filip howled and bandied about like an idiot, the stymph nearly eating both of them before Tedros finally beheaded it. He'd been giving his friend wary looks ever since.

"Not my fault the bird's demented," Sophie insisted for the

fourth time, trying to sound as princely as she could.

The last day in the School for Boys had barreled by in a blur of panic. Desperate to answer Agatha's alarm, Sophie waited until nightfall, hoping to abscond to the girls' castle, but Castor slept right outside the Doom Room to ensure the boys' team leader stayed in his cell and got his rest. Not that Sophie could rest if she wanted—Tedros spent the entire night drawing detailed maps of the Blue Forest, sharpening his father's sword, which Manley had grudgingly returned, and blustering strategy like he once had as Good's army captain.

"We'll be our own group, Fil. Let Aric and the princes take on the other girls while we go straight for Sophie and Agatha. No doubt they're fighting together, just like me and you," he said. "We have to slay them on the spot, or they'll kill us first."

"Can't we just hide under the Blue Brook bridge until sunrise?" Sophie moaned, pillow over her floppy prince hair.

"That's what I'd expect a girl to say," Tedros scoffed.

Now that girl, trapped in a boy's body, followed her would-be assassin through a tangled blue thicket. Tedros peered up at each turquoise oak appraisingly before jumping onto the tallest trunk in the batch.

"What are you doing?" Sophie hissed.

"Agatha just entered at the west gate," Tedros said, monkeying up the tree. "First thing she'll do is cross the Fernfield and find Sophie. Come on, we'll have a good view of the ferns up here."

Sophie had never climbed a tree before ("Only boys could enjoy such a low form of entertainment," she'd said), but the thought of seeing Agatha sent her bounding up the oak even faster than Tedros. She found her footing on the highest bough, icy breeze numbing her face, and tried to squint over the dense treetop as the prince climbed up next to her.

"Can't see anything," she grouched.

"Here, take my hand."

Sophie stared at Tedros' open palm.

"Relax, mate, I won't let you fall," he said.

Sophie put her big hand in his firm grip as he inched forward towards thinner foliage, pulling his cell mate behind him. Sophie's stubbled face blushed red-hot, remembering the feeling of Tedros holding her hand, the way he had a year ago when they were first in love . . . when he asked her to the Ball right here in the Forest . . . leaning forward in moonlight just like this . . . lips reaching for hers. . . .

"You sweat like a hog, Filip," Tedros snorted, letting go of her clammy palm.

Sophie jolted from her trance, silently screaming at herself, and grabbed on to a branch, off-balance.

"Can't see any of the girls," Tedros said. "Can you?"

Sophie peered through leaves at a wide view of the north Forest. The Fernfield, Pine Shrubs, and Turquoise Thicket were amply lit with the same wintry glow, but she couldn't see any of the girls' sapphire uniforms—just a few shadowy boy cloaks prowling through the shrubs. She felt a sharp sadness at not seeing Agatha, then relief that Tedros couldn't either.

"She and Sophie must be hiding scared," Tedros said. "We'll wait here until one of them moves—"

A blast of white fireworks shot up into the sky from the south Forest, signaling the first surrender. Tedros and Filip swiveled, almost careening off their branch, and saw treetops rustling far away, near the pumpkin patch. Screams echoed, boy and girl, along with a monster's shrieks, as blue pumpkins flew over the trees like kicked balls, followed by a flurry of red and white fireworks in one long, frightening detonation.

Then it went quiet.

"What happened?" Sophie gasped.

"One of the teacher's traps," said Tedros. "Only it got kids from both sides, whatever it was."

Sophie whirled to the scoreboards. *Please. Not Agatha.*

Vex, Ravan, Mona, and Arachne all went dark.

Sophie sighed with relief—then tightened. "Didn't kill any of them, did it?"

Tedros shook his head. "Fireworks are different if you die instead of surrender. I asked Manley."

Sophie felt a sharp wave of nausea. The idea that Tedros would actually kill her had never quite sunk in. But him asking Manley that simple question suddenly made it real.

Footsteps crunched in the thicket below, and the two boys looked down to see a pair of princes, one burly, one whippet thin, lurking down the path, both armed with battle-axes.

"Nevers are crap at fighting monsters—too used to having 'em on their side," the burly prince said. "Even with our help, those Neverboys dropped their flags like ninnies."

"Ah well, more chance at the treasure for us," said the thinner one, gritting his teeth from the cold. "No sign of those Reader girls, though, and we've combed the whole south Forest."

"Probably hiding under the Brook Bridge like cowards. Come on."

Sophie watched them leave, heart sinking deeper.

"Filip?" Tedros said, seeing his friend's face.

"Turning princes into assassins? Wagering treasure on two girls' lives?" Sophie turned, pallid and scared. "This isn't you, Tedros. No matter what you think's happened," she said, low voice breaking. "You're not a villain."

Slowly the prince's face weakened, as if finally seeing himself through his friend's eyes. "You don't know me," he said quietly.

Sophie could feel the branch wobbling, then realized it was her own trembling legs. "What if this is all a mistake?" she rasped. "What if Sophie just wants to go home with her friend?"

Tedros' jaw clamped as he looked away, fighting himself.

"What if she just wants their happy ending back?" Sophie said.

Tedros' body slacked deeper, like a shell about to crack . . .

Then his face hardened again like a mask.

Sophie followed his eyes past her, to the top of a girls' tower looming over the Blue Forest, directly in line with their tree. Tedros squinted at Honor's open-air rooftop, lit up by torches and dissipating fireworks in the sky.

"Come on, let's go," Sophie said quickly, knowing what was on the Honor roof—

But Tedros didn't move, peering at a menagerie of hedges once dedicated to the father he revered . . . now remade in the image of the mother who'd abandoned him.

"Tedros, whatever it is, it isn't worth looking at," Sophie hassled.

Tedros tore a big blue leaf off the tree and turned it to ice with his gold fingerglow. Holding it up to his eye, he magically melted the ice's edges until it curved like a binocular lens, magnifying his view.

"Tedros, please," Sophie entreated.

But he'd already found the last sculpture near the balcony, framed by a wall of purple thorns. The vision of his mother drowning her baby prince with inexorable hate. A mother who wanted her only son dead.

"It's not true," spoke Sophie softly, seeing through his lens. "You know it's not."

Tedros said nothing, staring at the scene, shallow breath fogging the air.

"You want to know why those girls have to die?" he said. "For the same reason my father left a price on my mother's head."

He turned to his friend, eyes wet. "Because it's the only happy ending left."

The hope drained from Sophie's face like a dimming light. "Now you really sound like a villain," she breathed.

The two boys glared at each other, chests touching on the branch, tears in both their eyes.

Tedros shoved by Filip and started climbing down the tree.

"Go hide if you want," he said. "But I'm finding those girls."

Sophie watched him stiffly, sweat chilling as it dripped down her back. Everything in her wanted to run and cower under the bridge until sunrise, to save her own life.

But she couldn't let him find Agatha.

Legs shaking, she followed the prince.

Agatha knew many things about Sophie, from her favorite color (primrose pink) to the strawberry birthmark on her ankle to the way she always blushed red before she laughed. But most of all, Agatha knew Sophie would have one and only one tactic to survive this Trial.

Hide under the bridge.

Knowing Tedros would be hunting her from the moment she entered the Forest—even spying from a tree, for all she knew—Agatha mogrified into a black lynx cat and carried her clothes in her mouth as she slunk through the Fernfield. As she reached the Blue Brook, waters babbling quietly beneath the gray stone bridge, she reverted back to human and dressed in the blue mint bushes before sneaking onto the brook's shadowy bank. The waters were pitch-dark under the bridge, but she couldn't light her fingerglow for fear of attracting boys.

"Sophie?" Agatha whispered, wading into the frigid knee-high water, fish flurrying away from her. For all she knew, Sophie had turned herself into a stingray. "Sophie, it's m-m-me," she hissed, teeth chattering—

An ice-cold hand grabbed the back of her neck and pulled her down into the water. Gasping to the surface, Agatha opened her mouth to scream for help—and saw Hester, Anadil, and Dot looking back at her, faces camouflaged with mud, hidden waist high in water beneath a hollowed-out part of the bank. Agatha could have collapsed in relief.

"Told you she'd come here," Dot humphed to the witches before offering Agatha two handfuls of sardines turned to spinach and Swiss chard. Agatha tended to think of vegetables as rabbit food, but she was too hungry to care. "Where's Sophie?" she snarfled, mouth full of spinach.

"Thought she'd be with you," frowned Anadil, rats peeping out of her collar, their furry faces camouflaged too. "Instead we're all here trying not to die while that wench is off fighting on the wrong *side*."

"Not for long. Yuba's spell will wear off any second," Agatha said, tensing. "We have to find Sophie before she turns back into a girl."

Even Hester's demon looked worried now.

"There's more," said Agatha ominously.

Keeping her voice low, she recounted everything she'd glimpsed in Evelyn's memory, until the witches were practically hyperventilating.

"Bringing the School Master back?" Dot shrieked. *"How?"*

"Keep your voice down, you imbecile!" Anadil spat. "Look, it doesn't make sense. Even a seer can't bring a ghost back from the dead for more than a few seconds—"

"Unless she's found another way," Hester pondered, eyes lifting to Anadil. "Only she needs help to do it."

Agatha's spine prickled, remembering Evelyn's cryptic

words before the nymphs came, implying the Dean wasn't the only Evil in this story. But who else then? Who could help her fulfill such a deadly plan? Who would end up the *villain*?

She thought of the tortoise's message, warning her of this Trial . . . the recipe in the Dean's office, flaunting a spell she'd led them to . . . Evelyn's wicked smile, knowing exactly where Sophie was all this time . . .

"She wanted Sophie and me to come into this Trial apart," Agatha said, suddenly understanding. "That was her plan all along. She wanted Sophie to go in with the boys."

"But why?" asked Dot. "Why would she want Sophie fighting with Tedros?"

Hester had that mulling, thoughtful look again before she glowered up at Agatha. "It's the last time I'm going to ask you this, Agatha. You're sure Sophie's Good?"

Agatha looked up at the boys' scoreboard, FILIP's name glowing in firefly lights.

"The old Sophie would be hiding right here to save her own skin. All of us know it," she said, almost to herself. "But Sophie's out there instead, staying with the boys. . . ." Agatha gazed up at Hester. "Making sure they don't find me."

Hester exhaled, finally convinced. "Then you have to find her before she turns back into a girl, all right? Find Sophie and hide with her until sunrise. Leave fighting the boys to us. If you win the Trial, we'll get another chance to find the Storian. It *has* to be in that tower somewh—"

She stopped cold, eyes narrowing.

Agatha heard the voices now too.

"Millie, we should hide here," said Beatrix, from the bank above them.

Her bald head came into view as she stepped her blue slipper down into the water and waded in shivering, her sapphire cloak floating behind her like a cape. "The boys will assume we're here like cowards," Beatrix said. "If we wait under the bank, we can attack them first."

Millicent treaded in behind, dirty red hair tied up. "I still say we mogrify and wait in a tree."

"And end up naked in a forest if we have to revert back?" Beatrix groused, scanning the banks for a hiding spot. "That won't be *noticeable*—"

Her voice petered out as she glimpsed her own reflection in the dark brook. Only there was something reflected next to it . . . a pair of eyes . . . no, two pairs . . . three. . . .

She looked up with a gasp—Agatha put her hand over her mouth and pinned her against the bank with Anadil, while Hester and Dot held down Millicent.

"Where's the Storian!" Agatha barked, ungagging her.

"In case you missed it, we're on the same *team*," Beatrix spat.

"Where'd you hide it!" Agatha hissed. "Why couldn't Sophie find it!"

"First off, I have no idea what you're talking about. Second, since when did Princess Agatha turn into a bullying henchman!"

"The snakeskin cape under your bed—the boy's uniform—you were *in* the boys' castle—"

"The only thing under my bed is a trunk of makeup and hair extensions, which I miss quite much, if I have to be honest—"

"You're *lying*," Agatha harassed. "We know the Dean sent you!"

"The Dean barely knows me, no matter how much I suck up," Beatrix retorted. "Came into this Trial top ranked, and she hasn't paid the slightest attention. Figure if I win the Trial, she might actually learn my *name*."

Agatha stared in surprise. She searched Beatrix's face until her grip finally loosened, and Beatrix wrenched free.

"Come on, Millie. Let's go hunt boys," Beatrix snapped, tramping down the brook, her freckled friend hastening to catch up.

Agatha gawked glassily at the brook waters, lost in thought. She looked up at Hester, skin pale.

"Hester, if that boy's uniform wasn't Beatrix's . . . then whose was it?"

But Hester wasn't listening, nor were Anadil or Dot. All three were gaping past her, paralyzed.

Agatha slowly turned around.

Downstream, a burly prince had his axe to Beatrix's throat, while a thin prince had his blade to Millicent's. Aric stood between them, grinning at Agatha and the witches, a rusted, jagged dagger in his hand.

"Let them surrender, Aric," Agatha rasped, trying to stay calm. "Let them drop their flags."

"Are those the rules at the School for Good and Evil?"

Aric smiled at Agatha, violet eyes storming. "Too bad I'm not a *student*."

"Then you have no place here," Agatha scowled, voice starting to shake as Beatrix and Millicent whimpered louder. "Nor do any of the princes you've brought in."

"You see, my mother used to tell me that true villains only have one Nemesis. One person who stands in the way of their happiness." With his rusted dagger, Aric combed his spikes of black hair, gleaming like raven beaks. "Only my Nemesis, it turns out, is in your *school*. And if war won't bring me to them, then a bit of carnage might bring them to me."

"Your *Nemesis*? *That's* why you're here?" Agatha blurted in horror, watching the princes' axes chafe the two girls' throats. "B-b-but who? Who at this school could warrant hurting innocent people?"

Aric paused, looking right at her. "It's the danger of fairy tales." He glared up at the girls' castle, his purple eyes clouding with a strange sadness. "Sometimes one story opens another."

He turned back to his princes. "Kill them."

The princes raised their axes. Beatrix and Millicent gasped, about to die—

"NO!" Hester screamed. Her demon tattoo exploded off her neck, swelling bloodred to the size of a shoe. Just as the axe blades scraped the two girls' necks, Beatrix and Millicent choking, Hester's demon yanked the girls' white flags out of their cloak pockets and flung them to the ground. Both Evergirls instantly disappeared as the axes cut through thin air, white fireworks rocketing up from their vanished bodies, singeing

the princes and sending them howling to the ground.

Enraged, Aric hurled his jagged knife at Hester, only to see it turn midair to carrot and boomerang smack into his face, knocking him down.

"Run!" Dot cried at Agatha and the witches—

The girls all twirled to flee, but there were six more hooded boys charging out of the Fernfield for them, brandishing weapons. Agatha's eyes flared wide. None of them was Filip . . . or Tedros.

"Go find Sophie!" Anadil barked at Agatha, huddling against Hester and Dot.

"I'm fighting with you!" Agatha shot back.

"Agatha, *go*!" said Dot, boys twenty feet away. "Sophie needs you before it's too late!"

"No! I can't leave you to die!" Agatha cried—

"Don't you get it!" Hester spun to her, eyes aflame. "A coven isn't *four*. We don't *want you*!"

Tears stinging, Agatha sprinted away into blue trees, glancing back to see Hester watching her, white-faced with fear. Then Hester turned, finger glowing red, as the boys converged and Agatha lost the view.

High on the teachers' balcony, Lady Lesso and Professor Dovey clenched teeth as they watched the boys' and girls' torch-lit scoreboards, their only clue to what was unfolding in the dark, veiled Forest.

Out of the corner of her eye, Professor Dovey watched the butterflies circling above the teachers and Pollux guarding the door. There was no sign of Evelyn on any of the balconies or in the Clearing below.

A loud cheer went up from the boys' school, celebrating BEATRIX's and MILLICENT's names vanishing off the scoreboard. The two girls reappeared in the Clearing, quaking and sobbing, before nymphs flew them back into the castle for magical treatment.

As the boys thundered a cocksure chant, the girls down to only six competitors, Professor Dovey sidled closer to Lady Lesso. "Your shield protects the south gate," she whispered quickly. "You can break it and enter—"

"For the last time, Clarissa, if a teacher goes into the Trial, the terms are *void*," Lady Lesso hissed. "All the boys and princes would storm our castle. It'd be a massacre."

"Only you can get through that shield! Unless you help them, Sophie and Agatha will die!"

Lady Lesso whirled. "I intervened at your insistence once before because of Evelyn," she seethed accusingly. "You'll never know the price I *paid*."

Professor Dovey fell quiet a long moment before speaking again.

"She attacked Agatha, Lady Lesso. Right there in her classroom, in a school that should have been ours to protect. And now our usurper threatens our only hope for peace, and you suggest Agatha fend for *herself*? That isn't Evil, Lady Lesso. That's *cowardice*," Professor Dovey said, her voice a low hiss. "There is no School Master this time to save us from Evelyn Sader. There is only you. And whatever Evelyn's ending is, it is worth *any* price to stop it."

Lady Lesso met her colleague's vehement eyes. Then she quickly cleared her throat and turned away. "You're overplaying as usual, Clarissa. Agatha has my best witches at her side protecting her. Hester and Anadil are more than capable allies."

Sparks shot past their heads from the Forest, a detonation of fireworks showering their dark balcony with white light. The teachers wheeled to see HESTER's name vanish off the scoreboard and the tattooed witch materialize in the Clearing, her face and blue cloak a mess of blood. She tried to stagger up, then buckled to her knees.

"What's happened!" Professor Sheeks cried, barreling past Pollux's unwieldy bear into the castle, followed by Professor Anemone and a few of the Forest Group leaders.

Professor Dovey stared at Hester trailing blood across the dead grass as the nymphs helped her into the tunnel. Hands shaking, she spun to Lady Lesso—

But Lady Lesso was already gone.

Agatha saw HESTER's name disappear on the scoreboard, the white fireworks signaling a surrender, and felt a palpable relief. Hester was still alive.

Agatha sprinted through phosphorescing blue tulips, doing a count of the girls still left in the Forest . . . *Anadil, Dot, Yara, Sophie. . . .*

And yet Sophie hadn't been in that group of boys attacking the witches . . . *nor was Tedros.*

Agatha's heart rattled faster. Was Sophie *with* Tedros right now? Why would Sophie be anywhere near him if she could turn into a girl any second?

A needling dread crept into Agatha's stomach. She ignored it.

Of course she's with Tedros. She's making sure he doesn't find me, she assured herself. *She's protecting me.*

But now the dread was festering, worming deeper. . . .

A snakeskin cape and a boy's uniform, balled under a bed . . .

A wrist full of spirick marks two weeks before . . .

A friend so desperate to get her home . . .

Agatha stopped dead in the pine shrubs.

A pink spell.

Her chest hammered, remembering Tedros pulling away from her in the tower, hunting madly for someone who wasn't there.

No . . . impossible . . .

Sophie couldn't have been there! Not the new Sophie, the best friend as faithful as Agatha once was to her! Not the Good Sophie, risking life and limb for her right now! This Sophie *couldn't* have torn her and Tedros apart and then pretended to be on her side. Not even the Witch of Woods Beyond could be so devious, so traitorous, so . . . Evil.

Agatha burst into a sweat.

Could she?

Boys' yells echoed nearby, followed by an ogre's grunts and explosions of red fireworks over the Turquoise Thicket. CHADDICK'S and NICHOLAS' fireflies fizzled and extinguished on the boys' scoreboard.

Agatha veered away towards the south gate, more desperate to find Sophie than ever.

"South gate?" Sophie followed Tedros through snowy, glittering-blue willows, her boy's boots dwarfed by giant footsteps left by a troll or some other hellish creature. With the lumpy path, her stiff calves, and tight breeches wedging up her behind, she stumbled along like a newborn. "What's near the south gate?"

"Pumpkin patch," Tedros said a ways ahead, slashing a few branches out of their path. "Clearest part of the Forest. We can see Sophie and Agatha if they sneak through. If you ever catch up, that is."

Sophie grimaced, deliberating ways to protect her best friend from Tedros when he found her. She'd have to stun him before he could hurt Agatha. She'd have to steal his red flag and drop it to the ground . . .

Sophie's heart suddenly beat faster, seeing the flash of red silk in Tedros' cloak pocket . . . his back turned . . .

This was her chance.

Sophie felt her pink fingerglow heat up, fear burning it bright. Chest pounding, she raised her finger slowly, pointing it at Tedros' broad back—

"Even though you're a crap fighter, I'm glad you're with me, Fil," Tedros said ahead. "Always wanted a best friend to team up with. You know. Like those two girls."

Sophie's fingertip dimmed.

Tedros turned with an arched brow. "But seriously, do I need to carry you?"

Sophie's heart fluttered and she hurried forward, trying to stiffen her gait to a boy's. "Odd that we haven't faced any of the teacher's traps—"

"Pfft, beating monsters is easy, Filip. The devil you *know* is the one to be scared of."

Sophie stopped, watching Tedros caressed by the sparkling, long-branched willows, as if saluting a knight off to war.

The prince sensed the silence and turned. "What now?"

"Have you ever killed someone, Tedros?"

"What?"

Sophie glared at him, ten feet away. "Have you ever *killed* someone?"

Tedros stiffened, looking at his elfish, clear-eyed friend. "I've killed a gargoyle," he puffed.

"That's defense, Tedros. This is revenge," Sophie said coldly. "This is *murder*." Her princely face darkened with pain. "No matter how Good you try to be after, you'll never escape it. It will haunt your dreams and make you afraid of yourself. It will follow you like an ugly black shadow, telling you you'll always be Evil, until it just becomes . . . part of you."

Tedros bristled, shifting in his boots. "Right. How would you know? Filip of Mount Honora who can't even fight a *stymph*."

Sophie's eyes cut into his. "Because I've killed worse than you'll ever know."

Tedros stared at his friend, stunned.

Moonlight seeped through the ice-blue trees, spotlighting the two boys, their breath misting towards each other.

Tedros cocked his head, seeing Filip in the glow. "That's

odd. Your face looks different."

"Huh?"

"It looks . . . smoother," Tedros said curiously, stepping towards his friend. "Like you've shaved . . ."

Sophie gasped. *The spell!* She'd grown so used to being a boy she'd forgotten the spell! She'd be a girl any second! She had to get away from him!

"Just the light," she prattled, goading Tedros ahead. "Let's go, before a troll eats us."

A soft groan echoed above their heads, and Tedros stopped short. "What was that?"

"I don't hear any—"

But it came again, a rasping wheeze like a punctured balloon.

The two boys slowly looked up into the weeping willow.

"Who's there?" Tedros called.

Between the spindly branches and shimmery blue leaves, they made out the edges of something hiding high in the tree. Tedros squinted harder, his eyes adjusting to the dark, until he saw a shadow . . . a human shadow . . .

. . . in a sapphire-blue cloak.

"A *girl*," he sneered.

Fireworks whipcracked behind them, and the boys spun to see white light lash across the sky, as two more girls' names erased off the scoreboard.

DOT.

ANADIL.

Sophie exhaled with relief. The two witches had survived

long enough to drop their flags.

But then she saw Tedros' pupils locked on the tree, glimmering darkly. Because if those two girls had surrendered, then chances were that the girl trapped up in that tree right now was . . .

"I'll get her!" Sophie shrieked, leaping onto the tree—

But Tedros was faster, prowling past his friend like a panther towards the hidden girl. Sophie scrambled up branches behind him, knowing she had to get to Agatha first. She lunged through sharp, tangled branches and yanked Tedros' cloak collar. The prince ricocheted backwards, watching his friend pass him.

"What are you doing!" Tedros hissed.

Sophie levied every ounce of power in her boy body to swing up the tree towards the hidden girl. Just as she got close, Tedros tackled her from behind.

"She's *mine*, Filip," he growled, shunting his friend aside. Panicked, Sophie shoved her boot in his backside, and Tedros face-planted on a lower branch.

As Filip fumbled past him, Tedros swung up and grappled him, Filip gave him a hard slap, and the two boys wrestled forward along dense branches, biting and kicking each other like animals until Tedros flung Filip back just as they got to the cornered girl. Heaving breath, cheeks scarlet, the prince gnashed his teeth, raised his sword over his prey, and drew back her hood with a snarl—

Then he slowly lowered his sword.

"Who are *you*?"

Sophie came up beside him and looked at a red-haired girl ensconced in blue leaves, moaning softly, eyes barely open, her long-nosed, freckled face deathly pale.

"Yara?"

"You know her?" Tedros said, agog.

"Heard someone call her name in the Clearing before she went in," Sophie lied hastily, remembering none of the boys had seen Yara before.

"Well, find her white flag and drop it," Tedros growled. "We need to be looking for Sophie and Agath—"

His voice petered out as he noticed a splotch of dried blood on Yara's chin. Slowly Tedros peeled back her cloak to reveal a rust-flecked jagged gash deep across her neck, already bled out.

"Aric," Tedros breathed, watching Yara pant and wheeze, her windpipe cut. "That's his knife mark."

Sophie looked at him, the two boys' faces filled with the same helpless fear. Yara was about to die.

Sophie cradled Yara's head while Tedros frantically ransacked her pockets, finding nothing. "We need to send you back to your teachers, Yara," he pressured. "Where's your white flag?"

Sophie shook her head, bereft. "She doesn't speak."

"Yara, we need to help you!" Tedros said manically, grabbing her shoulders—

"I told you, Tedros—"

"YARA!" Tedros screamed.

Yara stirred in his arms, her eyes still closed. "I'm . . . not . . . Yara," she whispered.

Sophie and Tedros recoiled in surprise.

Slowly Yara's blue eyes struggled open, gazing into Tedros'. She smiled as if looking at her best friend. "I—I—I . . . never was."

The prince let go of her, for Yara's face had started to change. Her cheeks roughened to ginger stubble, her jaw chiseling and squaring, her long beakish nose refining, her wavy red hair shrinking back into her skull until it was cropped short. Sophie went pale, watching a spell undone that she knew so well. Tedros went paler, looking back at a boy he knew even better.

"T-T-Tristan?" Tedros spluttered, stunned. "But that's impossible—how can—how could—"

"I'm . . . sorry . . . ," Tristan gasped, back in his boy skin. "Their school . . . was so . . . *beautiful*. And the boys—the boys were so mean . . . except you, Tedros . . . You were my only friend. . . ."

Eyes wet, Tedros couldn't speak. He just looked at Tristan, then at Filip, so confused.

"Tristan, we need your flag," Sophie strained.

"She let me stay in the girls' school—" Tristan said, shivering. "She said I could stay as long as . . . as long as I—"

"Who let you stay?" Tedros asked, still in a fog.

"The Dean . . . as long as I hid it for her . . . that's why I moved it from under the t-t-table . . ."

"Shhhh," Sophie said, touching his cheek. "Just tell me where your flag is."

Tristan's eyes found hers and suddenly twinkled with recognition. He looked deeper into her face and smiled weakly. "It's you."

Sophie's heart imploded.

Tedros peered at Tristan, puzzled. "But Filip came to our school after you left. How would you—"

"He's delirious," Sophie blurted quickly, then clutched Tristan harder, flashing him the F on her collar. "I'm *Filip*, Tristan. *Filip* of Mount Honora. And I need your flag—*please*—"

"The Storian," Tristan said, still smiling at her. "I . . . I hid it in your storybook . . . like she told me to . . . she knew you'd never look there . . ."

"What's he talking about?" Tedros asked nervously.

"I have no idea," Sophie lied, heart thundering.

"It's in . . . in your book . . . ," Tristan choked. "She's . . . she's coming for it . . . she . . . she needs it for your end-d-d. . . ."

But there was no more breath for Tristan to give. The red-haired boy convulsed, then stilled, his heart finally finished, and his eyes slowly closed once more.

Inch by inch, he started to glow like a halo, burning hotter, hotter, to the color of molten gold. In a flash, his body splintered to light and rocketed into the sky, drawing out Yara's face in a constellation of orange-gold stars, before the lights faded and fell over the Forest like raining fire. Then YARA's name went dark on the girls' scoreboard, and Tristan was gone.

Tedros shoved past Filip and stumbled down the tree. He leapt into shadowed blue grass behind it, and doubled over, gagging. "How could Aric kill her! How could Aric kill a girl!" he cried. "And it wasn't a girl—it was T-T-Tristan! A boy like any of us—but no one talked to him, no one was nice to him—no wonder he wanted to be in their school—" Tedros couldn't breathe, collapsing to his knees. "He just wanted to be happy!"

Sophie put her hand on his back.

"He must have been so scared, Filip," Tedros whispered. "Alone in that tree . . . dying . . ." He buried his face in his hands. "I can't watch anyone else die. Please. Not like that." He sniffled and smeared at his eyes. "You're right. I can't—I can't hurt anyone—"

Sophie knelt before him. "You don't have to."

"Those girls will kill me if I don't kill them first!"

"Not if you promise me," Sophie soothed. "Promise me you'll let them live."

Tedros looked up at her, cheeks wet. He shook his head as if he was dreaming. "Every second you look different, Filip. Softer, gentler . . ." He turned away, flushing. "Why do I keep wishing you were a princess? Why do I keep seeing one in your face?"

"Promise me you'll let Sophie and Agatha go home," Sophie begged, voice tightening. "A prince's promise."

"On one condition," Tedros said, their eyes locking. "That you won't go back to your kingdom, Filip. That you'll stay here with me."

Sophie burnt red, gawking at him. "W-w-w-what?"

Tedros gripped her shoulders. "You keep me Good, Filip. Please. I can't end up like Aric, angry and Evil. You're the only thing that keeps me Good."

Sophie's whole body went to butter, staring at the only boy

she'd ever loved, asking her to stay with him forever.

As a boy.

Slowly Sophie felt herself pull away from him.

"Listen to me, Tedros," she said. "Sophie needs to go home alive with Agatha. That's the only way to end this. That's the only way to stop anyone else from dying."

"And I need *my* best friend," said Tedros, holding her tighter. "You said it yourself, Filip. You don't want to end alone like your mother." His blue eyes weakened. "And I don't want to end alone like my father."

"I have someone waiting, Tedros," Sophie rasped. "Someone who knows the real me. Someone I wouldn't trade for any boy in the world."

"I wish you were a girl," Tedros said, hand moving down his friend's back. "That's why I keep seeing one in your face."

"Promise me you'll let them go," Sophie pressed, heart racing—

"You're all I have left, Filip," Tedros pleaded. "Don't leave me alone. Please."

"Just promise me—" gasped Sophie.

"Even stranger," Tedros breathed, lost in a daze. "Now you sound like a girl too."

Sophie held out her hand to stop him, but Tedros caught it. Sophie looked up into his wide, confused eyes as he leaned in, touching his lips to hers. . . .

"Oh my God," a voice cried behind them.

The boys spun in shock.

It was Agatha.

24

Villains Unmasked

Tedros broke from Filip and jumped back, the prince's face wildly red. "No no no no—" he stammered, whirling to Agatha. "It was an accident—"

But Agatha had her finger raised, glowing bright gold at the elfish, fluffy-haired boy beside him.

"Agatha, listen to me," Filip begged, retreating against a blue willow—

"You snake," Agatha hissed, advancing on him. "You lying snake."

Tedros instinctively shielded Filip, pointing his own glowing finger at Agatha.

"Leave Filip alone, Agatha. Your fight is with me."

But Agatha still wasn't looking at him. She was glaring daggers at Filip, her finger burning brighter. "You tried to kiss him! You tried to stay here with him and send me home!"

"It's not true!" Filip cried—

Tedros spun to his square-jawed friend. "You know each other?"

"*You* were there in the School Master's tower that night. *You* attacked us. *You* set him against me!" Agatha spewed at Filip.

"And you promised me you wouldn't see him!" Filip fired, pitch wavering. "I couldn't lose you, Agatha! Not without trying to win you back!"

"So you tried to get us home on a lie?" Agatha lashed.

"Why are my princess and best friend talking?" gaped Tedros, delirious—

"I had to show you your wish was wrong," Filip assailed Agatha, fighting tears. "That a best friend means *more* than a boy."

Agatha shook her head angrily, thinking of the dreams she'd cursed, the heart she'd maligned, trying to tell her the truth about her friend all along. "Can't you see?" she said, voice cold. "The more you try to stop us, the more my wish for him is true."

Filip fell back a step, cut to the core.

"I really don't understand what's happening," Tedros croaked, eyes wide.

"You'd choose him over me?" Filip rasped to Agatha, his

dimpled chin quivering. "After I risked my life to save us?"

"Is that what kissing him was?" Agatha mocked. "An attempt to *save* us?"

"He kissed me!" Filip screamed.

"H-h-hold on—it was a bad moment—" the prince fumbled. "We're friends—like you and S-S-Sophie—"

"Some friend," said Agatha, glowering at Filip.

"You have to believe me, Aggie," Filip stressed. "I chose you, even if Tedros could want me, even if I could be his forever—"

"It was so dark—and his face looked different—" Tedros moaned, slumping onto a rock. "Any boy would make the same mistake—"

"You said you wanted to forget this place," defended Filip. "You said you wanted our happy ending back!"

"*Happy!* Because of you, a boy is *dead*!" Agatha yelled. "Because of you, we could both still die!"

"I just wanted us to go back to the way we were. Before we ever came here. Before we ever met a prince!" Filip implored. "I just wanted us back to real friends."

"Real friends let each other grow up," Agatha seethed, neck searing red. "Real friends don't hold each other back from love. Real friends don't *lie*."

Tedros launched off his rock. "That's it!" he spat at Agatha. "I don't care how you two know each other, whether you're long-lost cousins, secret pen pals, or hiking buddies in Mount Honora, but Filip isn't your concern anymore, all right?" he snarled. "So go find your treasured Sophie before I change my mind about killing you."

Agatha goggled at him before spurting a laugh.

"What's so funny!" Tedros barked.

"You really don't see it, do you?" Agatha marveled. "You still think he's your friend."

"My *best* friend," retorted the prince. "And for the first time, I finally understand why you'd choose Sophie instead of me. Because Filip *knows* me. He backs me up and fights for me in a way no girl ever could. I always thought love was about a girl . . . but a friend like Filip is deeper than love. Because I'd choose as Good a friend as him over you, again and again and again."

"Let me tell you about *Filip*," said Agatha witheringly. "Filip's about as Good a friend as Lancelot was to your father."

Tedros bared teeth and drew his sword. "*What* did you say?"

Agatha searched his face, softening. "Never could tell between Good and Evil, could you?"

Tedros' whole body stiffened, dread slithering through him. He turned to see Filip backing past Agatha, out of shadowed grass and against the glittering willow tree. Now, in the frosty, spangling light, Tedros could finally see his best friend's face, terrified, trembling. . . .

Only it was no longer a face he knew.

Each new second, every pore of Filip's features shape-shifted with the tiniest changes, like a sand sculpture burnishing, grain by grain. Filip's sloped nose softened and rounded to a button, his eyelashes thickened and grew out luxuriously, his elfish ears shrank and pinned back, his eyebrows arched like delicate brushstrokes. Changes spread down his body, faster and faster, like a spell unraveling at the seams. Filip's thick, veiny muscles sleeked to creamy skin, his floppy hair flowed out in cascading blond ringlets, his hulking legs thinned and smoothed, his hips regained their curves . . . until there, in icy moonlight, a beautiful blond girl cowered and shook in a boy's black-and-red cloak, gaping plaintively like a scared cat.

Tedros collapsed against a tree. "Why does everyone lie to me?" he whispered. "Why is everything always a lie?"

"Not everything," Agatha said quietly.

Sophie backed up from Tedros, trying to smile.

"Don't kill m-m-me, Tedros," she stuttered. "See? Still Filip, still your friend . . . just different . . ."

She saw Tedros staring at her, his blue eyes glazed and frozen over, as if reliving every moment of the scene that just happened, parsing every word. Little by little, a golden glow dawned over him, like a warmth awakened inside, melting the darkness and edges.

Sophie slouched with relief—

But then she saw Tedros wasn't looking at her at all.

He was looking at his ghostly, dark-haired princess, standing beneath a sparkling willow.

"Y-y-you . . . you loved me the whole time?" he said softly.

Agatha nodded, tears streaming down her cheeks.

"And everything you said in the tower was true?" said Tedros, eyes wet.

Agatha nodded, crying harder.

"Why didn't I kiss you?" Tedros said, voice cracking.

"Why didn't I trust you?"

"You're . . . so stupid," Agatha wept, shaking her head. "Why are boys so stupid?"

Tedros smiled through tears. "Maybe a world without princes is a good idea after all."

Agatha choked a laugh, finally letting her heart flutter unashamed.

Standing between them, Sophie stood helpless, watching true loves reunited . . . more invisible than she'd ever been.

A blast of purple light flew past Tedros like a warning shot—

Lady Lesso stormed out of the trees, smoking finger raised menacingly at Tedros. "Agatha, Sophie, get away from him now!" she hissed, backing towards the south gate. "I'll hide you in the Woods until it's safe!"

Neither girls nor boy moved.

"What are you doing!" she spat at Sophie and Agatha. "The other boys will be here any sec—"

But now Lady Lesso's eyes widened, for Agatha was backing away from Sophie towards the prince, who took her protectively into his arms. Clutching each other, Tedros and Agatha glared at Sophie in her boy's uniform, standing in tree shadow, all alone.

"What's . . . what's happening . . ." Lady Lesso said, head whipping between the two girls.

"I thought stopping your wish was Good, Aggie," Sophie wept, voice faltering. "I thought I was doing Good."

Sophie saw even Lady Lesso retreat from her now, violet

eyes chilling with understanding. "A boy killed . . . students hurt . . . a Trial to the death . . . because of . . . *you*?"

"Come on," said Tedros, taking his princess's arm. "Let her fend for herself."

"I didn't want to be like my mother. I didn't want to end all alone," Sophie begged Agatha, cheeks wet. "I never meant to hurt anyone—"

"Let's go, Agatha," Tedros said harder.

Agatha looked up at her prince, as pure and devoted as he was in her dream . . . then at Sophie, sobbing repentantly across the willow glen.

No tricks. No more secrets.

This time the choice was for real.

A jet of red fire rocketed into the middle of the glen, sending Agatha and Tedros reeling back in a cloud of red smoke. Dazed, they swiveled to see red and white fireworks blast through the sky from every direction, ricocheting out of control, like a raining meteor shower. Instantly, the fireflies on the boy's scoreboard combusted to flames, scorching all the remaining names, TEDROS' and FILIP's included. . . . With a deafening crack, the board erupted in a blinding fireball. Across the forest, the girls' scoreboard detonated in another shattering explosion, billowing black plumes of smoke over the west gate.

"What's happening?" Agatha breathed, ears ringing.

She and Tedros sensed a low, dull rumble behind them, growing louder . . . louder. . . .

Faces draining blood, they slowly looked up.

The enchanted haze over the castles broke like mist, revealing the boys' and girls' schools overrun with roaring, descending bodies like swarming ants. Charging girls leapt onto broken Halfway Bridge from the balconies, wielding weapons and glowing fingertips, clamoring at the edge of the severed gap. Across the bay, hundreds of rabid boys and mercenary princes thundered onto the Bridge from the other side, lethally armed and bellowing for blood.

"They know I'm here," a voice said behind Agatha and her prince.

Agatha looked up at Lady Lesso, her violet gaze fixed on the castles.

"I broke the terms," her teacher rasped. "Trial's over."

Agatha swallowed. "What does that mean?"

They peered up at four hundred boys and girls raring to kill each other, separated only by a hole in a bridge.

"War," said Tedros. "It means war."

Over their heads, the willow branches began to glimmer brighter like blue tinsel until the glimmer detonated like a storm cloud, sweeping down over the trees. In the moon's glow, they saw the sparkles were butterflies, thousands of blue butterflies, that had given the willows their neon glow. Like locusts, they swarmed through the glen in a violent gale. Agatha shielded her face, while Tedros hacked uselessly at them with his sword and stumbled to the ground—

A loud gasp suddenly flew behind them, and Agatha spun to see Lady Lesso pulled off the ground by a cloud of butterflies.

"Evelyn—" Lady Lesso said, horror-struck. "She heard everything—"

"Wait!" Agatha cried, trying to hold on to her—

Panicked, Lady Lesso pressed her lips to Agatha's ear as the butterflies dragged her off. "Kiss him, Agatha!" she whispered. "Kiss him when the time comes!"

And then she was ripped away, as butterflies kidnapped her back to school, her last pleas to Agatha drowned out by the roars of war.

Agatha froze in the moonlit glen, gulping shallow breaths.

"What did she say?" a voice spoke.

Agatha looked down at Tedros staggering up, golden hair mussed.

"Agatha?" said another voice.

Agatha turned to see the last of the hellish red smoke dissipating through the trees, Sophie revealed behind it.

"What did Lady Lesso say?" her friend asked, face tense.

Agatha stared at Sophie across the willow glen, a moonlit stage, boys' and girls' war cries echoing far away like a chorus.

Overhead, the treetops suddenly began to rustle and sway, a heavy, crackling sound tearing towards them—

Agatha recoiled in shock as the School Master's silver tower crashed through into the willows. The moving tower glided into the moonlight and skidded to a stop, rupturing the ground with its force—splitting Tedros on one side, Sophie on the other, across a long, ragged crack in the ground, with Agatha straddling the fault line between them.

From the tower's window, a last throng of butterflies

fluttered down behind the three students, magically congealing into form as they touched ground. Like an actress on cue, Evelyn Sader stepped into the Clearing's spotlight, her long nails clutching a red cherrywood storybook that Agatha knew.

It was her and Sophie's fairy tale.

"'Trial,'" the Dean cooed. "Such a delicious word. So many relevant meanings. An experiment in service of a conclusion, for instance. Or a test of faith and stamina. Or a difficult moment in one's own life. And yet . . . I prefer the more formal definition." She paused dramatically, taking in Sophie and Tedros on opposite sides, dark brows knitted over her forest-green eyes. "A formal court before witnesses to determine *guilt*."

Her eyes moved to Agatha in the middle. The Dean smiled cryptically.

"Now the *real* Trial begins."

With her sharp nail, Evelyn slit open the sewn binding atop the book's spine. The gleaming Storian ripped free, glowing furious red, as *The Tale of Sophie and Agatha* magically floated out of the Dean's hands and into the moonlight. The pen flung the floating book open with its razor-steel nib, spilling ink across pages as colorful scenes filled in the gaps in the story. At last the pen slowed on a final page, taking its time as it painted Agatha between Tedros and Sophie. . . .

Only this Sophie didn't look like the Sophie in front of Agatha now.

The Sophie on the page was a bald, warted old witch.

Beneath the witch, the pen wrote a single line:

"The villain had been hidden all this time."

Agatha and Tedros slowly looked up at Sophie, milky beautiful in the moonlit glen.

"You see, Agatha, you thought I conjured Sophie's symptoms. That *I* was the villain." Evelyn sat on a stump at the glen's dark fringe. "When it wasn't me at all, was it?"

"Agatha, I'm not a witch . . . you know I'm not a witch . . ." Sophie scoffed.

But Agatha took a step back from her friend, crossing into Tedros' side of the glen. Sophie's face reddened with surprise.

"You think I can still be Evil?" Sophie breathed. "That I could hurt you?"

Agatha's hands were shaking. "Witches ruin fairy tales, Sophie. Witches lie to get their endings."

Sophie appealed to Tedros. "I was a good friend to you, wasn't I? A friend like that could never be a witch! Tell her!"

"A good *friend*? A friend built on lies isn't a friend," Tedros blazed across the divide. "The School Master went to the ends of the earth to find someone as Evil as him. Now we see why he picked you, Sophie. You'll *always* be Evil as long as you live."

"I'm not E-E-Evil! I'm trying to be Good! Can't you see? I'm *trying*!" Sophie cried. "The School Master was wrong! He was wrong about me!"

Agatha stared at the terrifying hag in the storybook, as she backed farther towards Tedros. "The Storian doesn't lie, Sophie. . . ."

"No—Aggie, please—" Sophie said. "You know the truth—"

Devastated, she ran to Agatha across the cracked glen—but a blistering pain in her neck made her cry out, before more pain seared through her wrist and forearm.

Agatha and Tedros cowered from her, eyes wide, and Sophie's stomach went ice-cold. Slowly Sophie raised her arm and saw it marred with two gruesome black warts. More warts sizzled through as her skin started to wrinkle like curdling milk, mottling with liver spots.

"No . . . it's her . . . it's the Dean . . ." Sophie choked, but she couldn't see Evelyn at the fringe. "She's doing this to me!"

Agatha retreated next to Tedros, fingers both raised at Sophie with matching gold glows, as Sophie's blond hair fell out in clumps, her back swelled to a hump, and her legs spindled to bony sticks.

Agatha shook her head, torn between pity and anger. "It was you, Sophie. It was always you."

"I'm sorry . . . for everything I did . . ." Sophie wept, writhing in pain. "But I'm not *this*!"

"You can't be here anymore, Sophie," Agatha said, misting up. "We'll only be happy apart."

Tedros looked at his princess, stunned.

"Agatha, *no*!" Sophie screamed.

The Storian suddenly glowed redder, sensing The End.

Agatha hesitated, as her friend's teeth blackened and dissolved, her hair shedding faster, faster. Agatha's face softened with anguish—

"We'll be happy as long as we live, Agatha," Tedros pressured. "But we have to do it now."

Agatha nodded, tears in her eyes.

"YOU HAVE TO BELIEVE ME!" Sophie begged—

"I can't, Sophie," Agatha said, holding Tedros. "I can't believe you anymore."

"NO!" Sophie cried, charging for her, but more pain sent her buckling.

Agatha gripped Tedros tighter as Sophie shriveled with a howl, her warted scalp gleaming, her face gnarling to an old, Evil hag's—

"*Now*, Agatha," Tedros said, for Sophie was crawling towards them across the crack.

"Agatha, I don't want to be like her," Sophie pleaded. "I don't want to end like my mother!" She reached out her shriveled hand for her only friend . . .

Agatha met her eyes with deep, terrible sorrow. Then she turned away.

Sophie recoiled, watching Agatha in Tedros' arms. "No . . . not this . . ." Sophie gasped—

Tedros' blue eyes pierced Agatha's with a promise. "Forever."

Agatha heard her wish for him, echoing louder in every heartbeat, begging her to trust it.

This time she listened.

Agatha gave herself to her prince.

"Forever."

Tedros clasped her cheeks and kissed her, their lips touching for the first time. Agatha's head went light, a blinding glow coursing through her veins. As his warmth spilled through her, Agatha heard Sophie's animal scream recede behind her, softer, softer, into silence. Holding Tedros closer, Agatha felt her heart floating, time expanding, fear crumbling to ash, as if at last she'd found her Ever After, as if at last she'd found an ending that couldn't be taken away. . . .

Their lips finally released, as prince and princess broke apart, each panting for breath. They looked up at their open storybook in the light of the moon, a vision of their sealing kiss splashed across the page, a witch vanished from their story . . . two last words penned beneath . . .

THE EN

Evelyn Sader had her fingertip under the pen's sharp nib, blood dripping as if she'd pricked it on a spindle—

The *D* left unwritten.

Agatha's eyes slowly lowered to the ground in front of her.

A bald, wrinkled witch gaped up at her and Tedros from the grass, her decayed face a mess of tears. Then, just as quickly as it had happened, Sophie melted back into her own young, beautiful skin, and the witch was gone, replaced by a betrayed, broken-hearted girl.

Agatha's heart caught in her throat, gawking at the friend she'd left behind . . . still right here. A friend who'd just witnessed a kiss that failed to banish her home, loveless and alone.

But there was no appeal in Sophie's eyes, no forgiveness. Just a blank distance, as if she no longer knew the dark-haired princess in front of her.

Doom rising, Agatha looked up at the Dean.

"Some might consider conjuring witch symptoms and then blaming them on a poor innocent girl as conduct unbecoming of a Dean. But then again, I do have a weakness for good *endings*," Evelyn simpered as a crowd of butterflies took the flailing Storian from her finger and restrained it in midair. She sucked the blood off her fingertip, eying the halted pen. "Funny thing about endings, you see. The story isn't quite over until the Storian writes 'The End.' And as you can see, you are in fact, one letter *short*. Meaning, we haven't reached 'The End' after all." Evelyn smiled at Agatha. "And now that you've had *your* ending, dear princess, it seems Sophie should have a fair chance, don't you think? After all, it is her fairy tale too."

Sophie gazed up at her, eyes big as emeralds.

"Give us the *pen*," Tedros spat, pulling his sword—

Evelyn stabbed her finger at him, and a willow tree magically grabbed him by its branches and lashed him against the trunk.

Tedros struggled angrily. "What are you—" A branch gagged him.

"You see, Agatha, my butterflies led you both back to school because I heard a wish worthy of ending your fairy tale. But it wasn't *your* wish," the Dean said, circling Agatha. "It was Sophie's."

"W-w-what?" Sophie spluttered.

"Oh yes, you made a wish too, dear," said the Dean. "Don't you remember?"

A butterfly fluttered off her dress, a disembodied voice playing back as its wings pulsed neon with every word:

"I wish I could see her again," echoed Sophie's voice. *"I'd do anything.* Anything."

Agatha remembered the words . . . spoken near a grave . . . the two of them in each other's arms. . . .

"My m-m-mother?" Sophie gasped, suddenly brightening. Then the light in her face dimmed. "But my mother's dead . . . nothing can bring her back. . . ."

"And yet you're in your own fairy tale, dear," the Dean offered. "Wishes are powerful things if you're willing to do anything for them."

Agatha's heart stopped. She stared at the Dean, her big bug eyes widening.

"The villain had been hidden all this time."

But it wasn't Sophie. Or Evelyn. It was—

"NO!" Agatha launched towards Sophie. "Sophie, *no*! She's using yo—"

Willow arms snatched her, gagging the princess with her prince on the tree trunk.

Sophie ignored Agatha's garbled cries. Her eyes lifted back to the Dean's. "What do I have to do?"

Evelyn leaned over, sharp nails caressing Sophie's face. "Only be true to your wish, Sophie. Be willing to pay any price to see her again."

Agatha screeched through her gag, but couldn't get words out—

"What price?" Sophie frowned.

"Agatha kissed a prince, Sophie. She tried to banish you forever and made you *watch*," Evelyn said darkly. "You have no one anymore. No prince. No friend. No father. No one to go home to. No one to trust."

Sophie looked into her eyes, crestfallen.

"Isn't seeing the only person who loves you worth any price?" Evelyn coaxed.

Sophie didn't move, listening to Agatha's muffled screams behind her.

"I can really see her again?" Sophie asked.

"Your wish can end your fairy tale just as much as Agatha's," replied Evelyn. "All you have to do is mean it."

Agatha tore against the willow tree, the branches lacerating her arms—

"I'm ready," Sophie nodded, swallowing.

Evelyn grinned toothily. Reaching towards her breast, she magically drew out a long, blue sliver of glow from her heart that lit up the night sky. As she did, the butterflies on her dress turned scarlet red. . . .

Agatha howled in horror, but Sophie's eyes stayed on the blue light as it swirled into a hypnotic, hovering orb.

"Now close your eyes and say your wish out loud," the Dean wheedled.

Sophie closed her eyes. "I will do anything to see my mother again," she rasped, trying to ignore Agatha's cries.

"*Mean* it," the Dean said wolfishly. "The wish only works if you mean it."

Sophie gritted her teeth. *"I will do anything to see my mother again."*

Then there was silence, for even Agatha had gone quiet.

Sophie peeked open her eyes to see the orb begin to spin in midair, expelling a sweep of eerie blue light. Inch by inch, the light morphed and sculpted, taking on dimension, until Sophie staggered back, seeing a human phantom take form. Two ghostly, delicate bare feet floated above the navy grass. Sophie's eyes slowly moved up the billowing blue robes, the pale stick-thin limbs angled from its sleeves, the long white-swan neck . . . and then a face that could have been a mirror, with ageless vanilla skin, a small rounded nose, and cool green eyes. The ghost smiled lovingly at her, and Sophie fell to her knees.

"Mother?" she whispered. "Is it really you?"

"Kiss me, Sophie," her mother said, her voice distant and foggy. "Kiss me, and bring back a life. That is the only price I ask."

"Bring back a l-l-life?" Sophie stammered.

Behind her, Agatha screamed until her voice broke—

"Just as once upon a time, you were brought back to life by your friend's kiss. A kiss of love," Sophie's mother said. "But that ending didn't last, did it? Now it's your turn to find your *real* true love."

"But no one loves me," Sophie breathed. "Not even Agatha."

"I love you, Sophie. But you don't have to end like me," consoled her mother. "For there is someone who loves you more than Agatha ever did. Someone who loves you for who you really are."

Agatha frantically chewed her willow-bark gag—

"Is it you? Are you my true love?" Sophie asked her mother, eyes wide.

Her mother smiled. "You'll just have to trust me."

"I do trust you," said Sophie, tears running. "You're the only one who knows who I am."

"Then kiss me, Sophie, and do not break it," Sophie's mother warned. "Break the kiss, and you will lose your last chance at love."

Agatha bit harder on the gagging branch, trying to snap it—

Sophie stepped towards her mother's ghost, heart hammering.

Agatha felt the willow splinter—

"Kiss me *now*, Sophie," said her mother. "Before it's too late."

Agatha spit out the gag. "SOPHIE, *DON'T*!" she screamed—

But in the waning moonlight, Sophie pressed her lips to her mother's, Sophie's face softening, glowing with the faith that happiness was coming . . . that this, her very first kiss, would at last bring her the end she deserved. . . .

But then the kiss turned colder, harder, and Sophie saw her mother's phantom face shriveling and rotting as if turning a thousand years old, its skin flaking off a maggoty, pockmarked skull. Alarmed, Sophie wanted to break away but, remembering her mother's warning, held her lips to the icy chill, praying for love that would never leave her, love deeper than a prince's or a friend's. Slowly, the skin started to firm over like white marble, as the face lost its phantom glow, smoothing younger, younger . . . until Sophie jolted with recognition, and stumbled back, a boy's real lips parting from hers.

Bare, ivory-fleshed feet stepped onto the ground, dark-blue grass prickling between the toes. The School Master raised his head, unmasked in his draping blue robes, his young chiseled face flawless and ghostly pale, his hair a shock of thick white.

Agatha and Tedros both quailed breathless against the tree, finding each other's hands beneath their binds.

Sophie looked up at the School Master, restored to life, more beautiful than any boy she'd ever known. "You . . . you did all this. . . ."

"For you," the School Master whispered. He touched her cheek with long glacial fingers. "I told you, Sophie. You'll always be mine."

"You don't want him!" Agatha screamed out from the tree. "He's Evil, Sophie! Pure Evil! You can still take it back! It isn't The End yet!"

Sophie finally looked at her, tears falling. As she met Agatha's scared eyes, reflecting a venomous villain, the moment was suddenly real. Sophie shook her head, heart breaking. Agatha was right . . . she had to stop this, she had to disavow this Evil, she had to take all of this back . . .

But then Sophie saw her friend's small hand in the strong, warm palm of a prince.

And she knew there was no Agatha anymore.

As the School Master pulled her closer into his hard, icy grip, Sophie didn't move.

Agatha blanched in surprise.

"What about me?" a voice said.

The School Master turned to Evelyn, blushing anxiously. "Brought your true love back," she preened. "Just like you asked, Master."

"Indeed. No doubt your brother foresaw you'd be useful for this purpose." The School Master grinned, frost-blue eyes meeting hers. "Ensuring my true love returned safe and sound."

Evelyn smiled back at him proudly. But then her face began to change . . . as the School Master's eyes inflamed red, burning deeper into hers. Evelyn seized at her heart as if it'd stopped beating, choking a last, empty breath.

"And now that purpose is fulfilled," said the School Master, clutching Sophie tighter.

Evelyn fell to the ground, shattering to a thousand dead red butterflies. The swarm trapping the Storian shriveled and plummeted too, dropping the Storian into the School Master's ready hands.

He looked up at Agatha and Tedros bound together to a tree.

"Now where were we?"

He released the Storian from his grip, watching the pen somersault to the suspended storybook and erase the aborted last words below Agatha and Tedros' kiss. Instantly it conjured a new page, sweeping a brilliant painting of Sophie and the School Master's kiss across it, recarving once bold, erased words beneath . . .

THE EN—

"Sophie, *no*!" Agatha roared—

The Storian carved the final, unmistakable letter, and the storybook closed, falling gently into the grass with barely a sound.

Agatha slowly raised her eyes to see the School Master leering at her, his arm around Sophie's waist.

"One . . . ," he smiled.

The two schools above the Forest suddenly rotted vulturous black, neither one distinguishable from the other, both darker, scarier than the Evil of old—

"Two . . ."

The gap in Halfway Bridge instantly healed, and boys and girls charged at each other, weapons drawn, accelerating towards war—

The School Master grinned at Agatha. "Three."

Agatha instantly started to shimmer, about to disappear.

"Wait!" Tedros screamed into his gag—

"It's sending me home!" Agatha shrieked to her prince, her body fading faster. "Sophie's kiss! It's sending me back home—" She whirled to Sophie, hearing a town clock toll, growing closer . . . closer . . . "Sophie, help me stay! Take my hand and help me stay!"

But Sophie stayed by the School Master's side, her eyes welling with grief.

"He chose me, Agatha," she said softly. "And you didn't."

Agatha cried out in horror, her body almost translucent now . . .

"I do believe I owe your dear friend a favor," the School Master smiled, prying off Sophie. "After all, Agatha did take *my* true love once upon a time."

The School Master pulled Tedros' sword from the ground. Terrified, Tedros thrashed under his binds.

Agatha gasped in shock—

"Fitting," the School Master mused, inspecting Excalibur. "Dying on your father's sword." He raised it high over the prince and stabbed, eyes flashing red.

"*NO*!" Agatha yelled, splintering to light—

As the blade split open Tedros' shirt, Agatha seized her prince's hand, and the sword slashed through thin air, Tedros shimmering safe in Agatha's arms.

Vanishing home with her stunned prince, Agatha watched the School Master sneer at her and clasp Sophie in his cold, stone grip as they floated together off the ground, receding towards his tower in the sky. Sophie and Agatha locked eyes one last time, but neither screamed for the other.

Once true loves, two girls now pulled apart like strangers, each in the arms of a boy, Good with Good, Evil with Evil . . .

Both of their wishes granted.

Deleted Scenes from
The School for Good and Evil

A Chat with Soman

Deleted Scenes from *The School for Good and Evil*

The School for Good and Evil was my very first book. I was just so ecstatic to be writing about Sophie and Agatha (so ecstatic to be writing at all!) that I was a volcano of energy and exuberance, unleashing enough material to fit into six books, let alone one. The first draft of Book 1 that I turned in to my poor editor was nearly 150 pages longer than the final version, featuring a number of scenes I loved deeply but ultimately had to cut in order to keep the story skipping along.

But that doesn't mean those scenes are lost forever . . .

BIGGLE AND BOGGLE

About halfway through Book 1, Sophie and Agatha are tasked to solve a riddle from the School Master: "What's the one thing Evil can never *have . . . and the one thing Good can never do without?" While Agatha struggles with the riddle in the School for Good, here is a scene you never read where Sophie tries to solve it in her own way. Warning: hold your nose.*

Remarkably enough, Sophie was much further along toward solving the riddle.

Her first-place rank in Uglification had silenced the hobgoblin taunts and reminded the Nevers that they were still dealing with a villain who had vanquished a Golden Goose and beaten all their Special Talents. Throwing her nervous looks as they slogged to the belfry, the Nevers arrived to find Castor looming over two horned billy goats.

"This is Biggle," he said, pointing to a white goat with black streaks. "And this is Boggle." He nodded to a black goat with white streaks. "Your challenge is to make them attack each other!"

The students stared at Biggle and Boggle, nuzzling each other sweetly as they shared a bale of straw.

"They're snuggling," gaped Hort.

"Forgot that part," said Castor. "They're brothers."

Everyone tried Castor's Henchmen Training tactics to make the two brothers fight. Vex tried to "command" them, but animals don't understand Nevers. Ravan tried to "taunt" them by kicking their hay around, but the goats just took a nap. Hort "bribed" them with a carrot, but Boggle pinned him down while Biggle ate it. Hester "bullied" them by knocking their heads together, but Biggle spit in her eye, and Boggle peed on her foot. Finally the goats had had enough of all this and rammed Beezle around the belfry ("Devil's goats!" he screeched).

"You're the sorriest pack of losers I've ever seen," growled Castor. "And that's sayin' something considering your school ain't produced a winner in two hundred years!"

Everyone stared at their shoes, shamefaced.

"Henchmen have to know you're their Master. Then they'll do whatever you ask, even if it means fighting their own blood. Now, most creatures respond to a few basic moves—"

While Castor demonstrated, Sophie tuned out and chewed the School Master's riddle.

What does a villain never have that a princess cannot do without?

Her first instinct was "Rumpelstiltskin," but that didn't make much sense. "Class" was her second, but there were plenty of villainous queens with good breeding. Villains lacked proper skin-care regimens, but that didn't mean they could never have one. Same went with pink dresses and cucumber juice.

Crap riddle solver this one is, came a voice.

Total crap, said another.

Sophie saw the two goats staring at her. Like the goose, they could apparently hear her thoughts.

What's the answer, then? Sophie asked.

What a princess got that a villain don't? said Biggle. *Easy.*

Good bowels, said Boggle.

When in doubt, poo it out, said Biggle.

They burst into hoary laughter. Biggle clutched his stomach. *Carrot gave me rumbles.*

Then why'd you eat it, you tosser? said Boggle.

Biggle scowled. *Should have shoved it up Weasel Boy's—*

Now my tummy's turnin', said Boggle.

What I'd do for Mummy's tea, said Biggle, and passed gas noisily.

When they gonna let us do our business? said Boggle, ripping his own fart.

Sophie held her nose. Once again, her ability to hear animal thoughts had yielded more trouble than use. Did every 100% Good Princess have to deal with this?

Evers feed us good, said Boggle.

Evers are pretty and clean, said Biggle.

Evers can solve riddles, said Boggle.

Not like this clown, said Biggle.

Sophie's chest tightened. Did she put on too much blush?

Dumb bird ain't ever gonna solve that riddle, said Biggle.

All that chat of cucumbers and diets, said Boggle.

Needs an Ever, said Biggle.

Needs a good poo, sounds like, said Boggle.

The goats collapsed in bleating laughs. Sophie's hands tightened into fists.

Why we even here? moaned Biggle.

Numpty Nevers.

Nosy Nevers. Why we here? Biggle called out.

Yeah, clown face, yelled Boggle. *Why we here?*

Sophie whipped around. *Because we're going to kill one of you. And we're trying to decide which one.*

The goats stopped laughing. They looked at each other

nervously. Then at Sophie.

Have you, uh, decided? choked Biggle.

Sophie nodded.

Which one? trembled Boggle.

Sophie smiled. *The weaker one.*

Well, I'm stronger! bellowed Biggle.

No, I'm stronger! howled Boggle.

You lying, stinking—

And just like that, the two brothers attacked each other, sparking a braying, murderous brawl. As Biggle gouged Boggle's stomach, Boggle bit Biggle's neck, and horns slammed and splintered, Sophie turned around and put her fingers in her ears, finally able to focus on the riddle—

Only, the whole class was staring at her.

"You made them . . . *fight*?" Castor asked, flabbergasted.

With another first-place rank, Sophie was only a few places from overtaking Hester in the race for Class Captain. Hester sprang into action.

"How about poison in her food?" she said as she stomped to her room with Anadil and Dot.

"She doesn't eat far as I can tell," said Anadil.

"How about poisoned lipstick?" said Hester.

"Or black widows in her bed?" asked Anadil.

"They'll lock us in the Doom Room for weeks!" fretted Dot.

"I don't care how we do it, or how much trouble we get in," Hester hissed. "I want that snake *gone*."

AGATHA'S AWAKENING

After Agatha is duped by Professor Dovey into thinking she's been turned beautiful by magic, Agatha realizes that the simple act of smiling awakens something deep inside her. If I could put one scene back into Book 1, it would be this one: Agatha's deepest thoughts as she experiences the School for Good in a brand-new way.

For all the spells taught at the School for Good and Evil, Agatha had found something more powerful in a smile. Overnight the snooty looks and snide barbs ceased, replaced by slack-jawed stares, baffled whispers, and girls trying to mimic her magical beam. Soon Agatha saw she too had been bewitched. For it was on her way to classes one day that she caught herself looking forward to them.

The other changes came just as slyly. She noticed that she didn't dread taking a shower now or spending a few minutes to brush her hair, iron her uniform, or polish her clumps. She listened to Professor Dovey's lecture on "Why Beauties Must Save Beasts" and didn't blush once at the word "beast." She got so caught up in Ball dance rehearsals she jumped when the wolves howled to end class. And where she once did her Good homework practically holding her nose, now it felt like food to her soul.

Curled up in the Library of Virtue, she read in *The Joy of Courtly Love* that princes might flirt with the most beautiful girls in the room, but ultimately they chose a "soul match": a girl precisely as pure or impure as they were. Over the years this word lost favor as too fixed and was replaced with "true love," so princes could believe they had free will to find their mate. In fact, Agatha learned in History that the first Balls began because kings and queens didn't trust their sons' wills. To test them, they held formal dances called "Hundreds" that they filled with ninety-nine girls of their choice and one girl who was their son's pure soul match. In the end, whether the girl was rich or poor, beautiful or ugly, the princes found this hidden jewel every time. Entranced by these trials of Goodness, Agatha would stay up after curfew, candle to *Princess with a Purpose*, reading of heroines who cut off fingers to save birds, scarred their face rather than marry a depraved king, and sacrificed their lives for true love. As she drank in these tales, so rich with feeling and mission, she felt the once potent allure of Evil dissipate and die.

Suddenly her life was full without Sophie. With Kiko stressed over whether Tristan would propose, Agatha distracted her with walks along the lakes, and midnight steals into the Groom Room. The more time Agatha spent with her, the more she realized Kiko wasn't stupid; she just covered insecurity with babble and gossip, like Agatha had covered hers with scowls and solitude. How many other girls at this school had she shortchanged? Sure, Beatrix and her fawns were awful as usual ("I heard she got a new nose," Beatrix swore), but in the Supper Hall, Agatha looked around at tables of girls—Mia, Therese, Marcela, Nicoline, Carmen—she'd assumed were the same. But now she smiled at them and won a smile back, as if they'd just been waiting for her to give them a chance.

Even the boys stopped leering at her. Like monkeys at a zoo, they reflected the face you gave them.

Lying in bed, Agatha looked out at fairies decking the Blue Forest with starry lanterns for the Ball. It was beautiful, really, what Good could do. She wouldn't have been able to admit that a few weeks ago. But somehow this School, which once embodied everything Evil to her, now felt like home. Agatha thought of her room in Gavaldon and couldn't remember how it smelled. She couldn't remember which side of her mother's face had the hairy brown mole. She couldn't even remember which of Reaper's eyes was black and which was gray. . . .

Before she knew it, it was two days before the Ball.

DOT AND THE BEES

This will throw you for a loop, but once upon a time, in an old version of The School for Good and Evil, *Dot wasn't a new student to the school at all. In fact, she'd failed her first time there, and her father, the Sheriff of Nottingham, had pulled strings to get her a second go at being a Never. Here is the scene where we find out about Dot's past history, while she tries to prepare Sophie for facing the Trial by Tale.*

The scene starts with Sophie attempting to find out how her witchy roommates are planning to kill her in the Trial. . . .

Sophie didn't go to History of Villains. She didn't care if she failed another challenge. She couldn't look at that wicked Sader—not after he kept her in the Trial and left her to die.

But Sophie had another reason to skip class. Since she'd left Room 66, surely Hester and Anadil had been plotting her murder there with impunity. Suppose they had left evidence? If Sophie could find out the trap they had planned, then Tedros could help her thwart it, even if she *did* have to go into the Trial first.

Stealing through the halls during class was no easy task with wolves prowling for truants. But without the Doom Room, the wolves had lost their aura of threat and apparently their motivation too. Sophie had glimpsed them bowling hedgehogs in halls after curfew, whispering to fairies behind trees during lunch, waking up late for morning call (and throwing both schools completely off schedule as a result)—she even caught one reading Sader's *History of Curses* in a broom closet. Of course when the wolves did snare a wayward villain, they roared louder and whipped them harder, as if to remind the students that they were still the disciplinarians of the school. To avoid becoming such an example, Sophie slipped out of her shoes and tiptoed up the staircase. Halfway up, she inhaled the strong scent of beer. She peered between the balusters and saw four wolves in the hall, playing cards, drinking from flasks. Sensing something, they looked up, but Sophie was already scampering through the sixth floor, clutching high heels in one hand, searching pockets for her old room key with the other.

Sophie slipped into Room 66 and closed the door. With the room pitch-black, she found the matches on the torch holder, where they always were, and lit a flame. She jumped back. The gilded mirror had been shattered to slivers. Her bed had disappeared and been replaced by bloody words on the floor.

RIP SOPHIE
LIVED WITH STYLE
DIED IN A TRIAL

Gasping, Sophie cowered against the wall. Something grazed her hair. She looked up and screamed.

All her old outfits hung by nooses, shredded, mutilated, like a gallery of headless corpses.

Sophie frantically put on her shoes and skirted around glass, trying not to look back up. Anadil's desk was clear, except for a mound of alarmingly large rat droppings. Hester's desk had a detailed, hand-drawn map of the Blue Forest, with "Central Clearing" circled and arrows pointing to each of its entrances. Sophie could see scrawled notes around its edges—

Fall 1—Winner: Fabian—Shapeshifting Siths; Frost Giants; (Vex's sister can't remember 3rd)

Spring 1—Winner: Fabian—Werewolves (Mona's brother says "man-wolves"); Baby Dragons; Firestorms

Fall 2—Winner: Jasira—Bugbears; Carnivorous Crows; Bloodsucking Bees

Sophie frowned. Most of these were creatures that Sader, Castor, and Lady Lesso had talked about in class. Is this what the School Master conjured in previous Trials? If so, then bloodthirsty Nevers were the least of her worries.

There was one more thing on Hester's desk. A soggy, faded library book. *How to Train Your Demon*. Sophie noticed one of the pages was dog-eared and opened to it. At the top, two sentences were underlined:

The biggest mistake you can make is to use your demon to kill. He is not strong enough to kill. But he is strong enough for you to sever your

The rest of the page had been ripped out. Sophie's breath shallowed. Sever *what*? Was Hester planning something with her demon? Sophie shook the book for the missing page, but nothing fell out. Was Hester carrying it with her? Was there another copy in the libra—

A grunt.

Someone was under the bed.

Sophie whipped her head toward the door. If she tried to run, they could catch her from behind. Panic numbed her body. Her heart was beating so fast it felt like one long detonation. Sophie held her breath—then pounced and kicked the bed aside—

Dot looked up meekly. "I thought you were a wolf."

"You almost gave me a heart attack!" Sophie roared.

"A heartbeat away from Hench Captain," Dot sighed.

"Dot, why are you *here*?"

"I just can't sit through another class about the Trial," Dot whimpered. "It makes me anxious."

"You're not even *in* the Trial, you twit!" Sophie snapped,

collapsing on Hester's bed. "Meanwhile, I have the whole school trying to kill me— Wait. Dot, surely you've heard! How are Hester and Anadil planning to—"

"I don't know," Dot said, crawling from under the bed.

"But you must—"

"They don't talk about it here," said Dot, leaning against Anadil's lumpy mattress.

"I think it's something with her demon—"

"I came here to get away from talking about the Trial," Dot said quietly.

Sophie watched her try to turn a sliver of glass into chocolate, but Dot's hands were trembling too much.

"Dot, you said Bane failed like all the other Readers. But he didn't, did he?"

Dot froze.

"He died in the Trial," Sophie said.

Dot clutched the glass tighter. "I can't tell you!"

"Bane was from my village," Sophie pleaded. "If I know what happened to him in the Trial, it might save my life."

"I can't!" Dot whimpered.

Sophie took Dot's hand and gently staunched the bleeding fingers. Dot looked up at her.

"Please," Sophie said softly. "I need your help."

Dot's eyes welled. "You can't tell anyone! Or they'll try to kill me too!"

"Dot, I promise."

Dot wiped her tears. She was quiet for a long while.

"We're not as different as you think," she said finally. "We both like to feel pretty. We both don't fit very well here. And we both have a weakness for . . ." Her voice tightened. "Boys."

"Well, life's pointless without boys, isn't it," Sophie smiled.

"But that's where we're different. I don't like the kind of boys you do."

Sophie's eyes widened. "You liked . . . *Bane*?"

Dot nodded.

"But he punched girls and called them names and—"

"I like boys who treat me badly," Dot said.

"So you liked Bane," Sophie prodded, trying to look understanding. "And you both made it into the Trial?"

"Oh, please. I was a worse student than I am now. But Bane was like you. He wanted to get into the Trial to impress someone. That's why I liked him. He thought Nevers could love." Dot forced a smile. "I did too."

"So he liked you back," Sophie smiled.

Dot shook her head bitterly. "He liked Leticia. Prettiest Ever in school. She made the mistake of smiling at him."

Sophie remembered smiling at Bane as one of her Good Deeds and being rewarded with a barrage of pinches and kicks.

"The Neverboys wanted to punish Bane during the Trial for breaking Evil's #1 rule," Dot said. "I found out they were planning to strip him naked and tie him to a stymph. I tried to tell him. He wouldn't listen."

"So you snuck into the Trial?" Sophie said.

"The wolves make crap guards if you haven't noticed. When I got into the Forest, no one spotted me. The Evers were fleeing from Bloodsucking Bees—those things love sweets and there's hardly anything sweeter than Evers' blood. Nevers were up in trees to kill a flock of Carnivorous Crows. I looked for Bane's red glow until I found him all alone, battling a Bugbear in the brook. He was wounded and about to throw up his flag . . . but I saved him. I told him to hide. That the Nevers would come for him soon."

Tears flooded Dot's face. "He said I had made it all up because I liked him. He said he'd never like me even if I was the last girl in the world. He said that I'd end up a warted toad, that my dad must be ashamed of me, that I was fat, stupid, worthless—he was getting so red, he was spitting in my face—I heard voices coming, and he said everyone would see I snuck in for him, and everyone would hate me as much as he did, and I got so scared that I . . . I . . ."

"You what?" Sophie pushed.

"I . . . just . . ."

"What?"

"I . . . I . . . ," Dot choked through tears. *"Chocolate."*

Sophie didn't understand. Then her face went white.

"You turned Bane into *chocolate*?"

Dot exploded into sobs.

"But surely you know how to turn something back—" Sophie gasped. "Surely the teachers—"

"They like sweet things . . . ," Dot bawled into her hands.

"The teachers?"

"Sweeter than blood . . . ," Dot heaved. "Sweeter than Evers' blood . . ."

Sophie shook her head. "I don't under—" Her eyes flared open. "No!"

Dot nodded in her hands.

"Bees ate Bane!" Sophie screamed.

"The teachers tried to save him but there was nothing left," Dot convulsed.

"But they wouldn't have let you back! They would have punished—they would have failed you!"

Dot let out a wail.

"They *failed* you?" Sophie shrieked. "But then how are you here!"

"Because they thought I'd tell the others!"

"The other children?" Sophie cried—

"No, the other ones who—" Dot stopped suddenly. "I can't—"

"Dot! What happens to kids who fail!"

"If I tell, my heart will stop beating," Dot wept. "He casts a spell to make you keep the secret."

"Who? Who casts the spell?"

Dot crumpled into heaves. "I killed him, Sophie! I killed the boy I loved!"

Sophie shrank against the wall—

"You shouldn't be in that Trial!" Dot cried. "I don't know how you made it! But you'll learn the same lesson I did. Villains can't love, Sophie! In the end, we're just too Evil!"

Sophie shook her head in horror.

"Say something, Sophie," Dot whimpered.

But Sophie couldn't look at her.

"We're still friends . . . aren't we?" Dot reached for her hand—Sophie pulled away, repulsed.

The wolves' call thundered through the tower.

"Go," Dot said softly. "Hester and Ani will be back."

Sophie didn't move.

"Go!" Dot cried.

Legs shaking, Sophie opened the door.

"Kiss Tedros now," said the voice behind her. "Before it's too late."

Sophie turned, but Dot was already back under the bed.

A Chat with Soman

Soman, you've written a bestselling series called the School for Good and Evil. You've toured all over the world, spoken at conferences, and met a lot of your fans. Do you get asked a lot of questions?

I love meeting the fans whenever I have the opportunity and yes, they have a lot to ask! In person and on my site, www.schoolforgoodandevil.com, I've been absolutely bombarded with questions about the books, the movie, and my personal life—over 2,000 questions on the website alone.

Do the fans ask any particular questions more than others? What are they really anxious to know and can you tell us the answers?

The kids want to know everything, but two questions pop up more than any others. The first is whether the end of book 2, *A World Without Princes*, is the end of the series. . . . Everyone seems to be worried about whether there's a third book or not. I always find this startling, because I can't imagine abandoning the series where *A World Without Princes* ends. How sadistic! If I left Sophie and Agatha hanging there, that'd be grounds for banishing me to author jail forever. So yes, there is a third book on the way.

What's the third book called, and can you tell us a little about it?

It's called *The Last Ever After*, and it's the biggest volume of the series, with the story exploring the aftermath of Sophie and Agatha's separation at the end of Book 2. In the first book, it was easy to peg Agatha as the hero and Sophie as the villain—but after reading the second book, it isn't so clear, is it? Is Agatha truly as Good as she seems? Is Sophie truly destined for Evil? In Book 3, both girls, as well as Tedros, will answer those questions and face their fates once and for all. This time the three of them will find the *real* ending to their fairy tale.

Since I started writing the series, I've been carefully planting little seeds in Books 1 and 2 that will all come to fruition in Book 3. The series was always designed as a trilogy, but it's really one big story. One day, I'd love for the three books to be combined together in one beautiful hardback volume, so that it can be read in one sweep.

So you've answered the first most popular question. What's the second?

The movie! Everyone wants to know more about the movie, including my mother, brother, nephew, dentist, tennis coach, and mailman. They're getting impatient, and I don't blame them! The process can be quite slow, especially when everyone involved wants to get it just right. But there *will* be a movie soon, from Universal Pictures, and produced by the team of Joe Roth, Jane Startz, and Palak Patel, who combined are responsible for *Maleficent, Snow White and the Huntsman, Alice in Wonderland, Ella Enchanted,* and *Tuck Everlasting.* I wrote the screenplay with my friend and former professor Malia Scotch Marmo (screenwriter of *Hook*), and we had a rip-roaring time. All our favorite scenes and all the love we have for this world are in the script, which we truly believe will give both the book fans and those new to the series a good, old-fashioned fairy-tale epic.

That said, making a movie involves a lot more people than writing a novel, so I don't control the outcome entirely. (Trust me, I'd love to.) But even if it isn't ultimately my film to make, I am as involved as an author can be, and I've made sure the producers are well aware that the fan base is as passionate as it is wide. I've come to think of myself less as an author during the moviemaking process and more as a Spokesperson for the Fans—or the Ever Never Army, as they call themselves. And I'm keeping a running tab of their desires: the actors can't be too old; Sophie has to have her

"Empress's New Clothes" fashion parade; the Trial by Tale has to be super scary; and most of all, Dot has to turn a lot of things into chocolate.

But the most popular request from fans is open casting for the movie, which would allow kids around the world to audition for their favorite characters. I'll certainly be advocating on their behalf. I'd love for readers to get their chance to try out for the movie, whether it's online video submissions or in-person auditions.

A lot of readers keep asking why you're not directing the movie yourself, since you're a filmmaker as well as an author. Then you could make sure the movie looks just like the book.

True . . . but then there'd be no more books! Directing *The School for Good and Evil* would take all my energy, given how large scale the project is. I have to choose, and I choose to keep writing and leave the moviemaking to the absolutely brilliant director I know we'll find.

One day, after I'm done with the School for Good and Evil series, I'd like to bring a new book from the seed of an idea to a story on the page and then onto the screen exactly as I imagined it. But in the meantime, I'm sure readers would prefer that I'm focusing all my energy on Book 3.

Because the movie process may take awhile, what can fans do to learn more about the movie?

The best thing they can do is get involved in the worldwide fandom for the series, and to check out the series website at www.schoolforgoodandevil.com, where I blog at least three times a week, keeping readers from all over the world in the know on the latest news. Plus, if you are on social media, you can find me on Twitter, Tumblr, Instagram, Facebook, and YouTube.

Because there are no movies without the books, let's go back to those. Will the third book, *The Last Ever After*, be the final book in the series?

It will complete *this* particular fairy tale, meaning Sophie, Agatha, and Tedros will find a lasting ending—though I can't guarantee they will all survive. What I can guarantee is that there will be no cliffhanger at the end of the third book. *The Last Ever After* will sew all the loose ends of the story into what I hope will be a fulfilling conclusion.

But will that conclusion be The End? I definitely plan to revisit the School for Good and Evil world in the years to come, so don't think of it as The End Forever. This is a world I love so deeply that I can't spend too much time away from it—so even as I go on to new things, I know that the school and its universe have many stories left for me to tell, and I look forward to writing them all.

You've given us a peek at *The Last Ever After* with a teaser of the first two chapters in this edition of *A World Without Princes*. Anything else you'd like to share?

This two-chapter teaser gives you an idea of what to expect in the third book. Instead of Good vs. Evil in Book 1 and

Boys vs. Girls in Book 2, this time we're looking at the battle of New vs. Old. We think we know exactly what those two words mean. But looking deeper, they're both just artificial ideas. What does it really mean to be young or new? What does it mean to be old? And is there any in between?

The Last Ever After is a monster book, a true epic across the Endless Woods, but it's also an intimate story that really lets us spend time with our two main couples, each facing different challenges. Can Sophie believe that the School Master is now a young, handsome, and charismatic boy who she can love and trust? And are Agatha and Tedros truly compatible once they have to live out the day-to-day of their Ever After? What happens when both of these couples are tested? And more important, what will happen when they all meet again?

Readers can also expect loads of new characters, enormous new worlds, and, as usual, plenty of mischief and wickedness. Oh . . . and blood.

Lots of blood.

Both *The School for Good and Evil* and *A World Without Princes* are *New York Times* bestsellers and will be translated into nearly twenty languages across six continents. Why do you think these books have found such a strong international audience, and how do you feel about it all?

The support for *The School for Good and Evil* staggers and humbles me. The readers have truly made this world their own, which is the reason I work so hard, trying to live up to their expectations. (And the reason I'm still single. My mother is livid about this, by the way. "You can't marry a book!" she yells.)

My favorite thing to do in the morning is check the Good versus Evil scoreboards on the homepage of www.schoolforgoodandevil.com. Each day, the five highest Good and Evil soul scores from the "Are You Good or Evil?" online school entrance exam are posted on the site, along with the city and country the reader is from. Without fail, it's a smorgasbord of users from around the world. I'm looking at it right now: Idaho, Los Angeles, Dubai, London, Canberra, Pakistan, Brazil . . .

I'm at a loss to explain it, except for the fact that the kids seem to love the idea that in the world of SGE, they can be truly themselves. You don't have to be perfect. You don't always have to do the right thing. You can just be you, neither completely Good nor Evil, but somewhere in between.

You've mentioned before that you enjoy talking to fans when you are on tour. Can you share with us one of your most memorable moments while touring? Do you like doing it?

I *love* touring. I'm not sure if I'll ever have kids of my own, if only because I put so much of myself into my work that I'm afraid I'll be a rather neglectful father. Because of that, and because I know the kids have made a big effort to come and meet me, I'm passionate and fully present during all the time I have with them on tour. And the things they say! I've been left speechless many times.

One girl asked me what happens if you're not Good or Evil, but just . . . "normal." (Book 3 has the answer to that question!) Another boy told me I can't possibly have any friends if I'm producing such large books all the time. I've had kids bake cakes in the shapes of the castles, paint tattoos of stymphs and crogs, dress up like Agatha and Sophie, and serenade me with "Let It Go" from *Frozen;* I've had mothers propose marriage, religious organizations denounce the book, religious organizations endorse the book, and rural-dwelling, tractor-driving, tobacco-chewing fathers add me on Facebook. Touring is always an adventure, no matter where I go.

With all that's going on, are you ever just staring at a blank page when you sit down to write? What do you do if that happens?

Some people call that writer's block, though I can't remember a time in writing the three books where I've been blocked for more than a few hours. When that happens, I've found that it means I'm coming at a problem from the wrong direction or just trying to force a storyline that's not working. That's a sign I need to get away from my computer for a bit and clear my head . . . whether that's hitting the tennis court with my very tall German trainer, Christoph, or settling into a sweaty, hot yoga class or listening to bouncy pop music on a walk through the park or going to see a movie like *Guardians of the Galaxy* (which I've seen five times). By the time I come back to the page, I usually have a fresh, new perspective.

Do you have any advice you can give to anyone who wants to be a writer—something that helps you?

It's all about getting a reader wanting to know what happens next. Read your work out loud to a boy who doesn't like books. If he fidgets after the first paragraph or looks bored, then you need to keep working on that opening. Character, story, theme . . . that all comes later. First you need to draw the reader in. The voice of your story has to feel authentic, real, and make you care about what's happening. If the boy you've chosen isn't saying "What next?" after every single sentence, then you still have more work to do.

Soman, what's next for you?

Besides planning further explorations of the School for Good and Evil universe, I'm looking forward to directing a movie soon and diving into a brand-new series in the near future that's just as big and epic as SGE. Readers can stay in touch at www.somanchainani.net for all the latest news, as well as find me on virtually every social media outlet.

Writing is such a solitary adventure at times that I relish every chance to interact with readers, whether it's handwritten letters, emails, fan art, videos, blogs, or anything else that comes my way. It's their creativity, commitment, passion, and intelligence that fuels me every single day.

Photo by David J. Martin

SOMAN CHAINANI's first novel, *The School for Good and Evil*, debuted on the *New York Times* bestseller list, has been translated into languages across six continents, and will soon be a major motion picture from Universal Pictures.

As a graduate of Harvard University and Columbia University's MFA film program, Soman has made films that have played at over 150 festivals around the world, and his writing awards include honors from Big Bear Lake, New Draft, the CAPE Foundation, the Shasha Grant, and the Sun Valley Writers' Fellowship.

When he's not telling stories, Soman is a die-hard tennis player who never lost a first-round match for ten years . . . until he started writing *The School for Good and Evil*. Now he loses all the time.